CRUCIFIED

Also by Lynda La Plante

Jane Tennison series
Tennison
Hidden Killers
Good Friday
Murder Mile
The Dirty Dozen
Blunt Force
Unholy Murder
Dark Rooms
Taste of Blood
Whole Life Sentence

DC Jack Warr series
Buried
Judas Horse
Vanished
Pure Evil

Widows series
Widows
Widows' Revenge
She's Out

Getting Away with Murder: My Unexpected Life on Page, Stage and Screen

For a complete list of Lynda's works, please visit:
www.lyndalaplante.com/books

Lynda La Plante was born in Liverpool. She trained for the stage at RADA and worked with the National Theatre and RSC before becoming a television actress. She then turned to writing and made her breakthrough with the phenomenally successful TV series *Widows*. She has written over thirty international novels, all of which have been bestsellers, and is the creator of the Anna Travis, Lorraine Page and *Trial and Retribution* series. Her original script for the much-acclaimed *Prime Suspect* won awards from BAFTA, Emmy, British Broadcasting and Royal Television Society, as well as the 1993 Edgar Allan Poe Award.

Lynda is one of only three screenwriters to have been made an honorary fellow of the British Film Institute and was awarded the BAFTA Dennis Potter Best Writer Award in 2000. In 2008, she was awarded a CBE in the Queen's Birthday Honours List for services to Literature, Drama and Charity.

✉ Join the Lynda La Plante Readers' Club at
www.bit.ly/LyndaLaPlanteClub
www.lyndalaplante.com
 Facebook @LyndaLaPlanteCBE
 @LaPlanteLynda

Lynda La Plante
CRUCIFIED

ZAFFRE

First published in the UK in 2025 by
ZAFFRE
An imprint of Bonnier Books UK
5th Floor, HYLO, 103–105 Bunhill Row,
London, EC1Y 8LZ
Owned by Bonnier Books
Sveavägen 56, Stockholm, Sweden

Copyright © La Plante Global Ltd, 2025

All rights reserved.
No part of this publication may be reproduced,
stored or transmitted in any form by any means, electronic,
mechanical, photocopying or otherwise, without the
prior written permission of the publisher.

The right of Lynda La Plante to be identified as Author of this
work has been asserted by her in accordance with the
Copyright, Designs and Patents Act, 1988.

This is a work of fiction. Names, places, events and
incidents are either the products of the author's
imagination or used fictitiously. Any resemblance to
actual persons, living or dead, or actual
events is purely coincidental.

A CIP catalogue record for this book is
available from the British Library.

Hardback ISBN: 978-1-83877-990-0
Trade Paperback ISBN: 978-1-83877-989-4

Also available as an ebook and an audiobook

1 3 5 7 9 10 8 6 4 2

Typeset by IDSUK (Data Connection) Ltd
Printed and bound in Great Britain by Clays Ltd, Elcograf S.p.A.

www.bonnierbooks.co.uk

To my dearest, talented and beloved friends, Amy Zerner and Monte Farber. Their ENCHANTED WORLD spills over to everyone fortunate to know them.

PROLOGUE

Week after week, eventually turning into months, Detective Sergeant Jack Warr had been recalled to the stand and subjected to the Defence's onslaught. They queried everything, questioning him until he was exhausted, but their main focus was the fact that the bodies of the four murder victims had not been found, despite the wealth of forensic evidence linking them to the basement. Jack was forced to describe the discovery of the horrific scene time and time again.

'You have stated that you pursued Rodney Middleton even after he was arrested for a lesser crime, which he freely admitted to. He had handed over the weapon he used in the assault on the owner of a shop he frequented. Is that correct?'

'Yes,' Jack replied.

'So, even though he pleaded guilty to the assault charge and handed over the weapon, you still requested a search warrant for his premises. On what basis?'

'My evidence has been submitted, it's in front of you, and the judge agreed that I had reasonable grounds. My intuition told me . . .'

'So, on the basis of your intuition,' the Defence interrupted in a disparaging tone, 'you obtained a search warrant. But it would have been days later when the search was carried out. So, all this time his basement apartment would have been vacant?'

'His girlfriend was still living there and she gave us entry.'

'The reality is, there could have been other people present or moving in and out of the basement property, couldn't there?'

Jack was getting sick of being treated like an inexperienced rookie.

'I can see where you're going with this, but what I discovered inside that basement couldn't have been recently deposited. Four young girls were butchered and decapitated over a lengthy period of time, leaving extensive forensic evidence: blood, hair, clothes, skin, nails . . .'

At this point the Defence attempted to interrupt but Jack refused to be silenced. Gripping the wooden edge of the dock, his voice strained and hoarse, he didn't pause for breath.

'He had cut them into pieces in the coal bunker. When luminol was used to detect if blood was present, the whole area, floor to ceiling, lit up. It was literally a blood bath.'

Jack was eventually released from the witness box, walking past the glass partition surrounding the dock where Rodney Middleton was smiling and raising his handcuffed wrists as if applauding. The hideous gloating expression never left his face as the judge called for a short adjournment.

Thirty minutes later, with the court back in session, the bereaved families were finally allowed to read out their impact statements. Middleton laughed, jeered and pulled clown faces, mocking their endless pain, until the judge was forced to intervene.

'Your antics will not save you from hearing their words, Mr Middleton. The families want you to understand how your actions have impacted them. Whether you care or not.'

Jack found the time immediately after each court session just as emotionally draining. Other families constantly approached him outside the courthouse, weeping and pressing photographs of their dead daughters to his chest, begging him to find out if they were also victims of Rodney Middleton's heinous crimes. Jack's team had found further blood stains, not linked to the four young girls they knew had died in that basement. There were definitely more victims, but so far the police had no idea who they were.

When the guilty verdict was delivered and Rodney Middleton given a life sentence, for Jack it felt almost meaningless. Against legal advice, and despite being refused the first time of asking, Jack persisted in his request for a ten-minute face-to-face meeting with Middleton in his cell before he was taken to prison. Jack argued that this was his best chance to gain more information about the as yet unidentified victims.

He was given five minutes. Jack was taken down to the holding cells, accompanied by an officer who agreed to remain outside the closed but unlocked cell door. As Jack waited for Middleton to turn and face him, his right hand slipped into his pocket and felt for the tough leather shoelace – he knew he'd have to act fast.

Middleton looked surprised to see him. Before he could speak, Jack said, 'I know you can give us the identity of more victims, Rodney. Let me give some peace to their families.'

Middleton smiled. 'You have no idea how much pleasure I get from being the only one who knows where they are and how they died. So you, Jack, can go fuck yourself.'

Jack didn't react. It was nothing more than he'd expected. Then he stepped quickly up to the bench where Middleton was sitting. In the blink of an eye, Jack had the leather shoelace round Middleton's neck, pulling it tighter with all his strength. Middleton tried to scream but no air could escape Jack's garrotte. He clawed at the shoelace as Jack dragged him across to the stainless steel toilet in the corner of the cell, forcing his head down into the bowl.

Middleton's bulbous red, oxygen-deprived eyes were now full of fear. It was Jack's turn to smile. 'I will find those girls; I don't need you.' This was the moment Jack should have let go. But he was enjoying the fear in Middleton's eyes too much and he knew that another twenty seconds would be enough to kill him. Middleton squeezed his fingers under the garrotte, took in a lungful of air and screamed. Jack whipped the shoelace from round Middleton's neck and deftly slipped it back into his pocket before yanking the cell door open.

As two officers rushed into the cell, he said, 'Mad bastard tried to scratch his own throat out.'

'He tried to kill me!' Middleton screamed.

Jack shrugged. 'If I had ... you'd be dead.' He exchanged a wordless look with the two officers, trusting that whatever they suspected had really happened would not be reported.

As he walked out into the corridor, Jack knew that if he ever got another chance he wouldn't be able to hold back. He would kill Rodney Middleton.

CHAPTER 1

Having been told Doctor Kenneth Hargreaves was running late for their appointment, Jack sat patiently in the Harley Street waiting room not knowing what to expect. It was his first visit to the clinic.

It was nearly 9.30 a.m. when the door opened and the receptionist informed him that Doctor Hargreaves had arrived. Hargreaves had actually arrived ten minutes earlier and had quickly scan-read the initial consultation report. Normally he would have studied a patient's file thoroughly, made notes and carefully considered his approach before meeting them, but today he just hadn't had time.

Jack entered Hargreaves' office and the doctor stood up, offering his hand.

'I apologise for keeping you waiting, Mr Warr. My train was cancelled. Please take a seat.' He pointed to a comfortable-looking chair in front of his desk.

Jack glanced around the bland, almost featureless room. Hargreaves flipped open his leather notebook and removed a slim silver biro from the grip, which he placed to one side. Jack settled into the chair as requested.

'It was my wife's idea to have a private consultation. She spoke very highly of you.'

Hargreaves hesitated while trying to recall the phone call with Doctor Warr. 'Ah yes, I have an NHS practice at the hospital where she works two mornings a week. She's on maternity leave now, I believe.' Hargreaves knew that Jack had walked out on two previous sessions with NHS therapists. 'But I believe you were not enthusiastic about coming to see me.'

'Correct.'

'Are you happy to talk to me today?'

'That's why I'm here,' Jack said non-committally.

Hargreaves found Jack's dark eyes unnerving, almost challenging, but it didn't disturb him. He had spent years as a prison psychiatrist so had extensive experience of troubled and dangerous individuals. Jack's physically relaxed demeanour was slightly at odds with his steady eye contact, but he showed no tension with his hands resting on his crossed legs. Hargreaves started slowly.

'This must be quite a challenging time with a new baby?'

'You could say that. But Maggie is incredible.'

'What's your son's name?'

'We're still arguing about that. I want to call him Horatio, but Maggie hates it.' Hargreaves looked as if he was about to say something so Jack quickly went on. 'When Maggie took maternity leave, she went into nest-building overdrive and decided we needed a kitchen extension. She organised it all. It's open-plan with a glass roof and fitted blinds. She chose the flooring tiles, lights and all the kitchen appliances. Now she wants a load of inside plants from the garden centre.'

'It all sounds very costly,' Hargreaves said.

Jack nodded. 'I had to take out a bank loan and sell my car. Well, Maggie thought it was my car . . .' Jack knew he was about to say something revealing but felt oddly comfortable with that. Perhaps because he knew his words would never leave this room. 'It was a debt someone felt they owed me. Nothing illegal, but Maggie wouldn't have approved.'

'Jack . . .' Hargreaves gave Jack a knowing smile. 'Why are you here?'

Jack was about to go off on another tangent, then stopped himself. 'I worry I might hurt Maggie.'

'Just Maggie? Are your children safe?'

'Of course they are.'

'The aggression you feel – is it verbal or physical?' Jack frowned as he struggled to find the answer. 'Have you ever hit out? Lost control? Jack, have you ever physically attacked your wife?'

Jack looked horrified by the very thought. 'Of course not!'

Hargreaves persisted. 'But you think you could?'

'Yes. It's got so bad that some nights I sleep in a different room. I have no control over it. And recently, it's got a lot worse. Punching, shouting and kicking out in my sleep.'

Hargreaves leaned back and sighed, wishing his train had not been late. Wishing he'd had time to read Jack's notes more thoroughly. 'You're talking about night terrors.'

'What did you think I meant?' Jack said through clenched jaws. 'That I'm a wife-beater?'

'Sorry. I misunderstood what I read in the report.'

'What did Maggie say to you?'

'Not that, Jack. It was my error. I understand now. You're in a deep sleep when these episodes occur. Do the nightmares occur frequently or just periodically?'

'More frequent now. When I punch or kick out, it usually wakes me up. I've fallen out of bed plenty of times.'

'Do you sleepwalk?'

'No.'

Hargreaves nodded and made a note. 'Have you had these problems since childhood?'

'Not that I know of. Maggie said it started a few months ago.'

'It could be due to the stress in your life right now. The upheaval in your home and a new baby. I want to book you an overnight appointment at a sleep clinic as soon as possible.' As Hargreaves made a note of this, Jack rolled his eyes. He wanted answers now. Not in a week. A month. Longer? 'You will be wired up to monitor your brain activity, as well as heart rate and eye and leg movement throughout the night. They will also watch your sleeping behaviour on CCTV. What we find out will allow me to understand your sleep disorder better, then we can discuss how best to control it. How does that sound?'

'Whatever it takes to stop the nightmares,' Jack said. 'And to keep Maggie safe.'

'You're still on leave at the moment?'

'My sick note's almost up, I think. Do I get another from you?'

Hargreaves smiled. 'Ironically, they are now called fit notes. Speak to your GP about that.'

The session continued for another thirty minutes, but Jack didn't invest too heavily in any of it. Once he'd discovered that Hargreaves was too stupid to read his notes properly, Jack had kept things quite superficial. He had given no indication of the torment that sometimes felt like a hurricane raging inside his head. He'd decided to keep that hidden or he'd be written off as mentally unstable. He was surprised Hargreaves had not asked about the content of his nightmares, not that Jack would have told him. Revealing that he had tried to strangle Rodney Middleton with a shoelace and felt an uncontrollable compulsion to destroy him on behalf of the unidentified victims would definitely not be a good idea.

* * *

Maggie, dressed in leggings and a vest top, was in the newly built kitchen extension checking on a pot roast. She beamed when she saw Jack.

'Hannah is at the park with Penny. The workmen have another couple of days on the loft extension before they start decorating, and Piglet is flat out after his last feed. I'm going to start feeding him bottled milk as well.'

'Why?'

'Because he's constantly hungry and I can't express enough milk... And I miss wine.'

Jack wrapped her in a bear hug and kissed her neck. 'You're back in terrific shape and looking gorgeous. We deserve the odd glass of wine in the evening. Just me and you.'

Grinning, Maggie squirmed free and flicked a tea-towel at him. 'Before I forget, I got an email from Hargreaves. You have an appointment at a sleep clinic at ten tomorrow. I printed it out... it's on the table.'

Jack went to the table to read the email. He'd got used to their cramped kitchen and it felt strange to have so much space now.

'So, what did Hargreaves say?' Maggie asked as she stuck a thermometer into the pot roast.

'Reckons I have some sort of sleep disorder which, let's face it, isn't exactly news! Apparently the sleep clinic monitors my brain and stuff while I'm sleeping, so I'll have to stay the night.'

'Did you explain what the nightmares are about?'

'He didn't ask. He was late for my appointment. And he didn't read the report you sent him. He thought I was attacking you when I was awake.' Maggie shook her head – she'd hoped Jack would have been impressed with Hargreaves, making him more likely to go back.

'Well, at least he booked the sleep clinic. They'll help find answers.'

'Let's hope so. Oh, and I need a sick note from our GP, or did he say from the sleep clinic. Can't remember.' The baby monitor kicked in, emitting a low gurgling sound.

'Can you go check on him? He might settle when he sees you. I'll prep the veg then come up.'

Jack deftly circumnavigated the dust sheets covering the stairs and landing. Stacks of paint tins and tools were propped along the walls and stairs leading to the second floor where the men were still working on the loft extension. Jack edged around them to move aside a plastic sheet covering the door to the newly refurbished nursery, which had once been Hannah's bedroom. It had now been extended to include an en suite bathroom. An alcove led into the next room, where Hannah's bed, wardrobes and toys occupied one side. There was a new carpet, freshly painted walls, pretty curtains and blinds.

When Maggie had first returned from the hospital, Hannah had thrown a tantrum and demanded that she take 'the piglet' back. But as the days passed, she'd become more accepting of her brother's presence and even seemed to like being a big sister. She was also excited to be starting prep school and especially looked forward to getting her new uniform and hat with a band and a badge on it.

Leaning over the cot, Jack stared at his handsome son lying on his back, his arms splayed out to the side and fists curled like a cherub. He had a robust, healthy appearance, with a round face, blue eyes and thick, curly blond hair, though his eyelashes were dark. He was growing quickly, and Jack knew it wouldn't be long before the bassinet was too small for him. Jack jumped as Maggie slipped her arms around his waist. She had watched from the archway, touched at the look of adoration on his face.

'Are we going to decide what to call him tonight?' Maggie asked.

'I'll open a bottle of wine then,' he said, kissing her. 'We might need it!' He made his way carefully downstairs, stepping over the paint tins which reminded him he was running very short of cash; he would have to find some more from somewhere to pay the builders and decorators to finish the work.

Unbeknownst to Maggie, Jack had used up his secret store of illegal cash which he had hidden in the garden shed. The money, which he hadn't asked for, had been left as a 'thank you' pay-off in his car after he had helped the four women involved in the mammoth train robbery to escape.

Along with the hidden cash had been jewellery acquired from another robbery investigation. He had sold it piece by piece over the past year and again used the money to pay the builders in cash. The only item left under the floorboards in the shed was the painting rolled in the cardboard tube given to him by the elusive artist Adam Border. Jack doubted it could be an authentic Giacometti painting as he had seen so many fake works in Border's studio. He'd also done some research on the internet and had been amused by the fact Giacometti only completed around five hundred works of art, yet it was estimated there were over thirteen thousand on the market. He was amazed by the number of famous artists whose works were routinely faked. In one exhibition of the artist Modigliani in Genoa, twenty paintings had been revealed to be counterfeits. The amount of money to be made from forgeries was astonishing.

Trying not to think about their financial situation, Jack checked the pot roast and turned the oven down. He selected a bottle of wine then vainly searched the kitchen's unfamiliar new layout for a corkscrew. He had only just found it when his mother arrived home with Hannah. Hannah came hurtling into the kitchen, screeching when she saw him and, with blind faith, she leapt into the air, knowing he would catch her.

'Daddy, Daddy, I met a puppy in the park and we played together! I really want a puppy – can I have one?' He swung her around and told her that it would have to wait as she would be starting at her new school, and it was not nice to leave a puppy on its own. Hannah wriggled free then glared up at him, hands on her hips. 'It wouldn't be by itself. Mummy, Nana and you are here. And I can play with it when I come home.'

'What about all the new friends you are going to make? You'll want to play with them, so maybe a puppy can wait until you're a bit older?' Hannah stamped her foot and looked as if she was about to throw a tantrum when Maggie called down for her to come and help bathe the baby.

'I'm asking Mummy about the puppy!' Hannah shouted as she stomped upstairs. Jack and Penny shared a quiet laugh as they listened to Hannah shouting 'Mummy!' all the way upstairs. Jack opened the wine and Penny put on an apron to make Hannah's tea and help finish dinner.

'Hannah has talked non-stop about a puppy ever since we left the park,' Penny said. 'She even suggested we swap the baby for one!'

Jack shook his head, smiling. 'Do you want a glass, Mum?'

'No thanks, dear.' Penny scooped up the veg prepared by Maggie. 'I'll get these on, set the table and sort Princess's tea.'

Jack poured himself a glass of wine and sat at the table. 'I love this new kitchen. So much more space. I think they should finish the loft conversion in a few days, too. Marius has just got to collect the glass for the loft skylight.'

'He's a lovely man, I must say, and I think he's done a great job so far,' Penny said. 'Those Romanian workmen of his seem very professional. You know the carpenter is related to his sister's husband?' Jack smiled. He knew Marius and Penny saw each other socially, not just around the house. He had taken her to the theatre, and she had introduced him to bingo which, to everyone's surprise, he thoroughly enjoyed. Jack and Maggie had tried to ascertain if their relationship was more than platonic, but neither wanted to ask Penny directly about it, so were left guessing.

Jack's mobile rang. He didn't recognise the number so he went into the living room and closed the door before answering.

Jack had just finished the call when Maggie burst in and told him off for promising Hannah a puppy. He raised his hands defensively.

'I never said she could have one! If she told you I did, she's lied.'

'Well, you need to tell her off then. "No name" is sleeping, so do it quietly.'

'Josh, from the US, just called. Remember, you met him when I was on that drug investigation . . . he came round for dinner.' Maggie dropped heavily onto the sofa.

'Oh yes, he was nice.'

'He's coming to London on some lecture tour. He wondered if he could stay for a night? It's a strange coincidence actually, as I was just thinking about the search we had on tracing . . .'

Maggie interrupted him. 'You're at the sleep clinic tomorrow night.'

'No, no, it's the following weekend Josh is coming.'

She frowned. 'Anyway, it's not exactly convenient with all the building work. The house is such a mess.'

'He can sleep in my office. I'll blow up that inflatable bed. It'll only be one or two nights.'

'Well, that doubled quickly! You said one night a minute ago.' Maggie sighed. 'I know you've already said yes. But don't just leave the extra cooking and food shopping to me and your mum. From memory, he eats like a horse. I see you've already started on the wine.'

'It's my first glass. Mum's finishing dinner, so you grab a drink and we'll name our son.'

Maggie stood up. 'Slow down a bit, Jack. You're drinking more than usual lately.'

He shrugged. 'It helps me get to sleep.'

Maggie raised her eyes to the ceiling before heading into the kitchen. 'Well, it doesn't help with the nightmares.'

Maggie didn't care that Jack had done little to help with the rebuilding work, other than load a few skips when he was available. Most of the time he had been at the Middleton trial, which she knew had been emotionally draining for him. And the unpredictable swinging between dreadful insomnia and terrifying nightmares had also taken its toll. She was relieved that Jack would be having an MRI and blood tests as part of his overnight stay at the clinic. He'd lost a considerable amount of weight and it worried her almost as much as the punching, kicking and shouting while he was asleep.

Maggie had hoped that, after the birth of the new baby, with Jack on parental leave and then a further two weeks of annual leave to come, his nightmares would get better. But they hadn't. He was still attentive and loving, but his temper was short, and he had started drinking heavily at night, supposedly to help him sleep. She knew he was constantly tired, and she worried that his volatile moods would only get worse with alcohol. Jack had been reluctant to see the police therapist, snapping that his colleagues would think he was screwed up. How could he retain his fellow officers' respect if they saw him walking into the fucking police therapist's office once a week? So Maggie was very relieved when Jack had agreed to see Hargreaves.

Maggie finished making supper while Penny fed Hannah, then took her upstairs to read her a bedtime story and put her to bed. She'd set the dining table for two as she liked to take hers on a tray to her bedroom and watch TV. Maggie sighed. They were so lucky to have Penny living with them. But when Maggie returned to work, she was concerned that Penny wouldn't be able to cope looking after Hannah and Piglet. Maggie had put out feelers with a few people at the hospital who she knew used au pairs but hadn't said anything to Penny yet. They had to do something, though. Maggie needed to return to work. Jack was always vague about money, but she could tell he was anxious about it, and they badly needed her salary. She decided that after they'd discussed the baby's name tonight, she would also raise the question of their financial situation.

CHAPTER 2

Hannah was still awake when Jack went up to check on her. He sat on her bed and gently reprimanded her for telling fibs. When she burst into tears and said she was sorry, he hugged and kissed her. As she settled back, he said they were trying to think of a nice name for her baby brother and, as she was his big sister, did she have one she liked? He was unsure about Bob SquarePants but asked her to keep thinking about it.

When he came downstairs, Maggie had lit candles for the table and dimmed the lights.

'You know, Jack, we could move the big table from the dining room into here and get rid of this old kitchen table. Then we could use this as a kitchen diner, making the dining room obsolete . . . we hardly use it anyway.'

Jack closed his eyes; he knew where this was heading. 'Please, Mags, no more knocking down walls.'

'Not straightaway, but we could open up the dining and living room and make it one huge room. Maybe get a nice big fireplace to replace that hideous tiled thing we've got . . . or make a partitioned area for the kids to play in.'

'The loft conversion will be a nursery and playroom for them. We can't afford it anyway.'

'Well, we do need to talk about money.'

Jack sighed. 'Tonight is for baby names.'

'I know you took out an extension on the mortgage which will cost us another five hundred a month,' Maggie persisted.

'Look, Mags, I've avoided VAT by paying Marius cash, which saves us a lot. He reckons they should be finished next week, so I'll know the total then.' Jack smiled reassuringly, wanting to bring the conversation to a close. 'We'll manage. Having one car makes a big difference.' In truth, Jack didn't know if they'd be OK or not. But there was no point discussing it with Maggie – she didn't have the whole picture and he wasn't prepared to enlighten her. He deftly changed the subject. 'I'll miss driving the Tesla though. Nice while we had it.'

Maggie frowned. 'I think it's awful that Simon's not been in touch. He's Hannah's godfather after all.'

Jack immediately wished he hadn't mentioned Ridley's bloody car. 'He's abroad,' he lied quickly. 'I got an email from him about taking the car back to the dealers.'

'An email? That all? I thought you were better friends than that,' Maggie said, shaking her head.

Jack poured himself another glass of wine and tried to get the subject back on track. 'Right, time we settled our son's name.' He was relieved when Maggie left to fetch her list of the names they had discussed so far.

She checked the baby monitor, quickly turning up the volume to listen to the baby's breathing as it would soon be time for another feed. 'Any thoughts on godparents?' she asked.

'Not yet.'

'I don't know if you agree, but I think Marius might be a good idea. I'm sure Penny would like it.'

'Isn't he a bit old? I thought it was about being, you know, like a guardian if anything happened to us?'

'Perhaps you should remind Simon of that when he next surfaces,' she said, testily. 'Right, names. What sounds good with Warr?' She flattened the notes out and picked up a pencil. 'The names on the list are . . . Oscar, Nathan, Adam, Daniel, James, Vincent, Henry, Louis . . .'

Jack leaned back and kept shaking his head as she read out one name after another. 'Don't like any of them.'

Maggie pursed her lips in irritation; she knew what he was up to. 'Stop shaking your head . . . we are not calling him Horatio! What do you think about Michael? That sounds good with Warr.'

'Nope, I don't like that either.'

She was losing her patience. 'I like Jason, Jason Warr?'

Jack sighed and gulped down the rest of his wine.

Maggie slapped the table with her hand. 'We need to register his name, Jack. And book a christening and . . .'

'I want to call him Horatio. Horatio Hornblower was a brave, defiant captain who sailed his own path. His life was one big adventure. No compromising. He was also the son of a doctor,' Jack added.

Maggie began to waver. 'What if we name him after your father? Will that satisfy you?'

'What . . . call him Charlie?'

'Yes, then Horatio can be his middle name if you like.'

Jack thought about it.

Maggie continued nudging. 'You have to consider the ribbing he'd have to contend with at school if he was called Horatio. I mean, some of the names these film stars call their kids are farcical.'

'Axl's all right.'

'What?'

'Guns N' Roses singer's called Axl'.

'No,' Maggie said firmly, unsure whether Jack was being serious. 'But what about Adam? That sounds good with our surname – Adam Warr. I like that.'

Jack repeated Adam Horatio Warr twice out loud, which seemed to Maggie like a positive sign.

'Terrific, we'll sleep on that. I'll feed and change him.' Maggie quickly left the room before Jack could say anything else.

Jack had no intention of calling his son Adam. It reminded him of the criminal, Adam Border, who he had hunted obsessively for months, suspecting his involvement in a horrific murder and large-scale drug dealing. He had eventually tracked Border to Ireland and was then offered a bribe he didn't refuse. Jack accepted the Giacometti painting to end the investigation and let Border go free, hoping he would go underground and never resurface. No, the name 'Adam' had all the wrong associations for Jack.

Just after eleven, Jack finished another large glass of wine, went upstairs, showered and got ready for bed. Maggie had already packed a small overnight bag for his visit to the clinic and was now reading. He opened her bedside table drawer and removed a small medicine bottle.

'If you don't mind, I'll take one of your sleeping tablets to get a good night's rest before the tests tomorrow.'

She worried that Jack was becoming reliant on the sleeping tablets but equally didn't want him having a nightmare and lashing out. 'I'd like you here with me tonight so if it helps you sleep, that's fine. I'll give him his next feed with us here in bed.'

A minute later, when Maggie put down her book and rolled over to face him, Jack was asleep. She turned off his night light and placed her phone beneath her pillow on 'vibrate' to wake her for the feed without disturbing him.

Maggie was in a deep sleep when Jack suddenly started pushing her in the back with both arms. He kicked out, making hard contact with her legs. She jumped out of bed and saw the look of fear on his face as he shouted through clenched teeth. 'Stay away from me. Leave me alone, get back. I don't know you. I can't find you.'

She stood watching anxiously as he punched and kicked out, his body twisting and turning. She cautiously went to his side and shook his shoulder.

'Jack, Jack, wake up. WAKE UP!'

His eyes opened wide in fear, not knowing where he was. He was panting and gasping for breath as he pulled himself into a sitting position. 'Oh God, it happened again . . . are you all right, Mags?'

'I'm fine. You were thrashing about and shouting, "stay away from me", like you were seeing ghosts. God, Jack, you looked so scared.' The baby monitor crackled, followed by the sound of Piglet crying. Maggie went to him while Jack, feeling nauseous, sat up rubbing his throbbing head – he was so hot, sweating like he'd done a workout at the gym. He got out of bed, snatching a cotton throw from the floor and staggered into the bathroom. He lay down on the cold tiles and covered himself with the throw.

By the time Maggie returned, Jack was asleep and, not wanting to disturb him, she reluctantly left him on the bathroom floor for the night. She wanted him with her, needed him. But he wasn't ready.

* * *

Maggie was up and dragging on her dressing gown in the morning when Jack emerged sheepishly from the bathroom, looking dreadful.

'I'll just feed him, then make us some breakfast. You grab a shower, and I'll order an Uber to take you to the clinic.'

'I'm sorry about last night.' Jack's voice had little life to it. Being so out of control of his own actions had drained him.

Maggie wrapped her arms around him and kissed him. She felt so sorry for him. 'They will get this sorted. You'll be back to your normal self in no time.'

'I hope so because I can't go on like this . . . and it's not fair on you. I'm completely knackered, and my head feels like it's going to explode.'

Jack looked better after his shower, but he hardly touched the bacon and eggs Maggie had prepared. He was very attentive to Hannah, who was eating a bowl of cornflakes and splashing milk around her plastic mat that covered the gingham tablecloth. Jack did a shocked face every time a splash of milk came his way, and it made Hannah laugh.

Penny and Maggie were discussing different formulas for the baby, as he had vomited after the one Maggie tried the day before. She was still breastfeeding as much as possible, but she knew it wasn't enough.

'Can you see if you can find one with a low iron content?' Maggie asked.

As Penny made a note so she wouldn't forget, she was also side-eyeing Jack. She'd heard him scream out during the night, as he had done on many other occasions. But although he looked all right now, she wasn't going to ask him about it. He'd been short-tempered with her whenever she broached the subject, so she was now leaving it all to Maggie.

The Uber arrived and Jack would have left without his overnight bag if Maggie hadn't handed it to him. It was a routine goodbye, as though he was just off on a work trip. Maggie didn't fuss, didn't wish him good luck. She closed the front door and controlled the tears before heading back to the kitchen.

'Do you think they'll be able to help him?' Penny asked.

'God, I hope so. On top of everything else, he's had terrible headaches lately. They'll give him an MRI scan to see . . .' She saw the shock on Penny's face, so quickly put on her doctor's voice, kind but clear. 'It's a good thing, Penny. There's family history of brain tumours on his mum's side?' Penny nodded. 'Then we need to rule that out.'

Maggie was sorry for bringing it up. To all intents and purposes, Penny was Jack's mother, having adopted him when he was just a toddler. Pouring a fresh cup of coffee, Maggie sat at the table, lifted Penny's hand and kissed it. She whispered so Hannah couldn't hear.

'I'm sorry for asking, Penny. I'm just worried about Jack. His nightmares and insomnia started during that recent murder trial, so that could be the reason. Or the stress of that could have triggered a physical issue. It could even be depression or anxiety. But he avoids talking about it, and I don't actually think he wants to return to work. I want to talk to Simon Ridley, you know, his old boss, but he seems to have disappeared. He was a mentor to Jack ... what with all the pressure of the baby, I wish he had a man to confide in.'

'Well, let's hope the sleep clinic can help,' Penny said, trying to be positive. 'And we can distract ourselves by taking Hannah to get her school uniform later. It's a special morning when parents can look at second-hand uniforms. I put it in the kitchen diary.'

'Sorry, I forgot all about it,' Maggie said. 'I'll come with you. And there's something I haven't told you ... I think we've almost agreed on a name for the baby. What do you think about Adam?'

Hannah pushed a half-eaten slice of toast away, got down from the table, and clung to Penny's arm as she sipped the dregs of her coffee and frowned.

'Adam?'

'Yes, we think it sounds good with our surname. It's sort of a deal I had to make, so Jack can't call him Horatio – that'll be his middle name.'

Penny couldn't hide her disappointment. 'I thought he was going to call him after his dad.'

Maggie pushed her chair back, not wanting an argument. It was obvious Penny didn't like Adam. 'Right, I am going to get me and the baby dressed. Then we'll all go to get your new uniform, Hannah.'

Penny whispered to Hannah. 'What do you think of calling your baby brother Adam?'

Hannah shook her head vehemently. 'No. Bob SquarePants!'

Once they were ready, Maggie put the baby in his car seat and waited for Penny and Hannah to join her. She was thinking of talking to Penny about getting an au pair, but knew she would have to tread carefully as Penny was very protective of her position in the household. However, the original idea that Penny would learn to drive had not been successful and after a couple of lessons, she had decided against it. So hiring an au pair who could drive would make sense. Whether it would be a live-in situation would also have to be discussed, but they would have room when the loft extension was done.

* * *

Jack was in the process of having an MRI scan at the clinic before meeting a therapist to discuss his sleep disorder. He would have further tests throughout the day then be left in a room to monitor his sleep pattern. He was calm, quite enjoying the attention and hopeful of a positive outcome.

It was early evening when Maggie received Jack's text and selfie. He was standing by the bed in his boxer shorts, with an alarming array of wires attached to his head, torso and legs. His text said that he'd had the MRI and was now expected to go to sleep with hundreds of wires forcing him to stay on his back and a nurse spying on him via a camera link. He was certain that the whole procedure would be a waste of time.

The picture made Maggie laugh. She texted back, saying she hoped he didn't get an electric shock and ending with, 'I love you very much.'

That night, Penny had the baby monitor and would see to the baby. So, for the first time in months, Maggie slept straight through.

The following morning, Penny had taken Hannah to the park and Maggie had just settled the baby down for his morning sleep when Jack arrived home. He called out and she hurried down the stairs to greet him. He put his overnight bag and a second larger bag down in the kitchen and hugged her.

'How did it go?'

He flicked the kettle on. 'Like I thought . . . a waste of bloody time. I hardly slept, and when I did, all they recorded was me snoring and my eyes twitching. They've given me something called Melatonin, but if it doesn't help, I may have to go back for another sleepover. On the plus side, they gave me a two-week sick note – sorry, "fit note" – due to lack of sleep and stress.'

'What's in the other bag?'

'A CPAP machine.' Jack opened the bag and put the machine on the worktop. 'Continuous Patient . . . something.'

'Continuous Positive Airway Pressure,' Maggie said, having seen patients using them many times. 'So did they say you could have sleep apnoea?' Jack's nod was uncertain, and Maggie knew that he hadn't listened properly. 'This pumps a continuous flow of air through a long tube attached to a breathing mask.'

Jack found the mask and put it on, making Maggie laugh out loud. He spoke in a Darth Vader voice: 'Follow me to the dark side, Maggie Warr.'

Maggie hugged him. 'I'd follow you anywhere, Jack Warr.'

Jack took the mask off so he could kiss her.

'I don't think there's anything wrong with your breathing when you sleep, but we'll give it a go,' Maggie said. 'What about the MRI?'

'The results will go to Hargreaves since he referred me to the sleep clinic. He'll arrange another appointment after he's seen the results . . . if he can find the time to read them, that is!'

* * *

Jack slept well for the next two nights and it seemed the CPAP machine was helping. On the third night, he tore off the mask and began thrashing about, shouting and punching so violently that he fell out of bed and cut his head open on the bedside cabinet. After that, he decided it was best if he slept on the sofa until his next appointment with Hargreaves. When he phoned the sleep clinic and told them what had happened, the doctor said to keep using the CPAP machine, but to stop taking the melatonin and replace it with trazodone, an antidepressant which helps with problems like insomnia. The clinic doctor emailed Jack's GP and the next day Maggie collected the prescription and took it to the local chemist.

Doubtful that drugs were of any use, Jack started working out for two hours a day at the gym instead of his usual one hour, hoping that excess physical exertion would tire him out and make him sleep better. It didn't.

Anxious and feeling Jack was now stuck in a vicious cycle, Maggie made an appointment to see Doctor Hargreaves herself. She didn't tell Jack. She said she was going to the hairdressers.

Hargreaves had read the sleep clinic report and Jack's MRI results, and the first thing he said was that there was no tumour or other physical issues with Jack's brain. He asked if the antidepressant tablets were helping.

Maggie sighed and shook her head. 'He said they make him feel lethargic during the day and he's finding concentrating difficult. The CPAP machine has helped a bit, I think, but he's still having nightmares . . . which makes it even more dangerous with that mask attached to his face. He ended up with the tube wrapped around his neck the other night.'

Hargreaves made some notes then looked thoughtful. 'Did Jack have any sleep problems when you first met?'

'No. He can't recall ever suffering from insomnia or nightmares before. I even asked his mother . . . she said he was never a restless sleeper until recently.'

Hargreaves leaned back in his chair. He knew discussing a patient's medical condition was unethical, even with the spouse. However, Maggie was a friend and also a medical professional, so they were bound by the same oath of confidentiality. That blurred the lines sufficiently for Hargreaves to continue.

'In his sessions with the sleep clinic psychiatrist, Jack said he could never remember the content of his nightmares. But the situation only manifested during a recent trial?'

Maggie nodded. 'Yes, Rodney Middleton. He murdered several young women.'

'Then, rather than sleep apnoea, it's more likely Jack has parasomnia. His nightmares are troubling; intense dreams that cause anger, anxiety or fear. The punching and kicking occurs because he acts out his dreams. The disorder is associated with multiple triggers, including stress, anxiety, depression and post-traumatic stress.'

Maggie nodded. 'I knew Jack was under a lot of pressure even before the trial started. He doesn't like to talk about it . . . in fact, he loathes bringing his work home. We both feel that way, especially as time together as a family is precious. I also had to deal with a lot of darkness and tragedy during the pandemic. We put it aside.'

'Quite natural,' Hargreaves said. 'But you must persuade him to talk now, Maggie. To you, or me, or a therapist of his choice. Keeping it all inside isn't working. Hypnosis might be a good next step if you can get him to agree. Recalling nightmares is the last thing the sufferer wants to do, but he must face his fears out in the open if he's to move on.'

* * *

Middleton knew that all prison phone calls were monitored and recorded, with the exception of calls with people identified by Rule 39 – legal counsel, the courts, anyone from the law society. These calls were the only ones with a guarantee of privacy. After her release, Middleton's girlfriend, Amanda Dunn, had joined the zero-hours, slave-fucking-labour cleaning agency used by the firm of solicitors representing Middleton so that, after hours and using the name of one of the legal team, she could call him or be there waiting for him to call her. As far as the prison was concerned, the woman on the phone was paralegal Gail Leadbetter and not Middleton's partner in some of the most horrific murders they'd ever come across.

At this moment, Middleton was talking quietly into the prison's public payphone, instructing Amanda to bring him drugs, hidden inside a Kinder Egg toy capsule which she would insert into her vagina. He dribbled on the mouthpiece of the phone as he imagined taking the egg back to his cell, the drugs on the inside and the smell of her on the outside. As he spoke, he cupped his groin and squeezed rhythmically.

'Tell me you're listening. Let me hear you.' But before she could respond, Middleton's two minutes came to an abrupt end.

* * *

Maggie was on her way home with two full bags of groceries, sighing heavily. Getting Jack to even consider hypnosis would be a tough sell. She intended to spend one more month off before going back to the hospital and she prayed that during that time they would find something to help Jack's condition.

In the meantime she had the christening to arrange and either an au pair or nanny to hire, whether Penny liked it or not. As she was thinking, Maggie immediately hit the familiar brick wall of not knowing where their finances were at. Could they even afford to employ help? Her personal account was overdrawn, and she assumed their joint account had very little money left. When the loft was completed, there'd be another hefty cash payment to find. Then she remembered Hannah's school fees ... It was never-ending.

Maggie opened the front door, pausing to listen when she heard Jack's infectious belly laugh. What a lovely sound! And so rare in recent months. Then she heard Hannah's high-pitched squeal.

'Daddy, do it again!'

Opening the dining room door, Maggie saw the table and chairs stacked against one wall and, covering most of the floor space, a blow-up mattress. Jack rolled around laughing as Hannah jumped up and down in excitement. Each time she landed, Jack released the pump which created a loud farting sound.

'Daddy's doing bottom burps!'

Maggie grinned. 'I can hear! Where's your mum?' she asked Jack.

'Upstairs with the baby.'

'I've ordered a KFC. It'll save me having to cook,' Maggie said.

'I'll eat with Josh when he arrives.'

Maggie had forgotten his American friend was coming to stay. Of course! That was why he'd got out the inflatable bed.

'The spare duvet and pillows are in Penny's wardrobe. Sheets and stuff are in the airing cupboard. Where's the big table?'

'Ah, we moved that into the kitchen. The old pine table is in the garden.'

'Fine by me. Come on, Hannah. Bath time.'

Maggie bathed Hannah and put her into her pyjamas, then let her play in her bedroom while she settled the baby after his feed. Just after seven, she went back to the dining room where Jack was putting the fitted sheet onto the blow-up bed.

'I'll move the dining chairs into the kitchen,' she said. 'It'll be great we won't need a dining room when we have a big kitchen-diner.'

She was shocked when Jack suddenly rounded on her. 'I've made room for my friend to stay over, not agreed to knocking more walls down. Gimme a break. I've had enough of the place looking like a building site. Plus, Marius has cost a fortune, even cash in hand. And, let's face it, we won't know if the work is any good until they've all packed up and gone.'

This wasn't the first time recently Jack had snapped at her out of nowhere. 'I think they've been really professional,' she said evenly.

'Well I'm sick and tired of them being here. And of you acting like a fucking interior designer, getting them to do even more work.'

Maggie couldn't control herself any longer. 'Well, it's not as if you were any help, Jack! I've had to oversee it all.'

'Because you instigated it all!' he retorted.

She wanted to fight back but could see that it would just make things worse. He was getting more agitated by the second.

'Have you taken your medication?'

Jack threw his hands up. 'I'm not taking any more of those bloody anti-depression tablets. They made me feel like shit. So, what did Hargreaves say about me?' He waited for her to answer.

'Well, you've clearly not had your hair done, Mags. So, what did he say?'

'Fine, so you caught me out. I wanted to speak to him personally because things aren't getting any better. You'll be pleased to know the MRI shows you don't have a tumour, Parkinson's or ME. Hargreaves thinks you have parasomnia. It's a sleep disorder . . .'

'I know what it is!' Jack interrupted. 'The shrink at the clinic went through all the possibilities with me.'

'I have some leaflets from Hargreaves. They advise about self-help for parasomnia . . . they might be worth a read.'

Jack dropped his head and rested his hands on his hips. He seemed exhausted – physically and mentally.

'I don't think there is a cure, Mags.'

'We have to keep trying, Jack. Your nightmares are a danger to both of us.'

'Then I'll sleep on this blow-up bed when Josh has gone. That suit you better?'

Maggie knew that turning on her was just Jack deflecting. He was worried. She went on carefully. 'There was something else Hargreaves suggested.'

Jack didn't move, didn't ask. He almost looked like he was asleep standing up.

'He thinks hypnosis might help and . . .'

Jack looked up sharply. 'No fuckin' way. I've had electrodes plastered all over my body, been on one medication after another and tried that stupid breathing machine. He's clutching at straws. He's clueless.'

'He's used hypnosis with parasomnia patients many times and, in general, it was a success.'

'He'll have me regressing to God knows where, reliving God knows what . . .' Jack checked himself. He was starting to sound irrational. He took a deep breath and whispered, 'Fine, I'll think about it.'

It was like bashing her head against a wall, so Maggie changed the subject. 'When are you going back to work?'

'In a couple of weeks, when the sick note, fit note, whatever it is, runs out. But I don't know if I want to stay at the same station or apply for a transfer.'

'OK.' Maggie took over making the bed. Jack stood and watched, like a useless child. Maggie took a deep breath, knowing she had to broach another delicate topic. 'I can go back to work full-time in about four weeks. I could ask about part-time, but we need the money. Me being full-time would obviously mean a lot of extra work for Penny.' Maggie heard Jack sigh behind her. He knew what she was about to say, but it needed saying regardless. 'I know Hannah will be at school from nine till three, but someone has to take her there and back and the baby will be here all day.' Maggie stood up and faced Jack as she put on the duvet cover. 'It's a lot for your mum, Jack.'

'She says she's fine.'

'Of course she does. I haven't talked to Penny yet, but we will have the space now with the loft conversion. If we get an au pair that would be live-in, an experienced nanny would be part-time.'

'God, Maggie.' Jack rubbed his forehead hard. 'We'd both be working full-time to pay a stranger to help Mum, who can do it all for free. That doesn't make sense.'

Now Maggie was the one becoming frustrated. 'Jack, I'm overdrawn at the bank, our joint account has to be nearly at zero and we haven't furnished the loft yet.'

'Fuck the bloody loft! If there's no one living in it, we don't need to furnish it do we!' His booming voice made Maggie jump. Jack turned down the volume as he continued, but he was still just as intimidating. 'We're not getting a live-in au pair – or a part-time nanny for that matter. That's the end of it, Mags – I mean it.' Jack took a step forward and almost whispered his final comment. 'And I'm well aware that we don't have a pot to piss in.'

Maggie realised that she was holding her breath. Jack had stepped into her space and that scared her. She was relieved when Penny called out that the KFC had arrived. Maggie dropped the half-done duvet to the floor and left. She'd never seen him so angry . . . not with her. Whether it was down to his medication or lack of sleep, she knew she had to find a solution to his problem.

She needed her husband back.

CHAPTER 3

Jack opened the front door and was overjoyed to see his six foot four American friend, Josh, standing on the porch. Although he'd aged, and his thick black hair was now speckled with white, he still looked fit. They shook hands, gave each other a manly hug and patted backs. Josh only had one large rucksack, explaining that he'd put his cases in left luggage at Euston station. Jack noticed his limp was more pronounced as they walked to the kitchen. Josh whistled in admiration at the new extension and open-plan layout.

'Man, this is spectacular. What a difference, it's three times the size.'

'My mother's "friend" did all the work with his crew. He's also doing a loft conversion. Next time you stay, you'll have a bedroom with en suite.'

Jack opened a bottle of whisky and poured two large glasses. They sat at the table. Josh filled him in about his family life, said he was no longer working as an undercover officer for the New York Police due to his further hearing loss. But they still employed him and he was currently doing a lecture tour speaking to police and prison officers across the UK. Josh said he'd spoken with DCI Clarke, who told him Jack was on sick leave.

'What's the problem?'

Jack waved his hand. 'Oh, nothing, it's just a ploy to extend my paternity leave.'

Josh knew Jack was hiding something and was about to press him when Penny walked in.

'Josh!' Penny gushed. 'How lovely to see you again. How's Louisiana? Do you still have a healthy appetite for roast leg of lamb with all the trimmings?'

'Ha! Great memory, Ma'am. Your food was delicious, the best I've ever tasted. Talking of food . . .' Josh beamed. 'I wonder if you guys fancy going out to eat . . . on me, of course.'

Penny wished she could say yes. 'We had something earlier but thank you for the offer. If you're hungry, I can make you both something.'

'No need, Mum,' Jack said. 'I bought two big steaks this afternoon.'

As Penny made herself a hot chocolate, Josh showed her photographs of his daughters on his mobile. Jack was impatient for Penny to leave but she was clearly enjoying herself and so it seemed was Josh.

'Who's that beautiful woman standing next to your daughters?' Penny asked.

'I intend to marry her as soon as my divorce is through,' Josh said.

Penny tensed her shoulders disapprovingly but then forced a smile. 'I'll leave you boys to it, then.'

Just as Penny was leaving, Maggie walked in with the baby balanced on her hip. Josh leapt up, hands out, desperate to hold the newest addition to Jack's family.

'My God, he's perfect. No wonder you went off sick, Jack.' Josh held the baby in the crook of his arm and swayed from side to side. 'I'd never want to let this guy out of my sight either. What's his name?'

'I want to call him Horatio, but Maggie doesn't like it,' Jack said.

Maggie smiled, playing it down. 'For goodness' sake, Jack, don't start this again.' Then she addressed Josh directly. 'I think we're going to call him Adam.'

'I haven't said yes, Maggie. And Josh will understand why. Remember the case we worked on, that big drug bust?'

'Yeah, yeah, I remember. Adam Border. We spent months trying to track him down. He was suspected of killing his mother . . . dangerous bastard disappeared off the face of the earth.'

Maggie stared daggers at Jack. Why drop this bombshell for the first time in front of Josh?

'Well, in that case, of course we won't call our child Adam. Penny will be pleased. She didn't like it either. Perhaps we're back to naming him after your dad then.'

'My kids' names all start with J. So any inherited silver will have the same initials,' Josh said. 'Maybe call him Jake. Jake Warr. Or Junior.'

Jack raised his eyebrows in approval as Maggie took the baby back from Josh. She was not prepared to discuss her child's name with yet another person.

'Right, I'll leave you two in peace unless you need me to make you something to eat.'

'I've got it organised,' Jack said. As he stepped in to kiss his son, Maggie shook her head at him, still unable to believe he hadn't bothered to tell her why he was against the name Adam.

With Jack and Josh now alone, Jack topped up their whisky. 'I'll take you upstairs later to show you the loft extension. Maggie has been like a sergeant major, ensuring the bulk was done before the baby arrived.'

Josh pretended to shudder. 'Adam Warr. Imagine. That's the problem with our job, everything reminds us of someone we'd rather forget ... I suppose Border sticks in your mind as the one that got away, even more so nowadays as I'm here giving warning lectures about some new drugs which I reckon will be taking hold in this country soon if you don't do something about it.'

'What did you make of DCI Clarke?'

'Not that helpful. And quite evasive when I asked about you.'

Jack opened the fridge and took out two large T-bone steaks on a covered dish.

'Clarke said you'd had a lengthy trial to deal with, and the defence council grilled you good and proper in the witness box.'

'That's putting it mildly. Did you see Laura at the station?'

Josh nodded, sipping his drink and giving himself time to think. 'Bit awkward. We both knew that what we had going wasn't the real deal. I wrote to her a few times when I went back to New York. Maybe she wanted more from me, but at the time I was still married, and to be honest, it was really a sort of one-night stand that went on for many nights!'

Jack smiled, although he knew Laura had been seriously smitten.

Josh continued. 'We were on the Adam Border investigation when I met her. But I left the UK before it came to a conclusion. Laura said he was still on the run.'

'Yeah, yeah, that's right. How do you like your steak?' Jack asked, not wanting Josh to talk anymore about the wanted man he'd let escape.

'Rare. Can I do anything to help?'

'No, everything's under control. You just sit and relax.'

As Jack popped the chips into the air fryer, Josh poured himself another whisky. He took out a cigar, held a lighter to the tip and asked if it was OK to smoke indoors. Jack hesitated, knowing Maggie would loathe it, and the pause was enough for Josh. He got up, opened the conservatory door and stepped outside into the garden.

Jack set the table, opened a bottle of red wine to let it breathe, and then threw together a side salad. The T-bone steaks, one rare and one medium, took only a few minutes to cook, and the chips were done at the same time. The whole process had taken the same time as smoking half a cigar. Josh came in from the garden to see his host opening one drawer after another, looking for steak knives and napkins.

'My God, this is a feast. And the steaks are the size we get in the States. Very much appreciated. Thank you, Jack.'

With everything dished up, Jack poured the wine; they toasted each other and tucked in.

Even though they had worked together, Josh felt he didn't really know Jack all that well, and it had been a while since they'd had contact. Josh was a very experienced officer with an excellent ability to assess people quickly due to his years undercover. But he found Jack hard to fathom. There was a boyish enthusiasm to him and a charming openness, but he always felt Jack was holding a lot back. He definitely disapproved of Josh's affair with Laura, for instance. It was Laura who'd said that Jack was on sick leave, but no one knew why. She also said he had changed a lot recently, putting it down to the absence of DCI Ridley.

Josh noticed how reticent Jack was when asked innocuous questions about returning to work. He avoided eye contact while distracting himself with clearing the dishes. He opened another bottle of wine and asked Josh where he was going to be travelling. Josh gave a rundown of the various stations he had already visited, some work he was doing with the UK National Crime Agency and a few prisons where he felt his talks would be beneficial. Josh noted Jack's lack of interest, staring ahead as if not even listening. He instinctively knew something was deeply wrong, but didn't want to ask in case it was personal, having sensed the tension between Maggie and Jack earlier.

'I miss undercover work,' Josh continued. 'But it was getting tough with my hearing getting worse and then my leg. Sciatica is a bitch! And all you can do is stuff yourself with painkillers. My boss put this programme in my orbit, connected to stuff going on in San Francisco, and then after a few months there I was sent over to LA because they were in a similar situation.'

'Situation?' Jack asked, pouring them both another glass of wine.

'There's a fucking epidemic over there! Zombie drugs, killing thousands of young kids. Fentanyl is being sold mixed with cocaine and heroin. It's a plague.'

Josh got up and stepped out for a second, saying he wanted to show Jack something. He returned with a small medical box, opening it at the table. He held up one of the small glass tubes.

'When there's an opioid overdose, from heroin or prescription drugs like Vicodin, OxyContin or Percocet, this little vial literally brings them back from the dead. Naloxone. You don't even need a prescription. You can buy it from any pharmacy in the US. I'm not sure about here.'

Jack nodded. 'Pharmacies don't stock it here. But I think all emergency services carry it now. Police have been trained to use it since mid-2023. Well, that's what's supposed to be happening.'

'I've been visiting all the known drug hangouts, first in San Francisco and then in LA, to get naloxone out there and save as many lives as possible. Junkies started carrying a vial at all times. You can see them administering it to each other out on the streets ... Anyway, just as we're making headway protecting people against the fucking mixed street drugs we know about, a brand new one sweeps through the inner cities.' Josh's level of passion doubled as he continued. 'This one is strong enough to knock out an elephant. It's called xylazine and wreaks havoc on users. The body count keeps mounting. Naloxone doesn't have any reversal effect on xylazine; what happens with this poison is their flesh rots, and the skin opens up with horrific lesions that don't heal. Amputating the limb is the only way to stop the spread around the body.'

'But it's not here in the UK?' Jack showed proper interest for the first time.

'It's coming. That's why I'm here. You've already had some deaths for sure. Your prisons have seen it. It's sometimes known as tranq or sleep-cut. It's a common veterinary tranquilliser used on cattle, horses and elephants. They inject it, swallow it or even crush the tablets into a powder so they can snort it. The dealers are also mixing it with fentanyl to get a greater high. Sometimes the user has no memory because it can cause amnesia, and as it's a respiratory depressant, it causes the heart rate and blood pressure to plummet. They become total zombies, dying on their feet, and . . .'

Josh suddenly bowed his head, and his shoulders shook as he started sobbing.

Jack quickly pushed back his chair and moved to Josh's side. 'Hey, come on. Maybe it's time you got some sleep. Jet lag's messing with your head.'

Embarrassed, Josh covered his face with his hands as he wept, having kept in the horrors for so long. 'Sorry, man, I've just seen so much.' When he tried to get up from the table, he stumbled as his bad leg went from under him. Jack had to grab him by the shoulders and help him to stand. He guided Josh out of the kitchen, almost buckling under the weight of the big man, then helped him into the dining room and onto the blow-up bed. Josh flopped back, moaning. 'Sorry for losing it, man, but what this stuff is doing to kids is a nightmare.'

'Believe me, I understand when it comes to nightmares,' Jack said, putting the pillows behind his friend's head.

Josh adjusted his hearing aid. 'What did you say?'

'Nightmares. I have them too.'

'Try living in one, day after day, night after night. To be honest, I've been sent on this so-called lecture tour because I was losing it . . . reality is I can't take being at the centre of this sickness. In the past, I've always been able to handle it but . . . maybe twenty years is enough for any man. I've risked my life Christ knows how many times, even going undercover in Mexico to infiltrate a gang bringing the chemicals in from China to cook up the fentanyl.'

Josh looked over to Jack. He was staring into space, clearly no longer listening. Josh eased himself off the bed, pulling himself to his feet on Jack's arm.

'I need the bathroom, not drunk so much in years.'

Jack hurried ahead to hold open the door. 'Downstairs loo is next to the kitchen. If you want to shower, there's a family bathroom on the second floor, by the nursery.'

Jack watched as Josh unzipped his holdall and grab his toiletries bag.

'Downstairs will be fine.'

Josh pressed hard on his leg as he limped from the room. Jack felt bad about zoning out. With all this talk of drugs, maybe Josh was hitting a little too close to home.

* * *

From the outside, the abandoned school looked completely derelict. Only the back bumper of a white Ford Transit van suggested any signs of life.

Indoors, the old drill hall was a hive of activity as four heavy-set men were taking crates from the back of the room to the main doorway ready for transporting out.

In the dim light, a slender man leaned motionless over a canvas on an easel at the far side of the room. He was wearing a set of surgical binocular magnifying glasses for close examination of the brush strokes and a silk scarf covered his mouth and nose. He lowered the scarf briefly to take a drag on his cigarette. Every now and then, he glanced up to make sure his men were fulfilling his instructions to the letter. One of the men was cutting some bubble wrap from a ten-metre roll.

'No!' the slender man screamed. The men froze. 'Muslin. Only muslin touches the canvas. How many times? Muslin, then straw, then the fucking bubble wrap. Bubble wrap leaves indents in the oils, clear as fucking day!'

The slender man turned from the easel with a sigh, and stood over them, watching their every move as the last paintings were finally packed inside the crates. One of the men opened the main door and they started loading the crates into the Ford Transit.

The slender man began to relax a little as he lowered the silk scarf and lit another cigarette. 'Fucking imbecilic monkeys,' he muttered, as the doors closed behind them. He unwound the scarf, tossing it aside before shaking out his thick shoulder-length hair, then removed his magnifying surgical glasses, placing them carefully in a leather box on a trestle table. Finally, Adam Border smiled.

* * *

Maggie finished the last breastfeed of the evening, then changed her still nameless baby's nappy before taking him to his bassinet and tucking the blanket tightly around him. Then she went to collect a formula bottle for his next feed. Maggie paused on the landing; she couldn't hear voices but heard the downstairs toilet flushing. Looking over the rail, she saw Josh moving slowly and painfully along the hall into the dining room. Next, Jack came out of the kitchen with a bottle of whisky and two glasses.

'I'm going to bed,' she said quietly.

Jack looked up at her. 'I won't be long.'

'Will you bring the baby monitor from the kitchen? I'll probably crash out before you come up.'

'OK, goodnight.'

Jack went into the dining room with the whiskies, but Josh was already crashed out and snoring, so Jack turned off the lights and went upstairs.

Maggie woke at around 4 a.m., annoyed that Jack had not brought up the baby monitor. She felt like waking him and sending him to go and get it but decided to let him sleep. She crept quietly into the nursery and could tell by the baby's restless movements that he would soon want his next feed.

Maggie poured hot water from the kettle into a bowl and submerged the bottom of the baby's bottle, waiting for the milk to warm while her thoughts drifted. She physically jumped when Josh walked into the kitchen wearing only his jockey shorts.

'Oh, sorry, Maggie, I just came in for a glass of water.'

'Oh, that's all right,' she said, recovering herself. 'I'm just getting the baby's bottle. I left Jack fast asleep, which is a blessing. I don't know if he mentioned anything to you.'

Josh shrugged as he took a glass from a cupboard. 'I'm afraid I sort of dominated the conversation. I had some personal stuff to get off my chest. Got a little emotional.'

Maggie sighed. 'I wish Jack would. I was hoping he might talk to you. He has a sleep disorder. It got so bad I made him see a specialist. Such nightmares, Josh. It's been very frightening. He punches and kicks out in his sleep, screaming and shouting. After a load of tests, they've pretty much diagnosed him as having parasomnia.'

'Which is . . . ?'

'Oh, it's basically caused by post-traumatic stress.'

Josh shook his head in disbelief. 'Jack didn't mention anything like that.'

'That's Jack, he won't discuss it. I've tried to get him to tell me what these nightmares are about, but he says he can't remember. It all started after he worked on a horrific serial killer case. I was hoping that he might talk to you about that.'

'I have noticed a change in him, but the reality is we were never that close. And it's been years since I last saw him'.

Maggie tested the warmed bottle, wrapping a linen cloth around it.

She sighed as she started towards the door, stopping at the table. Josh's medical box was still open.

'Naloxone, right? It's an overdose reversal drug. A while back, we were given some training in how to use it. We've had some fentanyl problems at the hospital – we were even warned about discarding used dressings containing residue as it was being syphoned off by addicts. One of the specialists I work with told me about seeing young kids around Victoria station . . . at first, he thought they were statues, you know, kids trying to make a few quid, but they're drugged out of their minds.'

Josh nodded. 'That's why I'm over here, giving lectures about it.'

Maggie couldn't help checking out the other drugs in the box. 'You've quite a selection of opiates and tramadol patches.'

'I have severe sciatica, so they're prescribed for me. The reason I'm no longer working full-time for the NYPD . . .'

'I'm sorry. You're obviously in a lot of pain. But do please make sure this is not left here like this; we have a very nosey little girl in the house.'

Josh was about to reply when they both heard Jack screaming, then a crashing sound, followed by the baby crying.

'He'll have fallen out of bed,' Maggie said calmly. 'Can you go and see to Jack, please, while I check on the baby.'

Josh found Jack lying on the floor beside the bed with a fresh cut on his forehead. It seemed he had knocked over the bedside table and smashed the lamp, sending shards of glass across the wooden floor. Josh stepped on a jagged piece, swore loudly and staggered forwards in the dark. Still in the grip of the nightmare, Jack's arms started flailing as he tried to push Josh away, then started punching him.

'Jack, it's me, it's Josh . . . JACK!' Josh slapped Jack's face. After a moment Jack seemed to come to his senses. He looked like a frightened child.

'Sorry . . . I'm sorry. I didn't mean to hit you.'

Josh helped him up and sat him on the bed.

'Where's Maggie?' Jack asked anxiously.

'She's checking the baby. Let me see that cut on your forehead; the lampshade got broken.' Josh walked on the edge of his foot to the bathroom so as not to push the glass deeper into his flesh. He got a wet facecloth, plasters and disinfectant, then cleaned and dressed Jack's forehead before pulling the glass from the sole of his foot, disinfecting it and sticking on a plaster.

Neither said a word when Maggie walked in; Jack just gave her a helpless smile of apology. She gave Josh a pleading look, partly a thank you for taking care of Jack but she was also asking him for help.

'You want to come downstairs and sit with me for a while, Jack?' Josh asked, moving to the bedroom door.

'No, I'm fine. You go back to bed.'

'You're not fine. If Maggie had been beside you, and God forbid with the baby in her arms, you could have done them both some serious damage. Talk to me, Jack. Come downstairs and talk to me.'

Jack glared at Maggie, knowing she must have been talking to Josh about him. He went into the bathroom and slammed the door behind him. Maggie was almost in tears as she raised her hands in a gesture of defeat.

'I'm sorry, Maggie,' Josh said helplessly, 'but that little tussle has left me in a bit of pain. I think I'm going to have to go to bed.'

'Of course,' Maggie said, quickly recovering herself.

He moved slowly downstairs to the kitchen and picked up his medical box and a glass of water before limping back into the dining room. Lowering himself onto the bed, he removed a hypodermic needle, then breaking the seal off the morphine capsule, he filled the syringe. He cleaned the skin with a sterilised wipe before injecting himself. Next, sipping the water, he took two OxyContin tablets, before carefully wrapping the needle in tissue to dispose of later.

Josh took slow, deep breaths as the morphine gradually dulled the pain. He leaned back against the pillows and began to feel his body relax. He could feel rather than hear the soft footfalls as Jack came and sat on the edge of the bed.

'You need to talk, Jack, get whatever is tormenting you out into the open.'

Jack got up and started to pace around the bed.

'Maggie mentioned you had a gruesome murder case before the nightmares started. Is that what it's all about?'

Jack sat back on the bed and, in a flat, emotionless voice told Josh all about Rodney Middleton and the horrific things he'd done. The only time his voice started to crack was when he explained about the victims who were still unidentified.

Josh shook his head. 'What a monster. But he could have gone on to kill many more kids if it wasn't for you.'

Jack didn't seem to hear him. 'I had a meeting with my boss about the unidentified DNA found in the bastard's basement. I was told the case would remain on file as the cost of trying to identify every suspected victim would be financially unacceptable – it would be reviewed in a year or two. Even though Middleton got a whole life sentence and will never get out of prison, I pleaded that we should make every effort to find out who else he killed, but it fell on deaf ears.'

With the drugs kicking in, Josh was now feeling in desperate need to go to sleep, but Jack seemed to have just got into his stride.

'I twisted some arms and I was given five minutes to talk to Middleton in the Old Bailey cell while he was waiting to be taken to prison. When the cell door opened and he saw it was me, he looked proper scared. I told him all I wanted was for him to give me names, to give the families closure.'

'But he didn't,' Josh guessed.

Jack clenched his fists as he recalled the feeling of pulling the shoelace tighter and tighter around Middleton's neck – his red sweaty skin, his bulging, terrified eyes. Jack whispered more to himself than to Josh, 'I wanted to kill him.'

'I can understand how you must have felt, Jack. But take some satisfaction from knowing his life behind bars will be a nightmare. Even on the nonce wing, there's a hierarchy of filth and my guess is that he'll be close to the bottom.'

Jack didn't seem to hear him. 'The worst moment for me was when I left court, so pent-up with rage and frustration I wanted to scream. Then a woman came up to me clutching a photograph of her fifteen-year-old daughter who'd been missing for five years. She was certain Middleton had murdered her, even though her DNA wasn't a match with any of the blood traces we found in the basement. I'd seen that woman in court every day, alongside all the other grieving parents... I promised I would do everything I could to find out what happened to her daughter, so when the investigation was closed, I felt I'd failed her.' Jack finally rested his head in his hands.

'You need to move on, Jack,' Josh said gently. 'Try and put this awful case behind you. I know it's not easy, but...'

'You don't understand,' Jack said angrily.

'I'm trying to.' Josh was feeling utterly worn out and desperate for sleep now. The only thing keeping him awake was the pain gradually returning as the medication began to wear off. He felt relieved when Jack got up and opened the door. He slowly turned round with a pitiful smile.

'I'm losing it,' he said simply before closing the door behind him.

Josh took another syringe from his medical box and gave himself another injection of morphine. He rested back on the pillows, feeling the pain slowly fading, and closed his eyes.

CHAPTER 4

Josh slept until 9 a.m., then put on jeans and a white T-shirt before packing his belongings. He walked barefoot into the kitchen, where Maggie sat at the table forcing down a decaf coffee while the baby was sleeping in his carrier beside her.

'Penny and Hannah have gone to the park, and Jack has gone for a run. He popped in to see you earlier, but you were sound asleep. Would you like some eggs and bacon for breakfast?'

'That would be great, thank you. The mattress was very comfortable. Do you want me to let the air out and fold it up?'

'Leave it . . . if Jack's nightmares continue, he said he might sleep downstairs. Coffee or tea?'

'Coffee would be great.' Josh drew up a chair while Maggie prepared breakfast.

'I had a long talk with Jack last night.'

Maggie handed him a freshly brewed mug. 'Yes, thank you Josh. He seemed calmer when he came to bed and didn't have another nightmare, thank goodness.'

Josh hesitated, wondering how he could explain his concerns to Maggie without revealing what Jack had said about wanting to kill Middleton.

'He went into a lot of detail about the Rodney Middleton case. It's clearly had a big emotional impact on him, especially dealing with the families whose daughters had been murdered or gone missing. I hope I am not speaking out of turn, but I think Jack is suffering from vicarious trauma. Basically, it's caused by prolonged exposure to other people's pain.'

'I've heard of it,' Maggie said. 'I'm aware of medics suffering from it, mainly those working in emergency and intensive care departments.'

Josh nodded. 'It's the same for detectives like Jack, who investigate horrific murders and the sexual abuse of children. Dealing with the victims, their families and witnesses can go on for months, even a year or more. No wonder it leads to mental health problems.'

'And you think it's causing his nightmares.'

'I do. I also believe it's the reason he doesn't want to talk about it or go back to work and face investigating similar cases again. I think it's imperative he gets counselling before he does something he will regret.'

'He adamantly refuses to see therapy as a serious option. He thinks the man he saw was an idiot, but I think that's just his way of deflecting.'

'He needs to see a real specialist,' Josh said.

'I wish I could track down Ridley,' Maggie sighed. 'He was always such a mentor for Jack, but I have no idea where he is or, for that matter, the circumstances surrounding his disappearance. Something happened between them which I have never been able to get out of Jack, apart from the possibility Ridley has cancer again and is not coming back to the station.' Maggie returned to the cooker and plated the eggs and bacon with fried bread and baked beans. As she placed it in front of Josh, he gave her an appreciative smile. 'Where are you off to next?' she asked.

'Manchester, Liverpool and Leeds. I have quite a busy schedule giving talks at police stations and prisons.' He didn't mention that he had arranged to meet Laura first.

'You must miss your family.'

He nodded but made no reply.

'Is it your second marriage?'

'It'll be my third'.

'Do you have other children or just the two little girls?'

'I did . . . my eldest son died not long ago.'

'Oh, I'm sorry.'

Maggie waited a moment for Josh to say more, but he didn't. Instead, he tucked into his breakfast as Maggie checked on the baby before lifting his carrycot to take him upstairs.

'I need to give him a bath and another feed,' she sighed.

'He's a lovely little boy,' Josh said.

'Thank you. We need to organise the christening, never mind choose the name. I thought about it last night and decided we'll christen him after his grandfather – Charles. And keep Horatio as his middle name. This means Penny will be happy, and hopefully, it'll perk Jack up as well. Though we'll probably use Charlie like everyone did with his dad.' Maggie paused at the kitchen door. By now, the baby had started to wake, so she told Josh to help himself to more coffee and that Jack would hopefully be home before he left.

Josh finished his breakfast then went into the cloakroom to freshen up. In the room he'd used to sleep in, he put on a fresh shirt and clean socks and laced up his expensive trainers. He got dressed, then double-checked he had left nothing in the room before slipping the medical box into his rucksack. He grabbed his leather jacket from the back of a chair and checked his wallet and passport were inside. He stood in the hall momentarily, listening, before quietly opening the front door and closing it behind him.

* * *

Maggie bathed and dressed Charlie, then gave him another feed before she showered and got changed. She could hear Penny and

Hannah downstairs as they returned from the park. She put Charlie in his cot, rocking him gently until he fell asleep, then checked the baby monitor and went downstairs. She was surprised to find that Josh had left without waiting for Jack to get back from his run.

In the kitchen Penny was making pancakes, while Hannah jumped up and down, demanding that she toss one. Maggie smiled, leaving them to it, saying she was quickly going to check her emails. She left the baby monitor on the counter, picking up a stack of post.

In her bedroom, Maggie opened her laptop and Googled 'Vicarious Trauma'. The symptoms included lingering feelings of anger, rage and sadness, with sufferers often experiencing guilt, shame, self-doubt, sleeplessness and nightmares. She sighed. Jack seemed to have the lot.

* * *

Each time Jack's foot hit the pavement, it reminded him how desperately he needed a new pair of trainers. The average lifespan was around 400 miles and he had to be coming up to 600. No wonder he could feel the impact every time. He might as well be wearing plimsolls. But the air was cool, the streets were quiet, and he was beginning to get his second wind. Just as he prepared to put on a spurt, he noticed that one of his laces was undone.

'Bloody things.'

As he knelt to retie it, this time with a double knot, he noticed a young girl, no more than eighteen, across the road waiting at a bus stop. She was glancing at her watch and pacing nervously. A horrible memory of Rodney Middleton's voice surfaced in his mind: 'I can always spot a runaway. Train stations. Bus stops. All trusting and grateful. Just waiting to be saved.' Jack clenched his jaw, unconsciously twisting the shoelace round his fingers and pulling, harder and harder. He could see Middleton's terrified face in the shiny stainless steel cell toilet, and he wished to God that he'd never stopped pulling on that shoelace until the bastard was dead. The lace snapped, and he shot back to reality just as a car slowed to a stop alongside the young girl. The driver spoke to her, and she approached his open window. Jack filled with panic and, like a runner out of the starting blocks, he charged across the road, one trainer flying off, shouting like a lunatic:

'Hey! Hey! Stop! Step back!'

The now terrified young girl automatically did as he instructed but the driver of the car, instead of racing away, got out and faced Jack down. He was around Jack's size, but heavier set and more muscular; still Jack stroke towards him, shoulders back and fists clenched, forcing the man to back off, hands raised in surrender. When Jack turned his attention to the young girl his body language instantly changed; he softened, relaxed and spoken gently.

'You OK? You know him? Do you know this man?' As Jack got close, she brought her hands up in a defensive gesture and nodded furiously.

'Course she knows me. OK mate. I'm her brother. She knows me. Calm the fuck down. OK.'

Jack spun to the look at the driver, then back at the girl who was now trying to edge her way round Jack as though *he* was the threat.

'Shit.' Jack stepped out of her way, allowing her to run into her brother's arms. 'I'm sorry.' Jack took a deep breath, rubbing his head. 'I saw you stop . . . I thought . . . I'm sorry.'

The driver hugged his sister and guided her into the passenger seat. Then he turned to Jack with a look of both anger and pity and snorted.

'Fucking prick.' He got into the driver's seat and sped off.

Jack walked back into the middle of the road and reached down for his trainer, his hands trembling with adrenalin. What the hell was he thinking! A car horn made him look up. He glared at the driver for a moment, then slipped on his trainer and trudged slowly home.

* * *

Maggie, Penny and Hannah were just about to tuck in to the pancakes with fresh fruit and honey when Jack breezed in, all smiles.

'Pancakes,' he said, rubbing his hands.

'Me did them!' Hannah said gleefully.

Maggie was taken aback by his good humour. He went and collected a plate, giving Hannah a funny pleading look.

'Just a little, tiny bit, please?' Jack took a huge mouthful. 'Oh my goodness, these are the best pancakes I have ever tasted.'

'You missed Josh,' Maggie said. 'Oh, and I've made a decision, Jack. I have decided to call our son Charles after your dad; he will be Charles Horatio Warr.'

Penny was instantly in tears. Jack leaned down, kissed her, and then looked at Maggie.

'Sounds good to me. I'll go up and give Charlie a kiss right now. Then I'll have a quick shower and clear up the dining room. And if Hannah wants to help me, we can bounce on the mattress to deflate it.'

The next hour was taken up by two of Marius's men arriving in a van to clear away the boxes of junk, empty paint cans and stacks of old wallpaper stripped from the top floor. Maggie went up to the now finished loft extension, making a list of what they'd need to buy to furnish it.

Going downstairs to the next landing, Maggie went into the nursery. Penny was folding the washed and ironed babygros, ready to put away. Charlie was fast asleep.

'I've given him his bottle,' she said with a smile.

'Where's Hannah?'

'Jack took her to the park. To the playground, I expect; I'm not brave enough to let her climb to the top of that rope climbing frame, I'm afraid. Scares me to death!'

A short while later Penny heard the front door slam. Looking out the window, she saw Maggie walking to her car carrying empty shopping bags. Left alone, she felt she should remain in the nursery rather than go to her room in case Charlie woke, so she went and sat in the antique rocking chair. Rocking gently back and forth, she let out a deep sigh. It was obvious that Jack and Maggie were going through a terrible time. But she also knew that Maggie, a caring and exceptional doctor, was looking after Jack better than many wives would be equipped to.

Penny recalled Maggie asking if Jack had trouble sleeping when he was a child. He could not have inherited anything from them as he was adopted, but now, alone with her thoughts, she did remember a time when he'd had sleeping problems.

When Jack was first brought to them, he'd flung his arms around Charlie and they'd bonded immediately. However, for the first six months, he had some very disturbed nights, waking and screaming in terror. The only way they'd managed to calm him was for Charlie to sleep by his side, so he could comfort him if he had a night terror. It had worried them both, but after a few months, the nightmares had stopped. They had tried to find out from the children's home if anything untoward had happened to Jack when they first took him in to care, but all they were told was that Jack was an emotional child, difficult to handle and a restless sleeper. The few short months of sleepless nights had been followed by so many years of joy that Penny had honestly forgotten all about them. Still, she ought to tell Maggie about them now.

CHAPTER 5

Portobello Road, as always, was alive with a remarkably diverse range of people going about their lives amid the multicoloured buildings and stalls. But if Jack had been in this part of London at this very moment, he would have been stunned to see who was coming out of a framer's shop carrying a stack of old guilt and wood frames, bold as brass.

It was Adam Border.

He had made no effort to disguise his appearance, with a baseball hat pulled quite low but not really hiding his face, his blond hair tied in a ponytail, and wearing a worn denim jacket. He walked casually down the road, turning towards a parked Mercedes jeep. He bleeped it open to stash the frames and drove off towards Westbourne Grove, pulling off his baseball cap and putting on a pair of sunglasses.

* * *

While Laura prepared a Chinese dinner, Josh sat at her small kitchen table with a bottle of beer.

'So, tell me, how is Jack really?' she asked.

Josh gave her an edited version of what Jack had told him. Laura put the sliced chicken breast in the pan and added sweet and sour sauce.

'Yeah, that was the Middleton investigation. One of the most horrific cases I have ever been involved in.' Laura removed the fried chicken breast and began to make the various side dishes. Josh watched as she chopped chillies, garlic, onions and peppers.

She intermittently stopped and took deep breaths as tough memories caught up with her.

'It was horrific, Josh. He had murdered so many young girls. Honestly, it was a horror show. He dismembered them, wrapped them up and stashed them in rubbish bins. As CSI opened the drains underneath the shower and bath, they found more and more evidence. Trying to identify the poor souls that had been murdered took months.'

Laura initially blamed her tears on the onions, but once she had started to cry, that was it. Josh got up and took her in his arms. She clung to him, first saying she was sorry and then, between sobs, telling him that she kept on reliving the horror over and over. When she was calmer, Laura explained she had been seeing a counsellor the police medical officer had recommended, because she couldn't sleep.

'The defence lawyer made Jack relive the whole thing, over and over. Sometimes it seemed like he was the one on trial. And to watch Middleton loving the attention, smiling and laughing, was hideous. Added to that, we were being inundated with families trying to find out if their missing daughters were Middleton's victims.'

Laura toyed with the idea of not mentioning what was on her mind but eventually couldn't help herself. 'There was an incident, I've never told it to anyone, but . . . somehow Jack got permission, or not, I don't know, but just before Middleton was being taken from the court, Jack went down to his cell. I think he was trying to ask him about the other victims. Again, I don't know exactly what Jack was thinking, but . . .'

'Go on.'

'Jack went into the cell, with an officer outside. Then Middleton started screaming, claiming Jack had tried to kill him. Middleton was ignored, but I asked the officer what had happened and he just said not to ever mention it.'

Josh returned to the table as she carried on cooking. 'Where is Middleton being held?'

'He was originally sent to Frankland prison in Durham, but he demanded that he be sent to a prison nearer to his family.' Laura laughed. 'As it turned out, he made a big mistake, because he was transferred to Bellview, one of England's toughest prisons. I know all about it because one of the nurses working there used to be at Holloway, which is now closed. I heard her talk at a conference about offender rehabilitation.'

'What was her name?'

'Janet Williamson . . . anyway, I asked her about Middleton. She told me that he had to be banged up alongside sex offenders and paedophiles for his own safety. Weird, isn't it – the real scumbags want to kill him, but when he was on trial all these teenage girls hung around outside the court, like he was a rock star.'

Josh nodded. He recalled watching the trial of the Los Angeles serial killer and rapist Richard Ramirez on television, who had girls fighting to get seats in the courtroom, writing love letters and even trying to get him to marry them. He remembered Ramirez turning towards his fans, smiling and blowing kisses.

'Some killers are just pure evil, the devil incarnate, I guess. If you spend any time dealing with them and their crimes, you can't stay immune.'

'What do you mean?' Laura asked.

'What I'm trying to say is that facing up to such inhumanity at close quarters is bound to affect you mentally and physically.'

'Are you referring to yourself or what you think is happening to Jack?'

'Both of us, I suppose. I can still see Ramirez's face, but I knew after that trial I didn't want to work as a homicide detective anymore, so I joined the drug squad. Now after what I have seen in Los Angeles and San Francisco with these zombie drugs being sold on the streets . . . I genuinely don't know what's worse.'

Laura served the sweet and sour chicken with fried rice, but it took two glasses of wine each before their mood lifted. First, she apologised for breaking down in tears, and he said he was sorry for bringing up the sadistic killer Ramirez. Changing the subject to something lighter, Josh asked if Laura was seeing anyone. Her cheeks flushed and she made Josh laugh as she described how many dating apps she had been on, with farcical results.

'So, you are seeing someone,' he said with a cheeky grin.

'I've met a nice guy who works in advertising. Nothing to do with the police service. I went to an art gallery and spilt my wine over him. So far, we've had three dates. I really like him.'

'Have you consummated your new love?'

Laura went even redder. 'Mind your own business! And you, what about you? You were married last time we were together.'

'Divorced, almost remarried, two children from her previous relationship.'

Laura smiled. 'Sticky toffee pudding with ice cream or cheese and biscuits with coffee?'

'Just coffee sounds good. I just need to go to the bathroom.'

After using the lavatory, Josh slipped into the box room. He sat on the bed and opened his medical box. He injected himself and took two painkillers, then waited for the excruciating pain to ease before he was able to rejoin Laura in the kitchen.

As they sat at the table drinking coffee, Josh could not stop yawning.

'Sorry, I was up most of last night talking to Jack.'

'Did he say when he would return to the station? Everyone is asking.'

'I don't know. He was a bit evasive, but I'm sure it won't be long.'

'Did Maggie tell you anything?'

'Not really. But I think she'll be going back to work soon.'

'More coffee?'

'I think I need to crash out, if you don't mind. I have an early start tomorrow.'

'Oh, of course. By the way, I got out a file I kept on the Rodney Middleton case, mostly newspaper clippings and things. I found them useful when I went to sessions with the therapist.'

Josh picked it up from the sideboard. 'Can I take this and have a read before I crash?'

'Of course. What time do you need to leave in the morning? I'm on a late shift, so I can make you breakfast.'

'Quite early, but if you're not awake, I'll just let myself out.'

She kissed him on the cheek, a tad disappointed he didn't seem to want anything more, but then she was unsure how she would have reacted if he had done. It was almost eleven by the time she'd cleared the kitchen, loaded the dishwasher and headed upstairs. Going to her bedroom, Laura noticed the light was still on in the box room. She almost knocked . . . then told herself not to be silly and went to bed.

* * *

Adam Border parked his Mercedes jeep opposite the double garage doors and walked around the gravel drive to the front of the elegant property. Before he could use his key, the door was opened by a woman with waist-length blond hair, wrapped in a satin pink kimono. He lifted her off her feet and into his arms as he kicked the door shut behind him.

'I've missed you,' she said.

* * *

Josh was propped up in bed, reading through the file, thinking that it was no wonder Jack was traumatised. The horrors of the Richard Ramirez case had haunted him, and he knew Jack was now in the same terrible place. He thought about Penny, Maggie and the children and knew if Jack didn't get help, and soon, he could lose everything – not just his mind. Josh sighed through his drugged state. He just hoped he could make a difference before it was too late.

The following morning, Laura found Josh's thank you note on top of the Middleton file on the kitchen table. She was disappointed he'd left without a hug or a goodbye. When she put the file back on the shelf, she didn't notice that there were sections missing.

* * *

On Saturday morning, Maggie persuaded Jack to accompany her to the Portobello Road market while Penny stayed at home with Hannah and Charlie. As Jack drove she went over the list of items they would need from the second-hand shops and stalls. He remarked that there wouldn't be enough room in the car if they purchased all the items in one go, but Maggie already had it all planned out.

'Marius is back home, and he has a van. We could call him and ask if he or one of his workmates could come and collect the larger items we buy this morning.'

'We pay him by the hour, you do know that?' Jack objected.

'He's a friend now!' Maggie retorted. 'He'll not charge us for picking up a few things. He has done an incredible job, and at half the price we would have paid anyone else. Money is tight, Jack, I know . . . have you decided when to return to the station?'

'I'm still thinking about it.'

'Well, I've decided to return full-time as we need my wages. And when I do, Penny will need some extra help . . .'

'Bloody hell, Mags, we've already had this discussion.'

'Not properly. I've not mentioned anything to Penny yet because I wanted to go over it all with you first. Just listen, then you can bite my head off if you must. I've checked out some nursery places for Charlie and they're so expensive. I think our only option is for him to be at home with Penny. But she will also have to take Hannah to her new school and collect her; that would mean she would have to take Charlie in the pram if we're both on early shifts. With the new deep freezer, I've been able to stock up on food, and I can start doing online food shops but Penny will still want to do local shopping for fresh stuff.' Maggie turned to him as he was leaning forward over the steering wheel. 'Are you listening to me?'

'I'm looking for a parking space.'

'We are miles away from the market. Go to the Ladbroke Grove end and find a space near there. I think we'll get more bargains from that end of the market.'

Jack sighed. Maggie had not stopped talking from the moment they set off. Jack crept slowly along Westbourne Grove and eventually found a parking space. Maggie said they would need about three hours. He used his credit card to pay for the parking.

'Bloody rip off. They only allow two hours max,' he moaned, putting the parking ticket on the windscreen.

Maggie didn't comment. The last thing she wanted was for him to get into one of his moods. They'd become so frequent of late that it was like treading on eggshells all the time. They made their way to the second-hand shops and she quickly earmarked two small bookcases, a chest of drawers and a single old-fashioned bed with a carved headrest. She skilfully bargained the owners down and then got more money off by paying cash. The market was filling up as they neared the popular midway stalls and Maggie stopped to buy a coffee and bagel, while Jack said he would look at the nearby stall selling Indian fabrics, throw rugs, cushions and curtains.

It took nearly five minutes for Maggie to get served, then carrying the two coffees and bagel wrapped in a napkin, she looked around for Jack but couldn't see him by the fabric stall or anywhere nearby. She killed some time going into a small boutique selling pottery. Then, after a minute or two, she came out, having seen some lovely big ceramic pots for the conservatory which she wanted to show Jack, but still he was nowhere to be seen.

While at the fabric stall, Jack had seen the side profile of a suntanned man wearing dark glasses as he passed by. He had tied-back blond hair and wore a baseball cap, denim jacket and jeans. He looked familiar, but Jack didn't instantly recognise him. At first he thought nothing of it, but curiosity got the better of him, so he walked back down the market to find the man. Eventually he spotted him talking to the owner of a stall selling damaged oil paintings and old wooden picture frames. Jack kept his distance and watched.

As Jack eased forward to try and see his face, the man followed the stall-holder through the door of a small, tatty-looking shop with a cracked front window. Jack moved round to a stall selling antiques so he could see into the interior of the shop, picking up a china-faced Victorian doll as if he was interested in it. The framer's shop was dark inside, but Jack could see the stall-holder showing the man in the cap some old picture frames, though he still couldn't see his face. The man picked up a frame and held it up to the light, revealing a gold bangle on his wrist.

'Jesus Christ!' Jack muttered to himself, nearly dropping the doll. 'It can't be!'

The stall-holder, a large woman with heavy gold earrings and too much makeup, clearly thought Jack was remarking on the price of the doll.

'It's a good price for a handmade Victorian doll of that quality,' she said. 'She still has her original hair and shoes, too.'

'I'm looking for a doll for my daughter,' Jack said, keeping half an eye on the interior of the framer's shop.

'She'll love her, I'm sure,' said the woman. 'She is a collector's item, too, so she'll only increase in value . . . be a good investment.'

Jack smiled, pretending to think about it. Then he saw the two men exiting the framer's shop, the owner pocketing a wedge of bank notes while the man in the cap put on his sunglasses.

'I'll come back at seven,' he said.

Jack knew that voice. It was Adam Border.

'Glass eyes still in perfect condition, which is rare when they're this old. They often roll back into the head, but you can see, if you rock her, her eyes still close and open.'

Jack turned away to hide his face as Border walked past. He waited a few seconds, still clutching the doll, and was about to follow Border when Maggie appeared.

'I've been looking all over for you. Here's your cold coffee.'

'You interested in buying the doll for your daughter or not?' the woman said, finally losing patience.

As Jack sheepishly handed the doll back, Maggie shook her head – what would Hannah want with such a scary old doll! Jack quickly looked around, but Adam Border had disappeared into a crowd of shoppers.

'Tell you what, I can let you have it for a hundred and twenty, and that's a real bargain,' the woman said.

'I'm sure it is. Thank you very much, but our daughter's got enough dolls,' Maggie said firmly as she pulled Jack away.

As they moved off, the woman pursed her lips. 'Fucking time-wasters,' she muttered under her breath. As she put the doll back on the stand, one plastic eye was wide open, the other remained closed.

CHAPTER 6

Maggie and Jack's drive home, the car full to the brim with plants, pots and urns, was tense; partly because they had been given a parking ticket for overstaying the two-hour time limit, but mainly because Jack refused to discuss hiring extra help for Penny.

They carried the plants and pots, plus two bags of soil and fertiliser through the kitchen and into the garden in silence. While Jack carried on unloading, Maggie ordered a pizza, bathed Charlie, fed him, and put him to bed. Because Hannah was eating with them, Maggie couldn't really bring up the subject of Penny getting some help when Maggie returned to work, so Maggie got out her mobile to show Penny and Hannah the photographs of all the second-hand items they had bought for the loft extension but hadn't yet collected. Bored with looking at pictures of furniture, Hannah said she wanted to watch TV in her bedroom, so she was allowed to take a slice of pizza up with her.

'I'll be up in a minute and bring you a hot chocolate,' Penny said, getting up from the table.

'Sorry we left the kids with you for so long,' Maggie said. 'We didn't intend to stay at the market this late.' With Jack there too, she finally saw her opportunity to bring up the idea of an au pair. 'Penny, Jack and I wanted to . . .'

Jack immediately got up from the table. 'Just going to check I locked the car.'

Maggie couldn't believe Jack was sabotaging the conversation again. She tried to stop him. 'I saw you lock it, Jack.'

'No, you didn't. I was still unloading when you went to check on Charlie.' He walked out of the kitchen and the front door slammed behind him. Maggie snatched up the empty pizza boxes as though taking them to the bin, then hurried to the front door just in time to see Jack drive off. She marched back into the house and Penny could see the look of fury on her face.

'Are you all right, dear? I don't mean to pry but . . . if you need to talk.'

* * *

Jack had not planned to drive back to the market. He was so pissed off with Maggie, he just needed to get away and was driving on autopilot. But he found himself heading back to where he'd last seen Adam Border. As he parked up, relieved he didn't need to buy another parking ticket as it was after 6 p.m., he looked at his watch. In twenty minutes, Adam Border would be returning to the framer's shop.

Jack walked up the now stall-less market, lined with rubbish bags being collected by two council workers who were throwing them in the back of a wire mesh truck. Another vehicle was hosing the street down behind them. As he looked for the framer's shop, Jack chastised himself for such a stupid move. Why was he out here chasing ghosts when he knew he should be home making up with Maggie?

'Hello, Jack.'

Turning sharply, Jack came to face to face with Adam Border.

'You're a bit late if you want to buy that doll. But I was hoping you would make an appearance.' Border stepped closer, smiling, and Jack was taken aback when Border hugged him.

'I thought you'd clocked me in the market. But I wasn't sure until I saw you doing that routine with the doll. Was that your wife who came up and distracted you?'

Jack flushed, hearing Border's description of his clumsy attempt at surveillance.

'But I thought if I mentioned when I was returning to pick up my frames . . .' He grinned. 'And here you are.'

Jack pulled himself away. 'I don't know why I came back.'

'I think I do, Jack.' Border laughed. 'How about a drink and a chat for old time's sake?'

'What about the frames you need to collect?'

'I phoned the framer and arranged an earlier time. It's all done and loaded in the car. It's parked round the corner.' He started to walk off.

Jack knew he should walk away but found himself following Border round the corner to a black Mercedes Jeep with mud sprays over the sides and wheels. The back seats were down, and he could see the car was stacked with battered frames and tatty-looking oil paintings.

Border gestured for Jack to get in the passenger side. He hesitated before climbing in, still unsure why he was even contemplating going with him. The inside of the Jeep stank of oil and paint thinners. Cigarette stubs overflowed from the ashtray, and used coffee cups littered the footwell, along with crumpled takeaway wrappers.

'Your friend obviously doesn't clean his truck,' Jack said lamely as the car bounced over a road hump and the contents slid and crashed about in the rear.

'That's why it's unlikely anyone would steal it. This area around the market is notorious for car thefts . . . I leave it for hours sometimes while I shop around, but it's always here when I come back. I did real good today. That shop owner is one of my best dealers. He collects for me at auctions and house sales up and down the country.'

'Where are we going?' Jack asked, worried about leaving Maggie's car behind.

'I've got a warehouse space in a property due for demolition. It'll only be for another six months, then I'll get turned out, but it will suffice until I return home.'

'Where's home?'

'France. But I keep looking for properties that I can lease for cash – I just need space, electricity, good light and no other tenants.'

Jack tried to figure out where they were, as Border turned down one backstreet after another until they finally entered a cul-de-sac with a kid's playing field on one side and three small boarded-up terraced houses. Border pulled up by a barrier, then used a set of keys to unlock it before lifting it up. He then drove over rough potholed tarmac towards some old derelict buildings.

'It used to be a school before the land was sold off for a new high-rise block, but it suits me. I'm what might be described as the caretaker, but I pay for the privilege.' They continued past what had been the entrance of the school into a low-walled backyard. Border got out, gesturing for Jack to follow as he opened one of the large double doors into the building.

As Border went inside, Jack quickly snapped some pictures of the location with his phone. He knew what he was doing was foolish and potentially dangerous, but it felt good to have some adrenalin pumping through his veins once more.

Border was standing at the end of a corridor by a room with a DRILL HALL sign above it and a padlock and chain on the door handles. He unlocked it and walked inside. Jack followed him and was astonished by the number of frames lining the walls; long trestle tables were piled up with canvases, and one was covered with an array of oil painting brushes and thousands of tubes of oil paint, jars of chemicals and turpentine.

'My God, how long have you been using this place?' Jack asked.

'Just a few months. Anything of value I keep in that old safe in the corner. I sometimes get kids trying to break in and nick anything they think they can sell. The place used to be full of old school desks and chairs, but now they've all been taken, break-ins are far less frequent. Whether the fucking junkies around here or the builders took them, I don't know. You fancy a drink?'

'Er, thanks, but I really need to get going.'

'I'll take you back to the market when we've unloaded the car. I'll get us a drink first.' Border walked out of the hall and into another room off the corridor while Jack looked around. There was a generator and an array of lamps, and easels with drapes over the paintings. Jack recalled being in Ireland with Border years ago and seeing his paintings. He remembered how fast he had flown the coop when the police were about to arrest him. He knew back then Border must have had a team of people working for him to be able to clear out his studio so fast and so professionally, leaving no prints or evidence that he had even been there. Jack knew Border traded in forgeries as he had gifted him a so-called Giacometti. He had contemplated selling it at one time but knew that it could get him in serious trouble, so kept it hidden beneath his shed. It was obvious now to Jack that Border was back in business.

Hundreds of photographs decorated every wall – close-ups of paintings, frames, canvases, zooming in on every minute detail, in order to make the forgeries perfect in every way Jack assumed. In front of one canvas was a high-powered A4 magnifier and against the wall was what looked like a mobile X-ray machine. This was attached to a large screen, currently switched off. There were cameras, goggles, medical-style magnifying glasses and more painting equipment than the average art shop. Jack picked up a brush that had just one single bristle. He was looking at the painting next to it just as Border returned.

'Impressed?' he said smiling, holding up a bottle of Pinot Grigio and two fluted wine glasses. 'That one is all my own work.'

Jack couldn't quite say what he thought about it, except that it was somehow fascinating. 'It's . . . special. Is it oils?'

'Yep, can't get anyone even remotely interested.'

Jack tore his gaze from the painting. 'Are you here alone, or do you have people working for you?'

'Right now, it's just me. Much of what you see stacked up will be useless, but it'll make good firewood. I have to be very careful to find the right frame. Let me show you what you might think is a rusted pile of crap but actually has immense value.' Border placed the glasses on a table and indicated a row of small cardboard boxes containing nails of various shapes and sizes. As he poured the wine, he nodded to one box that contained only two nails. 'Fifteenth-century nails, next box sixteenth century, then seventeenth . . . I also have nails from the Edwardian and Victorian periods. It's taken me years to collect them – from all over the world.' He offered Jack a glass of wine.

'So you live here?'

Border made a nonchalant gesture towards a corner of the drill hall. 'Mattress and sleeping bag, but I use a local gym when I need to shower.'

Jack looked at a stack of paintings propped up against the table. He glanced at Border as if asking his permission to look over them.

'Be my guest,' Border smiled.

'These are very good . . . all forgeries I suppose.'

Border laughed. 'Actually, they're my original work. You wouldn't believe it, but countless galleries and art dealers around the world have rejected me. I can't sell a single one of them . . . so frustrating when I can knock out fakes which they buy by the dozen.'

'Do they know they're fakes?'

'I don't think so, it's not as if I advertise the fact. There was a pair of artists who worked together, painted forgeries – they came up with an ingenious con. They collected a stack of crap . . . broken frames, damaged canvases etcetera and included one of their forgeries among the dross. Degas being a favourite.'

'Is that why you went to the market trader's shop?'

'Yes, for the old frames. He's got stacks of them and hasn't a clue how valuable they are to an art forger.'

Jack shook his head, laughing despite himself.

'So, these two artists would dress up all scruffy and go to reputable dealers, saying they had a carload of paintings they got from house clearances, and they'd ask if anything they had was of value. They would watch the so-called art connoisseur look over their offerings almost in disgust, until their eyes lit up when they saw the fake. Do you remember me telling you about the importance of provenance, you know, proof of authentication . . .'

'Vaguely,' Jack said, trying to disguise his interest.

'They were in it for the money, of course, but like me, they also resented the establishment rejecting their own paintings.'

'I can understand the frustration.'

'I doubt you can. I would say nearly fifty per cent of all the so-called Old Masters in museums and galleries are fakes. Even King Charles displayed one from a US artist. But these days it's getting tougher because so many art experts have had their fingers burnt. My biggest fear is that a man named James Martin will be my nemesis. He's considered one of the world's top art forgery detectives.'

'Never heard of him.' Jack took another sip of wine.

Border picked up a magazine article with a photograph of Martin and handed it to Jack.

'Forgeries have got so good Sotheby's hired Martin to check any painting brought to them. In 2015, a big art gallery in Paris had a tip-off that one of the paintings on display was a fake. It was *Venus* by the German Renaissance master Lucas Cranach the Elder, originally purchased by the Prince of Liechtenstein for about six million. Tests confirmed it was a forgery. They discovered it had been put on the market by Giuliano Ruffini, a well-known art collector, which hoisted a big red flag of concern about how many fakes Ruffini had sold. It turned out to be around twenty-five works, from which he made a staggering hundred and seventy-odd million.'

'So, has this Ruffini been arrested?' Jack was fascinated by the world Border lived in and the exotic figures who inhabited it.

'Yes, in Italy. He was extradited to Paris and charged with fraud, money laundering and forgery but has yet to stand trial. Ruffini has always maintained his innocence.' Border's mobile rang; he glanced at the caller ID before answering. After listening for a moment, he turned his back on Jack and started speaking angrily.

'It's too soon ... I'll need at least two more weeks. If anyone so much as touches the fucking paint ... Just wait until it's properly hardened, or you'll fuck up the sale.' He ended the call slamming his mobile down, then kicked at the frame resting against the table. 'Fucking stupid arsehole ... I'd like to cut his throat.'

Taking a deliberate look at his wristwatch, Jack drained his wine. 'Look, if you want to get everything out of the Jeep, let's do it now. I should be home.'

Border quickly regained his composure, putting an arm around Jack's shoulder. 'I've got you interested again, haven't I, Mr Detective? We'll have dinner the next time we meet and catch up on everything that's happened since we last met.'

For the first time in months, Jack didn't feel a bubbling anxiety just beneath the surface. Being in the company of an art fraudster like Adam Border who was still on the wanted list could get him into serious trouble, but instead of making him feel stressed, it made him feel alive.

'Maybe,' he said with a smile.

* * *

With the children now in bed, Maggie sat in the lounge making a list of items still to be collected, hopefully by Marius, within the next few days. Penny came in carrying two cups of hot chocolate.

'Jack not back yet?' Penny already knew he wasn't.

'No, and I have no idea where he's gone. To be honest, I wanted him here when I talked to you, but as usual, he's off doing his own thing.'

Penny hugged the hot mug. 'It's all very worrying.'

'He's stubborn as a mule. He's refused to see any more specialists but he also won't say when he's going back to work.'

Penny was about to mention the fact that Jack had previously experienced nightmares as a child, when Maggie reached out and took her hand.

'We appreciate everything you do for us, Penny, and I don't want you to take this the wrong way . . . but now the loft conversion is finished, and we've bought the furnishings, I'm hoping to return to work in the next week or two. So, I was thinking . . .'

A beaming Penny interrupted. 'I'm so glad you want to talk about it because I agree . . . I was going to suggest something that might help ease the pressure on us all, but I wasn't sure it would be acceptable.' She paused and Maggie, glad this conversation was going more easily than she'd expected, nodded for Penny to continue. 'Marius will be back any day now and I was going to suggest, as he has been such a godsend, that he move into the loft. It'd be a double blessing as he can drive me back and forth to school and the shops and be at home with me to look after both Hannah and Charlie. At the same time, if needed, he can do more decorating and handiwork.' She sat back expectantly.

Maggie tried not to frown or look shocked. 'Um . . . I would need to discuss it with Jack.'

'Oh, I know that, dear. I want you to understand that Marius and I are very close, but purely on a platonic level. He's a good friend, and we enjoy each other's company. I would also suggest that he pay a bit of rent.'

'Hasn't he got a place?'

'Yes, a little flat, but I know he's looking to move, so this just seems . . . perfect.'

Maggie hesitated, trying to think of the best way to put things. She was not keen on having Marius living in the house, even though he had been doing a great job with all the rebuilding and Hannah liked him.

'Well, we're sort of thinking along the same lines I suppose. I was going to suggest that you might need some help with Charlie. He needs so much attention, and I don't really want him to be in a nursery.'

'Oh, Marius adores Charlie and vice versa.'

'What I was thinking, Penny, was maybe getting a part-time helper for the mornings and the school run or perhaps a live-in au pair . . . as you said, with the new loft extension, we have more than enough room.'

'Oh no, no. I wouldn't want anyone else looking after Charlie and Hannah. Besides, it would cost you more money to have a helper or an au pair. I wouldn't trust anyone else like I do Marius.'

Maggie smiled glumly, deciding she would need Jack to back her up on this one.

'Maggie, be honest, you're not concerned about me, are you? I would be very upset if you thought I was incapable of looking after the children.'

'I'd never think that, nor would Jack. I was worried it might be too much for you when Jack and I are back at work all day.'

Penny was near to tears. 'It isn't, it won't be ... I'm upset that you think I can't cope.'

Maggie put her arms around her. 'Please, don't cry. Of course we know you could cope.'

'Thank you, dear.' Penny wiped her eyes with a tissue. 'I think I'm off to bed.' She stood up then turned back to Maggie.

'Oh, I meant to tell you something, Maggie. You asked me a few days ago if Jack had any childhood sleeping problems. At first, I couldn't remember because it was so long ago, but now I recall he did.'

Maggie was all ears. 'Go on.'

'They didn't last long, a month maybe. Terrible screaming fits, and the only way he'd stop was if his dad held him in his arms. He would try to climb out of bed, fists flying, screaming blue murder, and sometimes he seemed still asleep. We asked the children's home if he had been like it when he was there and they just said he'd been difficult to handle.'

'Did they tell you the reason?' Maggie asked.

'No, but after a while, the nightmares ended and never occurred again. Jack was happy with us, very loving, always holding out his arms for hugs and kisses, and we knew we would never let him go. He was the son, the baby boy we had always wanted.' She dabbed at her eyes again. 'I'm so sorry I didn't remember when you first asked.'

'Well thanks for telling me now,' Maggie said. 'I'm sure it'll be helpful.'

Penny smiled. 'I do hope so.'

After Penny had gone upstairs, Maggie thought about what she'd just told her. She doubted that Jack's childhood nightmares were linked to his current sleep problems, which seemed so obviously linked to the trauma of the Middleton case. But perhaps Jack had always responded like this to traumatic events. Maybe something bad had happened to Jack before Penny and Charlie took him in. It was something she'd need to ask Jack, but only when the time was right.

* * *

It was almost eleven o'clock when Adam Border dropped Jack off by Maggie's car. He then headed south, across Putney Bridge and onto the A3 towards Haslemere. After an hour he turned off the A3, then drove along a private lane to an ivy-clad Tudor mansion set in 20 acres of land. It was colloquially known as the 'Rock and Roll' mansion, due to the many famous rock bands who had used it as a recording studio over the years.

Border drove past the neatly manicured gardens and outdoor pool, then parked in the large two-car garage. He walked to the rear of the house, passing a flourishing vegetable patch, before kicking off his boots outside the stable door. Inside was a bright, modern kitchen with a long row of copper pans hanging above a welcoming Aga.

Border threw his denim jacket over the back of a chair, flicked on the kettle and got a coffee percolator from the cupboard. He used an electric grinder for fresh coffee beans, and then, with the coffee brewing, he went to the double-doored fridge and removed a bowl of salad.

Helga walked in barefoot, wrapping a silk kimono around herself. Her long blond hair was braided into a thick plait.

'I was right,' Adam said. 'Jack Warr came straight back to the market. I drove him to the old school and had a glass of wine with him.'

'Taking a risk, aren't you?' she said in a strong German accent.

'Better the devil you know. I thought he'd recognised me at the market, but I needed to be sure.'

She gave a long sigh. 'I hope you know what you are doing.'

* * *

Maggie was woken by the sound of the front door slamming, then Jack coming up the stairs. She hoped he wasn't drunk or in one of his black moods.

'Are you awake?' he asked, opening the door.

'Yes. I've been worried about you all evening. You could have at least rung me or answered my text.'

'Sorry, I got caught up.'

'With what?'

'Tell you in the morning.' He went to the bathroom. She heard him whistling. She had not seen him so relaxed and pleased with himself in ages, as if the boyish quality she loved in him had returned. He came out of the bathroom wearing only boxer shorts. He threw his jeans and T-shirt onto the floor, then sat on the bed to remove his socks.

Maggie turned off her bedside lamp, lay back and let him put his arms around her. They hadn't been this comfortable with each other for a long time, so she decided it was not the time to discuss her conversation with Penny.

'Sorry for leaving the house earlier,' Jack said. Then he sighed and leaned back against the pillows. 'I didn't intend to go back there, Mags, but I thought I recognised him and I was right.'

'Who are you talking about?'

'Adam Border. That's who I've been with.'

'Adam Bo . . . the man Josh was talking about?'

'Yes, he took me to his studio.'

'Oh my God, what are you going to do?'

'Nothing. Listen, Mags, years ago I made a deal with him for evidence that closed a huge case. That's all. I doubt anyone's going to be interested now. I had an interesting conversation with him.'

Maggie wanted to know more but Jack appeared to have gone to sleep. She, on the other hand, was wide awake now, remembering how Josh had described Adam Border as a murderer. She wondered if having Jack's 'old self' back was going to be a good thing or not.

CHAPTER 7

Janet Williamson lived alone in a small, rented flat above an estate agent in the local village. It was a temporary rental as her retirement date was only a few weeks away. She was a fully qualified nurse who had worked most of her career in UK prisons. After Holloway closed, she'd been offered numerous placements, and she chose to be the senior nurse in the hospital wing at Bellview prison in Southeast London. It was a Category A men's prison, with a high security unit housing some of the UK's most dangerous and violent criminals in squalid single-occupancy cells. It was overcrowded, run-down and in need of refurbishing, as well as having a reputation as a brutal prison, with constant gang fights and assaults on staff – but the pay was consequently very good.

Added to that, Janet had seen it all during her career, and there was little that surprised or disturbed her, having treated Category A inmates and others who were drug addicts, alcoholics or who had mental health issues. Working in the hospital unit for inmates who were too ill to be examined on their wing suited her just fine.

The only downside was Doctor Zardari, the new prison doctor, who worked as a local GP two mornings a week and spent the rest of his time at the prison. He seemed unsure of himself and couldn't get the hang of the prison rules and regulations.

On Sunday morning, Janet had a lie-in until 11 a.m. before going shopping at her local Tesco. She filled her trolley with frozen meals, one for every day of the week, and was just reaching for a carton of milk when she heard a voice behind her.

'Sorry to bother you . . . but is your name Janet?'

She ignored the voice and walked towards the cold meat section, but the man followed her.

'My name's Josh Logan, a friend of Laura's, the police detective. We met at that big Met event some time ago. I'm a detective on the New York drugs squad.'

She turned, frowning, having no recollection of him, although she vaguely remembered meeting a policewoman called Laura somewhere. She had no idea that he had followed her from her flat to the supermarket.

'Oh, do you live round here?' She noticed his shopping basket contained a bottle of wine, crisps and prawn crackers.

'No, I'm staying at a B&B down the road. I'm doing drugs awareness lectures at prisons across the country before I retire. I remember you said you were a prison nurse.'

She nodded. 'At Bellview. But I'm retiring soon too.' Looking at him properly, she realised he wasn't bad looking. 'I'm sorry I didn't remember you straightaway.'

'And there was me thinking I was unforgettable,' he smiled, and she laughed.

As they headed to the car park, Josh helped carry Janet's groceries. She noticed his limp and asked if he had a bad knee. He explained he'd been shot on an undercover assignment and his knee had got worse over the years.

'Family?' Josh asked.

'Divorced. My daughter lives in New Zealand.'

'Long way,' Josh commented.

'I'm going to visit when I retire,' she said. 'Marion went over there to be with the love of her life, but he dumped her and broke her heart, as well as leaving her six months pregnant. It's hard for her, being a single mother. She's got a good job as a bookkeeper for an insurance company, though.'

She was, by now, very chatty and offered to give him a lift. He did his best to make her laugh describing the underwhelming B&B he was staying in, and was rewarded when she asked if he would like to have lunch at her flat. *Still got it*, Josh thought to himself.

Janet's kitchen was as bland as the rest of the flat. Josh opened the bottle of Merlot and sat at the table with its worn plastic tablecloth while Janet put a frozen bolognese in the microwave and two small baguettes in the air fryer.

'I've not had anyone here since I moved in,' she admitted. 'I like my own company, but I do sometimes feel like an inmate doing time ... I suppose I am in some ways. Bellview houses some horrific bastards, mind. You wouldn't want to be in the same room with them if you knew what they'd done, but it goes with the job.'

The microwave pinged. Janet removed the bread from the air fryer and got two dinner plates out.

'Not like dining at the Ritz, I know, but help yourself.'

'It smells delicious.' Josh poured them both a second glass of wine and tucked in. When they were finished, Janet made them both mugs of instant coffee.

'So, tell me, why does a big shot New York detective like you want to go round giving talks at shithole prisons over here? Because I can guarantee there won't be any of the buggers listening. If they turn up at all, it'll just be an excuse to get out of their cells.'

Josh explained about the horrors of synthetic opioids and the havoc they were wreaking in the US. 'If I can do anything to stop it happening here, it'll be worth my time. Maybe some of them will listen. Can I ask – how many fatalities have occurred in Bellview from fentanyl overdoses?'

'Listen, love, ours OD on heroin, Vicodin, OxyContin and Percocet, and stopping drugs from being smuggled in is a losing battle for prison officers. They're so short-staffed it's impossible to do strip-searches and watch the visitors all the time. Some inmates deal drugs, and if they are in a cell 24 hours a day, they have plenty of time to devise clever ways of getting relatives and friends to smuggle the gear in.'

Josh nodded, knowing virtually every prison in the US was in a similar situation. 'There is a new drug exploding onto the market you may not have heard of. It's called xylazine or "tranq". It's a veterinary tranquilliser. Dealers are mixing it with fentanyl, methamphetamine, cocaine, and downers. In the US, it's being found more and more in lab-tested samples of seized heroin and fentanyl. The problem is, it literally eats away your flesh from the inside out, and the only way to stop it from spreading is by amputation.'

'I've not come across it. We definitely haven't had any flesh-eating cases in Bellview yet, thank God.'

'People are even taking xylazine on its own. Being a powerful sedative, it makes them appear physically unresponsive or 'zombified', which leaves them vulnerable on the street. Naloxone has no effect on it. In fact, there is no approved antidote for a xylazine overdose.'

For the first time, she looked genuinely shocked. 'Bloody hell. To be honest, I don't think we've got much of a problem with fentanyl. That said, God only knows what's coming in.' Janet picked up their empty mugs and took them over to the sink.

'Do you think the staff and inmates at Bellview might listen to me?' he asked.

'Well, the prison doctor, Doctor Zardari, is quite young and inexperienced. I'm sure he could learn a lot from you about these new drugs. And I'm sure the inmates will love that accent of yours . . . where are you from?'

'Louisiana. But I've been in New York for nearly twenty-five years.'

'Married?'

'Divorced a couple of times,' he laughed.

'Any kids?'

'Two girls.' Josh was pleased Janet was asking all these personal questions. It suggested he'd managed to kindle a spark between them. But he still had some questions of his own. 'As a matter of interest, do you know who the biggest dealers are in Bellview? I might have encountered them when I worked in London a few years ago on a big drugs case.'

'Drug dealers are always kingpins in prisons, but it'd be a bit unethical of me to name them. No offence, but I don't want to risk getting into trouble when I'm about to retire and get my pension. I've always gone carefully, even when I worked in Holloway.'

Josh knew not to push it. 'Sure. Understood. The last thing I want to do is cause you any problems.'

Josh stood up from the table. 'Thanks for the delicious lunch, Janet, but I should be getting back to do some work on my talk.'

'Thank Tesco, you mean,' she laughed.

He smiled. 'I'd like to take you out for dinner to say thank you properly.'

'Well, we're short of restaurants around here, but there's a good Turkish one open on Sundays.'

'That's a date, then. I'll come by about seven?'

Janet wiped her hands on a tea-towel, smiling. 'I'll give them a ring and book a table.'

After Josh had left, Janet decided to take a bath, wash her hair, and perhaps even wear it loose, not having done so for years. She went to her bedroom, pulled off her sweater, unzipped her skirt and kicked it to one side. Her underwear had seen better days, and the elastic in her waist-training pants had long gone. She stood in front of her bedroom mirror and wondered what Josh would think if he saw her naked.

'For God's sake, Janet Williamson,' she said quickly. 'Pull yourself together, your imagination is running away with you. Face it, you are well past a time of any man wanting you and have been for twenty years.' She glared at herself, a woman so used to dealing with untrustworthy and frankly disgusting men that she wasn't used to thinking about a man in that way. She couldn't even remember the last time she went out on a date.

Josh made it back to his B&B, more than ready for his medication and injection; his leg felt as if it was on fire. He lay on the cramped bed in his awful room, with dreadful flowery wallpaper, and closed his eyes. It would be a lot harder than he thought to do what he planned. Janet was a tough nut to crack, but he needed her. He sighed, knowing he had fucked a lot worse in his life, and if that was what it was going to take, then that was what he would do.

He slept for a few hours before getting ready to meet Janet for dinner. He sprayed some aftershave on his neck and armpits and made his way to Janet's flat in a taxi, to save his leg. She opened the door, and he stood back admiringly.

'Hey, you scrub up well, Janet . . . you look lovely.'

She blushed, unable to recall the last time a man paid her a compliment.

They walked to the Turkish restaurant, which was bigger and more modern than Josh expected, and ordered a large mixed grill to share. Janet had brought a photo album to show Josh pictures of her daughter and grandchild and said she couldn't wait to go and see them, so Josh ordered a bottle of New Zealand Sauvignon Blanc to go with the meal.

As they clinked glasses, Janet said she hoped her daughter's new partner was going to turn out better than the last one.

'What about you, Janet? Are you seeing anyone?' Josh asked.

She laughed. 'No, not for years. I'm not interested in a relationship, either.'

'What about Marion's father?'

'He's been out of my life for twenty-five years, thank God. I don't know or care where he is. He was a heavy drinker and used his fists when he'd had a few. The final straw was when he knocked me about in front of Marion . . . I kicked him out, changed the locks and got two friends of mine working in the prison to beat the shit out of him.'

Josh nodded sympathetically. 'Good for you.'

'What about you?' Janet asked.

'Well, like you, I'm single now and ready to retire, but I wanted to make one last-ditch effort to do something good. I believe this country will be overwhelmed with xylazine unless people wake up to the threat. And I don't just mean the authorities. I want my message to get through to the drug traffickers, particularly the top dogs doing long sentences. If I can get them on my side . . .'

Janet shrugged her shoulders. 'Waste of time, love. They don't give a damn what happens to the people they sell their drugs to.' She drained her glass which Josh refilled for her. 'I should watch it. I'm over my limit already. But it'll take more than a couple of glasses of wine to get me to tell you who the dealers are.'

Josh waved his hand dismissively, as if that was the last thing on his mind, and they chatted about other things until it was time to get the bill. After paying, he walked her home, wondering if she'd ask him in, but no luck.

'Thanks for a lovely meal,' she said.

'My pleasure. Maybe see you tomorrow when I give my talk.'

Back at his B&B, Josh quickly medicated himself before turning in. He'd hoped to get Janet into bed but in the end was relieved it hadn't happened. He doubted he could have got an erection. As for his plan, he'd just have to play it by ear the following morning.

CHAPTER 8

Jack was up in the loft on a stepladder with a tape measure, checking if the little wardrobe they'd seen the market would fit in the alcove, when Maggie took the opportunity of mentioning Marius possibly moving in.

Jack shook his head vigorously. 'No way. Look, I like Marius, but I don't think having him move in here is a good idea. Jeez Mags they're not . . . you know . . . are they?'

'Not so loud, and no, Penny said it was a purely platonic relationship. But he'd be useful around the house, and he could drive her around in the van. He might even pay rent.'

'I don't want him living in. And he's not all that anyway! I'm going to have to top and tail some of his paint work, and I am very wary of the plumbing; you turn on the shower late at night and it makes a hell of a racket.'

Maggie persisted. 'It's just if we get an au pair or part-time nanny, we will have to pay for it. An au pair could live up here in the loft, though.'

Jack sighed. 'Let me talk to Mum about it. I don't want anyone else living here . . . So, if we must have someone, it would be best if we got a part-time nanny.'

As Jack measured the space for the chest of drawers they had also purchased, Maggie asked him about another of her concerns.

'Will you be seeing him again?'

Jack zapped his tape measure home as if he'd stopped listening.

'I'm talking about Adam Border. From what Josh said, he sounds like a nasty piece of work. And he's still on the wanted list for God's sake.' She thought Jack was going to argue, but instead he said simply,

'I have no intention of seeing him again.'

'Good. That's one thing I don't have to worry about, then,' she said before going downstairs.

Once she was gone, Jack frowned to himself. He seemed to find lying to Maggie very easy these days.

* * *

The next morning, after a brief meeting with the governor, two prison officers led Josh down the dank stone corridors to the inmates' wing, where he was to meet the prison doctor before talking to a group of prisoners in the library. The pervading stench he had smelt many times before was present: the rancid mixture of stale vegetables, Dettol and urine. Together with the constant screams and howls from the prisoners in their cells, it gave the place a hellish feel. In the hospital wing, Josh found a young Asian man talking to Janet.

She was checking over a trolley laden with medications and instructing a female nurse in how to ensure they were actually taken by the inmates and not retained in the mouth to be spat out later and sold to other prisoners.

After briefly making eye contact with Josh, she introduced him to Doctor Zardari and Josh explained what he wanted to talk to the prisoners about.

Zardari shrugged his shoulders. 'You're welcome to try, of course, but I doubt it will be of any benefit. Nurse Williamson has warned them many times about the dangers of using drugs smuggled into the prison which could be mixed with anything. The prison staff try to separate the new arrivals from the hardcore users, but they are so short-staffed that it is virtually impossible to protect them.'

Josh nodded. 'Well, I'm going to see if I can get their attention anyway.'

Janet finished with the medication trolley and gestured for Josh to accompany her to the prison library, accompanied by two prison officers. She walked ahead briskly as they passed through numerous gates, each requiring the control room to unlock one bolt before Janet unlocked a second with a key from a chain attached to her belt. Josh was eventually ushered into a shabby room with walls of battered paperbacks lining the shelves and a semi-circle of folding chairs in front of a whiteboard.

Josh opened his folder and started sticking photographs onto the board. After a few minutes, a disappointingly small group of men dressed in prison-issue denim jumpsuits shambled in and sat down. The library doors were locked. One uniformed officer stood beside the prisoners, while the other stood to one side with Janet. Josh took a deep breath and began to speak.

* * *

Maggie leaned across the kitchen table and gave Jack a kiss. 'You handled your mum perfectly, thank you.'

They'd waited until Penny had got back from dropping Hannah off at a playdate and then invited her to sit down for a coffee. Jack had explained why he didn't want anyone else living in the house, while assuring Penny that he had nothing against Marius personally, and had then announced – to Maggie's surprise – that he intended to return to work the following week. Realising that she would be left running the house on her own, Penny had suggested getting in a cleaner, so she could focus on the children.

'I can ask for cleaners at the hospital,' Maggie said.

'I'll do the same at the station,' Jack nodded.

Maggie clapped her hands. 'Right, let's get started. I'll write a little advert.'

'And I'll go and do some grocery shopping. I'll just get that list on the fridge door,' Jack said. He drove off, giving Maggie a cheery wave, happy to have an excuse to get out of the house. It was time to go and see Adam Border again.

* * *

Josh was beginning to feel that Janet had been right. When he'd described the horrifying effects of xylazine, the only reaction he got from his audience was when one of the prisoners asked if he'd brought any with him because it sounded like the business. Then a couple of them started doing zombie impressions. And before he was able to get things back on track, his time was up.

A young blond prisoner helped Josh take down his photographs. As they stood by the board, Josh quietly asked the boy who the main drug dealers were on his wing. The boy was nervous and said he wasn't sure, but that some prison staff could not be trusted.

'You mean they're supplying the drugs to the prisoners?' Josh whispered.

The boy looked around furtively then nodded. 'One of them is the main supplier.'

Josh started putting the photographs back in his briefcase. 'All I need is a name.'

Janet clapped her hands. 'Come on, Eric. It's time to get back to your cell, love. I've not got all day for you to chit-chat.'

Eric nodded and shuffled out without looking back at Josh.

Janet turned to one of the officers. 'I've got to go back to the hospital wing. Can you escort our guest back to the main gate?'

'Thank you,' Josh said, zipping up his briefcase.

'Well, I told you it would be a waste of time. Having seen our lovely inmates and the state of this shithole, I'm sure you appreciate why I want to get the hell out.'

Josh smiled. *Maybe not a complete waste of time*, he thought as he followed the officer out.

* * *

Jack quickly bought the items on Maggie's shopping list, and then drove to Adam's studio in the old school drill hall. The barrier was down, so he parked up and was about to go and lift it when he saw a Mercedes sports car parked next to the mud-splattered jeep. He hesitated before walking around the barrier and heading towards the drill hall on foot.

Jack paused when he heard raised voices. There was a boarded-up window with a chink left at the bottom. Bending down, he looked into the studio and could see Adam Border's cowboy boots. There was another man, wearing stylish fawn trousers and highly polished ankle boots. Then he saw Adam kicking out and putting his heel through a canvas on the floor.

'You are a fucking greedy son of a bitch. I'm not prepared to do any more than what we have already commissioned. I want out.'

'Come on, Adam, I've offered you double the price we agreed,' the other man said calmly. Then his voice hardened. 'And I say when you can leave.'

Adam picked up the painting and hurled it aside furiously. 'You think I care about your threats? Never mind warning me, I am warning *you* . . . I will fucking slit your throat if you do this to me again. Take your cash and shove it up your arse. I am not for sale.'

Again, the softer-toned man said something, but all Jack heard was Adam shouting for him to get the hell out. Jack moved fast, running back to his car and making a quick exit.

* * *

After returning to his B&B, Josh packed his bag, paid the bill and walked to Janet's. He saw no one as he headed along her street and turned into her drive. There was no security camera at her front door; the last CCTV was on the main road near his B&B, but he made a detour to avoid it. He opened the main front door in seconds, with a set of skeleton keys, then walked quickly up the stairs to Janet's flat and, this time, took his time to open her flat door as she had two different locks fitted. He felt vulnerable standing on the landing, but luckily no neighbours appeared.

Inside the flat, he stood listening for a minute with his back against the door. Silence. For his size, Josh moved stealthily, even with his bad leg. He first searched the kitchen, pulling open drawers in the cheap cabinets and feeling along the tops. He even did a search of her fridge-freezer, often a hiding place for drugs, but it was mostly filled with microwave dinners.

Satisfied the kitchen was clear, he moved to the bathroom, opening the toilet cover to make sure no drugs were stashed in the cistern. In one of the bathroom cabinets, in a plastic container, he found hundreds of empty capsules, a pair of scales, a measuring scoop and a garlic crusher. He paused, listening for any new sounds before making his way to the bedroom. He slid his hands beneath the mattress and under the bed but found nothing, then opened the wardrobe and bent down to examine the rows of boots and shoes, before patting down all the garments on the hangers. He then focused on the dressing table. There were three drawers on each side containing underwear and sweaters, and a small leather box containing jewellery. The last one was locked. It only took a few seconds to prize it open.

Inside were stacks of envelopes with New Zealand stamps, all addressed to Janet. Another stack of bank statements was tied with an elastic band, and Janet's passport and tickets for her trip to New Zealand were in an envelope.

Taking out all the items and laying them on top of the dressing table, he felt into the back of the drawer and withdrew stacks of twenty- and ten-pound notes along with a thick wad of fifties. He reckoned there was at least twenty thousand, but more interesting was the thick red notebook wrapped with a green elastic band. By this time, the pain in his leg was getting bad, so he had to sit on the edge of the bed. Opening the book, he saw pages and pages of initials and numbers. Some initials, which he presumed were names, were crossed out. Some pages had scribbled dates, beginning with when Janet worked in Holloway.

He next went through her bank accounts. There were substantial transfers over the years to the same bank in New Zealand, with amounts varying from ten to thirty thousand. However, there was only four thousand pounds in her own account. Frustrated, he went laboriously through every item, including her wage slips, even reading the copies of letters from her previous Governor extolling her professionalism and years of exemplary work with the incarcerated women. There was even a note from the prison doctor who praised Janet's work as a nurse and her assistance in many procedures.

He began to put all the documents back into the drawer, apart from her passport, the tickets and the cash. The drawer stuck as he tried to close it. He pushed harder, certain he had replaced everything as he had found it. He pulled out the drawer, reached inside and felt something stuck at the back with duct tape. He carefully pulled off the tape and drew out the dark maroon ledger, with 'Medical Prescriptions' on the cover in gold letters.

Inside were details of the drug supplies required for the prison hospital, and Josh instantly realised he'd hit paydirt: this was how Janet was bringing drugs into the prison in plain sight. When she found a prisoner to sell drugs to, she would get Dr Zardari to prescribe them with something that came in a capsule. Anything. It didn't matter. Because she then emptied the capsule and refilled it with their drug of choice.

'Gotcha,' he whispered.

CHAPTER 9

Jack parked up a street away from the old school, waiting to see if the Mercedes drove out. After fifteen minutes it passed him. He couldn't get a clear view of the driver, a man wearing dark glasses, but he used his mobile to take a picture of the licence plate.

Driving back to the school, the barrier pole was up, so he was able to drive straight into the empty forecourt, parking beneath the lean-to shelter by the jeep. He looked around for the exit he had used previously, then began walking further around the building and paused by a broken-down bicycle shelter. He moved cautiously around until he could see Adam Border, wearing torn jeans and a T-shirt, hurling broken wooden frames onto a fire.

'Bit early for Bonfire Night, isn't it?' Jack said, moving closer.

Adam turned towards him, showing no surprise at his appearance.

'I was going to collect some of the stuff I'd bought in the market,' Jack lied, then shrugged, smiling. 'They were closed, so it was a wasted journey. Then I remembered you hanging out here.'

Adam nodded and continued stoking the fire. Jack moved closer, watching as wooden frame after frame was set alight.

'Why are you burning all the frames?'

'Not good enough for my use. I only want the authentic period frames. You can give me a hand if you want but mind you don't get splinters.'

Jack picked up some of the broken frames and tossed them onto the fire. Adam was sweating, his blond hair clinging to his face, and Jack removed his jacket as the fire burnt more fiercely. Adam used an old dirty rag to wipe his face and hands then kicked down the corrugated iron roof to lie on top of the dying fire, placing a large jam jar on the top.

'I'll need some of the ashes when they've cooled down.'

'What do you do with them?'

'Grind them into the canvases to age them. Fancy a cold beer?'

Jack picked up his jacket. 'Sounds good.' He followed Adam to the rear entrance and along the corridor, until he opened one of the double doors onto the drill hall. Jack glanced towards the boarded-up window he'd been looking through when he overheard the argument. He stared around the hall.

'Are they pulling this place down because of that old cement that's been on the news?'

Adam nodded. 'That, along with the asbestos, will see the whole place flattened. Two school rooms have collapsed ceilings, and I don't know how long the drill hall will be safe, to be honest.'

'Built in the fifties, was it?'

Adam turned and looked at him. 'What's with all the questions? Who gives a shit when it was built.'

'Just making conversation.'

Adam walked into the little office room he used beside the kitchen area as Jack stood looking around the large drill hall. He saw the painting Adam had been stamping on earlier and realised it was his own work.

Adam returned with two ice-cold bottles of beer and handed one to Jack. Jack turned to look over the long trestle table, gesturing to a white cardboard box that had a large stone inside cushioned in tissue paper.

'What do you do with that?'

'Lapis Lazuli. Very valuable. In the 13th and 14th centuries it was used to make ultramarine, an intense blue pigment. Titian was famous for using it to show off his wealth, since it was so expensive.' Beside the box was a big stack of used fifty-pound notes, held together with elastic bands. A mobile rang with a strange musical ringtone. Adam casually tossed a rag over the money as he searched for his phone. Eventually he found it hidden buy a stack of old books, snatched it up and took it into the kitchen.

Moments later, Jack heard him laugh. 'Great. That's terrific news.' He came back out, smiling, and gestured to three framed canvases draped with a white sheet.

'I have to get them ready to be shipped out as soon as possible. We've got buyers in China and the U.S. Do you want to see them?'

Jack nodded. 'What's your ringtone, Adam? It sorts of sticks in your head.'

'Ah yes, it's the Harry Lime theme from *The Third Man*. Orson Welles' brilliant movie set in Vienna. Now stand back while I line these up for you.'

Jack watched as Adam carefully removed the old sheet and stood the three paintings against the wall.

'These are Modiglianis. Most of his portraits are kind of flat, very simple in style, making him a favourite among forgers.'

Jack stood in front of the three seemingly identical paintings depicting a woman with slanting eyes.

'What do you think?'

'They all look the same.'

'If I were to tell you one of them is authentic, which one would you say it was?'

Jack bent down to look closer, moving from one to the other. 'Is it this one?' He gestured to the painting in the middle.

'Excellent, Jack. You've got a very good eye. Now I've got work to do, crating them up.'

'Do you want a hand?'

'Why not. The crates are stacked in the room off the corridor.' Together they carried back the wooden crates, just an inch larger in all measurements than the paintings themselves. They were laid out flat on the floor as Adam went over to the table and opened a box full of labels, all different sizes. He picked out several, placing them to one side, close to a bowl of brown liquid. 'Cold tea,' he said. 'I use it to age them.' There was also a large drawing pad, next to a bottle of ink and a handful of quill pens. Jack turned a page on the pad. It was covered in signatures. Hundreds of them.

'That's my homework; I do fifty to a hundred every night. Recognise any of them?'

'Not sure. Yeah, this is Leonardo da Vinci.'

'You are learning fast, Jack. Turn to an empty page, go on, keep going.'

Jack found the empty page as Adam picked up a black sleeping mask. He slipped it on as far as his forehead and drew up a stool. Adam chose a quill and dipped it in a pot of ink, then pulled the sleeping mask down over his eyes.

Fascinated, Jack watched as Adam, after a moment's thought, fluently made a signature, then quickly two more, before removing the mask.

'Pretty good huh? Forgeries are often caught out because they copy letter by letter, so it doesn't flow. I've done this since I was a kid.'

'I'm impressed.'

Adam grinned. 'That's nothing. Take a look at this.' He drew Jack over to an easel and pulled off the sheet. Underneath it was a half-finished canvas depicting an exotic-looking dark-haired woman, shimmering with inlaid gold sections. Adam then went over to the table and gestured for Jack to look over a stack of clippings. All referred to a painting by Gustav Klimt which had been found on his easel when he died and eventually sold for eighty-three million pounds. Jack recognised the woman's face from the painting he had just seen.

'What are you going to do with it when it's finished?' Jack asked.

'Wait a bit, then switch them,' Adam laughed.

'What about your own paintings?' Jack asked.

It was as if he'd flicked a switch. Adam's whole personality suddenly changed as his body tensed. He strode across the floor, picked up the painting Jack had seen through the crack in the window and hurled it across the room with such force it crashed against a wall. Not satisfied, Adam went over and kicked what was left of the frame.

'Let me tell you, it's just a question of time before I prove what I am capable of. No matter the cost.'

'What do you . . . ?'

Adam pulled himself together, clearly realising he had almost revealed too much. 'You should go and let me get on.' He started sorting through labels as if Jack wasn't there.

'Thanks for the beer,' Jack said, turning to go.

Adam didn't reply.

* * *

Jack arrived home to an irate Maggie. But before she could let rip, the doorbell rang and Penny hurried down the stairs to let Marius in. Jack had a brief respite while Maggie gave Marius the receipts for the furniture they'd bought and the addresses of the shops to collect it from.

'Jack will go with you,' she added.

'Not a problem,' Marius said, putting the receipts in his pocket.

'Sit down and have a coffee,' Penny said, as Maggie hustled Jack out of the kitchen and upstairs to his office.

'You are one selfish bastard, you know that, Jack?' Maggie seethed when they were alone. 'Imagine this. I go out for a small shop in the afternoon, and by 7 p.m. I'm not home. I've not texted. My mobile is off. 8 p.m. I'm not home. 9 p.m. I'm not home . . .'

'All right, I get it. Something cropped up.'

'Which is fine. But, fucking hell, all it takes is one text message, Jack. I've been worried sick.'

'I'm not a kid who has to give you a rundown of everything I am doing,' he frowned.

'Have you any idea how ill you have been? Anything might have happened to you,' Maggie insisted. 'It's not just selfish, it's reckless. Last night you slept like a log with no nightmares by the way – but I was wide awake because all I could think of was you meeting up with . . . what's his name . . . Adam Border. The murdering drug baron.'

Jack had been prepared to apologise for not texting, but now Maggie was going too far. 'He's neither of those things,' he said angrily.

'Is he still wanted?'

'No, the case is over . . . closed a couple of years ago.'

'So why did you go back to the market then?'

'Curiosity. He was . . . is . . . a fascinating character and a very good artist in his own right.'

'So, what happened?'

'We got talking. And he invited me to go round to this old school where he's living until it gets demolished.'

'Why is he showing you around his studio? Don't you think that he might have an ulterior motive? You're a police officer for God's sake.'

Before he could answer Penny tapped on the door.

'I'm off to bed. Charlie's had a feed, but he's a bit ratty, and Hannah is fast asleep.'

'Thanks, Penny.'

She hesitated before leaving. 'Everything all right, is it?'

'Yes, Mum, thanks. We'll be down in a minute.'

Maggie kissed Penny at the door and turned back to Jack. 'I'll just go and check Charlie, then fix something for dinner.' Her anger seemed to have cooled. 'Maybe you can open a bottle of wine. And then we can talk some more about your new friend.'

* * *

Josh had taken more medication and was resting on Janet's bed, waiting for her to return home from her all-day shift at the prison. He dozed for a while as the morphine kicked in but woke up when he heard voices from the street below. From the bedroom window, he could only see the back of the terraced house, so he went into the kitchen, looking out to see Janet with a bag of groceries at the garden gate. She was talking to an elderly woman and it sounded like she was giving her safety advice about credit cards.

'You must be careful when you use them, love. People can use a scanner now and get your card numbers when you pay for something or withdraw money at a cashpoint. You need to get one of them special credit card holders.'

'I'll ask my son. He's a security guard at the Co-op.'

'You do that, love. Stay safe now.'

Josh listened to her heavy footfall on the stairs, thinking it ironic that such a good neighbour to some poor old dear across the street could also be a major drug dealer.

Janet opened her flat door and kicked it closed before easing off her heavy shoes. She took off her coat and walked into the lounge with her groceries. When she saw Josh sitting on the sofa she didn't flinch.

'I know I locked my front door, so you are breaking and fucking entering. You've got two minutes to get out, or I am calling the police.'

'Sit down, Janet. I don't have long so we need to cut to the chase. I am going to make a deal with you . . .'

'I am not sitting down, sunshine, and you had better shift your arse or you're going to be arrested.' She opened her handbag and took out her mobile phone.

'I wouldn't make that call, Janet. I've enough on you to put you away for years.'

Janet hardly even blinked. 'I don't know what you are bloody talking about, just get the fuck out.'

Josh shook his head, smiling. 'Damn, you're good, Janet. But I have your passport, plane tickets and that nice stack of cash you had squirrelled away. Without them, you won't see your daughter or granddaughter any time soon . . . now put the phone down like a good girl and sit.'

She slowly sat down opposite him, her mouth drawn in a thin, hard line.

'I know you are dealing drugs to the Bellview inmates and did the same at Holloway. From what I've seen, it's been going on in plain sight for years.'

She folded her arms tightly across her chest. She looked strong, but her eyes betrayed her, and he could hear her grinding her teeth.

'Here's the deal. If you agree to help me, I keep your secret. Then when the job's done, if it's all gone my way, you get your passport and clear out, never to be seen again. If you don't agree, I hand your little notebook to the police.'

Now Janet was certain Josh did actually know everything. For the first time she sounded afraid.

'I wouldn't last two minutes if I gave up my dealers. These are gang lads, street thugs even the cops don't mess with.'

'I don't want your dealers.'

'So, what the fuck do you want? I can't give you my stash, they'll kill me.'

'Other way round, sweetheart. I'm going to give you my stash.'

Janet looked confused. Josh opened his folder, took out Rodney Middleton's photograph and put it down in front of her. He then prodded it with his finger forcing Janet to look.

'Yes, I know who he is,' she said, 'but he's not after anything from me, except his legit medication: OxyContin and anti-depressants. He got beaten up, see, and they damaged his shoulder. He doesn't mix with the junkies 'cause they'd punch him out for his tabs.'

Josh took a deep breath. 'We have a week, at a stretch, two.' Janet sat in stunned silence as she watched him pull on a pair of surgical gloves and take several numbered sachets from the folder. 'Give him sachet number one first. It's fentanyl. Not enough to kill him, but enough to scare whoever finds him. Give him naloxone to bring him round. I want everyone to think he's using. Next, give him sachet two. This is fentanyl with a tiny amount of xylazine. Again, not enough to kill him. He'll find it harder to remember what happened this time. Use the naloxone again. Next, sachet three. Then four. Then five. You get the idea. None of these should kill him but, by now, he'll be starting to bleed and ulcerate because each sachet contains a slightly higher dose of xylazine. He'll be asking you for more pain relief, so dosing him can happen in plain sight . . .

just like it always does. You be on shift, Janet. You be the one to check on him. You be the one to ignore the zombification if it happens. You be the one to treat his ulcers, keeping them covered, making out they're fine. Sachet number eight is the final one.'

Janet remained impressively calm in the midst of this litany of horrors.

'I know you can do this. He's a piece of shit.'

She leaned forward. 'How do I know I can trust you?'

'You have no alternative but to trust me. Do what I say ... and you get to go to New Zealand.'

She took a deep breath. 'Who was the fucker that tipped you off about me?'

'No one tipped me off, I'm just a fucking great detective. You oversee the inmates' medication. You got empty capsules and pill crushers hidden in your home. You use Dr Zardari to write legitimate prescriptions, mainly painkillers or sleepers I guess, making sure they're capsules. Then all you gotta do is empty the capsules out and refill them with whatever it is you're selling. Then you've got a legit bottle of prescription medication containing pills filled with your street drugs. No one would ever guess. It's so simple, it's genius.'

She laughed, shaking her head. 'I thought it might be that young Eric you were having such a pleasant chat with, sugar and spice and all things nice ... evil little prick carved up his siblings you know. Anyway, look, I only have two weeks till I retire. It's impossible.'

'Nothing's impossible.'

'No, no,' Janet panicked. 'You'll fuck off and leave me in the shit.'

Josh paused to think for a second. 'Janet, all I want is for Rodney Middleton to get what he deserves. That's all I care about. I don't give a damn about what you've been doing.'

Janet put her hands flat on her knees to stop her foot from jiggling. Josh could tell she was thinking, weighing up how much he was guessing and how much he could actually prove. But without her passport and cash, none of that mattered. Josh took out a burner phone and put it in her hand.

'No one else gets involved; it's just you and me.'

She wrapped her fingers around the phone and shut her eyes for a moment. When she opened them again she seemed to have made a decision. 'Then I guess we have work to do. Turning your drugs into capsules. It'll take a while. We can have a microwave dinner while we work.' Janet stood up. 'I suppose a fuck's out of the question?'

Josh howled with laughter as Janet headed into the kitchen. She was definitely a piece of work. Which was good in one way: she'd be more than capable of giving Middleton the send-off Josh wanted. But she'd also be capable of double-crossing him if she could.

'Hey Janet,' he called out, 'don't go poisoning my ready meal. I've scanned your notebook to my phone and sent it to a friend of mine. He'll only send it to the cops if I don't call him every day for the next two weeks.'

It was a lie, but it wasn't a bad idea.

CHAPTER 10

In the end, Jack and Maggie didn't talk about Adam again that night. They'd simply shared a bottle of wine, talked about nothing important and then headed to bed. Neither of them had actively decided to avoid the subject; they were just fed up of arguing.

It was gone midnight as Maggie lay in the curve of his body, his arms around her waist. Maggie felt more content than she had for a long time.

'I do love you, Jack, and I'm sorry if I sounded like a pain in the arse earlier. It's just that I was worried. I know I've been a bit over the top. I thought it could be baby blues . . . that was part of my stress for a while.'

Jack didn't reply although she knew he was listening because his thumb stroked her forearm. He just let her talk. 'Recently, you've not been sleeping too badly and have been more like your old self, so it could be really good for you to return to work. It feels like we've turned a corner. Especially now the building work is finished.'

'Just promise me no more extensions or walls being knocked down,' he said.

Maggie laughed. 'I promise the dining room arch can wait.' She pulled Jack's arm tighter around her. 'I'm really looking forward to going back to work. Penny will have her help, you and I will be earning again. It's all coming together, Jack.'

Jack reached out to turn off his bedside light as Maggie turned around to face him.

'So, isn't it a bit unwise for you to go and meet up with this Adam Border again?' In the darkness, she could feel him tense.

'Mags, it's over. I'm not getting involved again.'

'You got involved again by going to see him. Please don't get angry, Jack. I'm just trying to understand. Isn't he just an art forger?'

Jack tossed the duvet aside and moved to the end of the bed. 'Do you know who Gustav Klimt is?'

'I think I've heard of him,' she said dubiously.

'They found a finished painting on his easel called *Lady with a Fan*. In June 2003 it sold for eighty-five million. When I was in Adam's studio at the school, he showed me these cuttings about the painting and the auction and then he goes over to one of the easels and whips off the sheet like a magician ... and there's the painting.'

'What, the real one?'

'No, a fake. But he said he's going to switch it for the eighty-five million job.'

'Surely they'll spot it,' Maggie said dubiously.

Jack warmed to his theme. 'Adam reckons that in every gallery around the world, fifty per cent of the paintings are fake, even more with old masters.'

Maggie was taken aback. 'And that's what Adam is doing, faking old masters?'

Jack couldn't hide his enthusiasm. 'Yes, he's collecting old canvases, frames and even nails. He's got boxes of them from different centuries, and when I was over there earlier today, he was burning frames in a bonfire. When I left, he had a jar to collect the ashes, which he was going to use to age the canvases.'

'Bloody hell, Jack, can you hear yourself? He's faking paintings, and you seem to admire him. You should walk away as fast as you can. What if he's not as smart as you think? What if people do know he's back and he's being watched? You could be caught up in what he's doing.'

Jack sighed. 'You still don't understand . . . I'll be right back, don't go to sleep.' As he hurried out of the bedroom, Maggie lay back and closed her eyes. She felt herself dropping off. She jumped when Jack barged back into the bedroom with his laptop.

'I was looking at stuff on the internet with him and it got me Googling for myself . . . honestly Mags, when you start to look at it, you'll be amazed'. He got into bed beside her and propped the laptop between them. He opened an article about fakes and famous artists. At first Maggie just wanted to tell him she'd look at it in the morning, but after reading a couple of paragraphs she quickly got sucked in.

'This one, Tom Keating: can you believe he faked over two thousand paintings by over two hundred artists. He even did a Rembrandt. And look at the next guy, John Myatt. He's done Chagall and Giacometti, and look . . . here's his copy of a Matisse with the real one beside it.'

'OK, I'm impressed.'

Jack smiled as he returned to the screen. 'I thought you would be.'

'No . . . I'm impressed with you. Listen to yourself reeling off artists' names as if you've been an expert all your life.'

Jack grinned. 'Look at this guy, he's Dutch and got fed up with critics dismissing his artistic ability so decided he'd show them up by faking a Vermeer. He was going to admit it was his work but then decided to fuck them all by painting six more. He sold them worldwide for around sixty million dollars.'

Maggie was properly hooked now, looking at the photographs of famous fakes as Jack scrolled down through the article. 'OK, now look at this guy's work, Modigliani. Just as I was about to leave tonight, Border showed me three identical paintings. He asked me which one was the original, and it was almost impossible to tell them apart, but I said I thought it was the one in the middle, and guess what? I was right.'

'How much is it worth?'

'Hang on.' Jack did a quick search. 'Bloody hell, the original would set you back millions. Adam's dealer rang while I was there, and I think he said they were all sold. I helped him get them ready to be shipped.'

Maggie laughed. 'So my policeman husband has been helping an art forger pack up his fakes!' She lay back and closed her eyes. 'Right, I really am going to sleep now. Maybe when I wake up I'll find this has all been a dream.'

CHAPTER 11

The next morning, after another peaceful night, Jack woke up feeling refreshed and energised. After a quick shower he went into his office and spent the morning looking at videos about forgers and ordering books from Amazon, along with *The Third Man* DVD. At 11 a.m. he wandered down to the empty kitchen, dressed in old jeans and a T-shirt, as he was expecting Marius to drive them to collect the larger pieces of furniture for the loft.

Maggie got back from her run with a sleeping Charlie in his pram to find Jack eating a bacon and egg sandwich and wondering where the hell Marius was.

'Oh, yeah. I forgot to say. He had a problem with his van. He'll call you when it's fixed. Sorry.'

'Oh, right.' Jack pretended to be disappointed, thinking he could go back to his office to watch more videos.

'And me and your mum are interviewing some cleaners this afternoon,' Maggie added.

'Daisy had eight puppies last night!' Penny shouted from the hallway, closing the front door behind her. She came into the kitchen, taking off her coat. 'Ah, they are cute, Jack. You should have seen Hannah's face light up at the sight of them.'

'No way,' Jack said as he forced his breakfast plate into an already full dishwasher. 'There's quite enough going on here without getting a puppy.'

Penny wasn't quite ready to give up though. 'It's a Labradoodle. The poodle side means they are very clever. Mind you, the Labrador side can mean they're also boisterous.'

'I don't care what breed it is. We are not having one. You need to make sure Hannah knows it, Mum. No umming and ah-ing or she'll talk you round.'

'I'm afraid Jack's right,' Maggie said.

Jack wrapped his arms around her. 'You see, we agree on something. I'll disappear when you two start interviewing the cleaners unless you need me to do anything.'

Maggie hugged him back. 'You can make me a nice cup of coffee.' She surprised him by adding in a whisper, 'Then I'd like to sit with you in your office and watch one of those art fraud videos.'

He grinned. 'You go up and I'll bring your coffee.'

* * *

Janet Williamson was in the prison infirmary when the alarm went off, signalling an emergency in cell block four, cell fourteen. She quickly picked up her medical bag to accompany the male nurse and prison officers onto the wing.

They found Rodney Middleton face down on his bunk bed, as she knew they would. Janet waited for the male nurse to examine him. Middleton appeared comatose, his eyes wide open and staring, while his body was stiff.

'He's OD'd on God only knows what,' the nurse said. 'His pulse is very low. We need to get the doctor.'

'He's not on duty until this afternoon,' Janet told him, moving to Middleton's bedside as the nurse turned him onto his back. She removed a vial of naloxone from her bag then, gently moving the male nurse aside, bent over Middleton, broke the seal and squeezed the contents into his nasal passages.

'Come on, Rodney,' Janet spoke quietly and calmly. 'There's a good lad, just breathe in. You're going to be all right. Come on, big breaths. There you go.'

Rodney jerked upwards, blinking rapidly, and then fell back against the pillows. Janet checked his pulse and blood pressure as he slowly began to regain his senses.

'Back with us, Rodney? How are you feeling now?'

'What happened? What the fuck happened to me?' he gasped.

Janet turned to the male nurse. 'I've spoken to Doctor Zardari about making naloxone a stock drug. It was lucky I had some on me. We had so many ODs at Holloway.'

With the emergency over, they headed back to the infirmary.

'I'll report it to the doctor when he gets here. And someone will have to talk to Rodney to find out what he's been using. He's prescribed some heavy-duty painkillers, so he could have stored them up to get high. Or maybe he's being passed something at visiting. Sneaky bastards, all of them. All we can do is make sure he swallows his meds, so if you're on duty handing out the tabs to that wing, check his cheeks and under his tongue. I'll check who he's got visiting him.' The male nurse nodded his understanding before leaving Janet to write up her incident report. Once she was alone, she closed her eyes and sighed heavily. She put her hand in her pocket and pulled out the sachet with '1' written on it. 'Come on Janet, come on,' she whispered to herself. 'Think of New Zealand.'

* * *

Jack stood outside Boots on the phone to Maggie explaining that he was hanging around for a bit as the baby formula she wanted had just been delivered, but they had to book it into stock before they could sell it to him. She spoke quickly, explaining they were busy interviewing the third applicant for the cleaning job and the fourth had just arrived, with two more expected soon.

'I thought we'd cracked it with the first woman, but when I told her that I was a doctor and you were a detective, she legged it. Actually legged it. Anyway, no need to hurry back. I'll be busy for at least another couple of hours.'

It took half an hour for Jack to drive to the old school. Just as he reached the open barrier, a large white van drove past him. As he parked, he could see Adam pushing a heavy-duty trolley carrying a huge frame wrapped in a tarpaulin.

'Good timing, Bro. Help me with this and be careful you don't damage the canvas. I've been waiting months for one this size.' Together they lifted the frame off the trolley and hefted it into the old drill hall. 'Careful,' Adam warned as they eased it along the corridor and through the double doors then laid it on the floor. Adam carefully pulled back the tarpaulin to reveal a painting of a battle scene with cannons and dead horses strewn among the soldiers, torn flags and wagons. The paint was cracked and chipped in some places, showing the canvas beneath. The heavy gilt frame was broken and had missing corners, but Adam seemed thrilled, pacing around it, clapping his hands.

'You have no idea how long I have been trying to find a canvas this size and the right age. It's perfect. Now help me turn it over to check out the back.' Together, they gently eased the canvas over to lie face down on the tarpaulin. Adam got down on his hands and knees to inspect the back of the frame, looking closely at the rusted nails hammered in to hold the canvas in place.

'It's perfect,' Adam gushed. 'Bloody worth the wait.' He went over to the trestle table and came back with a scalpel which he used to ease off a section of cracked paint.

'There's an even older painting underneath. That's the reason it's cracking so badly. It'll take me hours to get it down to the bare canvas.'

'Did you get this from the same framer's shop in Portobello Road?' Jack asked.

'You must be joking. This has taken Christ knows how long to track down. I've found a few that were almost perfect, but they weren't the right size. No, this is the one I've been waiting for. In fact, it's one of the reasons I'm back in the UK.'

'This dealer knows his stuff then, does he?' Jack asked.

'He certainly does. And this cost me a good few quid, I can tell you.'

'He looked like a bit of a thug to me.'

Adam frowned, becoming edgy. 'Who are you talking about?'

'That dealer in the frame shop, the one I first saw you with.'

Adam shook his head, smiling. 'He's just a delivery man, not the owner. He wouldn't be around on Saturdays, more than likely he'd be at his gallery or abroad.'

'What's his name, this owner?'

Adam narrowed his eyes. 'What's with all the questions, Jack? What are you fucking after? You going to shop me?'

'No. And I could ask you the same question . . . what are you fucking after?'

Adam gave a sly smile. 'You never know.' The tension between them disappeared as quickly as it had arrived.

'I've been watching loads of documentaries. I've even got my wife interested. Did you know this about Picasso? Sometimes, when he was presented with a copy of his work and he thought it good enough, he'd sign it.'

Adam laughed. 'Yes, he's one of the easiest to copy. His later works are the best. So, who else have you been researching with your wife? Did you mention anything about me?'

Jack slightly flushed as he nodded. 'She was not that pleased about it at first, but I mean, it's not like you're on a wanted list.'

Adam nodded, now focusing on carefully removing the rusted nails from around the frame. 'Making a painting look like the original – that's the easy part in a way,' Adam mused. 'It's really all about the materials. You've heard of Wolfgang Beltracchi? A real genius as forgers go. But he got sloppy. He'd run out of zinc to make white paint. So he went and bought a cheap over-the-counter tube and got caught.'

'How?' Jack asked.

'Because when it was tested, it contained titanium, which had not been used as a white pigment since 1914. It blew his provenance because the artwork he was forging was supposed to have been painted in the 1920s. It was about to be sold for two and a half million when the inconsistency emerged. Lesson learnt, eh?'

'So, artists like you, do you get a percentage of the sale price of the fakes?' Jack asked.

Adam looked up, smiling. 'I get a big cut, but he must get God only knows how much more. And it's tough to say no to a job, because he's got you by the balls.'

'Surely he can't threaten you or he could be exposed too,' Jack said.

Adam shrugged. 'It doesn't always work like that. He's a top dealer with galleries all round the world. His partner's a good artist actually but a very frustrated one as his work doesn't sell. They're a bit like Joe Orton and Kenneth Halliwell as a duo. Anyway, I'm sick of him controlling me. Some days I'd like to fucking strangle him, or better still, stick a paintbrush down his throat.'

Jack decided to be more careful when questioning Adam. He seemed quite at ease explaining about art frauds, but quickly changed the subject or became angry whenever Jack asked about the other people involved in his 'business'.

Adam carried on minutely inspecting the canvas. 'Wow, wait a second.'

He carefully lifted a section of cracked oil paint from one side of the painting. 'Well, look at this Jack. It's a crucifixion. See, that's part of the cross.' His bad mood suddenly gone, Adam came and put an arm around Jack's shoulder. 'This is going to be my crowning glory. I've been working towards it all my life, and just when I thought I would never find the perfect materials, this came along. You have no idea how it makes me feel ... all the years of practice, perfecting my work, will culminate in this one. It's going to be faultless.'

Adam turned away abruptly and went across the drill hall to a small, hard-backed chair stacked with large art books. He carried one over to the trestle table and started flicking through the pages. He waved Jack over.

'See this? It was stolen in 1965 from the altar at the cathedral in Palermo. It was never recovered, and the empty space where it had hung was a constant reminder of the loss until, many years later, they commissioned this, a copy, which is still hanging there today.' He turned the page to show the copy, and Jack stared, unable to see the difference. Adam slammed the book closed and went and put it back on the chair. 'I am going to find the original, Jack,' he said with a wink.

Before Jack could say anything, Adam's mobile rang, and he turned his back on Jack to answer it, waving a casual goodbye to Jack as he did so.

As Jack returned to his car, he could still feel the afterglow of Adam's intense excitement. He realised he had never felt that way about anything in his own life. But he desperately wanted to feel that joy for himself.

CHAPTER 12

Janet was discussing Middleton with Doctor Zardari.

'Do you think he was trying to commit suicide?' Dr Zardari asked.

She shook her head. 'Accidental overdose, I reckon. Men like him are too narcissistic to kill themselves.'

Dr Zardari sighed heavily. 'And where's this stuff coming from?'

Janet's face gave nothing away. 'Good God, smuggling's rife. Visitors bring all sorts in, hidden in all sorts of places! It'll be happening right under our noses.' Janet didn't need to dissuade Zardari from the idea of someone smuggling drugs in for Middleton, as long as he never imagined it could be her. In truth, Janet knew that the perfect scapegoat was already in the mix.

Amanda Dunn had spent two months in Holloway for a minor offence. She was bullied throughout her stay and had come to Janet to be patched up on a couple of occasions. She quickly saw that Amanda was weak, easily manipulated and destined to make terrible mistake after terrible mistake. Regardless, she always had hopeful eyes. This is what Janet recognised through the disguise she wore when visiting Middleton. Here she was again, doing the bidding of a murderer. If they thought someone else was involved in Middleton's death, it wouldn't be Janet they homed in on. It would be Amanda.

Janet looked at her watch. She was on early evening duty, delivering medication from their secure annexe, and the prisoners were starting to line up in the corridor before, one by one, they came to the small security booth, protected by a Perspex screen with an open stainless-steel section for the medication to be passed through in small paper cups. The evening deliveries often ended in violent arguments as prisoners complained that their dosages of painkillers had been lowered, or they were no longer being prescribed sleeping tablets.

Janet was ready for Middleton with his cup containing the weaker painkillers prescribed since his 'overdose'.

'Rodney, we're putting you on a lower dose of the same medication to see how it deals with your back pain. If it doesn't help, then you will need an appointment to see the doctor tomorrow.'

Middleton kicked the base of the booth and the officer standing by took a step closer.

'You take these for tonight, Rodney, and see how you go.' Janet passed him the small paper cup containing two large white capsules, then handed him a paper cone-shaped cup with water. She watched Middleton tip the capsules into his mouth, sip the water and then open his mouth and lift his tongue to show they'd been swallowed.

'Thank you, Rodney.'

Middleton leered at her before he turned away to be taken back to his cell. The next prisoner stepped up, and Janet continued dishing out the meds. She would be off duty in another few hours, knowing that Josh would call for an update as he always did each evening. Just thinking about him made her come out in a sweat, but so far, it was going to plan. She had five more days to slowly up the dosage before administering the fatal one.

* * *

Jack knew he would be in for a grilling from Maggie as he'd been gone nearly all afternoon. But when he walked into the kitchen, excuses at the ready, there was another sort of drama going on.

Hannah was having a major meltdown, screaming and crying, thrashing about on the floor.

'She's been like this since we told her she can't have a puppy, so you can take over, Jack, because we are both drained,' Maggie said.

Hannah kicked out with her legs, her head buried in her arms, wailing. Jack squatted down beside her, relieved he wasn't being interrogated about his absence. Hannah slowly lifted her head, her eyes red-rimmed from crying, her cheeks puffy. When she saw Jack, she lifted both arms to wrap around him.

'You said I could have a puppy, didn't you, Daddy?'

'I didn't say that.'

'You did. You said when I'm older. And I'm older now. You promised. You did. *Yes you did!*'

Jack had never seen his little daughter in such a ferocious temper. She was definitely beyond the point of no return as she flailed with both arms, her hands bunched in little fists, trying her best to punch him.

'I hate you!'

Jack rolled away from her, curling up and howling,

'That hurt me, you hurt me, how could you be so nasty to me.'

Hannah crawled over to him, and, to his astonishment, she gave him another punch. He had thought she would be devastated to think she had hurt her daddy, but clearly that was not the case. He jumped up and scooped her into his arms. She struggled and screamed, kicking him in the nuts, almost making him drop her as he marched into the hall. Holding her under one arm, he managed to open the new closet that Marius had built under the stairs and pushed Hannah inside as she let loose with a screaming howl. Jack drew the small bolt across the door as Hannah let loose a screaming howl, banging and kicking at the closed door.

'Listen to me, Hannah. You will stay in there until you are quiet, and I will not let you out until you have apologised.'

There was silence and then a pitiful wailing as Hannah screamed for her mummy. Then, between sobs, she said she was sorry. Jack felt something suddenly swamping him, a memory of darkness that consumed and terrified him. The cries from inside the cupboard brought everything flooding back as he pulled the bolt back and lifted his daughter out. He remained on his knees, rocking her in his arms, asking over and over for her to forgive him, promising he would never ever lock her in there again. She clung to him, exhausted, pressing her face into his neck as she gradually calmed.

'I'm sorry, Daddy, I don't want a puppy anymore.'

'Listen to me, Hannah, I am sorry. One day I promise you will have a puppy.' He lifted her in his arms and she smiled, kissing him frantically.

'I love you, Daddy,' she said, bright-eyed.

'I love you more,' he said, his voice cracking.

His heart raced as she wriggled out of his arms, as if the incident had been instantly forgotten, and ran up the stairs. He slowly felt his heart rate slowing, his breathing steadying as he entered the dining room, closed the door, slumped in an easy chair and put his head in his hands.

Jack had been in the same position for ten minutes before Maggie walked in. 'Well, you've done it now, promising Hannah a puppy. Penny and I have been adamant about telling her she can't have one. Why on earth did you tell her she could . . .'

Jack sat back in the chair and Maggie knew instinctively something was very wrong. She quickly went to him and bent forward, looking into his face.

'What is it, Jack? You're shaking.'

He sighed. 'I just did an unforgivable thing. When Hannah punched and kicked me, I grabbed her and chucked her into the closet under the stairs. I locked her in.'

'Oh God Jack, that was . . . So, it was a guilt promise from you. Not exactly teaching her the right way to behave, is it?'

'You don't understand,' he said, turning away, his chest heaving.

She sat beside him, taking his hand. He tried to pull it away, but she tightened her grip.

'Tell me what it is, Jack. Explain to me what happened to make you like this.'

He remained silent for a long time, leaning against her shoulder, trying to find the right words. Something buried deep inside him had just been released, a torment he had never allowed to surface until now. Just as he had calmed Hannah, gently rocking her in his arms, Maggie now cradled him with both her arms around him, his head still buried in her shoulder.

His voice sounded hoarse when he eventually started to talk, as if each word caused him pain. He was at the care home, no more than four or five, when it started. He recalled how he cried for his mother, not wanting to eat or sleep, and that was when the punishment had started. Jack had been locked in a cupboard in the cellar of the old house, for hours and hours, left in the dank darkness, and if, when he was eventually released, he continued to be disobedient, he would be beaten. He could not recollect how long the terror had dominated his life, always afraid of being shut away, and that he would never be let out.

'Dear God, how long did this go on for?' Maggie asked.

'Until I was fostered. Not many families wanted a boy my age, especially one they thought had mental health issues. Mum and Dad saved me, and for the first time I was shown love. I had never known any kind of affection, and for a long time, I was terrified they would send me back. So, I always tried to be a good boy.' Jack sighed, unable to believe what he had done to his daughter.

Maggie, however, saw a positive in what had just happened. She was certain now that Jack's nightmares stemmed from his childhood. Maggie didn't want to talk anymore about what Jack had done to Hannah, she just held him tight.

'It's over. Hannah will be fine. And you're going to be fine.'

He smiled and nodded, finally feeling he could breathe properly again. 'Thank you.'

'Oh, by the way,' Maggie said, 'me and your mum employed a nice lady called Gladys today. Five mornings a week. She's from Ghana and has the most amazing dreadlocks. She was the best one by a mile.'

'Great,' Jack said before heading upstairs to see if Hannah really was OK.

Maggie sat for a minute, wondering if Jack had told her the whole story. Had he been sexually abused too? It would not be uncommon where physical and psychological abuse were present. She was happy that Jack had shared his memory . . . but was now worried what other issues were going to come out into the open.

* * *

An odd side effect of what Janet was doing to Rodney Middleton was that he had become a far more pleasant man to deal with. He was not as aggressive and had even started to take an interest in the art department. But Janet knew it wouldn't last.

She was on duty more often than not and was therefore usually the one who administered his white capsules. These were a growing cocktail of fentanyl and xylazine, plus his Ibuprofen, plus whatever his girlfriend might be smuggling in for him. Janet didn't care about Amanda fucking Dunn. She'd got away with murder, quite literally, so if she got dragged into any investigation into Middleton's death, Janet wasn't going to lose any sleep over that.

Middleton was also now seeing the on-duty medics in relation to a wound that had appeared on his right leg, which had to be cleaned and dressed daily. He could not recall falling or hurting himself, but Janet made sure it was documented that when he overdosed, he could easily have fallen and not known about it.

Josh insisted on daily updates on her progress, and every call made her nervous because time was running out before her departure. Middleton was changing daily, becoming more addicted to his cocktail of drugs while his leg wound slowly changed from a scratch into an ulcerated hole. Janet worked hard at being the medic who most frequently dealt with Middleton, so that she could monitor his reaction to the drugs.

As Josh's return date to New York got closer, he started pushing Janet to administer more fentanyl and xylazine as he wanted the job done before he left the UK.

'I can kill him in the blink of an eye, Josh, with one special capsule,' she told him. 'But you wanted him to suffer. We have just under one more week. Let's use it.'

After their conversation, Josh put in a call to Laura at the station asking if Jack had returned to work yet.

'He's expected next week,' she told him. 'Everyone's really looking forward to seeing him. How's the tour going?'

'I've just got two more events before I go back to London, then home,' he told her. 'It would be good to see you . . .'

As he'd hoped, she offered to let him stay at her flat.

* * *

On Portobello Road, Marius and Jack had spent the morning stacking the van with the larger items they'd bought at the stalls: bookcases, large ceramic pots, a bed and two shelving units. It was already looking full, so they reckoned they'd need another trip for what remained. Marius fancied a bacon roll and coffee, so Jack said he'd check on the mattresses Maggie wanted, then they could meet back at the van.

Heading along Portobello Road, Jack stopped to enquire at a small shop selling beds. They didn't have the right size in stock but would have a big delivery the following day and would likely have the one he wanted then. He was about to head back to the van when he did a U-turn, heading further down Portobello to the framer's. The door was open, letting in enough light so that he could see inside. It was stacked to the ceiling with frames, but Jack's attention was immediately taken by a massive cross dominating the entire room, looking like a theatrical or movie prop. Jack edged further into the shop, looking over the mountain of frames. He bent down to check one.

'What you lookin' for?'

Jack turned. The man leaning on the doorframe from the inner room was the one he had seen selling frames to Adam.

'I have an unframed picture and was just checking if one of these might be suitable.'

'What size?'

'Ah, that's me being stupid. I don't actually have the measurements with me.'

'Then come back when you do. We're not open right now, we're just waiting for a delivery.' He was very muscular, about the same height as Jack, wearing dirty denim overalls with a washed-out T-shirt beneath. His balding head boasted the odd strand of greasy blond hair.

'Thanks, I'll do that.'

'Only open Saturday from ten till two.'

Jack gestured to the massive cross. 'That's really something, isn't it?' For the first time, he noticed the heavy black chains hooked to a ring at the back of it. 'Have to have a big room to stand that in.'

He received a cold glare from the man's small, flinty eyes. He obviously didn't want to have any further conversation . . . which was enough to make Jack continue.

'It's probably from a theatrical production, I suppose. I can't remember if they had a big cross in *Jesus Christ Superstar*. Or maybe from a biblical epic?'

Jack received another dismissive stare, so he backed away towards the entrance. 'This your shop?'

'No, I just work here. Shut the door on your way out.'

'Do you have a card?' Jack persisted, 'Maybe when I get home and measure the picture, I could ring to find out if you have a frame that'd fit.'

'No cards. Go on, out now, mate.'

Jack nodded and smiled as he left, closing the door behind him. As he made his way back to Marius and the van, he paused, wondering if he should have said he was Adam Border's friend. He also thought there was a possibility that Adam could have ordered the cross for his new painting.

'Hurry please, Jack,' Marius shouted as Jack approached, 'I need to get everything unloaded. I have a job this afternoon.'

'Sorry, I was asking about mattresses. Might be coming in tomorrow.'

'I can't do it tomorrow. It'll have to be the day after.'

'Fine by me. I can help . . . I don't start work until Monday.'

By the time they had unloaded the van and carried everything up to the loft extension, Jack was hungry. A note on the kitchen table informed Jack that Penny was out with Hannah, and Maggie had taken Charlie to the clinic for his check-up. The large ceramic planters stood empty beside the plants Maggie had ordered. So Jack decided he would surprise her.

When Maggie arrived home, she was thrilled to see all her plants in their new pots, looking wonderful. She chose not to point out that, now full of soil, they'd be much harder to move into place. Jack rolled the pots on the rims of their base as Maggie directed him into the conservatory, where he left the planters on either side of the sliding doors into the garden. 'Kew Gardens has got nothing on us,' he joked.

Jack felt in good spirits. Whether or not it was connected to opening up about what happened to him at the care home, he just didn't know. What he did know was that he was looking forward to returning to work.

When Maggie went upstairs to bathe and feed Charlie, Jack ducked into his office and started Googling the stolen painting Adam had told him about. There it was: Caravaggio's *Nativity with Saint Francis and Saint Lawrence*, painted in 1609, stolen from the altar of the church in Palermo. One article provided the exact measurements – explaining why Adam had been searching so long for a canvas measuring eight feet eleven inches in length and six feet five and a half inches in width.

Apparently the whole city celebrated when the copy was put in its place, but the worldwide search for the missing masterpiece went on. Some people believed the Mafia had stolen it to use as a bargaining tool in exchange for the release of jailed Mafiosi, then it had been burnt when it became too dangerous to hide. Witnesses had come forward to say they had seen it rolled up in a carpet, while others maintained it was hanging in a Mafia don's villa.

Jack's phone rang. It was Laura calling to ask if he would like to join her for dinner when Josh returned to London, as she had offered to let him stay before he returned to New York.

'That would be great, Laura, thanks. If his staying with you is . . . awkward . . . last time he was here, he slept on a blow-up mattress, but now we have a loft extension. Up to you.'

'Wow, you've been busy!' Laura laughed.

'You wouldn't believe the work that's been going on here. As well as the loft, we now have a kitchen twice the size with a sort of conservatory attached.'

'No wonder you've not come back to work.'

'Truth is, I've just been a bystander. Maggie did all the planning, and my mother's boyfriend and his mates did all the work.'

'How's the new baby?'

'Charlie is fabulous. Maggie is organising a christening celebration. You'll be invited, of course.'

'I'm looking forward to seeing the baby and you on Monday. We've all missed you.' Laura hesitated. 'Is everything all right now?'

'Yeah, terrific.'

'It's not been very exciting around here without you. Heard anything from Ridley?'

'Nope, not a whisper. I'm sure one day he'll just turn up.'

'See you Monday. Love to Maggie.' Laura hung up.

Jack sat staring at the laptop. It did feel strange at times not to have heard from Ridley, but it had now been so long that, in truth, he rarely thought about him. He hoped that wherever he was, he was enjoying his retirement. He returned to reading up about the Caravaggio. If the Mafia were involved in the disappearance of the original, Adam would have to be very careful.

CHAPTER 13

Jack spent Saturday morning painting the bookcases in the loft extension and finishing off some areas that needed another coat of emulsion.

Gladys, with the extraordinary hair extensions, came by for coffee, to get to know Jack and Hannah. Penny showed her round the house and gave her a run-down of what was expected when she started work on Monday, then showed her how to use all of the appliances.

In the afternoon, Marius and Jack went back to the market to check whether the right-sized mattress had come in and were soon hefting it back to the van. Marius said he would like to check on a stall selling some second-hand electrical tools, particularly a paint stripper, and Jack agreed to meet him back at the van in twenty minutes. Once alone, Jack hurriedly returned to the framer's. The door was slightly ajar, and he could hear an angry exchange from inside. Jack eased himself behind the woman selling vintage dolls, to be less conspicuous as he listened.

'You're supposed to be taking the crates to Southampton. You got paid upfront, so don't give me your bullshit excuses. If we miss the delivery, that'll be another week lost . . . All right, let me close up and I'll get on the road. There's no need for you to come here threatening me. Lugging that fucking cross here nearly broke me back, so you tell him that whatever he's going to be using it for, it's not going to be me that moves it again.'

Jack pressed himself against the wall as the door banged open. A handsome black man wearing an elegant fur-collared leather coat, his hair swept back from his face, walked out. Jack could smell his cologne from where he was standing. Jack waited until he was out of sight before stepping into the shop, just as the thuggish man was about to close the door.

'I've got the measurements for the frame I was looking for,' Jack said.

'Sorry mate, we're closing.'

'It'll only take a minute,' Jack said with his best winning smile.

'Come on then, I'll give you sixty seconds. Then I'm closing up.'

Jack stepped around the cross to a stack of frames heaped on a cabinet. The man went into the back room, and Jack picked up a small gilt frame – then noticed a stack of envelopes on the side of the cabinet. Without thinking, he slipped one into his jacket just as the man returned. He snatched up the envelopes and stuffed them into a leather shoulder bag.

'Stupid bastard forgot them,' he muttered.

Jack held up the frame.

'Ten quid, lowest I can do.'

Jack shrugged, shaking his head. 'Not worth more than a fiver.'

The man had no time for bartering. 'Time's up, mate.' He grabbed the frame, tossing it back onto the pile, then walked towards Jack, forcing him backwards and out of the door. Jack heard the bolts being drawn across from inside. Then the sign flipped from 'open' to 'closed'.

* * *

Back in his office, Jack took out the blank envelope he'd picked up in the framer's shop. Inside was a gilt-edged invitation from Detmar Steinburg to a private viewing at a gallery on Bond Street in two weeks' time. Jack was hopeful that Detmar Steinburg was the collector Adam had been railing against. He tapped the invitation against the desk, trying to recall another name Adam had said. Was it Jim or Joe . . . Orton? Maybe that was the elegant black guy he had overheard arguing at the shop.

Jack Googled Detmar Steinburg and found he definitely matched Border's description, with galleries in Berlin, Los Angeles, Florida and Dubai. There were numerous photos of him taken at high society functions in *Tatler* and *Vogue*, at film and theatre premieres. Jack peered closely at the elegant, neatly coiffured man, always dressed in fashionable designer suits. He had shoulder-length, glossy dark hair receding slightly from his high forehead. No age was mentioned in any of the articles, but he looked to be in his late forties or early fifties, reminding Jack of a younger Karl Lagerfeld.

Maggie called out to tell him that an Amazon delivery had arrived, so he slipped the invitation into a drawer and went downstairs. The box was on the kitchen table, and when he opened it, he couldn't help grinning.

'What is it?' Maggie asked, looking into the box. 'More books about art forgery?' She picked them up and read out the titles. '*Confessions of a Master Forger . . . The Art Forger's Handbook . . . Art Crime and Its Prevention*. My, you are getting very serious about this, aren't you?' she said.

'I know it interests you, too,' he said.

She smiled. 'We've never had a sort of hobby together, have we? I suppose if we do, then I ought to meet Adam Border myself, don't you think?'

Jack laughed. 'Fair enough, Mags. The next time I see him, I'll invite him round for dinner.'

* * *

Jack arrived at the station early on Monday morning and was welcomed back by DCI Clarke, who took him into his office for a private chat about whether or not he needed any help or counselling. He was impressed with how Jack explained his semi-breakdown, assuring Clarke that after the trial of Rodney Middleton, he had felt emotionally broken but was now eager to get back to work.

Returning to the incident room as everyone arrived, Laura welcomed him back, updating him about any staff changes and associated gossip. He was pleased to be told that Anik had moved on to another station, and she primed him about his replacement. DI Brianna Armani had only been at the station a few weeks, but Laura hinted that she had already ruffled a few feathers.

'She's very keen on ethnic diversity.' Laura leaned in close and whispered. 'There's a feeling she's selected a few black probationary officers who are not up to scratch.'

Jack found the CID office running very smoothly, but DCI Clarke's list of 'rules' pinned on the noticeboard, along with his obsession that every officer give details of their whereabouts throughout the day, was a tad irritating. Also listed were the specific times the detectives and civilian staff could take refreshment breaks to ensure the offices were continuously manned. Clarke had also instigated an office briefing in the boardroom every Monday at eight o'clock.

Jack spent the morning sifting through all the cases currently being investigated and those already assigned for court appearances. He did not meet Anik's replacement until late afternoon, as she had been at the Old Bailey. She was tall, wearing a smart tailored suit, a stiff collared shirt and high heels. Her dark brown hair was swept back and tied in a short ponytail. She acknowledged Jack's presence with a polite nod and placed a very expensive briefcase on her desk before going directly into DCI Clarke's office.

It was after five and Jack was about to call it a day when Armani came out from Clarke's office and walked briskly towards him. He promptly stood up. She was slightly taller than him, and her handshake was strong. She was attractive, with dark eyes, arched eyebrows and a wide, thin-lipped mouth.

'Jack, I've heard very good things about you and look forward to working alongside you. We have nothing too demanding right now, but you know it's always that way ... the calm before the storm.' She cocked her head to one side, giving him a tight-lipped smile. 'No doubt that will be a relief as I believe you have had some emotional issues.'

'Everything is fine, back to so-called normal,' he said lightly, trying hard to conceal his irritation.

'Good to hear it, and you know I am always open to an informal chat if you feel concerned about anything or how we've been running the station since you've been on sick leave.'

Jack managed to keep his cool despite her heavy-handed reference to his sick leave. He already knew she would be the last person he would ever want to have any informal bloody chats with.

The CID room had slowly become busier, with a number of young officers of varying ethnicities entering the briefing room. Jack never normally noticed the ethnicity of his colleagues, but the ratio was clearly tipped in the direction of minorities which suggested an operation that required this specific approach. Jack felt the adrenalin build as he waited to find out more. He definitely felt ready to get stuck into work again. And, as Armani approached his desk, he hoped she was about to get him up to speed ahead of the new recruits.

'Ready to get back on the horse, Jack?'

He smiled and nodded, but, again, wasn't very happy with her choice of words.

'We have a female victim,' she continued, 'subjected to a vicious attack from her husband, called 999, and he was arrested, but she later refused to make a statement. She said it was an accident, and her husband was released from custody.'

'A domestic?' Jack glanced towards the briefing room, still filling with officers clearly about to be briefed on a big operation of some kind.

Armani couldn't help noting his lack of enthusiasm. 'If you read the report you will see that she suffered substantial injuries which required an ambulance to attend. I believe she lied about it being an accident through fear of further abuse by her husband. I'm sorry you feel she might be a waste of your time, DS Warr. I was hoping you might be able to allay her fears and change her mind. Or maybe your people skills have been exaggerated.' She ended with a glare.

He raised his hands in a submissive gesture. 'I have read the report and I'm sure you're right about being afraid of her husband. I'll be there first thing in the morning and see if I can persuade her to change her mind.'

Jack couldn't help noting that the victim's address was near Ladbroke Grove, a stone's throw from Portobello Road.

* * *

Maggie had had a very long, hard day at the hospital and arrived home after Jack, who was in the kitchen with Penny as she made a stew. Hannah was in her room watching TV, and Charlie was already in his cot. Maggie slumped down in a dining chair, and Jack put a glass of chilled white wine in her outstretched hand.

'There's a bottle of formula ready for his next feed. You enjoy your wine.'

Maggie sighed. 'Oh boy, do I need this. I've had a nightmare day. We're so short-staffed, we have patients lined up in corridors with no beds because they are all filled with old people who are chomping at the bit to go home. But getting their transport and social services organised is impossible. What about you?'

Jack described his interactions with DI Armani.

'I bet she's well dressed, at least,' Maggie quipped.

'She is, actually,' Jack said. 'Apparently, she's got a psychology degree. She's the kind of person who likes you to know that she knows everything. According to Laura, she was fast-tracked to get a promotion, and she has DCI Clarke in the palm of her hand.'

'Well, don't you antagonise her. Keep your head down.'

'I will. But I think she's already picking on me. She's got me on a bloody domestic.' Jack handed Maggie a DVD. 'Fancy a movie night? It's that film I was telling you about, *The Third Man*. Watch it in bed?'

Maggie smiled. 'You watch. I'll sleep.' Then she went upstairs with her wine to have a shower.

By the time they'd finished dinner, it was almost ten. Penny went to her bedroom as Jack cleared the kitchen and Maggie was pouring the remains of the wine into two glasses.

'You sure you're too tired to watch the movie?' Jack asked, closing the dishwasher.

Maggie picked up the DVD and read the back. 'It's black and white. What's so special about it?'

'I don't know. The theme tune is Adam Border's ringtone, remember, so we just got talking about the film.'

Maggie rolled her eyes. 'I can't wait to meet the man who has such an effect on you, Jack. Come on, let's get into bed and watch it.'

They were both propped up with pillows as the film started. Neither said a word as they watched for half an hour. Maggie turned to see that Jack was fast asleep. She sighed because, as tired as she was, she had decided to watch it all. When the credits rolled, she turned the movie off and lay back. Something about the movie disturbed her, and even after closing her eyes and settling down, she could not get to sleep.

* * *

Jack woke early and went down to the kitchen to make Maggie a cup of tea so she could drink it in bed. When he returned, she was frowning.

'I watched the entire bloody film and then, when I was trying to sleep, that bloody theme tune kept on playing in my head.' Jack smiled and kissed her as he handed over the tea. They could hear Penny and Hannah laughing, but thankfully Charlie was still asleep for now.

'Do you need the car today, Jack?'

He hesitated before answering, 'I wouldn't mind. I have to interview the domestic assault victim. But if you need it then I'll go by tube.'

'You take it. I might be home late again tonight. We have a new surgeon, and he'll certainly have his work cut out for him, to coin a phrase. I've got a late start, so I'll get an Uber.' Maggie cupped the mug of tea in her hands as Jack sorted out what he would wear. 'You know the film was quite good. It's about lies and betrayal and people hiding from the truth, and from themselves, I guess. But mostly it's about friendship, or what this one guy thought was a friendship ...' Maggie sipped her tea. 'It's about ... who can you trust?'

He nodded absently. 'I'll watch it tonight then,' he said before kissing her and hurrying out.

Maggie sighed. He didn't seem to have heard a word she said.

* * *

Jack started to hit traffic as he neared Ladbroke Grove. He had Waze on his phone for directions, but he'd decided to rely on his own local knowledge. He used the backstreets to avoid the heavy traffic at Shepherds Bush and eventually found himself entering a large council estate. Parking his car, he placed a Met police card on the dashboard and headed towards a fifteen-storey tower block, looking for 151 Willow Court.

The first thing he saw was an OUT OF ORDER notice on the lift, so he reluctantly started up the stairs. He was out of breath as he reached the eleventh floor and rested for a minute before heading down the dank corridor. He could find 149 but not 151. He rang the nearest bell. He waited a few seconds and rang it again before he heard the latch chain being pulled back. A thin girl in a nightdress opened the door.

'Sorry to bother you, but I'm looking for number 151. Do I need to go up another floor?'

'This is the top floor, and we got no 151.'

'Is this Willow Court?' He showed her his notebook with the address.

She looked at it and laughed. 'That says Willow Court*yard*. It's right at the end of the estate. It happens all the time with deliveries. With the lift out of order, it's a big schlepp up here.'

Jack squinted at his note, furious that he had misread the address.

'Should have gone to Specsavers,' she said, closing the door on him.

Jack trudged back down the stairs. Returning to his car, he noticed a big gob of spittle running down the windscreen. He got in and slammed the door, now annoyed with himself for putting the police card on the dashboard *and* misreading the address. He turned the window washer spray and wipers on, but that just spread the spittle across the windscreen. He kept the wipers going as he drove down the estate to the far end. There were the usual low walls surrounding the big blocks, patches of brown grass, then there was a narrow archway which he turned into. The low mews houses had attached garages but no gardens and appeared well-maintained with flowering tubs on their doorsteps.

He parked in front of 151, reluctantly leaving his Met card on the dashboard as he was on a single yellow. It was ten past ten as he rang the doorbell. Stepping back, he looked at the drawn curtains on the ground floor window. He rang again, and a woman's voice from behind the door asked what he wanted.

'I'm Detective Sergeant Warr from the Met Police. I want to speak to a Mrs Barras, Maria Barras.'

She took her time before replying. 'Thank you, but I don't need to see you.'

'Mrs Barras . . . I'm not here to cause you further distress. I'd just like a quick chat, then I'll go. Please. This won't take more than a few moments.'

The chain was removed, the door unlocked and the woman slowly opened it wider. Jack smiled through the small gap she'd created.

'Can I come in, please?' Jack showed her his warrant card, and she stepped back, allowing him to enter, before gesturing for him to go into the room to his right. He entered a comfortably furnished sitting room and she followed. Jack could see she had a swollen lip and a deep bruise around one eye that was already turning dark purple as well as surgical tape around two fingers of one hand. She was obviously nervous, shaking as she gestured for him to sit down.

Jack opened his briefcase to remove a copy of the incident report. Attached were details of two previous domestic incidents and police reports. Jack felt a bit guilty as he had not done more than glance through the file. 'I'm just here to ask a few more questions about the 999 call you made and the subsequent investigation,' he said. 'You suffered quite nasty injuries, Mrs Barras.

Two broken fingers, facial bruising . . .' He also knew some of her hair had been torn out and he realised that she was now wearing a wig. 'I see you reported incidents of domestic abuse on two previous occasions. But, like this last time, you refused to make a formal statement or press charges. I understand, of course, you are frightened, but making a statement will . . .'

She interrupted. 'Thank you, but I really do not want to waste your time. I made that clear to the detective who first interviewed me . . . she was very kind, and I appreciate your concern.'

'I can't force you to make a statement, but there are domestic abuse agencies, social services and other support groups that can help you.'

'I'll be fine, thank you.' Mrs Barras half rose from her chair as if the interview was over.

'I would like to talk to your husband as well. Is he home?'

'He's at work. I did explain that he is on a lot of medication because he suffers from depression and insomnia.'

'I understand how debilitating that can be,' Jack said, noticing how she was constantly glancing over to the doorway.

'What line of work is your husband in?'

'He was a security guard, but he had to retire.'

'Before that?'

'What?'

'Well, has he always been a security guard?' She looked even more nervous, so he continued thumbing through the report. 'What security company did he work for?'

The front door slammed shut and they both looked up. After a moment, a dark haired, muscular-looking man walked in.

'What's that car outside? You a police officer?'

'Detective Sergeant Jack Warr.' Jack stood up, showing his ID.

'What do you want?'

'Are you George Barras?'

'You got a warrant to be inside my house?'

'Your wife kindly invited me in.' Jack made no effort to hide why he was here. 'I am following up on an allegation of assault made against you.'

'I wasn't charged with anything,' Barras said with a half-smile. 'No harm done, Officer. You can go.'

Jack glanced at Maria, who was clenching her uninjured hand to stop it from shaking. 'I would say considerable harm was done, Mr Barras. I'm concerned for your wife's safety, so it's my duty to come and make sure she's OK.'

Barras had dark, expressionless eyes matching his black, greasy hair and he stood beside his wife with his muscular arms folded and his legs apart, not quite goading Jack but certainly showing no respect.

'Be assured that I will continue to monitor your wife's well-being,' Jack said calmly. 'I have several support agency contacts for you, Mrs Barras, should you need to call for assistance or seek advice.' Jack handed her a typed list of the agencies, on which he had also written in biro the clinic he had used for his insomnia condition. She took it from him with her good hand.

'I also suggest, Mr Barras, that you contact the number I have written down for a clinic that can help with your insomnia and depression.'

George scowled, clearly angry that Jack knew about his problems. 'This isn't the usual follow-up visit. I know the procedure, so you can't bullshit me.'

Jack ignored the comment. 'Barras is a Spanish surname, isn't it?'

'What's it to you? I was born here, she was brought up here. Is there anything else you want to poke your nose into?'

Jack put the file back into his briefcase, snapping it closed. 'I suggest, Mr Barras, you seek help and consider yourself fortunate that your wife did not press charges.' He left before Barras could respond.

Jack had been longer with the Barrases than he had intended, and it was now too late for him to pop over to Adam Border's school.

As he headed back to the station, Jack wondered again why DI Armani had insisted that he visit Mrs Barras, and whether she had another agenda.

He went straight to her office to report back on the interview, explaining that George Barras had also been present.

'What did you think of him?' she asked.

'Cocky. Arrogant. Thinks he's got away with it again,' Jack said. 'I made sure he knew we were onto him, and his wife is now on the radar of social services and the domestic abuse agency.'

'Well, thank you for that,' Armani said, apparently pleased with the way things had gone. 'Now, I'd like you to check over the suspects we have earmarked in this gang war operation. It's likely all down to turf boundaries, but the last knife attack was outside a primary school. You have the details on your desk; draw up a priority list of those who have criminal records for violence, then others who are known to us.'

Jack nodded and went back to his desk. There was a stack of files beside his computer, but before he tackled them he decided to write up his report from the Barras house.

He took the file from his briefcase and began to put the pages back in order. He knew he had been lax by not reading everything before speaking to Mrs Barras, but he still didn't know why he'd been sent to interview her at all. Once he got the file sorted, he read through the details of the previous assaults. The first one was comparatively minor: Mrs Barras had a bruised arm and red cheeks from being slapped by her husband. He admitted he lost his temper and received a caution for common assault but wasn't charged. The second incident had been called in by a neighbour who heard Mrs Barras screaming and rang 999. When police arrived, they noticed

Mrs Barras was clutching her stomach and had bruising on her legs and arms. They suspected George had kicked and punched her, so arrested him and took him to the station to be interviewed.

With her husband out of the way, the officers spoke with Mrs Barras again but she was still adamant she had fallen halfway down the stairs and landed badly in the hallway, which was why she screamed so loudly. George told the same story at the station and was released without charge.

Jack then looked at the most recent incident where Maria Barras was taken to hospital and George Barras was again arrested. He read the attending doctor's statement, which had an envelope attached to it with a paper clip. Jack opened it, and inside were photographs of Maria's broken fingers, split lip and extensive bruising to the right eye, with the doctor expressing concerns about damage to the cornea. Lastly were two photographs of the scalp with a large area of hair torn out by the roots. Jack leaned back in his chair. This was clearly a vicious assault and no accident.

Jack turned on his desk computer and entered George Barras's name and date of birth on the criminal records database. As expected, he found the caution for common assault and two other incidents where George hadn't been charged. He was about to close it when he noticed a 'next page' marker at the bottom of the screen. He pressed it and discovered George also had an assault charge against him from five years earlier. The case officer was DS B. Armani.

'Well, well,' he said to himself. He still didn't know what Armani's agenda was, but now he was determined to find out.

CHAPTER 14

The prison staff had organised a farewell drinks party for Janet at the local pub that evening. She had been on duty all day and was touched by the surprise announcement. Another few days and she'd have served her time... then she'd be off to New Zealand. But she couldn't start to relax yet; she still hadn't quite fulfilled her part of the deal made with Josh. Sachet eight would have to be administered today.

Arriving home after her shift, she spent time clearing away her drug equipment, taking everything that could be incriminating and dumping it all in a bin two streets away. She then changed into a smart black cocktail dress before joining everyone at the local pub. They had taken a small room above the main bar. A wobbly trellis table brimmed with wine and titbits, and all available staff had gathered to thank Janet for her work at the prison. They had all chipped in and bought her a silk scarf as a farewell gift. As she had a glass of wine and chatted about New Zealand, for a second she almost forgot what she had done.

Just after shift change on the affectionately named 'nonce wing', the night officer, Don, did his rounds, peering into every cell through the door hatch to make sure everyone was alive and well. As normal, most were reading, sleeping or masturbating. Middleton, however, was seated on the edge of his bed, bent forwards with his head between his knees and his knuckles dragging on the cell floor.

Don smirked. 'Trying to give yourself a blowie, Rodney? Oi, Middleton, stop mucking about and get in bed. *Now!*' When Middleton didn't respond, Don called for a second officer. The cell door was opened and they entered, again instructing

Middleton to do as he was told. Losing patience, Don pushed hard on his shoulders to make him sit up, but he rocked back, frozen in that grotesque shape, hitting his head hard on the cell wall before coming to rest on his side, head still between his knees and his hands down by the side of his feet, his fingers frozen in claws. They could now see bloodstains on the thighs of his trousers. 'Jesus, what the fuck's wrong with him?'

As the Governor stepped up to make his speech, Janet downed her umpteenth glass of wine.

'Janet, love. What can I say? Our loss is New Zealand's gain.' His speech continued in the same meaningless vain, mainly because he'd never actually met Janet and didn't know anything about her.

After he'd finished and everyone could thankfully go back to drinking, a call came through from one of the on-duty officers, requesting Doctor Zardari return to the prison. As he passed, Janet asked what had happened. 'I don't know,' Zardari smiled. 'But the prisoners are no longer your responsibility. You forget about them and enjoy your night.'

* * *

The male duty nurse fumbled with the naloxone kit, desperately trying to remember what Janet had done a week earlier. The vial was prefilled so all he needed to do was attach the needle, but his fingers refused to work and he dropped it onto the floor saying that he'd now need another as that one was no longer sterile.

'Fuck that,' Don snapped as he picked up the needle and handed it back. 'Look at him. You ain't got time to worry about health and fucking safety.'

The nurse finally attached the needle then stabbed it into Middleton's leg and pushed the fluid in.

'You'll be all right any second now, Rodney. This stuff works fast.' The nurse was expecting Middleton to snap back to life, straighten up and maybe even punch him for wasting his fix. But nothing happened.

'You must've done it wrong, you idiot,' Don snapped.

'I didn't,' the nurse insisted. 'He's supposed to be OK!'

Don shook his head. 'Does he *look* OK? Do something else.'

'He might need another dose.' As the nurse prepped a second dose of naloxone, Don cut Middleton's trousers to expose the injuries that were bleeding through. The bleeding, oozing ulcers were repulsive and, once exposed, they stank.

'Fuck me!' Don slapped his hand to his mouth, trying to control his gag reflex.

'God, they're infected.' The nurse gasped. 'They're all infected. I don't understand. He fell. That's all.' As the nurse injected Middleton for a second time, the bodycam on Don's shoulder was recording everything. Middleton's bizarre frozen shape, his petrified, panicked eyes, his bleeding ulcerated thighs and his total lack of response to the naloxone. The male nurse raced from the cell shouting that he was going to call an ambulance. Middleton's breathing became more and more laboured, and his face became distorted by excruciating pain. Every muscle in his body was tightening and freezing, including his heart.

Don's bodycam caught the very moment that Middleton's eyes glazed over, and his own muscles squeezed the life out of him.

* * *

Janet had left her own party shortly after Zardari because she knew if she'd stayed, she'd have fainted or puked or had a fucking heart attack. She called in to the prison surgery just after eight thirty, asking if she could be of any assistance. She was told Rodney Middleton had been found in a zombie state, unable to move, bent over on his bunk bed. He had died at the scene, but the paramedics had still attempted to revive him with epinephrine and a defibrillator. Zardari had arrived moments later and pronounced him dead.

Back at her flat, Janet had to sit down and take several deep breaths before she picked up the burner phone Josh had given her and reported that the deed was done. As usual, he spoke tersely, simply giving her the location of her passport and plane ticket and her fifteen thousand pounds. To her annoyance, they had all been stashed in her own kitchen under a floorboard by the fridge.

'Get rid of the phone,' Josh said. 'And I mean right now. Have a nice flight,' he added.

After Josh hung up, Janet sat with her knees jiggling and her hands shaking as the adrenalin slowly left her body. It was not until she had retrieved her stuff that she began to calm down properly. Packing the money into her case and the passport and ticket in her handbag, she took a hammer and smashed the burner phone into pieces which she would throw into different bins. She was too nervous to make any further calls to the prison, but she knew Middleton's cell would be searched, and perhaps they would find something that could incriminate her. She told herself she had been very careful in the dosages, always making sure he swallowed the capsules and did not hold them under his tongue to either retain for later or sell to another inmate. But she needn't have worried; in the end, Middleton couldn't wait to get his hands on the fentanyl-filled capsules as he was gripped by his new addiction. He hadn't noticed that it had been eating him alive for two weeks.

Janet left her keys with the landlady and took the train to London, booking in to a Holiday Inn near Heathrow. She still had two days before she got on the plane, but until then, her life was in the hands of the one person who knew she'd just committed murder.

CHAPTER 15

It was ten thirty and Jack was just pulling into his driveway when his mobile rang. It was Laura: 'Are you up for a drink?' But it didn't sound like a casual invitation or like he really had a choice. Penny had seen Jack's headlights and was now standing in the open doorway, smiling. He opened his car door and held his mobile in the air.

'Laura needs to speak to me. I'll be an hour, tops.' Penny waved her understanding then went back indoors.

They sat in a corner booth of a pub not far from Jack's house. He had ordered a gin and tonic for Laura and a half pint for himself. 'OK, out with it, what's up?'

She hesitated, sipping her drink before she began. 'You know I said Josh could stay over on his way back to New York, and you said he could always stay with you. Well, I'm a bit concerned as I had a date on the night he wanted to stay over, so I tried to contact him via the drug squad. I spoke to Dave, the detective involved in that huge drug case, the one at the big house in Kingston. You remember him?'

Jack frowned. It sounded as if she thought he'd lost the ability to recall anything. 'Yeah, of course, I remember. That case was how we met Josh.'

Laura nodded. 'I asked Dave if Josh was back in London and he didn't know what I was talking about. He hasn't seen him for ages. When I mentioned he was doing this lecture tour of prisons, talking about the flood of fentanyl coming into the UK, Dave said it was news to him; maybe something Josh had organised with his US drug unit. He also told me that Josh was retired.'

'He mentioned that to me. I think he said he's semi-retired on medical grounds: you know, with his leg.'

'What else did he tell you?'

Jack shrugged, having no idea where this was all going. 'Not a lot. We had a few drinks. Caught up. He left early the following morning.'

'From what Dave said, I got the impression Josh is very sick. He was not that forthcoming but said he was told Josh was having major mental health issues. Apparently, his youngest son went to San Francisco a few years ago. Josh found him on the streets, but it was too late. He was addicted to fentanyl and this new xylazine drug they call tranq.'

Jack was shocked. 'He never mentioned anything about his son.'

'Today I tried to talk to the New York drug team I knew Josh worked with, but they didn't say much; protecting their own, I guess. But I got the impression he was actually forced to retire, because he'd become obsessed with tracking down his son's dealers, like some sort of vigilante.'

Jack shook his head. 'He never said a word about any of that to me. God, it makes me feel terrible. Going on about my own problems.'

'I tried to catch you at the station but Armani's had us doing different stuff all day. Jack, I saw a memo on DCI Clarke's computer screen when I was in there collecting a file . . . his emails were just open, and it pinged through as I was right there. Well, when something pings, you look, don't you? This is hot off the press, Jack.'

'About Josh?'

'Rodney Middleton was found dead in his cell. They've only just completed the postmortem. It was a fentanyl overdose, but they also discovered he had been taking this new drug, xylazine.

And he had open wounds on his body. It's terrifying because they don't heal and, when someone ODs, they can't use naloxone to reverse it.'

Jack was speechless, hardly able to comprehend what Laura had just told him. But he straightened out fast when she asked him if he knew if Josh had been at the prison Middleton was in. Laura drained her glass and sat twisting the stem.

'There's more, Jack . . . they have Amanda Dunn in custody, suspected of supplying the fatal dosage.'

'You are joking!' Jack barked, before checking his volume. 'I thought she was inside for her part in the murders. She was his girlfriend for God's sake.'

'She got a year. But as she had been held in custody before the trial and then turned Queen's evidence, she was only inside for six months. She did have orders not to contact or fraternise with Middleton, but of course they checked all his visitors once he'd OD'd and there she was – wig, fake tan, contacts to change her eye colour. Signed in as a Gail Leadbetter, a paralegal from the firm of solicitors representing Middleton. So she's been rearrested. I don't have all the facts, but they found drugs in her B&B and in her handbag and coat pockets I think.'

Jack was shaking his head, trying to take it all in.

'Do you know which prisons Josh was supposedly visiting?' Laura asked.

'How the hell would I know?' Jack responded angrily, then checked himself. 'I'm sorry Laura, this is hard for me to take in, but I don't like you inferring that I was privy to whatever Josh was up to . . .' He hesitated, then lied. 'I never discussed Rodney Middleton with him.'

Laura sighed and bit her lip. 'I think I did. In fact, I think I showed him a file I had on Middleton, newspaper cuttings and stuff.' She was becoming upset. 'Jack, I think the best thing is for neither of us to mention any contact we've had with Josh. Walk away from it . . . it's nothing to do with us. And anyway, Rodney Middleton was a vicious killer of innocent young girls who deserves what he got. And I'll be glad if that precious lying girlfriend of his goes down again, too.'

Although he offered to get another round in, it was obvious they both wanted to end the evening. Laura even refused a lift to the nearest tube station, preferring to walk. Outside the pub, he gave her a hug.

'If you still have any files on Middleton at home, get rid of them. Like you said, we walk away from this. It's over.'

On his way home, Jack slowly went over the evening he'd spent with Josh. He remembered the stash of drugs Josh had in his medical bag. He also thought about how long he had talked to Josh about the Middleton trial. But by the time he arrived home, he no longer felt any anxiety, and a new emotion had taken its place: relief.

* * *

The following morning, the household quickly fell into their new routines. Penny was on the school run; Gladys was out with the hoover by eight and Maggie was taking the car to work. Jack got a lift to the tube and waved her off as he hurried down into the station. It wouldn't do any harm to be early, to impress his new boss.

Laura was already at her desk, and as soon as she spotted him, she gestured for him to come with her to the canteen.

'I've already had breakfast.'

'Well, let's use the boardroom, then. I need to update you.'

He hesitated. 'Didn't we agree not to delve into it any further?'

'Well, I lied,' Laura whispered. 'It's important and won't take long, but I don't want anyone overhearing.' Laura hurried out, with Jack reluctantly following.

He closed the boardroom door as Laura pulled out a chair, opening her notebook from her briefcase.

'Right, I couldn't sleep thinking things over. OK, firstly, when Josh stayed over with me that one night, he was asking me a lot of questions about Middleton, including which prison he was in. I also recall mentioning a woman I had met at one of the Met functions, Janet Williamson; she was a nurse at Holloway, then when it closed, she went to work at Bellview as the senior staff nurse. I'm seriously worried, and I think you are too, that Josh could be involved in this.'

'I never said that, Laura.'

'Just listen. I called the prison on the pretext of contacting Janet only to be told she had retired and had left no forwarding address. But apparently she was flying to New Zealand to live with her daughter.'

Jack was starting to get annoyed. Laura had not stayed out of it at all. Instead, she had been busy making very fucking traceable phone calls.

'You want the good news?' Laura asked. He shrugged. 'I did a bit of digging on Janet . . . she was at her leaving do when Middleton was found dead. And she flew out of the UK this morning, but that flight was bought ages ago so it's not like she was fleeing. I also got confirmation that Josh returned to New York. His last lecture was at Strangeways Prison, and he flew from Manchester Airport to Kennedy.'

'For God's sake, Laura . . .'

'There's more. They found capsules of fentanyl hidden in the lining of Amanda Dunn's coat; the coat she had worn for her visits to Middleton. They also found a container of fentanyl in her room at the B&B ... and here's the kicker, Jack ... it's the same B&B Josh stayed at. Amanda might be innocent, and I might have given Josh everything he needed to ...'

Jack stood up, put his arms around her shoulders and leaned forward to kiss her on the cheek. 'You didn't and Josh didn't. All you need to remember is that Amanda Dunn aided and abetted that piece of shit in the murder of young girls. Middleton's dead. And I'm glad.'

The boardroom door opened and DI Armani was framed in the doorway, looking at them with pursed lips. She clearly thought she'd caught them in a compromising position. 'DCI Clarke was asking for you, DS Warr,' she said tersely. Jack hurried out, scowling.

'I was just giving DS Warr an update on a case we had previously worked on,' Laura said lamely.

'It is not advisable to have a relationship with a senior officer, Laura, especially a married one,' Armani said. She turned on her heel before Laura could reply.

Clarke gestured for Jack to sit in the chair in front of his desk. 'I wanted a quick word with you as I've been given some information regarding Rodney Middleton, which will no doubt get some press coverage.' He handed Jack the memo. It was almost word for word what Laura had told him. He gave an appropriately shocked response, shaking his head as if in disbelief.

'The postmortem revealed high doses of fentanyl,' he read, 'along with a drug I've never heard of – xylazine?' He looked up at Clarke.

'It's a veterinary sedative, which is actually quite fitting since Middleton was an animal. They've arrested Amanda Dunn. Local CID will handle it, and I doubt they will require any information from us. However, I felt that you should be pre-warned in case there's some journalist wanting an interview, given your conspicuous involvement in the Middleton investigation and trial. That said, I am also aware that it did take quite a toll on you emotionally. If I do get any further information, I will make it a priority to ensure you are given all the details.'

'Thank you very much, Sir, I appreciate it.'

'It's a pleasure to have you back with us, Jack. I hope you settle in with the new probationer detectives and, obviously, with DI Armani. I think she will be a big asset to the team.'

'Thank you again for giving me the heads-up, Sir, I really appreciate it. There's just one thing . . . as you said, it will no doubt have press coverage, but I wondered if we should give the victims' families the news about Middleton before it becomes public?'

Clarke frowned. 'I know you felt strongly about other potential victims of Middleton, but there is no reason for further involvement. It's over. Do you understand, Jack?'

Jack nodded. 'Yes, Sir.'

After leaving Clarke's office, Jack went over to Laura's desk and repeated what he'd just been told. 'That goes for you too, Laura,' he whispered. 'It's over.'

'I get it, I get it,' she assured him. 'But look, watch out for Armani. She gave me a dressing down about being over familiar with a married officer, which really pissed me off. As if I'd go for you!' Laura and Jack shared a smile.

As Jack went back to his desk, he clocked Armani just as she was entering the incident room with a coffee. He gave her a beaming smile and joined her at her desk.

'I've just been told Rodney Middleton was found dead in his cell from a drug overdose.' Armani's blank expression told Jack that she didn't know the name. 'Serial killer, young teenage girls he picked up at Euston station.'

'Ah, yes of course.'

'Me and Laura both worked on the case and the subsequent trial. We discussed Middleton's death earlier this morning as she had heard the rumour, but now DCI Clarke has verified it. It was an emotionally difficult investigation, and I was thankful for Laura's constant dedication and support. You should know that any inference our relationship is anything other than friendship is an insult to me, Laura and my wife.'

Armani's mouth dropped open for a moment before she regained her composure. But before she could reply Jack had walked back to his desk.

CHAPTER 16

That afternoon, Jack got stuck into the pile of files on his desk relating to Armani's gang war. After three hours of concerted reading, Laura passed his desk and saw what he was doing.

'She's brought you in on this now then?'

'Yep. And I'd better stay in.'

'Jack Warr, that sounded like a threat.' Laura sat down next to him.

Jack slid his chair closer to Laura, so their knees touched beneath the desk.

'You know that domestic she sent me on.' Laura nodded. 'Detective Sergeant Armani was the investigating and interviewing officer in an assault case against George Barras five years ago. It's got to be DI Armani before she was promoted.'

'There might be another Armani in the Met.'

'The report is full of psychology and profiling jargon . . . it's her. The odd thing is that it's incomplete; missing key details I'd normally expect.'

'That's not like her . . . she's normally boringly thorough with her reports.'

'I knew something was up when she sent me to interview Maria Barras, and I'm going to find out what it is.'

Laura nudged Jack when Armani appeared behind him. 'Well, here you both are again, whispering in corners. I'd prefer you to concentrate on the gang war case and the list of suspects I asked you to look through, if it's not too much trouble.'

Jack flushed with anger but controlled himself. 'I was just asking Laura if she could recommend any of the new young probationers to assist me.'

Armani frowned, then nodded. 'You can use the boardroom for a briefing. They are all very keen and have been carefully selected; they should be of particular value for the case in question. I hope it will be beneficial, as your performance since your return to work has not particularly impressed me so far.'

'Yes, Ma'am.' He wanted to tell her to fuck off but knew it would be better to bide his time until he'd discovered whatever she was hiding from her past. For now, Jack was just glad to be on board with the meatier operation of gang wars.

The meeting in the boardroom started with Jack introducing himself to the six new officers DI Armani had brought onto the team. They were five strapping lads and a young woman he'd seen showing signs of nerves in the canteen. Jack linked his laptop to the digital whiteboard to show images of the known and suspected gang members. Ranging in age from twelve to their early twenties, and mostly males, they had previous convictions for assault, robbery, possession of an offensive weapon and drug offences. Some were known to police but had no convictions. Jack had just brought up the picture of the suspected leader of one notorious local gang when Armani entered the room. The young officers all stood up. She crossed the room, stood beside Jack, and addressed them.

'I will oversee this operation, and DS Warr will be my deputy supervising officer.' Jack tried to mask his delight with a blank expression. 'I know that none of you have ever worked on this division before, but that is why I selected you all.' The young officers looking at each other with confused expressions. 'You have been selected for your ethnicity. This operation is about learning as much as possible about two rival gangs operating in our division. Some of you will infiltrate the community and covertly gather information about the young men and women on the list so we can identify which gangs they belong to and who the ringleaders are. We need to know as much about them as possible: where they live, who their parents are, what street corners they frequent etcetera. Others of you will speak with headteachers at the local schools and find out who's been expelled or is a regular truant ... these kids are so easily sucked into gang life. Find out who the weaker members are, as they may have been enticed into a gang and be a useful source of information. Check out and photograph all local graffiti ... identifying a tag to a name on the list of suspected members will help us to identify who's who and hopefully identify others not yet on the list.'

The young officers remained attentive, and the glint in their eyes revealed how pleased they were to be part of the team.

'Kids as young as twelve are being used as drug runners. They deal in any and all drugs, from feeding local junkies to supplying high-end parties.' Armani's tone became more serious. 'I want you to understand that *any* drugs on my streets are unacceptable. Cannabis and Skunk are class B, but they still kill people. Get behind the wheel of a car with that in your system, with the paranoia and hallucinations, and the reactions of a snail, you get the picture. Your job is not to arrest the couriers or dealers; it's to work covertly and gather information to build the bigger picture. Then we'll regroup, move to phase two, and take the ringleaders off the streets, disrupting the gang's way of life.'

Jack was impressed with her knowledge and the confident way she spoke, underlining the need for them to be totally covert. This also kept them as safe as possible. No challenges, no confrontations. He knew that once the 'bigger picture' was complete, search warrants would be obtained for simultaneous early morning home raids, followed by the arrest, interview and charging of as many of the gang members as possible. The only problem, as Josh had told him, was that dealing and drug-taking was as rife inside prison as it was in the outside world.

* * *

PC Nala Coley had been called 'Fishy' since arriving at Hendon police college two years ago. She'd married her childhood sweetheart who unfortunately had a terrible surname for a probi copper. But Fishy was an old head on young shoulders and had the makings of an exceptional officer. She, along with PC Kwame Abara, had been tasked with working undercover at the local snooker hall as general dogsbodies doing bar work and cleaning. Although both were in their early twenties, they easily looked late teens. They used their real first names for simplicity and Kwame quickly made it known that he was a user by allowing himself to get caught smoking weed in the backyard. Within days of starting work, Kwame and Nala were sitting at the bar having a beer when Denny, a lad high up in one of the local gangs, approached with three other boys, none of whom could have been more than sixteen.

'You ain't selling on my turf are you, blood?'

Kwame was instantly submissive so as not to cause trouble. 'Shit, no man. I didn't know this was your patch, but I figured it was someone's. I don't sell. I just use a little.'

One of the lads looked Nala up and down, smirking and licking his lips. As his eyes came all the way back up her body, she spoke strongly and firmly. 'I don't go for jailbait.' Her comment made the others laugh which really pissed him off. Kwame put a hand on her knee as if to say, 'be respectful', but she ignored him.

Denny sent the others off to play snooker while he discussed business with Kwame, but the three lads knew to stay close, hovering with cues in their hands. 'The top three tables over there are mine,' Denny explained. 'On weekends the school kids come in wanting to hang out with the big boys. Talk to them. Find me some customers, yeah.' Kwame said that he didn't want to get involved with anything illegal but was quickly put in his place. 'Then you came to the wrong place, blood.' He stared Kwame straight in the eyes, unblinking, and put his hand on Nala's thigh. This time, she knew enough to be frightened. She froze as Denny slid his hand towards her groin.

'All right,' Kwame said quickly.

Denny smirked, removed his hand and bounced away as if nothing had happened. 'Be in touch, yeah.'

Nala couldn't believe how much she was shaking. 'Jeez, K,' she whispered, 'what the hell have we agreed to?'

* * *

Jack and Maggie both slept late on Saturday morning. Maggie was still getting used to her hectic schedule at the hospital but she was relieved Penny and Gladys were coping well with the children. She also noticed Jack made no further complaints about DI Armani, who he was beginning to feel he'd misjudged. She'd certainly been more respectful towards him since they'd been working directly together, even giving him the weekend off as he had been working long hours late into the night. He seemed impressed with her leadership and with the progress of the investigation, as they were making a lot of headway.

After breakfast Maggie asked Jack if they could finish painting the bookcases in the loft extension, as they now had the new bed and mattress installed. He was not that eager but agreed to get the job out of the way and was mixing the paint when she came to look over the room.

'Do you remember that place selling the mattresses? Next to it was an Indian shop with a stall and some nice carpets and rugs. With the pine floor, it might be nice to have a rug beside the bed, and we could do with another little chest of drawers. What do you think?'

'Do you want me to paint this now or come back and do it?'

Maggie grinned. 'Marius is downstairs; he can take you in his van.'

'My God, you've already organised it,' Jack smiled wryly.

'I didn't organise it really, he came by to fix the showerhead upstairs and, well . . .'

Half an hour later, Jack and Marius left for Portobello Road. Their first stop was the carpet shop, where Jack bought a rug, and then managed to find a nice six-drawer cabinet with brass handles.

Jack was sweating as he carried the heavy cabinet, while Marius had the rug over his shoulder. Getting to the van, they removed the drawers from the cabinet to stack beside it and laid the carpet on top.

'What about the paint you need?' Marius said. 'There's a good place halfway up the market.'

'Screw that, I've had enough for one day,' Jack said grumpily as he slammed the van doors.

'Give me a few minutes. I'll run and see what I can find. If you go home without it . . .' Marius shook his head. 'Let's get the job done and dusted.'

Jack climbed into the passenger seat as Marius went off towards the market. He had not been gone long when he came hurrying back, yanking open the driver's door.

'Something's going on down the road. Loads of police cars and they're putting up crime scene tape. I can't get down.'

Jack hesitated as Marius got into the driving seat. 'Hang on, Marius, I'll go see what's happening.'

'I'll turn the van around and wait here for you.'

Jack headed back towards the market. After a couple of minutes he could see that the framer's shop was sealed off with yellow crime scene tape while squad cars were blocking off the road. Jack watched as two white-suited SOCOs with their equipment bags got out of a forensics van and entered the shop.

Keeping well back, Jack turned to a woman with a shopping trolley and asked if she knew what was happening. 'Well . . .' she said, 'I heard one officer say murder.'

Jack took a few steps backwards, telling himself to get away and not get involved. He returned to the van and told Marius vaguely there had been an accident. As they drove home, he hoped there might be something on the lunchtime news about it. Already he had a sinking feeling that Adam Border was somehow involved.

CHAPTER 17

Maggie was delighted with the chest of drawers but not that keen on the rug. Having lugged it up to the loft, Jack would have been annoyed, but he was more concerned with finding out what had happened at the framer's shop.

He went downstairs to his office and brought up the latest local news on his laptop. There was a video of what looked like a hectic scene with forensics and uniforms going in and out, but, frustratingly, no further details.

Jack went down to the kitchen to make a coffee. Penny was tucking Charlie into his pushchair, ready to take him to the park with Hannah, as Marius stirred some paint outside the kitchen with a stick. Maggie gave Jack one of her sour looks then said, in that flat tone of voice he hated, 'Don't worry about painting the chest, Jack. We are doing it, so there's no need for you to bother yourself!'

'Fine,' Jack retorted. 'I need to go out. I won't be long.'

'Please yourself,' she said. Jack grabbed the car keys as Penny opened the front door and pushed the pram out.

'It would be nice if you took Charlie out with Hannah one day. She really loves the swings,' Penny remarked.

'Tomorrow, I'll take them both out tomorrow,' Jack said, squeezing past her.

In the car he began to feel bad and thought about going back to apologise but then thought better of it. He'd buy his mum a bunch of flowers instead. He decided to drive to Adam Border's abandoned school to see if he knew what had happened in the framer's shop.

There were police cordons blocking his usual route, so he did a detour using Waze. When he arrived at the school, the barrier was down, and it looked as if demolition had started on the smaller outer buildings. The lean-to shelter had gone, the bike shed and toilets had been flattened, and Jack, unable to lift the barrier, had to park on the road.

He made his way round the rear of the building to the double doors he had used previously. There was a NO ENTRY sign and a double chain was padlocked through the door handles. He went round to the rear of the building to find many of the windows were broken and some had been boarded up. Jack stood on some crates and carefully knocked out the broken shards before climbing through a window.

The kitchen had been stripped of anything of value, even the cupboard doors, and there was no electricity. Rubbish had been left in plastic bags and old coffee cups and takeaway food cartons were everywhere as he made his way towards the drill hall. It had been stripped bare. The vast room was desolate, but he could still make out the lingering smell of oil paint and terps. There was nothing: Adam's clothes, his sleeping bag and blankets had all gone. Just a layer of old dirty newspapers remained, which Jack guessed he'd probably used as insulation beneath his sleeping bag.

Jack made his way back to his car. He recalled the time he had instructed the Gardai to search the studio in Ireland for Adam. He was told there was nothing left, not even fingerprints. It was as if Adam Border had never been there. It was the same here. And the entire building would soon be flattened.

He started the car, did a U-turn, and headed back down the road. He tried to work out when he'd last seen Adam. Surely he wouldn't just have disappeared without a word? Unless something had happened that forced him to clear out quickly. But he would have needed more than just the jeep to move everything out: all the paintings, the table and frames, not to mention his equipment. Jack thought he might come back when the workmen were present to see what he could find out.

* * *

Maggie called out from the loft when she heard the front door shutting behind him. She caught Jack hurrying into his office. 'Come and see what we've done, I think you'll like it.'

'Not now Maggie, there's something I have to do.'

She could tell immediately something was wrong so followed him into his office. He was throwing his jacket off and pulling out his desk chair. 'What's happened? You look freaked out.' He tensed, at first not wanting to say anything, but then she came and put her arms around him. 'Tell me, Jack.'

He took a deep breath. 'OK, you know I went to the market earlier . . . well, part of the market was shut off with forensic guys and crime ribbons across the road. I spoke to a woman watching, and she heard there'd been a murder in the framer's shop.'

'Oh, my goodness. Is that where you went off to?'

'No, I needed to speak to Adam, so I drove to the school he was using as a studio. There was no sign of him or his equipment, and the place was being demolished.'

'You think he could be involved?'

'I don't know. It's just, there was nothing left.' Jack was struggling to make sense of it all. 'He would have needed help to move all his gear, he can't just have disappeared.'

'He did before, though, didn't he? Isn't there anything on the news?'

'I looked earlier but they didn't have any details.'

'Try now.'

Jack logged on again but there was still nothing beyond the fact that 'an incident' had occurred and police were investigating. Jack knew details were routinely withheld from the press in murder cases, while the family were informed.

'Is there no other way you can find out? Use that system thingy at work.'

'If I try, it'll flag up as me, then I'll need to explain why I'm after the information. I suppose I could say I was in the market . . . but then why didn't I make an approach then?'

'Surely Adam must have been staying somewhere else apart from the school?'

'He was living there, Mags, unless . . . hang on.' Jack picked up his mobile and began scrolling through the photos until he found the ones he'd taken of Adam's Jeep. It was hard to read the number plate because of the mud, but eventually, after enlarging all three images, he pieced together the entire registration. He phoned the CID office and asked to speak with Laura, but she wasn't there so Jack told the clerk he needed a vehicle registration check done for a car that may be connected to the street gangs operation. After giving her the number, he could hear her tapping the keyboard as he waited anxiously for the result. The clerk informed him the vehicle was owned and insured by Daniel Ferrato, with an address in Haslemere. Jack wrote the details down on a pad, thanked the clerk for her help and ended the call.

He typed the address into Google Earth and got a satellite image of a large, gated Tudor mansion house off a country lane, surrounded by woodland. A long driveway led up to the property, which had a double garage to one side, landscaped gardens, an enormous greenhouse and an outside pool. Jack switched from satellite to street view to see if he could get a better look at the front of the house, but it was too far up the drive from the lane. One thing was certain, though: if Daniel Ferrato owned the house, he was an incredibly wealthy man. Jack was about to switch the computer off when something on the wrought iron gates caught his eye. At first, he thought it was a 'private property – keep out' sign, but when he zoomed in, he could see it was a letting agent's sign with their address and phone number. Jack found the property on the agent's website, and his jaw dropped when he saw that the price for a week's rental was over ten thousand pounds. More than Adam Border could afford, which is why he was living in the old school. So what was his connection to Mr Ferrato?

Jack looked at his watch, it was almost five. He hoped the letting agency would be open on a Saturday. Calling them, he hung on for what seemed like an age and was about to hang up when someone finally answered.

'Firstly, my apologies for calling so late, but it's regarding a property you rent out in Haslemere, Surrey. I believe it might belong to Mr Daniel Ferrato.'

'I am sorry,' said a posh woman's voice, 'but I am unable to give any details over the phone. If you care to come into the office, we open at ten o'clock on Monday.'

'I am Detective Sergeant Jones from the Metropolitan Police,' Jack continued. 'Mr Ferrato's vehicle was involved in a hit-and-run incident, it is a Mercedes, registration number XE . . .'

She interrupted, asking him to hold on for a moment while she looked at her computer. Jack shook his head, smiling. With no proof of his ID at all, she was about to give him what he wanted. Just the mention of the word 'police' was enough.

'Mr Ferrato has been in Florida for six months, so I don't think he could be the driver. I can give you his contact details.' She handed over Ferrato's address and a phone number in Florida, but Jack didn't bother to write them down. He then read out the registered address of the vehicle owner and asked if Mr Ferrato owned the property.

'Yes, and his vehicle is, I believe, allowed to be used by the occupiers, but the lease expires in two weeks.'

'Could I have the names of the people currently staying there, please?'

'I'm not sure I can give out our clients' details,' she faltered.

'This is a serious matter,' Jack persisted. 'The pedestrian who was hit by Mr Ferrato's vehicle is in a coma. She may not survive.'

Jack could hear the woman tut and then start frantically typing again before she told him that Mr Adam Jessop and his wife were staying at the address. She asked Jack for his name and rank again so she could inform her boss, which was when he put the phone down on her.

Jack went up to the nursery as Maggie was finishing feeding Charlie. 'I have an address that Adam might be renting, so I'm going there tonight.'

'You sure?'

'Yes, very sure.'

Maggie smiled. She had her worries about Jack getting involved in Adam Border's world, but loved that he was once again engaged and enthralled by being a detective, even if it was nothing to do with his actual job. He was smiling again, sleeping again and that was all that really mattered to her. 'You be careful driving tonight. I'll leave your dinner in the oven if you're not back in time.'

* * *

As Jack drove, Waze estimated the journey to Haslemere would take an hour and a half. At first, he was uncertain whether to ask

Laura to help him, but he reckoned she might be up for it. She could never resist a Miss Marple task.

He put his mobile on speaker as Laura answered and Jack explained that he needed her to do some sleuthing for him about the incident at the framer's shop. 'I've searched the Met Web and other websites but can't find anything about it. The framer's shop is on Fulham's patch, and I know you used to work there, so maybe you could phone an old colleague and find out what's going on?'

'I was never at Fulham. I was in a relationship with Mark Morrison, the station DCI . . . well, he was DI back then. He dumped me, so thanks for opening that old wound. What's your interest?'

'You know me, I'm a nosey bugger. I was down the market to pick up some furniture but couldn't because the area was sealed off with crime scene guys milling about, and I wondered when the roads might reopen.'

'Wow,' Laura laughed, 'you must really want that furniture! You're a terrible liar Jack, but you're also hardly ever wrong . . . so if you've got a hunch about something or other, I'll call that arsehole Morrison. But he may not be very forthcoming. I'll ring you back if I get anything.'

Jack laughed. 'Thanks, Laura.'

The journey to Haslemere took longer than expected due to an accident on the A3. Jack drove down dimly-lit country lanes, passing expensive looking properties with high hedgerows and massive gates. He noticed virtually every property had an intercom system and CCTV security camera warnings on the gates. His phone rang, and Laura's name showed on the screen. He pulled over onto the grass verge and answered it.

'You owe me, Jack, big time. I had to listen to Morrison's bullshit about how much he regretted dumping me, blah, blah, lovely arse, blah, blah, and if we could try again, blah, blah, blah. I wanted to tell him to fuck off, but I couldn't because I had to get the info for you. I even had to agree to go for a drink with him!'

'You didn't mention my name, did you?'

'No, course not, I just said I knew someone who'd been at the market and overheard something about a murder. I said I was being nosey, which he agreed with a bit too quickly for my liking! Anyway, Fulham's working the case and Morrison's the DCI on it. He was full of his own self-importance, but I reckon he's shitting himself, the big baby ...'

'Can I please have the details, Laura?' Jack asked, trying not to lose patience with her.

'OK, they got the initial call from a stall-holder who leaves her trestle table inside this framer's shop and only works Saturdays. The bloke who runs it normally opens the frame shop before she gets there, but this morning she found the front door still locked. She knocked but got no answer, then went round to the backyard and found the rear door open. She called out but didn't get a reply and thought the framer might have gone to get a coffee, so she went in to get her trestle table.' Laura paused and Jack could hear her sipping on a drink.

He was getting frustrated. Again, Laura was going round the houses instead of getting straight to the hard facts. 'So, she goes in, and then what?'

'The guy was naked, and you are not going to believe this ... he'd been crucified.'

'What?' Jack exclaimed.

'I know, unbelievable. There was a giant wooden cross in the shop, and he was nailed and chained to it. They reckon he's been there for a day or two.'

'Jesus Christ ...'

'You can say that again ... he was beaten so badly his face was unrecognisable. Morrison said it was horrific. They're still trying to

ID him and that's why there's been no press release, because, unbelievably, he's still alive. So they need to find his family and protect him. Or all of them. Dunno. That's all I got.'

'Laura, thanks so much. I really appreciate it.'

'Oh, another bit of info for you: Morrison let slip that he and Armani had been an item and he dumped her too. Well, he didn't exactly say that, just that it hadn't worked out between them.'

'Interesting. That's another IOU.'

'Where are you?' she asked.

Jack sensed Laura's growing curiosity and decided to end the call. 'I'm at home with the kids. Talk when I get in on Monday, and thanks again.'

He sat in the car for a while before driving on to the house. A large padlock and chain were hanging loose on the gate, and from his position, he could just see the big house at the end of the driveway. The light was fading, so he got out of the car for a better look. He could see there were lights on.

Pulling open one side of the wrought iron gate, Jack returned to his car, turned the headlights off and drove slowly up the drive. As he parked in front of the garage, he noticed security lights on the house but to his relief, it wasn't quite dark enough for them to kick in. He walked around the garage and stood on tiptoe to look through a window. He could see the Mercedes Jeep, polished and pristine, as if someone had valeted it. Next to the jeep was a white Mercedes sports car and two electric scooters.

Jack walked back to the gravel drive and up to the front door, which was flanked by two white pillars. He pressed the bell and stepped back. To his surprise, the door instantly buzzed open. He walked into the hall, towards a wide staircase.

'You're rather early,' a woman's voice called out from upstairs. 'But you can start taking my cases down while I finish packing'.

Jack walked up the stairs, passing beneath a huge chandelier. He paused on the landing, then headed towards a room at the end of the corridor with its double doors half open. Jack pushed the door open wider. It was a huge bedroom. Lined up beside the bed were Hermès suitcases and a trunk. A woman appeared holding an array of silk blouses. She was dressed in a silk kimono, with her thick blond hair hanging loose to her shoulders. When she saw Jack, she swept one side of her hair back from her face with her hand.

'I'm not your driver,' Jack said, remaining by the door.

'Are you a replacement? You're very early. Take those cases down and wait until I call you to return for the rest. I have to finish and change.'

'Are you Mrs Jessop?' Jack asked.

'Why are you asking me that?'

'Because I know the house is leased to a Mr and Mrs Jessop.'

'Ah yes, well, that is correct, but I am leaving before the end of the lease. The house must be left in pristine condition. We had to leave an absurdly large deposit, and I was warned that they would also check the mileage on their cars. So, if you are here to do that, go ahead, but they should have warned me.'

Jack stepped further into the bedroom and took out his ID. 'I'm Detective Sergeant Jack Warr.' She straightened but otherwise showed no reaction. But he could tell she had recognised his name. Jack got straight to the point. 'I need to speak to Adam.'

'He's not here. He left days ago, so you have had a wasted journey.'

'Do you know where he is?'

'No, I do not.'

'I really need to see him.'

She shut the case on the bed and placed it beside the others. 'I'm sorry. I have no idea where he has gone. I need to change, so if you don't mind leaving me. Go down into the kitchen, have a drink of coffee or whatever you want. I won't take long. I am expecting a driver as I have a plane to catch.'

Jack hesitated. He found her precise way of speaking slightly disconcerting. 'Where are you from?'

'Germany. Go on, hurry out, let me get ready.' Without further hesitation, she slipped out of the kimono, revealing that she was naked beneath. Jack flushed with embarrassment at the sight of her perfect body as she strolled into the en suite.

Jack went back downstairs and into a luxurious kitchen filled with high-end electrical appliances. He took a moment to admire the floor-to-ceiling dresser filled with matching blue and white crockery, then grabbed a mug and poured some leftover coffee from a complicated looking percolator. The refrigerator was the largest and most modern he had ever seen. It contained several bottles of wine and champagne, yet the rest of the shelves were empty. He pulled out a chair and sat with his lukewarm mug of coffee. After a while, he became concerned that the beautiful Mrs Jessop might have left. Then he heard the click-clack of high-heeled shoes making their way across the hall towards him. He'd thought she was stunning when he first saw her, but now she looked breathtaking, with her makeup and lustrous hair coiled into a long, loose braid. But he had been mistaken about her age; she was older than he'd first thought, almost middle-aged. She was wearing thigh-high black boots over tight fitting fawn trousers, a white polo neck sweater, and slung around her shoulders was a cashmere fur-edged stole.

'He told me a lot about you, Jack,' she said as she placed a leather shoulder bag on the table. 'He told me about your visits to his studio.'

'Did Adam live here with you?' Jack asked.

'Of course. He liked his comfort and my being here.'

'How long have you been here?'

'It has been nearly two years ... but he had to leave like he usually does. He worked at the school so as not to be interrupted but needed time to relax in comfort also.'

Jack was at a loss, trying to come to terms with all the lies Adam told about living rough in the school hall and all the while returning to this luxurious house, never mind this stunning woman. She seemed totally at ease as she waited for him to process this new information. Pulling himself together, Jack realised he needed to take charge. 'Sit down,' he told her. 'I need some answers.'

She stayed standing. 'I don't have very long.'

'I need to know where he is. What's your real name?'

'Helga Meirling.' She opened her bag and tossed her passport towards him. He opened it and flicked through the pages, noting how many times she had travelled to Europe and the US. She was forty-two years old.

'You travel a lot. What work do you do?'

'I am a fashion journalist covering promotional and charity events for some of the big names in Milan.'

'Where did you live?'

'In Berlin, some of the time.'

'But you've been here in London for almost two years?'

'Yes, not all the time. But it has been very pleasant.'

'With Adam?'

'Yes, I would have thought that was obvious. It was much longer this time. We rarely have this length of time together. He is always on the move.'

'So where has he gone?'

'I have no idea. A situation came up about two weeks ago that made him become very agitated.'

'You know what he does, don't you?' Jack said.

'He's an artist, a genius, that's what I know. I have had to come to terms with his erratic behaviour and not question what he chooses to do.'

'So, he packs up, walks out and leaves you with no way to contact him? I don't believe you. I don't believe he just woke up one day and walked away from all of this. From you.'

'Believe me, it has been this way for ten years. He could be with his wife in France. He has three children aged two, four and six. It seems a child appears always after a length of time he has been absent. He leaves her pregnant, but I have no idea where she lives or any of the other women in his life. You may not be able to understand that I am content with what I have when I am with him. When we are together, he is everything to me, and I live for the next time he calls. That is all true.'

Jack didn't know whether to believe her or not. But he still needed to find Adam. 'Did you help him move his stuff from the old school studio?'

She sighed with impatience. 'Do I look like someone who would do that? You are so naive, Detective. Adam has many people working for him, ready to jump to it when he wants something done. They too enjoy the life he gifts them.' She could see the deepening furrow between Jack's eyes. 'Adam is worth a fortune, Jack. And don't ask me what bank, because I do not know. You have to believe that as much as I adore him, and love him, he guards his secrets with his life. I would never question him.'

'He pays you to be with him?'

'You are a very silly man, Jack. Some women are happy to be bought. Tickets, jewels, expenses, anything I needed. He is the most generous and considerate man.'

'I may be silly to you, but it's hard for me to grasp how such a beautiful woman can be at the beck and call of a man who just fucks off when he wants and picks you up again in the same way. Do you really think he loves you?' She tensed, declining to reply. 'Helga,' Jack's tone was gentler now, 'I am here because I think Adam's been involved in a terrible crime. So I really need to know where he is. I liked him too. All I am trying to do is find out if he's in danger.'

For the first time, she showed a flicker of emotion, though she hid it well behind the action of taking out a cigarette case and lighting a cigarette. 'Let me give you a warning, Detective. Adam has many friends, many helpers, and if you attempt to trace him, he will turn on you. Believe me, you don't want that to happen. Don't for a second think that you know him or have any idea what he is capable of. No one does.'

'Tell me about the last time you were with him. When he did his disappearing act.'

She hesitated, drawing on her cigarette before pushing the smoke out through the corner of her lips. 'Honestly, I had never seen him be so concerned. As you probably know, he was usually easy-going, but two weeks ago he came home in a terrible rage. I didn't really understand. He paced up and down, not really talking to me but more to himself.' She crossed to the sink and ran the water to put out her cigarette. 'As far as I can recall it was something to do with telling a forgery from a real thing. He said something about radiocarbon dating techniques to analyse paint chips from paintings too old to easily determine their age.' She smiled at Jack. 'I looked it up. Scientists have been working on carbon-14 radiation dating to detect fake artworks since 1972.'

Jack had never heard of this technique, nor did he understand what it meant.

'Whether or not it was this that had made him unusually anxious, I don't know. Then there was a phone call. I was on the landing upstairs when I heard him ... I've never seen Adam that angry. He was blazing, screaming abuse at the caller, saying that he was a leach and could destroy everything because of his greed. He repeated that he needed at least two years, at the very least, to accomplish what he intended to do and that any interference would cost him dearly. Adam was threatening to crucify this person on the phone.'

Jack could hardly believe what she had just said. 'Do you know who the caller was?'

'There was someone who acted as Adam's dealer. I never met him, but I know Adam hated him. I think he put pressure on him to produce more paintings.'

'Fakes.'

She gave Jack a cool blink of her eyes before turning away. 'I have no recollection of any fakes produced by Adam. To the contrary, he is a brilliant artist. His work is bought by many dealers around the world.'

This was the equivalent of Helga saying 'no comment' so Jack let it lie and changed the subject. 'Does the name Detmar Steinburg sound familiar?' Again he saw the slight glimmer in her eyes.

'No. Now I think this has gone far enough, Jack. I stick to my side of our bargain, he leaves, and I don't question when or where I will see him again. That's all I have for you.'

He was sure she was lying, but he had already gained a lot from her and didn't want to alienate her by asking any further questions. She picked up his mug of cold coffee, poured it into the sink and rinsed out the mug. 'Everything has to be left in perfect order, part of the lease specifications.' She picked up her passport and put it back in her bag.

The doorbell rang and she hurried to the door. 'That'll be my driver. Oh, I still need my cases bringing down.' Jack walked into the hall to see a burly man heading up the stairs, following Helga. Jack watched as the driver returned with two of the cases.

'Can I help?' Jack asked, looking up to the landing.

'There are only two more suitcases and my travel bag. He can do it.' The driver returned and hurried up the stairs. He came out of the bedroom with the last two suitcases and Helga turned off the bedroom lights, following the driver down the stairs clutching a small holdall and her shoulder bag.

She walked past Jack and slipped the house keys, car keys and a handwritten note in an envelope which she put on the hall table. 'There. That is it . . . unless you want to stay on here to look around?'

'No, thank you. You've been very helpful.'

'There was one thing, it may not mean anything, but after that night when he was so angry, he was different. Usually, that was a sign to me that he was going away, but he said . . .' She frowned, running her finger over her lips as she tried to recall Adam's exact words. 'He said the radiocarbon dating was no longer an issue. Then we had a wonderful night together. He was so excited, and for a while, I believed he wouldn't do his usual disappearing act. But I woke up the next morning and he had gone. I truthfully don't know where he is, Jack.' She was about to walk out when she hesitated. 'You haven't told me why you are concerned about Adam . . . other than rather dramatically mentioning his possible involvement in a terrible crime.'

'The shop he used to acquire the old frames for his paintings; a body was discovered there.'

She laughed in relief. 'Then it is obviously nothing to do with Adam. He would have already left England.' She waited for Jack to pass her before turning the hall lights off and closing the front door. Jack walked around to his car, watching as the driver opened the rear door of the Mercedes so that Helga could climb inside. After following them out, Jack drove past them, as the driver had stopped to close the big iron gate and attach the padlock.

* * *

Jack had a long journey home which gave him time to think over his interview with Helga. She had not asked when the body had been discovered before saying that Adam had already left the country. Did that mean she was lying? Did she know Adam was involved in the murder? Or . . . even worse . . . was he the man who had been crucified?

CHAPTER 18

It was after eleven when Jack arrived home. Maggie had left his dinner covered with cling film on the top of the oven. He wolfed down the congealed roast beef with soggy roast potatoes and veg before opening a bottle of wine. He filled two glasses and headed up to the bedroom. He elbowed the door open, relieved to see Maggie sitting up in bed reading Eric Hebborn's *The Art Forger's Handbook*. She lowered it as he slunk into the room.

'This had better be good Jack, and I don't want some lengthy excuse. Just get straight to the nitty-gritty.'

He handed her the glass of wine and took a long slug of his own before coming to sit beside her. 'This is going to be hard to believe. Sorry, but I have to begin back when Marius and I went to Portobello Road and saw the frame shop was a crime scene. Because of my association with the place, and obviously with Adam, I kept my distance, right?'

'Jack, you told me this earlier.' Maggie closed her eyes and leaned back on the pillow as Jack continued. He finally got to the crime itself. 'Crucified! Are you serious?'

'Yes, but he is, or was, still alive. So next I discovered from the registration of Adam's Jeep, and a bit of searching on Google Earth, that it was associated with a rented property in Haslemere. That's where I've been; a sumptuous bloody property leased by Adam and his girlfriend. She was pretty sumptuous as well.'

'You mean he wasn't living at that school hall place?' Jack nodded. He then told her all about his conversation with Helga. Then he went into the bathroom, cleaned his teeth, got into his PJs and joined her in bed to finish his wine.

'There is one thing I need to Google in the morning. Something Helga said about a radiocarbon technique that tells the ages of paintings ... whatever it is, it made Adam freak out. She said she didn't understand, and I don't either, but I'll research it tomorrow.'

Maggie turned off her bedside light and Jack did the same. 'So this gorgeous woman just accepts being picked up and dropped whenever he feels like it? I don't believe it.'

'Well, look how he drew me in. There's something about him, Mags.'

'I've listened to you going on about him,' Maggie said, 'and I must admit you had me convinced, too, but to me there was always something untrustworthy there. I mean, I know I never met him, but I can tell there's something evil about him. I can almost feel it, even if you can't. And you only have her word for it that he was not in London. You need to be very careful. I mean, how many times have you been in and out of that framer's shop? And the school. God forbid anyone finds a connection between you and him. Do you know which hospital the victim was taken to?'

Jack was fast asleep. She looked at him and sighed. She sometimes felt so protective of him, more than she probably should. At least he was sleeping these days; it had been a while since he'd had a nightmare or fallen out of the bed. As she drifted off to sleep, she tried to pinpoint what Jack found so fascinating about Adam. She decided that it was his knowledge, his passion, his cunning. All attributes Jack showed in his policework when his mind was in the right place. Suddenly the Harry Lime theme tune started up in her head. That bloody film! As the plot ran through her weary mind, she wondered if it was a sign ... a message even. Was Adam playing some sort of twisted game with Jack?

* * *

The next morning Maggie was up and getting ready in the bathroom while Jack was still sound asleep. She could hear Hannah and Penny moving around, so she pulled on a dressing gown and slippers before going downstairs to sort out breakfast. After preparing bottles for Charlie, she went up to the nursery. Hannah was having a bath and creating her usual mayhem with too many bubbles and too much splashing.

When Hannah was dressed she went to wake Daddy as he had promised her a trip to the park and the slides. He awoke with a start as she jumped on the bed and then sleepily put his hands up in a defeated gesture, begging for five minutes to come round properly.

Sunday morning was up and rolling in earnest by nine, with bacon and eggs for Maggie and Jack, pancakes for Hannah and Penny and Charlie was playing, wedged into a highchair with cushions as he was becoming more boisterous by the day.

Maggie was still in her dressing gown as Penny struggled to get Hannah into her puffa jacket, tie her shoes and give her a bag of stale bread for the ducks. Penny also stuffed Hannah's beloved skipping rope into her coat pocket.

'Are you taking Charlie as well, Jack?'

'No, Mum. It takes all my effort to not let Hannah swim with the ducks.'

An hour or so later Maggie had the TV on in the bedroom, listening to the BBC news, but there had been no bulletin regarding the incident at the framer's shop nor any police request for information. She dressed in a pale blue tracksuit, deciding not to do any further painting in the loft but to have a nice, relaxed Sunday instead. Jack had still not returned from his outing with Hannah, so she went to join Penny.

'Anything I can do, Penny?'

'No, dear, all under control. I was thinking I'll do lunch for about one thirty.'

'Fine by me, I'll set the table later. Just going into Jack's office.'

* * *

Jack bought several Sunday papers on the way to the park and was eager to look through them for any mention of the murder. First, though, Hannah wanted to feed the ducks.

Hannah delved into the bread bag and did exactly what Jack had told her not to do, hurling whole slices into the water with gleeful giggles. There was a flap of wings as a swan moved quickly to snatch a slice. Hannah screamed as the huge white wings flapped close to her head and, as she turned to run away, she slid in the mud and her feet went into the water. Jack quickly dropped his papers and grabbed her, hauling her back onto the path. The bread bag floated away while his newspapers lay soaked in the mud.

Jack shook his head at Hannah. 'You see what happens when you don't listen? Look at that feeding frenzy now.'

'My feet are all wet, Daddy!' Hannah wailed. 'And there's mud on my school shoes!' Jack sighed. So much for a restful Sunday.

Back at home, Hannah explained that it was Daddy's fault she'd fallen into the pond. 'You're a naughty fibber, Hannah,' Jack told her, wagging a finger. 'Those shoes were expensive,' Maggie said sadly.

Once lunch was served, everything quietened down. Afterwards, Jack retreated to his office to see if there was anything on the database about the murder. Maggie came in to say that Charlie had conked out after half a bottle, which must be down to all the bouncing he'd done after breakfast.

'I think we need to take Hannah in hand,' Jack said. 'She's becoming a spoilt brat. She doesn't think she has to listen to a word anyone says and Mum spoils her rotten. You should have a word. It was totally her fault she ended up in the pond.'

Maggie pretended she hadn't heard him. 'Did you read the thing I printed out for you? I've been reading that you can determine a painting's age by the ratio of carbon-14 isotopes it contains. There was an article about a painting supposedly painted in 1866. But by examining miniscule strands of the canvas, they discovered it had actually been painted in 1980 because the binder in the paint had higher than normal levels of carbon-14 isotopes.' Jack glanced at the printout, reading as Maggie continued to explain. 'It's something about the Hiroshima bomb being a definite point in history when the levels of isotopes in the air changed forever. So, it accurately dates certain things. Before August 1945, a certain level of carbon-14 isotopes were naturally occurring. After 1945, it was higher. That's how they spot fakes. Cool, right?'

'Yeah, very interesting.' Jack thought for a moment. 'From what Helga said, it sounded like Adam had found a way around it.'

Jack's mobile rang – Laura – bringing the conversation to an end. Maggie left Jack to it.

'You read the papers?' she asked him.

'Not yet. I took Hannah to the park.'

'Well, it's very much still under wraps. There's a couple of articles saying an incident occurred in Portobello Market and that the police were requesting that anyone with any information contact Fulham station urgently. And a man's in hospital. They don't even say if he's alive or dead.'

'That it?'

'Yep. It's not on any news channels either. The woman who found him is in a safe house but I think it's mainly to keep her from gossiping about it. With the victim alive and still unidentified, they need to find out who he is before revealing any information. The only update I have is that he is in a critical state and still in an induced coma.'

'Which hospital is he in?'

'St Mary's is probably the closest to Fulham, isn't it? Anyway, thanks to you, I'm having a drink with Morrison tonight, so I should get more details. I'll let you know. Bye.'

Joining Maggie in the kitchen, he repeated what Laura had just told him. 'What about fingerprints? Surely they could identify him that way?' she said.

'Only if he has a criminal record. But Laura might have more details after her drink with the detective in charge.'

Maggie raised an eyebrow. 'You should be careful. I hope you've told her to keep all this under wraps. The last thing you want is people knowing you're asking about Adam Border.'

'It can't be him,' Jack snapped.

'You don't know for sure, Jack. And don't get tetchy with me. I'm only trying to look out for you.'

'Sorry, Mags. I just hope to God it isn't him. I mean, it could be the thug running the shop . . . he was a nasty piece of work. I asked him about the cross last time I was there.'

Maggie banged down the cutlery box. 'Shit, Jack, how many times have you been in that shop?'

'Not that many,' Jack said, trying to sound reassuring. 'First when I recognised him, then again when I met up with him. Oh, and a third time, I went in with an excuse of looking for Adam. And the fourth time, when I went to buy the rug with Marius, I stopped there to buy a frame.'

Maggie couldn't believe it. 'Is there CCTV in the shop?'

'I don't know. But, if there's cameras, the investigating team will have the footage by now.'

'Well, Jack, you'd better stay well away from there from now on. I mean it. The most important thing is to find out from Laura who the victim is; it will at least tell us how worried we should be.'

Jack was about to reply when Penny walked into the kitchen, putting a stop to their conversation, and soon everyone was sitting down to eat. Charlie was bouncing away in his chair as usual, but Hannah was very subdued as she looked at her mud-stained shoes drying on the radiator. After lunch, Jack and Maggie cleared the dishes and made a pot of coffee as Penny took Hannah to her room to watch TV.

'I could make a few enquiries for you,' Maggie said, trying to mollify Jack. 'I know the top guys at St Thomas's and could check if your victim is there. If not, I could try St Mary's; I think I used to work with a surgeon there.'

'Could you do that?'

'If it makes you less anxious, of course. You take Charlie up to Penny for a sleep and I'll go into your office.'

Jack picked up Charlie with a smile, then made a face when he smelt the awful stench coming from his nappy. After guiltily handing his smelly son to his mum, Jack hurried to his office. Maggie was on the phone, so he sat and listened. 'That's really useful, Ken. I appreciate it. It's just that I like to be ahead of the game . . . Oh, totally overloaded. My concerns are that if we have an emergency, we'll be understaffed . . . Yeah, I know. We even ran out of oxygen in Resus last week with all the COVID cases.'

She continued to listen, then thanked whoever Ken was before hanging up. 'He's not been moved to St Thomas's, so he must still be at St Mary's. Let me see if Gareth Thomas is still the top dog there.'

'Are you sure this is all right, Mags? I don't want to get you in trouble.'

'I won't. I am doing my due diligence and basic risk assessments for work.' Maggie smiled as she picked her mobile again. She was enjoying playing detective. A moment later, she had the information they needed. 'He's there. In intensive care, in an induced coma. He has serious facial injuries that will require a massive amount of plastic surgery, but he's way off that yet. At the moment he's in a sort of face-cage that holds his bones together. From what Gareth said, it's doubtful he is going to survive as he also has internal injuries. He's in a side room with an officer outside his door round the clock. Gareth's leading his case . . . he's a loveable rogue sort of a guy, but a brilliant surgeon.'

From the sound of the injuries Maggie had just described, it felt like whoever attacked him didn't intend for him to survive.

'Nailed to a fucking cross . . . What sort of person does that?' Jack's question was rhetorical as there was no valid answer. He just hoped to God Adam was neither the victim nor the attacker.

'Someone full of hate, that's for sure,' Maggie said. 'Gareth described his face as being obliterated. Cheeks, nose, eye sockets, jaw . . . all smashed. Oh, he said something else too: he said that the victim's palms and fingers had been burnt.'

Jack shook his head. 'No wonder they're keeping the details out of the press! Burnt fingers means no prints I guess.' Out of nowhere, Jack leaned forwards and gave Maggie a kiss. 'I love you, Mags. You're amazing. Who else has a wife happy to chit-chat about art forgery and obliterated skulls.'

CHAPTER 19

Maggie was lying on the bed, reading the last few pages of Eric Hebborn's *The Art Forger's Handbook*. She was shocked when she read that the renowned forger had been murdered in Italy. No one had ever been charged with his murder, and there were rumours that the Italian Mafia were responsible, as he had sold many fake masterpieces to prominent Mafia-connected individuals.

Maggie was so engrossed in thought that she jumped when Jack walked in and clapped his hands. 'The painting is complete. It should be dry by the morning. Let's have a takeaway. Chinese? Peking crispy duck and those lovely fried prawns?'

'Sounds pretty good to me.'

'I'll check with Penny and see if Princess would like some fried rice and crackers.'

Maggie put the book down and got off the bed. She could hear Jack laughing upstairs as she went to splash cold water on her face. She decided not to mention what she'd just been reading about, not wanting to puncture Jack's good mood. But she couldn't help thinking about Adam Border.

The family evening was relaxed, with Marius joining them to play poker, using dominoes, marbles and the cards from the Happy Families pack instead of money.

Later, Maggie left them to go and settle Hannah and Charlie. After reading them a story and giving Charlie his night feed, she rejoined everyone in the kitchen. Penny was eagerly counting her winnings, having won the biggest pot yet. Jack and Marius shared a smile, having just let her win. They were about to play another hand when Jack's mobile rang. He picked it up from the table – Laura.

Jack quickly showed Maggie the screen. 'Sorry, guys. Got to drop out of the next hand.' He went to his office and sat at his desk. 'Hi, Laura.' She started talking but he was having difficulty making out what she was saying. 'Are you pissed?'

'Not as much as Morrison,' she said.

'He's such a cheapskate. I thought he might offer to buy me dinner, but he only bought a bag of peanuts all evening. He ordered double vodkas every time it was my round and got me singles when it was his! After the fourth round, it was just tonics for me but not him, so he was well pissed.'

'Did you get any new information?' Jack asked, trying not to sound impatient.

'Not that much. He was very cagey. They still have no ID, but the fella's not in good shape. They found no clothes that would help to identify him as he was bollock naked. No paperwork, no official documents, just a few receipts. They did get the name of the bloke that runs the place though.'

'Did they arrest him?'

'What?'

'You said they got someone that ran the shop.'

'Oh, right, yes. I had to be a bit careful, Jack, you know, not give away why I was interested, but eventually he said they'd picked him up in some bar. Claimed he'd been in Southampton and didn't know anything about it. Said he was just a hired hand who collected all the frames and he'd never actually met the owner. Oh, got paid in cash and not always by the same person and the cross was apparently used at S&M parties. You ever been to one of them, Jack?'

'Can't say that I have. Did they arrest this guy?'

'They did, but he was released when his alibi checked out. He'll be back in for further questioning though; Mr Norman O'Reilly has a sheet as long as my arm. He's done time for armed robbery, GBH, assault with a deadly weapon, handling stolen property, you name it. I checked him out.'

'OK, that's all very interesting. Thanks, Laura. Like you said, I owe you big.' Jack ended the call and pulled up the records on Norman O'Reilly as Maggie tapped on the door.

'Did Laura get anything useful?'

'Yeah, they still have no ID on the victim, but they arrested this guy, Norman O'Reilly. Apparently, he has a firmed-up alibi but remains, as they say, a person of interest. He's the nasty piece of work I met at the shop: long record, spent more time in the nick than out of it, but claims not to know who owns the lease or buys the frames.'

Maggie leaned in to look at the mugshot of the bullish face holding up his ID and number. 'I hope you can trust her, Jack. I mean, if she was drunk when she called you, I worry she was loose-lipped with this detective she was drinking with.'

Jack put his arm around her shoulders as they walked out. 'I'll know more in the morning. I'm on the early shift.'

'So am I. God, I'm knackered,' she said yawning.

'I suppose a fuck's out of the question?'

Maggie laughed. 'I didn't say that.'

CHAPTER 20

The station was unusually busy. Jack had arrived early to have breakfast in the canteen and hopefully catch Laura and check she was keeping her lips sealed. Today, the canteen queue seemed to go on forever as a large number of officers had been brought in for a major briefing in the boardroom. Apparently DI Armani and her team of probationary officers had gathered a lot of new information relating to gang members and their families over the weekend.

Jack had a memo left on his desk with a detailed report of the weekend's results and instructions to familiarise himself with the contents. He'd only glanced at it before taking off his jacket and going to the canteen. Returning to the incident room, Jack saw Laura, looking very hungover, flicking through a similar memo.

'Morning Laura, you look like you need a coffee.'

'I've already had three and I've still got a terrible headache. I blame you, Jack.'

'What is going on? All these extra uniforms in the canteen and a big briefing this morning.'

'Things have been moving at quite a pace over the weekend. The probationers are knackered. They've been on rotation, 24-7.'

DI Armani, wearing a very smart tailored suit and carrying a stack of files, appeared at the door. 'Five minutes before we kick off, everyone, please be prompt. We have a lot to discuss this morning.' She headed in the direction of DCI Clarke's office.

Jack was taken aback by the amount of information on display: photographs, addresses and other personal details and criminal record sheets took up three large whiteboards. Chairs had been arranged around the table, and more lined the walls. The room began to fill up. With a packet of paracetamol and a cup of coffee in her hand, Laura sat beside Jack.

'My God, they have been busy,' she said. 'Glad it was my weekend off.'

Soon, the available chairs at the table had been taken, so the remaining uniformed officers had to stand against the wall. DI Armani entered, the door held open by DCI Clarke. She took off her jacket, putting the file on the table in front of her. She picked up a pointer stick as DCI Clarke took one of two reserved seats at the front of the room. She did not need to ask for everyone's attention. The room had gone silent as soon as she entered.

'Firstly, I would like to thank our terrific group of probationary detectives who worked the weekend to gain a good deal of valuable information about these two warring gangs that have dominated the area for far too long.'

Using her pointer stick, she indicated board one.

'These are all the known members of the ZRDO gang, with photographs and, where possible, personal details and police records. These are the names of members still at school. The second board lists all the crew identified as belonging to LEPO. Again, you can see their details and records. We also have some undercover footage to show you from gang territories, occupied streets, fresh no-go areas including tags and coded graffiti warnings.'

Lastly, she moved to the third board. She stood, arms folded, with the pointer beneath her arm like a sergeant major. 'These are the addresses and contact numbers for parents and families of as many gang members as we're able to find. The names with a star denote single parents, and the ones with a black cross indicate family members incarcerated. As you can see, there are high levels of single parents and imprisonment, meaning parental control is going to be low.'

There were scattered murmurs of dissent, which Armani quickly dismissed: 'Targeting gang members and making arrests is one thing, but if we're going to have any chance of getting control of this situation in the long term, we need to get the families on board, working with us . . .'

Hands shot into the air as the officers started to voice their opinions. Jack exchanged a meaningful look with Laura and two other officers they worked with. What DI Armani was talking about felt like community outreach, not the sort of policing they were committed to, dealing with serious crimes.

The doors opened and a trolley with tea and coffee was wheeled into the room. Armani announced a five-minute break, grabbed her mobile and strode from the room. Jack waited for a couple of minutes then did the same. But he had no intention of returning. If asked, he would point out that someone of rank should be monitoring the incident room.

As Jack walked into the incident room, he immediately saw Armani. She looked as if she was about to ask him why he'd left the meeting but before she got a chance, the door banged open and Detective Sergeant Ed Burrows, an old hand who manned the intelligence cell on the ground floor, gestured urgently to her.

'Yes?'

'Mrs Barras has been taken to St Thomas's, and they've made an arrest, Ma'am,' he said, breathlessly.

She hurried over to him and conducted a whispered conversation.

'Everything all right, Ma'am?' Jack asked, approaching nearer so he could hear.

'Yes, yes,' she said dismissively.

'This is my case,' Jack said forcefully. 'If George Barras has been arrested, I should be the one to interview him.'

Armani nodded for Burrows to leave, then closed the door, and turned to face Jack. She took a deep breath. 'George has attacked Maria again. She's been taken to St Thomas's hospital and is in a critical state. He ran off, but a uniform quickly tracked him down. He's now in custody at Fulham station.'

Jack was fuming at this wholly avoidable situation. 'I warned you he was bloody dangerous. If you'd let me continue the investigation, I could have got Maria to change her mind, make a statement and press charges. George would have been in custody pending trial and none of this would have happened.'

She faced him angrily. 'I made the decision I felt was right at the time, with the information available to me.'

Jack quickly changed his attitude. 'I'm sorry. My tone was uncalled for, Ma'am. But let me go to the hospital and check on Maria. It'll mean you can continue your briefing. I can catch up on everything on my return.'

She considered her options before nodding. 'Yes, please do that. I will explain everything later.'

As she walked off down the corridor, Jack smiled to himself. An official visit to the hospital to see Maria would also give him the opportunity to check on the victim from the frame shop. As he grabbed his jacket from the back of his desk chair, Laura walked in, prizing open a pack of aspirin, popping two in her mouth and grimacing as she forced them down.

'What's going on?' she asked.

'That domestic I was looking into. The victim has been assaulted again, and Armani wants me to deal with it, so I'm not going back to the briefing room.'

Before Laura could ask anything else, he was out of the incident room and hurtling down the stairs to talk to Burrows. He learnt that the police had been called to the Barras house by social services, who were there to speak with Mrs Barras. As they knocked on the front door, George Barras ran out of the back door like a crazy man. They found his wife unconscious on the kitchen floor.

'She's in a bad way, Jack,' Burrows said. 'He used a fucking claw hammer on her this time.'

'And Fulham station called us?'

'Yeah. They wanted to talk to DI Armani. And only her.'

Jack thanked Burrows, then headed out. Burrows called out to him as he went. 'Put your foot down, Jack. It's a bad one.'

Jack took the unmarked CID car, turning on the sirens and concealed blue lights as he left the yard. Arriving at St Thomas's three-quarters of an hour later, he found a parking space and left the Met Police logbook on the dashboard to avoid getting a ticket. He went to the main hospital reception area, showed his ID and explained his urgent reason for being there. It was a few moments while the receptionist conferred with two others working on the desk. They located Maria Barras in the intensive care unit in a new building away from the main hospital. He was handed a red plastic lanyard and told he could take a shortcut by exiting and going through the staff-only entrance on the right-hand-side of the hospital.

Jack made his way along a narrow pathway and then turned into the entrance to the newly built section housing the ICU wings. He went down a long corridor, following the arrows, until he got to a midway cubicle manned by two nurses checking TV monitors. Jack identified himself again.

'The patient you're making enquiries about is being prepared for surgery,' one of the nurses told him. 'I'm afraid I am unable to give you any further detail.'

Jack tried to mask his frustration. 'Is there an area I could wait until the surgeon can speak to me?'

'Yes, we have a private visitors room. A duty nurse can take your details and give you information when there is an update. It may be quite a while as the team is only just preparing for surgery. Go down this corridor and take the third door on your right.'

Jack followed her directions, passing several white-coated doctors and nurses who paid him no attention. He stopped by a large glass-fronted map of the ICU with directions to theatres, private wards and the visitors' waiting room. Reaching the waiting room, Jack found a young man sitting in the corner reading a medical journal. Jack sat down. After a couple of minutes a nurse opened the door.

'Miles, you're wanted in X-ray. Like now.' The man dropped his journal and darted off.

'Things a bit hectic?' Jack asked with a smile.

The nurse nodded. 'We've got a lot of extra security around terminal one at the moment.' She glanced down at her beeper, then hurried out herself. Jack stood in the empty room for a couple of minutes, then made his way back to the map. If terminal one had extra security, it was a good bet that's where the frame shop victim was.

Jack studied the map for a moment, then took off at a brisk pace down the length of the corridor, turning into a large mushroom-shaped area. There were banks of monitor screens lined up on the desk, but to his relief, nobody was around. He was about to go round the desk and have a peek at the monitors when he felt a firm hand on his shoulder. He whipped around.

'Jesus Christ.'

A burly uniformed officer was grinning at him. 'It's Ralph, Ralph Jordan. We were on a training course together a while ago. What are you doing here?'

'I went to the loo and couldn't find the way back. There's a woman I need to interview but she's in surgery.'

'Come on in,' Ralph said, opening a door to the right of the desk. 'We've got decent coffee in here.' Jack hesitated for a second, not wanting to appear too eager. As Jack entered the room, Ralph introduced everyone. 'I'm relieving Tommy, and that's DS Collingwood. This is DS Jack Warr. We were on a Met training course years back. He's here on another case.'

The men nodded their hellos as Tommy put on his jacket. Ralph went to a table laden with sandwiches and two percolators and offered Jack a coffee, which he gladly accepted. 'See you tonight,' Ralph said to Tommy as he started to walk out.

'Maybe you won't. Word is he's failing fast and you know the rules, Ralph.' Tommy glanced to Jack, who he obviously thought shouldn't have been allowed into their waiting area. Ralph waved his hand dismissively as he handed Jack his coffee.

'I needed this, thanks. So, why are you lot here?' Jack sat in one of the easy armchairs and looked at the bank of monitors lining one wall. Most of the screens were blank, but on one he could see doctors and nurses surrounding a bed, with a lot of complicated looking equipment around it.

'It's that bloke found in Portobello Road,' Collingwood said. 'We've been on round the clock since he was brought in.'

'Oh yeah. I think I heard something about that,' Jack said, taking a sip of his coffee.

'I've never seen anything like it,' Collingwood continued. 'He was stripped naked, nailed to a bloody great cross, his face shattered. Knife wounds to his chest, punctured lungs.'

'Who is he?' Jack asked.

'Dunno. There were no clothes, identifying items or fingerprints. His palms and fingers had been scraped raw, and there were no teeth because they'd been hammered out. His jaw was hanging loose.'

'It's a wonder he's still alive,' Jack said.

Collingwood sighed and got up to refill his coffee. 'The only thing working, and it has to be bloody strong, is his heart. He's in an induced coma; can't breathe by himself. The machines are pumping day and night.'

'Bet you're chomping at the bit to talk to him.'

'Shit yeah. For now, it's a sterile room with only the surgeon and nursing staff allowed access to him . . . You were on that Rodney Middleton case, weren't you?' Collingwood asked, stirring his coffee. The question took Jack by surprise. 'I was at the trial, waiting to go into another court. You were very impressive, and I'm not telling tales out of school, but we could do with someone like you heading up this one.'

'Thanks. Who is running the investigation by the way?'

'DCI Mark Morrison. He's running around like a headless chicken because we've got fuck all after almost a week. We had a nasty piece of work brought in who appeared to be running the shop. At first, he said he wasn't the owner, then admitted he was. The shop mostly sells junk; old picture frames, that sort of shit. We had him in custody for twenty-four hours, but he's got a solid enough alibi.'

'Had the shop been broken into?' Jack asked.

'The rear door was left open, which is how he was found. Another stall owner found him . . . poor woman.'

'What's the guy's alibi?'

'He was in Southampton, shipping some frames out, and had missed a pick-up. So, he booked into a B&B for the night and got his girlfriend to meet him there. He was there the entire weekend.'

'And he couldn't help ID the victim? No identifying scars or tatts?'

'Nope. And no face to show him either! We even tried to get a court artist to see if she could give us an impression, but she said it would be impossible. I mean, we could only show her photographs, obviously, but whoever beat the crap out of the poor guy made sure he couldn't be identified.'

They fell silent as Jack drained his coffee and sat holding the empty cup. The monitor was still hiding the figure encased in the bed, and the nurses were standing in front of the camera.

'Could I get a look at him?' Jack asked.

'Hell no. I told you, it's a sterile unit. Any infection and he's gone.'

Jack was thinking he might be able to identify the man based on height, weight and build. 'What are the other monitors for?'

'After the medics leave, we switch all monitors on. There's a camera at the door, one showing the rest of the room, the patient. Anyone who comes and goes.'

'How tall is he?'

Collingwood thought a moment. 'I reckon five-ten maybe. I can tell you, he's quite muscular, in good shape. I reckon he'd recently been abroad as well. He's quite tanned.'

'Age?'

'Thirties. Forties. Hard to guess without the face.'

Jack hid his growing tension. The description could be Adam's. 'What about his hair?'

Collingwood looked over to Ralph. 'See what I mean, real detective we got here. I mean, have you heard Morrison asking about any of this? If he did, it's not in the notes. Shoulder-length, dark blond, at least it was before they shaved it all off for the operations.'

'The reason I'm asking is that I reckon you could put out a request for information; you've got quite a good description, even without his face.'

'It's on standby, but we have checked the missing persons reports. Nothing relevant. We'll check with Interpol next.'

Although Jack knew that Adam was at least six feet tall, the hair colour and his suntan matched. Collingwood suddenly stood up, gesturing to the screens which now showed the medics moving away from the patient's bedside.

'What would be your next port of call, Jack? You can see more of him now.' Jack stood next to Collingwood as the three other screens now showed the same room. There was a cage over the lower part of the man's body, breathing tubes attached to his mouth, but most disconcerting were the number of wires and steel rods coming from his chin, cheeks and jaw. All designed to keep his facial features in place and all covered with a fine mesh that hid his entire face and skull. But now that Jack could see the man's toned physique for himself, his instinct was that it wasn't Adam Border. Relief filled his body and he physically relaxed.

Jack now acted like a police officer, answering the question Collingwood has just asked. 'Somebody wanted to inflict the utmost pain on this guy, before making sure he was unidentifiable This assault took time. So, there's real hatred there. Your victim would have known he was going to die. He's defied the odds, perhaps by being found earlier than the killer predicted. Also, I reckon this attack could have taken more than one person.'

Collingwood looked to Ralph, gesturing for him to stand up. 'He was about two feet off the ground, ankles crossed and chained, the chain hammered into the wood. His arms were splayed out ... spread your arms, Ralph, that's it ... wrists bound and chained. His head was held up by another heavier chain that went round to the back of the cross, and there was a big iron ring hooked up onto what we think was some kind of stand for a heavy shelf.'

Ralph stood, arms stretched wide before he lowered them and, like Collingwood, he looked to Jack for his opinion.

'That would all take a lot of time, hours. And I definitely think it could have been two people; lifting and attaching your victim wouldn't be easy. I'd have fought like hell even if they had a gun on me. Then the place was cleaned up. Again, that takes time. Was there a substantial amount of blood?'

Collingwood nodded. 'Oh yes. We've questioned the neighbours, but a lot of the properties are used as business storage for the market, not many residents live in them, and to date, we've not had anyone come forward saying they heard or saw anything. I reckon we should have had a press release days ago.'

'I agree.' There was just a fraction of a second when Jack thought about mentioning his visits to the shop, but Collingwood looked at his watch interrupting Jack's chain of thought.

'I'm going to kick you out, Jack,' Collingwood said. 'We've got DCI Morrison coming in for an update. God forbid he finds out I've been spilling the beans to you. I trust you won't let on that I have. He's hard enough to work with without any further aggravation. Just in case you bump into each other, what are you doing here?'

'Questioning a woman who's been attacked by her husband with a claw hammer. She's been in theatre since I arrived. I was in the visitors' waiting room, needed to take a slash, and this place is like a rabbit warren. The next minute, Ralph slapped me on the shoulder and said he'd seen me wandering around on the CCTV monitors.'

Collingwood laughed. 'Yeah, this place they call the new build is already outdated and understaffed. At one point, they were going to move our patient to another ICU unit, but we needed to have this area to monitor his progress. Good to meet you, Jack. See you around. Ralph, walk him back to the visitors' section.'

Ralph took Jack back to where he had entered the mushroom-shaped section, now manned by numerous staff. As he headed down the almost familiar corridor, it was already after 2 p.m., but he didn't mind as his day had been more fruitful than he expected. He sat in one chair and drew another over to rest his feet on. Leaning back and closing his eyes, he once again thought that the victim was not Adam Border. That horrific sight of the victim clinging to life was shocking, but now Jack had to consider that, if it wasn't Adam . . . Jack swung his legs to the floor and rested his head in his hands. 'Shit, shit'.

He remembered what Helga had said about Adam, that Jack had no concept of what he could do and that he was very vengeful. Jack also recalled her saying that Adam had many helpers; he would have used these people to clear his studio in the school. Jack needed to learn who these people were.

But Jack was really getting palpitations remembering what Helga had overheard Adam shouting to someone on the phone.

'I'll crucify you!'

CHAPTER 21

Jack waited in the visiting room for an hour and a half and was eventually told by a male doctor that Maria Barras had undergone major surgery and was now in the recovery ward, heavily sedated. He would not be able to interview her for at least 24 hours. Frustrated, Jack had asked if Mrs Barras would recover, but the doctor was non-committal. He gave him his phone number and asked to be updated regarding her condition. Then he headed into work.

Jack went up to the canteen only to find the hot lunches had already been served, but limp salad and some dried-up cold cuts were still available. He decided not to bother and went into the incident room to find it half empty. The only news was that DI Armani had organised a community meeting at the YMCA hall the following evening. Jack threw his jacket over the back of his chair and started looking at the files left on his desk with a Post-it note asking him to appraise the contents. He was flipping through the reports when Laura came in, looking pissed off.

'She's got us schlepping round the high-rises delivering bloody leaflets. Everyone is pissed off. DCI Clarke seems to support her strategy for breaking up the gangs – but I'm not the only one who thinks it's getting out of hand.'

Jack gave Laura a quick nod as DI Armani walked in. Laura turned.

'Just filling DS Warr in on the leaflet distribution, Ma'am.'

Jack stood up as Armani gestured for him to follow her into DCI Clarke's office.

'What the hell have you been doing? Why didn't you contact me?' she said angrily as soon as he'd closed the door behind him.

'I'm sorry, but I have been waiting at the ICU unit for Mrs Barras to get out of surgery, but then I was told she was not in a state to be interviewed. And you can't use mobile phones in the unit.'

She waved his excuses away. 'Just tell me how she is.'

'They wouldn't give me any details, only that she was in the recovery ward heavily sedated, and it could be some time before we can speak to her.'

'So, you don't know her condition?'

'It's serious, I know that much. I presume by now you must have the details of her husband's arrest unless, of course, you were delivering leaflets and unable to . . .'

She pursed her lips in anger. 'That's enough, Detective Warr.'

Jack ignored her. 'If you'd allowed me to revisit Mrs Barras, I know I could have persuaded her to make a statement so her husband couldn't have . . .'

She glared at him angrily. 'I won't discuss this now.'

'I am aware, Ma'am, that as a DS, your name was attached to the report when George Barras was previously arrested.'

Armani suddenly seemed to stumble forward, grabbing hold of the desk chair as though she was about to faint.

'Ma'am?' Jack caught her and helped her to sit. She was shaking, then she put her head in her hands and started sobbing. 'Are you all right . . . do you want me to get some water?'

She sat up straight, wiping her face with the back of her hand, and remained silent. Jack didn't really know what to say next.

'If you want to speak freely with me, please know that you can. Nothing will leave this room.'

Armani took a series of deep breaths as the tension left her body. 'Dear God, how one wrong move can turn round and bite you.' She looked into Jack's eyes and somehow, she knew she could trust him. 'George is my sister's son,' she said quietly. 'As a family, we have tried to deal with his mental health problems, but he has suffered severe PTS after serving in Afghanistan. It's not an excuse, not anymore, but I am asking you to let me handle the situation. Maria will bring charges against him, and I will take care of her and ensure he remains in custody.'

Jack thought quickly about how he should react. 'I'll leave you to handle the situation, Ma'am. And perhaps after he's sentenced, he'll get the medical help he needs.'

'Thank you,' she said simply. Armani walked out of DCI Clarke's office and Jack followed. As she collected her coat and briefcase, she gave Jack a small nod. 'I'm going to the hospital if anyone wants to know where I am. I'll be back at the station in the morning.'

Jack watched her as she walked out. She'd made a mistake – a terrible one – but he trusted her to make things right, as she trusted him to keep her secret.

Laura's gossip sensors were twitching. 'What happened? You were ages.'

'You wouldn't believe me even if I told you, which I am not going to. Instead, I am going to be a very diligent officer and wade through all of this crap.'

Jack arrived home and spent time playing with Hannah and Charlie.

Maggie didn't get home until almost eight, and she was tired out, having had another rough day. Penny had made a shepherd's pie for dinner, and Jack helped her put the kids to bed before he sat down with Maggie to eat.

He told her briefly about the situation with DI Armani. He could see that she was doing her best to be interested, but at the same time, her eyes were drooping.

'Why don't you go to bed, love,' he said gently. 'I'll clear up down here and then I've got a bit of work to do. I'll come up in a little while.' She gave him a kiss, then went upstairs.

Shutting himself in his office with a large glass of wine, Jack began making notes. He wrote down as much as he could recall of his conversation with Helga, then everything he could remember about the description of the victim. Next he opened a drawer in his desk to remove the photographs he had cut from magazines after finding the invitation to the art gallery showing. He laid out all the pictures of Detmar Steinburg, the art dealer. Could he be missing and no one had reported it? That had to be doubtful, so he jotted down the gallery phone number from the invitation to call the following morning.

Jack then remembered the well-dressed black man he had seen at the framer's. He had to skim through his mobile to find the exact date when he and Marius had been at the market, the day he had taken one of the invitations. He also noted that he had seen the wooden cross. Lastly, he searched around in his desk drawers to find an old burner phone, which he could use to contact the art gallery.

Maggie was fast asleep when Jack got into bed beside her. As his brain would not stop ticking over, he took one of her sleeping tablets. He had a lot to do the next day and needed a good night's sleep.

* * *

The next day, Jack dressed in jeans and a sweater and his old leather bomber jacket, putting the now fully charged burner phone in his briefcase. Gladys could be heard hoovering the stairs, yanking the hoover cable after her and talking to someone on her phone. She gave him a beaming smile as he eased past her to collect the car keys and hurry out of the house just before nine thirty. He reckoned it might still be too early to call the art gallery, so he decided to get to the station and call from the car park.

By the time Jack was parked up, it was almost ten. He took the invitation out of the glove compartment along with his burner phone. Dialling the number, he waited as it rang three times before a posh-sounding woman answered.

'Steinburg gallery.'

'Good morning. I am just calling to confirm the gallery event is on this Saturday.'

'Of course, the doors open at six thirty. We will be showing a new collection.'

'Ah good, and I presume by black tie, that will be evening dress?'

'Yes, as usual. May I ask who is calling?'

Jack picked up an empty bag of crisps and crinkled it near the phone, simultaneously saying he was flying in from Zurich, before cutting off the call. He sat thinking for a minute. So he must have been wrong about the victim being Detmar Steinburg. But he still wanted to check out the gallery. He was trying to think if his old dinner jacket and dress shirt would pass muster because there was no way he could afford to hire a monkey suit. Someone rapped on his window, and he whipped around to see Laura holding a takeaway coffee and wrapped toasted sandwich.

'Get a move on. It's after ten.'

He stashed the invitation and burner phone in the glove compartment and they headed into the station.

'I don't suppose you've heard anything from Josh?' Laura asked.

Jack stopped in his tracks. 'I thought we had both agreed to let this go.'

She held up her hands. 'OK, yeah, you're right. If it makes you feel better, I've already got rid of all the files on Middleton. And so far there's been hardly anything in the press.'

Laura and Jack were the last to enter the boardroom to hear DCI Armani issuing instructions about the YMCA event, insisting officers record the attendees' details and their relationship to the gang members. They did their best to look attentive.

By lunchtime, it was business as usual again in the incident room, but nothing urgent was happening. Armani came and leaned on Jack's desk.

'I thought you might want an update. I was at St Thomas's most of last night and again this morning. Maria Barras has serious injuries but is recovering well from the surgery. The biggest concern is a skull fracture. She is going to remain in the ICU for the time being until I can organise a transfer to a private hospital.'

'Thanks for telling me, Ma'am.'

'George is being charged with GBH, and it will no doubt be a custodial sentence due to the previous assaults.'

'It's for the best.'

Armani nodded. 'I hope this can remain strictly between us, Jack.'

'Of course.' He gave her a reassuring smile. She turned to leave, then paused. 'I suppose you heard the news this morning? DCI Morrison was at the hospital and told me that their victim had died, so his case is now a murder investigation. A press release was issued this morning.'

Jack didn't want to overreact or show that he already knew who Morrison was. 'He's with Fulham CID, isn't he?'

'I believe so; I worked with him a while back. Right: onwards and upwards with our current investigation DS Warr, and let's hope we get some positive results from this evening.' She walked out of the incident room.

Laura swung round in her chair. 'Did I hear Mark Morrison's name mentioned?'

'You did. His unidentified victim has died. There was a press release this morning.'

Laura immediately went back to her computer. She signalled to Jack. 'It's on the database . . . I've got it up now.'

Jack feigned a lack of interest. He picked up a file and pushed his chair back. 'I've got to go and get this copied.'

Standing in the gents, Jack wished he had never mentioned anything to Laura about the case. She was quite capable of saying the wrong thing to the wrong person without even realising. He needed to quash any further discussion by providing a weighty distraction . . .

Back in the incident room, he made his pitch. 'I mean, we won't be offended if you say no, but if you would agree to be his godmother, Maggie and I would really love that.'

'Wow, Jack, I am really touched,' Laura gushed. 'Yes, of course, I would be proud to accept, and I promise to take it very seriously. I mean, I'm not that religious, but I was confirmed. Is it going to be at a church?'

'Yeah, and then there will be a bit of a party afterwards. Maggie is organising it, but we don't have a date set yet. I just wanted to make sure you'd be up for it.'

Laura put her arms around him. 'I am really moved, Jack. Please tell Maggie I will do anything to help organise the celebration.' Sitting back down with a broad smile still on her face, Laura seemed to have forgotten all about Mark Morrison and his mysterious murder victim. The rest of the afternoon was spent preparing for the event at the YMCA.

* * *

When Jack got home, it was after ten. Maggie had already gone to bed, and the kids were sleeping soundly. Penny had left some sandwiches under cling film on the kitchen table, so he tucked into them and had a large whisky before going up.

Maggie was reading when he walked in, shrugging off his leather jacket to toss on the floor by the wardrobe. 'Do you want the good news or the bad news?' he asked as he sat on the bed. Maggie didn't answer, letting Jack choose how to start.

'I have to say, Mags, Armani can be quite impressive when she tries. The YMCA Hall was only a quarter full, and there were a lot of no-shows, but those that did were very vocal. To start, a bloke stood up shouting that he wanted to know when Hammersmith Bridge was going to be working, as he was losing business.'

Maggie laughed as Jack kicked off his shoes.

'After dealing with that, she got the message across with some real emotion, but it was the video footage that really did the job: footage of many of the young knife victims who died last year, and then photographs of the kids hanging out by school gates and in the snooker halls. As you know, I really wasn't getting along with her, but I have to put my hand up and say she did a good job. She got a lot of positive feedback from the parents. And she got some press attention. Someone was there from the *Daily Mail* no less.'

'OK, so that has to be the good news,' Maggie said.

Jack, by now, had got down to his underpants and was standing at the open wardrobe door.

'I needed to get Laura to keep her mouth shut about me trying to find out about the victim from the framer's shop.'

'My God, yes. I heard the news about him dying.'

'I asked Laura to be Charlie's godmother.'

'What!'

'You know the last thing I need is for her to start blabbing about me trying to find out about the victim.'

'So, it's a bribe?' Maggie couldn't believe what she was hearing.

'She's over the moon, Mags. I'm sorry, I know I should have discussed it with you.'

'Of course you should have. I hardly even know Laura. And I was going to ask the matron I work with.'

'Well, I definitely don't know *her*!' Jack grinned. 'Look, we haven't even set a date yet. And she offered to help with organising it.'

Maggie sighed, tossing the book aside. 'Well, at least you have to start thinking about the christening now. We have to talk to the vicar and decide whether to do a buffet at the house or in a pub.'

'You know me, Mags. I'll go along with anything you suggest.' Jack removed his old, hardly used black suit, with dress shirt beneath, from the wardrobe. 'Do you think Mum could sort this for me? It's all creased up and has a few stains. Or do I need to send it away?'

'You won't need that for a christening, Jack.'

He hesitated, deciding now was not the time to tell her about visiting the art gallery. Instead, he went into the bathroom to clean his teeth. He was saved from explaining when the baby monitor kicked in, and Maggie jumped out of bed to check on Charlie. A few moments later, Penny tapped on the bedroom door to ask for Maggie's dressing gown. Charlie was very restless, and it could be the start of teething or colic.

'Mum, can you do me a favour? I need my dress shirt and suit. Can you spiff them up a bit?' He passed her Maggie's dressing gown, together with his suit and shirt. 'No need to tell Mags, eh.' Penny took the items without a word.

An hour later, when Maggie returned, Jack was asleep.

* * *

Jack was the first to leave in the morning as he was on early shift. When he got to the station, he found that Armani's YMCA event was already bearing fruit. The custody sergeant was asking for assistance as parents had been bringing in weapons they had found in their son's bedrooms. Two officers were assigned to collect, tag and store lethal knives and machetes. There were also plastic handguns, air rifles, baseball bats, even swords ... the list went on.

Armani was in high spirits, but no one was resting on their laurels. Everyone on shift had their work cut out as there had also been a break-in at a local jewellery shop. The thieves, wearing black hoods, smashed the window and stole a selection of top-end watches. Armani had Laura visit the premises and had discussed with DCI Clarke adopting the same strategy against the thieves as two other local stations. They were using undercover officers wearing Rolex watches, to draw out the thieves who were robbing in the streets, often in broad daylight.

Jack was having lunch when Laura found him standing in line. 'Jack, I was looking for you. Something's going down.'

'I heard. She wants undercover cops flashing gold watches acting as bait. I've been selected along with—'

She pulled at his arm. 'It's not that. I just saw Morrison and another detective in a meeting with DCI Clarke. You always know when something is up because he closes his blinds. He didn't see me, but I just thought—'

'No, Laura, you thought nothing.' Jack moved up in the queue, hoping Laura would take the hint, which she did.

Jack got his lasagne and sticky toffee pudding and was eating at the same table as Nala and Kwame, discussing the array of weapons coming into the station, when Armani walked in, pausing in the doorway before heading towards his table.

'DS Warr, you are wanted in the DCI's office. Sorry to disturb your meal.' Jack took a last mouthful of his lasagne before getting up and sliding his sticky toffee pudding across to the probationers to fight over. Passing Laura at her desk, she gave him a covert glance, but he ignored it and continued to DCI Clarke's office. He knocked and waited a moment before he was ushered in.

Mark Morrison was sitting in front of Clarke's desk, with Collingwood standing to one side. On the desk was a bulging file containing photographs and statements. Clarke made the introductions.

'I don't know if you are aware,' he said, 'but DCI Morrison has been leading the investigation into the now murder of an unidentified man discovered at a framer's shop in Portobello Road.' He hesitated, looking uncomfortable. 'Jack, new evidence has emerged in the form of some CCTV footage.'

Morrison interjected. 'You have some explaining to do, Detective Warr.'

Jack shrugged. 'I'm happy help in any way I can . . .'

'We have been reviewing CCTV footage from a camera opposite the framer's shop,' Morrison continued. 'Can you explain why, on three different occasions, you were caught on camera entering the shop?'

Morrison spread out some printouts of the CCTV images and indicated Jack's presence with his pencil. Jack leaned forward, looking intently at each picture with a date and time printed at the bottom.

'Is that where the victim was discovered?' he asked casually.

'You know the answer to that,' Morrison snapped. 'As you can see from this photograph, you're standing behind the crime scene tape.'

Jack hesitated a moment before asking if he could borrow Morrison's pencil. He handed it to him with a frown.

'The first time I was near the frame shop, I was with my wife Maggie and we were shopping for furniture for our loft extension. She can confirm that. There was a stall directly outside the framer's, and I was looking at a Victorian doll for my daughter. Again, my wife will be able to confirm this.'

Morrison nodded. 'We've talked to the stall owner.'

Jack then pointed to the second photograph. 'I did go into the shop then because I was looking for an old-style frame. My son's being christened soon and I wanted to frame a picture of him for my mum. She already has one of me at his age in an old frame and I wanted a matching one of Charlie. I spoke to a man who said he ran the shop; I didn't get his name. But as I didn't have the measurements, he suggested I come back when I had them, then he ushered me out. He was very abrasive, almost threatening.'

'Yeah, Norman O'Reilly. We brought him in and he identified you,' Morrison confirmed.

Jack leaned closer to the CCTV stills. He tapped the third one. 'That's when I came back with the measurements. I found a suitable gilt frame, and the same man asked ten pounds for it. I said it was not worth more than a fiver, and he snatched the frame from me. I obviously didn't want a full-blown confrontation, so I left.'

'Did you see a life-size cross in the shop?' Morrison asked bluntly.

'Yes. It looked like maybe two RSJs bolted together. I asked if it was a theatrical prop from *Jesus Christ Superstar*.'

'And you didn't think it was significant?'

'It wasn't mentioned in the news coverage and I'm not familiar with the case so . . .'

Morrison pursed his lips. 'So, talk me through the last photograph, Detective Warr. There you are, clearly standing with other spectators behind the police tape, watching the police and SOCO going in and out of the shop.'

'I had no idea what had happened. I was with my builder Marius that Saturday morning. We bought a carpet, more than likely from the same shop that you have the CCTV footage from. Marius and I were carrying the carpet back to his van – I expect that'll be on CCTV too – when he called my attention to the police cordon and the patrol cars. I assumed whatever had happened was connected to the man who ran the place. I can give you Marius's contact details.'

Jack could feel the sweat dripping from his armpits, but he remained calm and helpful as the tension in the room built. By now, Morrison was furiously gathering the photographs and shoving them into the file before snatching back his pencil.

He spat out his next words. 'You expect us to believe that your presence at the murder site, on several occasions, was just a coincidence?' Morrison glanced at Collingwood before continuing. 'I also have information that you were present at St Thomas's ICU unit, in the victim observation room with some of my officers, which was against my orders as we had not yet identified the victim.'

Jack glanced at Collingwood, who gave a tiny, almost apologetic shrug of his shoulders.

Morrison continued. 'Detective Warr, you gained access to the ICU where the victim was being cared for and asked numerous questions regarding his identity.'

Again, Jack glanced at Collingwood and, this time, Morrison slapped the desk with his hand. 'Don't look at him! Look at me! There is hospital CCTV supporting everything I've just said. Collingwood had no option but to identify you.'

Jack took a moment to think. Morrison smirked, sure he had Jack in a corner. 'DI Armani can confirm my reason for being at the ICU,' Jack started. Morrison's smirk vanished as he sensed Jack was about to slip out of this too. 'I was checking on Maria Barras in connection with a domestic. Mrs Barras was undergoing an emergency operation, so I could not take a statement from her. I waited in the private visitors' section for a considerable length of time before looking for the toilet. I don't know if you're familiar with the ICU building, but the layout is very confusing. After using the toilet, I mistakenly went down the wrong corridor on the way back to the visitors' section.'

Jack raised a hand apologetically towards Collingwood before continuing.

'I don't want to get anyone into trouble but, in the corridor, I bumped into an officer named Ralph Jordan, with whom I had been on a training course a few years back. He asked if I wanted a coffee and invited me into the ICU victim viewing room. I accepted. I was told why your team were there. Up until that point, I had no knowledge of the victim's location or the nature of his injuries. After finishing my coffee, I was asked to leave. I returned to the waiting room, where I waited another hour and a half before I was informed that Mrs Barras's surgery was complete, but that I still could not speak to her.'

Morrison took out another file and removed a stack of photographs. As he laid them on the desk, Jack held his breath as he tried to guess what Morrison was going to throw at him next. Many of these new CCTV images were blurred, but he could see they were customers entering and leaving the framer's shop. Inside, Jack started to panic.

'We have a number of photographs of this man.' Morrison tapped away at the images with his pencil. 'He is seen entering the framer's shop, then carrying out a number of frames.'

The first image showed Adam Border with his baseball hat pulled down low over his face, which was turned away as though he knew where the shop cameras were located. The second had him with the same baseball cap, sunglasses and again carrying two frames. Jack took his time, looking at the two photographs, then sat back.

'Well . . . without a full face of the bloke in the baseball cap it's hard to tell . . . but I'm pretty sure I don't know him.' Jack looked at Morrison. 'Is he the victim?'

Morrison shoved the photos back in the file with a scowl.

'Is he the suspect then?'

Morrison stood up. 'This is not over, Detective Warr. I don't believe in coincidences and by Christ I have a slew of them with your name on them!'

Jack looked to DCI Clarke, who nodded for him to leave. Jack walked calmly to the door, glad he was wearing a jacket because he knew his shirt would be soaking wet with sweat. As he returned to his desk, Laura rocked back in her chair, not even needing to ask.

'I'll fill you in later,' Jack assured her.

'Not good enough, Jack,' she said vehemently. 'Morrison hasn't seen me yet, Jack. Was that about me calling him the other day?'

'No, you weren't even mentioned. Do us both a favour, Laura, go into the loo, and stay there until they leave.'

Laura shook her head. 'How the hell will I know when they've gone? I'll go for lunch. I've been too worried to eat till now!'

'Great, go on then. Hurry up!'

Laura left the incident room and Jack remained at his desk for half an hour before Morrison and Collingwood walked out of DCI Clarke's office. Morrison strode out, without so much as a glance at Jack, allowing Collingwood to hang back for a second.

'Sorry to drop you in the shit, Jack. No hard feelings.'

'None. I hope you get your victim identified.'

Collingwood shook his head. 'You must be joking. All we've got is crank calls, the victim's physical description doesn't match anyone on any missing person's list. Morrison is clutching at every straw he sees. He reckons O'Reilly is our main suspect.' Collingwood smiled. 'After you.'

'He could be right about O'Reilly. He was a thug basically.' Jack was just about to suggest that they should check out what O'Reilly was shipping from Southampton docks when Morrison appeared at the doors, and Collingwood quickly joined him. Jack was relieved that Adam Border had been wise to the position of the shop's CCTV cameras. But why was he so concerned about having his image recorded? He also thought about the tall, well-dressed black guy coming out of the shop when he'd found the invitations. Perhaps the camera was only picking up people entering the frame shop from one side, as he had done. Adam Border had walked out the first time he had seen him and turned to the right, and so had the elegant black guy. He sighed, doubting he could do anything about it unless he returned to the carpet shop opposite the framer's and looked for himself.

For the rest of the afternoon, Jack found it hard to concentrate as he kept mulling over the meeting with Morrison. The shock of seeing the photos of Adam Border had really unnerved him. All it would take would be for one person to identify him from the investigation Jack had been involved in when Adam Border had been suspected of drug dealing and murder. Jack's nerves started to jangle as he tried to remember what photographs of Adam Border they had on file.

As the incident room thinned out, Jack went into the records department with the intention of skimming through what had been retained about the years-old drug investigation, and what information they had on Adam Border.

As Jack sifted through the file, he was unable to find any adult photographs of Adam, only the ones they had uncovered from his childhood. He also became aware that due to his friendship with his old boss, Ridley had deleted any record of his suspicions about how Jack had traced Adam to his studio in Ireland. When the studio was searched, they had found no evidence that Adam had even been there. It had been wiped clean because Jack had given Adam the time to do that and then escape. Adam was very good at disappearing without a trace.

Returning to his desk in the incident room, he packed up, ready to leave. Before he did so, he recalled Ridley's words: 'Be careful Jack,' Ridley had warned. 'Border is a smart, dangerous liar. He'll come back one day. Be ready.'

CHAPTER 22

On Thursday the whole station was in a celebratory mood following numerous arrests of gang members based on tip-offs and community support. The local newspaper showed a picture of DI Armani with a group of grateful parents and she made it clear that the police were committed to ending the local gang wars.

Jack, however, was clearly in the doghouse as far as DCI Clarke was concerned; the last thing he needed was one of his officers being connected – however tangentially – to a murder case. Jack noticed Armani was now keeping her distance, too. Whether it was because he'd mentioned her as his 'alibi' during his interview with Morrison, he didn't know, but he decided against bringing the subject up with her. She must know he hadn't divulged her connection to George Barras, because she would have been dragged over the coals by now. In the end he put her aloofness down to her being busy with her new-found media profile.

The covert programme to put officers on the streets wearing expensive watches had started to show results, with four arrests being made after receiving information from two other stations. Jack was in the thick of things but kept one eye on developments in the framer's shop murder investigation.

The still-unidentified victim was now being physically described using Collingwood's words in the ICU: five feet nine to ten, late thirties to early fifties, tanned, muscular, with collar-length dark blond hair. The media still made no reference to the crucifixion, but they did elaborate on the appalling injuries inflicted, suggesting that it was a possible hate crime due to the perpetrator disfiguring the victim's face. Jack knew that by withholding certain key details, the hundreds of officers manning the public phonelines would be able to more easily distinguish between nutcases and true potential leads.

To Jack's relief, so far there were no references to CCTV images of people seen entering the framer's shop. On his way into the station, Jack had checked the position of the CCTV camera across the road from the framer's. It was angled to show the carpet shop's display out in front, and it just took in the left side of the framer's shop entrance which was still covered in yellow crime scene tape. It was why the elegant black man had not been caught on camera, but Jack had been, along with Border who had been wearing his baseball cap pulled low and dark glasses.

Jack was packing up, ready to go home. Laura was at her desk and leaned back in her chair to indicate she had something to say. 'Guess what, DCI Morrison has asked me on a date. I couldn't believe it. I said to him was it just a drink and he said he was offering dinner.'

'And?'

'I accepted. You know what I think, it's because of what I told you about Cruella working with him. I saw the reaction when he saw her, and she was just as tense. I'm going over to Fulham after work tonight.'

'Well don't have too much to drink.'

'I won't, and I'll see what nuggets I can find out about his murder case.'

Jack was still shaking his head when he got to the car park. With Laura's total inability to be subtle, Jack often wondered how on earth she had managed to become a police officer in the first place.

* * *

When Jack arrived home just after six, Maggie was in the nursery with Charlie, while Penny and Hannah were having dinner in the kitchen. Jack asked about his evening shirt and Penny said it had been washed and ironed and it was in the bedroom with his pressed jacket. Jack rolled his eyes, knowing Maggie would see it and ask what he was up to. As he left the room, Penny called after him, 'You're welcome!'

Jack was looking for a bow tie when Maggie came in with Charlie balanced on her hip. 'Guess who just had a chicken and veg mush for his dinner?' Maggie handed Charlie to Jack so she could change her top which was covered in the aforementioned mush. 'So,' Maggie smiled, 'are you going somewhere posh?'

'I'm trying to find my bow tie. Not the velvet one, the black one that you have to tie for me,' Jack said, ignoring the question.

Maggie opened some drawers and soon held up a crumpled bow tie.

'It needs a bit of a press,' he said. 'What about trousers?' He watched her hunting through his wardrobe before bringing out a pair he hadn't worn for years. They even had a turn-up.

'These sort of match the jacket,' she said. 'Please don't tell me it's one of those Met retirement dinners. I don't have to come do I?'

Jack grinned. He should have thought of that. He passed Charlie back to her, then took the trousers and bow tie for Penny to press. 'All will be revealed in due course.'

By the time Hannah was bathed and settled in front of a cartoon, Maggie was rocking Charlie to sleep, and Penny already had the ironing board set up and was pressing Jack's trousers with a damp cloth. The bow tie still looked as if it had seen better days. Jack helped by putting the ironing board away, then took the trousers upstairs to hang them with the jacket and evening shirt. He passed Maggie on the stairs.

'Is it something to do with Ridley?'

'I wish it was. You know nobody has heard a word about him. Let alone from him.'

Maggie laid a gentle hand on Jack's arm. 'I'll open a bottle to have with dinner.'

'I'll be right down.'

While they ate, Maggie listened to Jack explain what had gone down at the station with regards to his jaunts to the framer's and to the ICU all being caught on CCTV. Maggie sighed as she cleared the plates.

'I hope this is a warning to you, Jack. You have to forget this obsession with Adam Border and look out for yourself.'

'It's not an obsession, Mags. I did think he could be their victim, but after I'd seen the victim in ICU, I knew that it wasn't Adam. But . . .'

'Please don't go into details of his injuries again. It's hard to even imagine the motive behind such an atrocious method of murder, and the crucifixion is just horrific. No wonder they have kept that out of the press.'

'The "but", Mags, is that I have a good idea who the victim might be . . . come up to the office and let me show you.'

'It's getting late, Jack.'

'You wanted to know why I've got the evening suit ready.'

Maggie cleared the kitchen before locking the front door and coming up to Jack's office. Fifteen minutes later she was sitting beside him, holding the gold embossed invitation in her hands. On the screen, Jack had Googled the art gallery in Bond Street.

'Apparently, Detmar Steinburg has galleries all over Europe and has exclusive viewings for his rich clients. Now look at all these photos of him. He's the right age, size, build, and I know he was Adam's dealer; well, I think it's him.'

Maggie sighed, putting the invitation back down on his desk.

'I called the art gallery to check the viewing was still going ahead, because if it wasn't, I reckoned I could be right that this Detmar was the victim. But when I rang, I was told it was happening.'

'So, if Detmar is there, your theory's wrong.'

'Yeah. But it could still be useful. It could be someone who works for him, like that black guy I saw at the framer's when I lifted that invitation.'

'Don't you think you're taking this too far, Jack?'

Jack swung back in his chair. 'This will be my last opportunity to see if I can come up with anything. Look at all my notes . . . I am not just arsing around, Mags; I think I'm on the right track. Which is better than Morrison who thinks I'm his fucking killer.'

She picked up his pages of notes. 'But what if you are on the right track? You're taking a big risk of being caught. And if you find a connection, what do you intend to do with it? This isn't your investigation. Would you just forward everything to this Morrison guy?'

'Maybe. I'd have to think about it. Right now, they have zilch, no identification and just one suspect: the thug who works in the framer's. And when Morrison was trying to implicate me, DCI Clarke sat on his arse giving me no backup whatsoever. He's virtually cold-shouldered me ever since, and now bloody Armani is circling around me like I'm contagious. I want some respect again, Mags. Some kudos.'

Maggie tapped the page she was reading. 'What does this mean: "Joe Orpen and his partner"?'

'It was something Adam said to me when he was describing his dealer, that he was like that fella, but I've not checked it out yet.'

'Is he an artist?'

'Probably. I'll follow it up properly when I've not got so much in my head. At this event, I have to come across as an art buyer or expert.'

Maggie laughed. 'Good luck with that!' She was at the door when she paused and looked back. 'You know, Jack, I'm finding it hard to keep up with you; first you tell me you're concerned the victim could be Adam, then when you learnt more at the ICU, you're certain it isn't. Next you're a murder suspect because they have you on CCTV visiting the framer's shop. That's supported by more CCTV from the ICU where you saw the victim. And now tonight you bring up someone else you saw in the bloody framer's who could be the dead guy on the cross . . . oh, that's right, the giant cross you saw at the crime scene!'

Jack frowned. 'What is all this, Maggie?'

'Jack, you need to straighten yourself out. Firstly, you're withholding evidence. Now you're planning to go to this dealer's gallery, because you think you know who the victim is . . . So what if you do discover who it is? How are you going to explain being at the gallery?'

'You don't get it, Maggie.'

'No. I don't. Surely the most important thing is that whoever did this horrific murder is found. Withholding the information you already say you have might prevent that.'

'I'm not listening to you anymore,' Jack said.

Maggie stood her ground. 'Why not? Why not, unless . . . right, I'm just going to say it. Do you think Adam Border killed that man? Is that why you're trying your best to pin it on someone else? Because the longer you keep silent Jack, the further away he's getting. Aided and abetted by you.'

Jack turned away refusing to answer, and he was shocked when instead of leaving she angrily stepped closer. 'You did it before.

You think I don't know, Jack.' Maggie then walked out, slamming the door closed behind her.

Maggie was in the bathroom splashing water on her reddened face when Jack came in and stood looking at her in the mirror. 'You make it all sound like a game, Jack. Just consider what was done to the victim. Whoever did it, is so very, very dangerous. You have a family and if anything happened to you . . . it doesn't even bear thinking about. Your job worries me at the best of times, but here you have no one backing you up. You're all on your own.'

Maggie hadn't seen it for a while, that steely anger when his eyes got dark. But she saw it now.

'You should have more faith in me. I know what I am fucking doing. Do you not think I have been planning this in detail? This *is* my job, Mags. Chasing a killer, not sitting at a bloody desk checking files on kids who'll get nothing more than a rap over the knuckles.'

Maggie shook her head sadly. 'Adam really has a hold on you. You're doing this for him, aren't you?'

'Wrong! I am doing this for me, all right, *for me*!' Jack stormed out.

Maggie got into bed and turned out the light. The following morning, with Jack's half of the bed empty, she assumed he'd slept on the sofa or in his office. By the time she went into the kitchen, Penny was clearing up the breakfast dishes.

'Jack left early,' Penny confirmed. 'He seemed to be in one of his moods and I asked if he was all right, but he just walked out.'

Maggie sighed and then did her best to smile. 'He'll be fine.'

CHAPTER 23

On Friday the incident room was busy with rounding up officers for magistrate's court appearances. Jack had a slew of statements to double-check and file, which took most of the morning. In his opinion, Armani was moving too fast, and he predicted there could be dire consequences.

Laura, who had been in court all morning, eventually came in after lunch. She looked over to Jack, making a 'C' shape with her hand. He nodded that he'd love a coffee, and she headed to the canteen to get them a proper one. Filing everything he had completed, Jack began checking another case that had been dismissed for lack of evidence. It still had to be documented, dated and filed, and placed alongside the other dismissed cases.

Laura returned with two coffees and a KitKat. She perched on the edge of Jack's desk and divided the KitKat in two.

'How was dinner?' he asked as she handed him his share.

'Italian. Not bad. But he kept me waiting three quarters of an hour 'cause he had some big meeting. I think they're trying to get on this new crime stoppers TV series. As far as I could make out, they're still checking out their main suspect's alibi; you know, the bloke that owns the framer's shop. Anyways one of his team, nice guy, Mike Collingwood, he looked after me till Morrison was free.' Laura nibbled her KitKat like a rabbit skinning a carrot. 'I had a look over their whiteboard. Proper old school, like we used to use before we got these techy ones. Three boards, all stacked with photos and notes. They had white paper covering the crime scene photos so I couldn't have a really good nose. But they had a row of blurry CCTV photos of people coming and going from the shop.' Laura grinned. 'You know your ugly mug was up there, right?'

'Tell me about it. That's why Morrison was here the other day. I was buying a frame for Charlie's christening, but I'm pissed off they have it on their board.'

'There was another photo, unidentified, guy with a baseball cap and shades. It was weird because he gave me déjà vu. Anyway . . . I told Collingwood that your photo should not have been on the board. He took me to one side, explained why Morrison really had it in for you. Apparently, he had overheard two of his team talking, suggesting you'd be better at handling the case than him, and saying what they'd gained from you being at the ICU. That was it. Once he found out you'd been in the ICU, he latched on to you as a suspect.'

'I had good reason to be there. Armani sent me.'

'Whatever. So, dinner mainly consisted of him asking about you, and whether or not I trusted you. He got tetchy when I said I did . . . how could I not after so many years of being one desk away from you.'

As Jack and Laura shared a smile of solidarity, Armani approached and reprimanded Laura for perching on a colleague's desk like she was a child in a school classroom. Laura immediately stood up.

'Sorry, Ma'am. I was just giving Detective Warr an update from the magistrate's court. I'll put my report in your office now.' Laura quickly moved back to her own desk as Armani continued towards her office.

Jack took a moment to gather the dismissed case files before following Armani. Her office was next to DCI Clarke's, but it was little bigger than a cupboard. Jack tapped on the open door. She looked up frowning. 'What do you want?'

'Sorry to disturb you, Ma'am, but I think there has to be some attention drawn to the number of cases building up which are being dismissed for lack of evidence. Due to the backlog, the magistrates are complaining. It could backfire and damage the good work you have been doing against the gangs. Especially if the press get wind of just how many of the juveniles we've arrested . . .'

She held her hand up to stop him. 'I am fully aware of the situation, and it is in hand.'

'There's something else, Ma'am. Laura happened to be over at Fulham station.'

'What was she doing there?'

'I believe a dinner date with DCI Morrison who inadvertently kept her waiting in full view of their crime board.'

'She was in their incident room?'

'Apparently so. Ma'am, she saw my photograph pinned on the board, alongside other people wanted for questioning.' Armani gave a dismissive shrug. 'I felt that I had very clearly explained my reasons for being in the ICU. It was quite by accident I went down the wrong corridor and into the unit that was caring for their victim.'

Armani knew what Jack was after. 'Yes, yes, obviously I backed up your statement. I was told that DCI Morrison also had a CCTV photograph of you entering the location where their victim was found, which obviously I couldn't comment on.'

'I understand that Ma'am, but I also explained why I was there, and with witnesses to verify my account.'

Armani shrugged. 'I'm not privy to any of that.'

'I just think that it is unethical for DCI Morrison – as I am a serving Met detective and attached to this station – to put my photo on his crime board.'

Armani didn't respond and Jack was beginning to find her lack of interest in his predicament more than a little annoying. He gritted his teeth and added, 'I suppose it was also unethical of me not to explain why you had insisted I personally visit Maria Barras...'

She pursed her lips, then held her hand out for the file he had brought with him. 'I will have a word with Morrison. Thank you.'

Back at his desk, Laura caught his eye with a concerned look, but he just gave her a thumbs up.

In her office, Armani put in a call to DCI Morrison. 'Mark, I just want to run something by you that's come to my attention.'

'I'm up to my eyes at the moment, but...'

'It won't take a moment. Apparently, you've got DS Jack Warr's photograph on your incident board. He really is an exceptional officer, and I believe your enquiries were satisfactorily answered by him and supported by witness statements. So, I think you should take it down.'

'I hear what you're saying. Anything else? I don't want any hard feelings between us.'

'Likewise. I hope you understand, I'm just protecting one of my team.'

Morrison started to laugh, but she had already hung up. His dislike of Jack Warr went up another notch.

Armani was despondently looking over the files of dismissed cases when she got an urgent summons to a meeting with DCI Clarke.

'There's been a fatal stabbing,' he said without any preamble. 'A sixteen-year-old boy, questioned three weeks earlier about gang affiliations and then released.'

* * *

It was after nine thirty when Jack arrived home. As he reheated cling-filmed sausage and mash, Maggie came down in her dressing gown. 'I'm going to have an early night, been a rough day. I'm going to treat myself to a haircut tomorrow. Do you still intend to go to the gallery?'

Jack opted to keep the conversation short as he didn't want another argument. 'Yes.'

'Then your suit is hanging up, all pressed. Penny's done a good job on the bow tie. Anything of interest happen today?'

'Not much. Armani's in the doghouse a bit, as her epic operation to eradicate the gangs looks like it might be backfiring. One of the kids she brought in has been found stabbed.'

'I'm sorry to hear that.' The conversation felt as if it was over. 'Penny is taking Hannah to the petting zoo tomorrow and Marius is coming over to check over the snags,' Maggie said before heading back up to bed.

After finishing his unappetising meal, Jack poured himself the remainder of an open bottle of wine and went to his office. He reckoned he'd spend a while there until Maggie fell asleep. He had only just settled down when his phone rang. Jack answered even though it was now gone ten thirty.

'Hello?'

'Hi Bro, just checking in. See how you're doing.' Jack recognised his voice immediately, but was so taken aback he didn't answer. 'It's Josh. All right to talk, is it?'

'Yes, yes, everyone's in bed.'

'So, how's things?'

Jack couldn't quite believe the low-key conversation they were having after Josh had disappeared so suddenly. 'Er . . . back to normal sleep-wise. Under the usual pressure at work.'

'Ah, so you're back at work?'

'Yeah, what about you? How are you doing?'

'Been better, Jack. I'm having to use a walking frame.' Jack thought Josh sounded almost ashamed of his physical decline. 'Moved to Tampa. How's that son of yours?'

'He's great, eating solids now. Hannah is quite a handful, though. In fact, something . . .' Jack paused, unsure how to continue.

Josh's gentle, reassuring voice soothed Jack's anxiety around opening up. 'Ready when you are, bud.'

'I'm so ashamed of myself, Josh . . . but the outcome was really important.' Jack took a deep breath. 'Hannah was screaming blue murder about wanting a puppy, kicking and punching me, and before I knew it I . . . I picked her up and locked her in the closet in the hall. God, I don't know why I did it.' Josh said nothing. He just let Jack explain in his own time. 'It triggered something in me, from my childhood. Before I was adopted, when I was put in a children's home. They used you lock me up in this dank cellar, leave me for hours, and I'd be screaming in terror. He was a bastard, what he did to me, and it all came out, Josh. My nightmares, my problems, and since then, I've been fine.'

'I can understand all of that. Facing your fears head on as an adult, that takes time. But when that one thing falls into place . . .'

'That's right.'

'You ever think about going to find that guy and giving him a good beating?'

Jack laughed. 'He's long dead.'

'Good. Listen, Jack, I feel bad about just hightailing it the way I did. Can you tell Laura I'm sorry not to have contacted her? I'd been at Strangeways Prison and was thinking about stopping by and staying another night at her place, but I found a cheap flight from Manchester back to New York, so . . .'

'I'll tell her. She was asking after you. Are you planning on coming over again?'

'I doubt it, not fit enough to be honest.'

'If I ever make it to the States, I'll come see you.'

'That would be good.'

Jack paused and then very quietly said. 'I owe you, Josh.'

'You owe me nothing. Going to hang up now Bro, you take care.'

Jack felt unexpected tears welling up as he hung up the phone. They hadn't mentioned Rodney Middleton, his death or the real source of Jack's torment. But even though Jack had told him that his childhood trauma was the root cause of his nightmares, he knew Josh understood the real cause. Rodney Middleton was gone from Jack's life and Josh's phone call felt like some kind of dark bucket list tick, as Josh checked to make sure his friend was free. Jack was definitely free now. From Middleton at least. Next on the list was Adam Border.

CHAPTER 24

Maggie returned from the hairdressers laden with shopping bags, having also done a larger than intended grocery shop. Penny helped her to load up the deep freeze and cupboards, dropping into conversation that Jack had watered the plants without being asked. Maggie shrugged as if uninterested. 'That's a first.'

Upstairs Jack took a long bath, shaved and washed his hair, splashed cologne over himself and put on his dressing gown. It was too early for him to get dressed in his suit, so he decided to go and find Maggie to apologise. The last place he looked was of course where he found her; as Jack walked into the loft, Maggie turned to look at him.

'You had a haircut,' he said, hovering nervously.

'I told you last night. You've overdone it with the aftershave by the way.'

'Look, I'm sorry I sounded off last night. I can't explain it, Maggie, but the first time I met Border, I connected with him somehow. He sparked my imagination. He's a genius. Imagine what it must feel like to have the ability to fake a Rembrandt and for it to be acclaimed as a genuine masterpiece when his own work is dismissed as worthless. Imagine being able to fool the smartest art experts around the world. And none of them even know you exist. In truth, Mags, I'm fascinated by art forgery, the incredible skill of it, not by Adam. There are many forgers doing what he's doing.'

She turned, cupping his face between her hands. 'Thank you for being honest with me.'

'I love you, Mags.' Jack took her hands in his. 'Do you think you could fix my bow tie?'

They went downstairs together, Maggie going into the nursery to check on Charlie. As she joined Jack in the bedroom, they could both hear Hannah whooping and shouting as she and Penny returned from the petting zoo. 'A tiny goat! I want a tiny goat to keep in my bedroom!'

Jack and Maggie's eyes widened in unison at the awful thought of Hannah now wanting a goat. Jack was wearing his suit, shirt and jacket.

He stepped into his trousers and tucked the dress shirt into the waist. Then Maggie stood on tiptoe to fix his bow tie.

'I'm afraid your old brogues aren't going to work,' she told him. She rooted around the bottom of the wardrobe for the slip-ons with toggles that he had worn at their wedding, eventually dragging them out and giving them a quick polish with one of Charlie's wet wipes.

Jack sat on the bed to put the shoes on. They were a very tight fit, which is why he had not worn them for years, but Maggie was right that they looked better with the trousers than the brogues. Jack looked at himself in the long wardrobe mirror and then turned to Maggie for her opinion.

'I forget how handsome you are, Jack Warr. You look amazing.' She began to hum the James Bond theme, but it faded quickly as she thought about where he was going and the dangerous game he was playing.

Jack checked that he had the burner phone, as well as his own mobile. He had the invitation in his jacket pocket and a wallet without any Met documents or insignia. At five thirty, it was time for him to leave. He kissed Maggie and was opening the front door just as Penny came out of the kitchen. 'My God, you look amazing! Where are you going?'

'Met function,' Jack lied. 'No wives unfortunately.'

'You should have a long white scarf to finish the look, darling. I've got one in my room if you want me to fetch it?'

'No, I've got to go, Mum. Don't want to be late.' He walked out, closing the door quietly as Maggie joined Penny in the hall.

'Doesn't he look handsome,' Penny beamed. 'You'd better hope it's men only, Maggie dear. If any ladies see him dressed like that, they'll be after him straightaway.' Maggie laughed, then remembered they had left the light on in Jack's office so went back upstairs to turn it off.

She rarely, if ever, spent time in there and certainly not alone, but now she glanced over his untidy desk with all his notes and photos cut out of magazines. She began to tidy them up, then, intrigued, sat down in his desk chair and started flicking through them. She stopped with a frown. Jack had written 'reference to dealer' and then scribbled 'Jo Ogden and partner', which was then crossed out.

Maggie was sure she had heard the name, maybe a famous pianist? But she wasn't certain. She put the notebook into the envelope with the rest of the notes and then into a drawer. She was about to use Jack's computer but wasn't certain what the password was, so she turned off his desk lamp and then the room light before going into their bedroom. But she couldn't stop thinking about it so went to her briefcase and took out her laptop.

Sitting on the bed, she Googled Jo Ogden, and was pleased to find she'd been right. There was a famous pianist called John – not Jo, as Jack had written – Ogden, who died in 1987. She skimmed through the details of his life and brilliant career, a self-taught prodigy who had been overwhelmed with the burden of genius and could not cope with everyday life.

Maggie then looked for an artist with a similar name and was taken aback when up came Joe Orton, a playwright born in 1933, who was bludgeoned to death by his live-in partner, a failed artist called Kenneth Halliwell. She started delving deeper and the more she read of the relationship between Orton and Halliwell, the more anxious she became. They appeared to have had a tortuous homosexual relationship that broke down when Orton became successful. Halliwell's failure as an artist drove him into a jealous rage, battering Orton's head nine times with a hammer. Maggie took a deep breath, trying to think exactly how Adam had phrased his description of his dealer. Did he sound like Orton?

She rang Jack's mobile. 'Has something happened?' he asked concerned. 'I'm almost at Bond Street.'

'Can you pull over, Jack? I need to talk to you . . . it's important.'

'For Chrissakes Mags, you know where I'm going. Can't it wait?'

'No, you have to pull over and listen to me.'

'Fuck's sake,' Jack murmured to himself. He drove on until he spotted a parking space in Berkeley Square and parked up. 'OK, this had better be good, Mags.'

'Jack, I need you to think back to when Adam said something derogatory about his dealer, and you made a note of it.'

'What are you talking about?'

'In your notes, you wrote down a name, Jo Ogden. I think you said that Adam had inferred his dealer was like him, or he and his partner were like them.'

Jack sighed, trying to piece together what she was asking him. 'As far as I can recall, it was after he'd had a call from his dealer putting pressure on him . . .'

'What did he say?'

'I'm trying to think, Maggie, what's so important about it?'

'You wrote down the wrong name, Jack. I think he was referring to a famous playwright named Joe Orton.'

'Maybe I did. I honestly can't remember it clearly. I still don't understand what the big deal is.'

'Joe Orton's partner was an artist called Kenneth Halliwell. Orton became hugely successful as a playwright, but his partner, the artist – he did collages with bits of paper and cut out stuff from magazines – anyway, he was not successful, and he became consumed with jealousy.' She heard him give an impatient sigh. 'Jack, Orton was hammered to death by his boyfriend. He tried to disfigure him with nine hammer blows to his head.'

In the blink of an eye, Jack understood the connection. 'Was this recent?'

'No, years ago, late sixties, he was only thirty-four. Halliwell committed suicide. Listen, Jack, if someone in the art world referred to someone else's relationship as being like Orton and his partner...'

'I don't know if this Detmar guy is gay, dead or alive, or even if he has an artist for a boyfriend.'

'What about Adam?'

'What?'

'You don't know him, Jack, I just thought you should know what I've found out. Think what he has told you, even that German woman said he'd threatened to crucify someone. Please be careful.'

He closed his eyes and took a deep breath. 'You're right, Maggie, thank you. Now I've got to go. I don't want to be late.' Jack sat in the car thinking over everything she had just told him. Something started to kick into gear inside him. He knew that compared to Adam he had a pitiful knowledge of the art world, and Adam had probably enjoyed dropping intellectual clues like the Orton reference for his amusement. Jack felt suddenly angry that he'd been so worried when he thought Adam might have been the crucified victim.

Jack waited until he was back in control of his emotions, then drove to the venue on Bond Street. Parking up, he had a good view of the gallery: four storeys, the windows brightly lit, a red carpet from the pavement to the glass double doors and a uniformed doorman standing to attention as the guests arrived. Rolls Royces, Mercedes and even a stretch limo drew up as Jack watched glamorous women and elegantly dressed men entering the gallery. He hid the family car down a side street, then hesitated only a few moments before heading across the road and entering through the gallery's gleaming glass doors.

CHAPTER 25

'Welcome to the gallery. May I have your name please, Sir?' The smartly dressed young woman on the desk in the reception area smiled warmly at Jack.

Jack waved his invitation as if insulted. 'Sotheby's, you should recognise me by now,' he said curtly.

She gave an embarrassed, apologetic nod as Jack picked up one of the leaflets from the desk and walked towards the first open doorway, picking up a glass of champagne from a tall young man holding a tray along the way.

The walls were adorned with large oil paintings from what Jack guessed was the eighteenth century, depicting women in full satin gowns and men in white powdered wigs.

More guests were arriving as Jack made his way to a corner to read the leaflet. The gallery had three open floors: the third floor would feature the exhibition of a new artist's work, and Detmar Steinburg would introduce the artist at eight o'clock. The fourth floor contained the private offices.

Jack walked out and noticed two men, who were not in evening suits, standing in opposite corners of the room. He assumed they were security guards. As he approached the wide staircase, he saw a glass-sided lift with a sign that read: 'Gate opens outward'. Jack stepped into the lift and got out on the second floor. The walls here were adorned with more modern paintings, and two men were examining them closely while referring to a catalogue. Another security guard in a suit was standing to one side.

After wandering around for a while, Jack managed to slip past the security guard while a group of people arrived at the same time.

He took the lift again, this time exiting on the third floor. There was no one stationed at the entrance to this part of the gallery, but a chain was attached to the long door handles. He was able to inch them open a little giving him a reasonably good view of the room. He was surprised to see that all the canvases were draped with muslin sheets and were on easels rather than hanging on the walls. At one end of the room, there was a small, raised platform with a microphone and a jug of water with a glass next to it. He guessed that this had to be the exhibition area, and Detmar would be introducing the artist from the platform.

He took the stairs to the next floor. There was a sign that read, 'Private: No Admittance', and all four doors were closed. Each door bore a small plaque indicating that it was a private office, a staff bathroom and toilet or a sales department. At this point, Jack was beginning to think he had been mistaken about Detmar, as it seemed that Detmar was definitely expected to open the exhibition.

He moved across the landing to the door at the end. Although it appeared to have some kind of digital lock requiring a code to enter, when he turned the handle, it opened. He quickly slipped inside, leaving it partly open, so he wasn't locking himself in. One window overlooking the rear of the gallery had the blinds partly open, giving the room a yellowish glow.

Although the light was dim, as he moved further into the room he could see an array of crates. These were stacked against one wall beside two large sacks. One crate, narrower and longer than the rest, was open and Jack saw it was filled with straw. Jack got down on his knees and pulled away the straw until he could feel the frame of a painting. Pushing aside the protective muslin covering, he could now see the edge of an oil painting, just making out a bejewelled woman's wig and part of her brow. He recognised it immediately as *Lady with a Fan* which he'd first seen at the abandoned school with Adam. He took out his phone and began to film.

He straightened up, dusting down his trousers, and turned his attention to the wall. It was covered in laminated sheets detailing storage units, shipments, dock numbers, drop-off points, customs and the different paperwork required for European ports: France, Amsterdam, Italy. One laminated sheet detailed shipments from Berlin, expected times and collection points, another had a list of Japanese customs regulations. Jack felt his heart rate increasing. This floor, this room, was clearly the heart of the operation.

Jack had started to take pictures of more canvases ready to be packed, making certain to get close-ups of the descriptions and destinations, when he heard raised voices. He listened at the door, unsure where the voices were coming from, then edged out onto the empty landing. As the voices got louder, he realised they were coming from the office. Jack barely made it into the staff bathroom before the door to the office opened.

'I am very concerned, Kurt. We were expecting him yesterday. I still have not received a text or return phone call – we should have cancelled.'

'This is my show, you understand me. He isn't here, so I am taking over and you can do nothing about it.'

'Oh, I can, Kurt, because you're drugged out of your head, as usual. You have not allowed any of the staff to organise the showing, let alone even see what we are exhibiting. I have worked here for ten years, and he has never allowed anyone else to take control of a gallery showing before. Have you any idea how many years of hard work it has taken to have these buyers and dealers here? It's his reputation that I am worried about.'

'This is my life, Ester, mine, not yours . . . you can go fuck yourself because he would never put his cock up your frozen cunt.'

'I am not taking that from you! *I've* been organising these events alongside Detmar. *Me*. Not to be allowed onto floor three is ridiculous. You've had it locked and barred – why?'

'If you don't like it, you know what you can do. Get the hell out! This is my night, and I am warning you not to interfere.'

Jack eased open the bathroom door and waited for the man she had called Kurt to come into his eyeline. As soon as he saw him, he recognised him as the black man he had seen coming out of the framer's shop. He was wearing a long, flamboyant white gown with embroidery and beads around the neck and sleeves.

The woman called Ester was shaking in fear and frustration. 'I am going to call him again right now. Believe me, he won't approve of this because I know exactly how he feels about your endeavours. He would never even contemplate giving you an entire exhibition. I will tell him . . .'

Jack tensed up as Kurt reached out and grabbed her throat, stopping her in mid-flow. He was a big man, and he shook her like a rag doll. 'Don't make me hurt you, Ester. Just stay out of it, or you will regret it.'

He pushed her hard against the open office door and her head cracked against the wood panel. She looked terrified as he calmly backed away, heading towards the stairs. Jack shut the door so Kurt wouldn't see him, then had to quickly go into one of the toilet cubicles as the door opened.

Ester came into the bathroom, bleeding from a cut on the side of her head. She was sobbing as she splashed cold water over her face and then soaked a wad of paper tissues to stem the blood. Jack slowly pushed open the toilet door. She could see him in the mirror and looked as if she was about to scream.

'Ester, don't, please don't. I'm here to help you. Take a deep breath, come on, breathe, that's it. Now sit down for a minute.' She had the tissues clamped to her head, staring at him fearfully. Jack helped her sit on a small gilt-backed chair with a velvet cushion. Dressed in a white silk blouse and tight black skirt, she had high cheekbones, dark brown eyes framed by thick eyelashes and her jet-black hair was pulled back from her face and coiled in an elaborate knot at the nape of her neck.

'I am looking for Detmar, it's urgent. I really need you to tell me what is going on and if you know where he is.'

'But why do you want to know this?'

'I'm a private investigator,' Jack lied.

She looked at him dubiously, then started to cry. 'No one knows where Detmar is,' she said. 'I've been trying to contact him for days. He was in Germany on business, due back over a week ago. He has galleries all over the world. None of them know where he is.'

'Tell me about Kurt?'

'He's Detmar's partner, although they have a very volatile relationship and lately he has been very difficult to handle. Detmar always leads these events, but without him here, Kurt has been running the gallery.'

Jack helped Ester to her feet and she led him into the office, an elegantly panelled room with an antique desk and numerous filing cabinets, along with a computer with a wide screen and a shredding machine beside the desk. She sat at the desk, powered up the computer and showed him all the texts, messages and calls she had made trying to trace Detmar.

'Can you tell me about Detmar's other business?' Jack asked carefully.

She looked confused. 'I don't understand what other business you are referring to.'

'Tell me about Kurt, then. Are they business partners? How is he involved with the galleries?'

'He's an artist. They have been together for years, but you know Detmar can be very promiscuous, and it infuriates Kurt. I think he is envious of his success, too, and he is often here arguing with him because he won't promote his artworks.'

'So, they live together?'

'Yes. Detmar keeps him in luxuries. They have houses all over the world, and Kurt wants for nothing.'

'Do you know an artist called Adam Border?'

There was not so much as a flicker of recognition. 'No, but I never deal directly with artists really. I handle the running of the galleries. My contact on the US and European side is always through someone equivalent to me.'

'What about shipping paintings around the world?'

'That is handled by Detmar, and he has numerous assistants to handle collections.'

Ester had gradually regained her composure, opening her handbag to remove her compact and check her face. Now that the blood had stopped and her face was clean, she could see that the cut on her temple was only small. She began using a powder compact to conceal the injury. Jack watched, pacing, as she put on fresh lipstick. If she knew about the forgeries, she was good at hiding it, Jack thought. She seemed to instinctively trust him, perhaps because she was in shock after Kurt had attacked her. But he was unsure whether he could trust her.

'I should go down to check on the guests,' she said, snapping the lipstick cover back on and putting it back in her handbag. 'Do I look OK?'

'I think you should be very careful after what just happened to you,' Jack said.

She pursed her freshly painted lips. 'I will be all right. Thank you.'

Almost as an afterthought, as Jack was about to follow her out, he asked, 'Do you know a Helga Meirling?' The question seemed to take her by surprise, and this time she reacted to the name. Jack quickly blocked her exit. 'How do you know her?' he persisted.

Ester sighed. 'She is a very wealthy client. I believe Detmar arranged a rental property for her'.

'Was that in Haslemere?'

She reacted again, just a slight flicker of her eyes. 'I am not sure. It was a private transaction. Ah, I suppose Helga must be the one who hired you then?'

Jack didn't deny it. 'If you know Helga, you must know Adam Border.'

'I have never heard of him. The reason I am aware of Helga Meirling is not because Detmar leased some property for her, it's because she recently contacted me about a cheque that she had been expecting from Detmar.'

'So, they are close friends?'

'I don't think so. She is a client who makes a lot of introductions.'

'How much was the cheque for?'

Ester hesitated, returned to the desk, opened a drawer and took out an expensive-looking black leather diary. She searched through it, then closed the diary before unlocking another small drawer to take out a large chequebook with the name of a private bank emblazoned on it.

'Three days ago. It was for a hundred thousand pounds. I told her that there must be some mistake and that I would tell Detmar to send a banker's draft instead. If you are working for her, you know she is a very astute businesswoman. He pays her on a regular basis.'

Jack sighed. The more he learnt, the less he felt he really understood. They left the office together as the sounds of the guests from below drifted up. Ester went to the lift, but Jack raised a hand.

'I'm not going in that thing again. I'll walk down.'

'It is an unusual lift, I suppose, to the layman. You see the gate has to open outwards for when we move the artwork in crates between floors. There is more room inside the lift and the crates cannot be damaged by the doors closing on them. But walk if you insist.'

She stepped back as the door opened, then entered the lift, while he went towards the stairs, watching it pass him. After a moment, he went back up the stairs and into the office again. He sat at the desk, picked up a silver letter opener in the shape of a dagger and broke open a small, locked drawer. The drawer was filled with chequebooks from different banks. Flipping through them, he found cheque stubs for hundreds of thousands of pounds in various currencies. The writing was neat and elegant. Next, he took out a diary and read through the most recent entries made in the same elegant handwriting.

The diary was filled with appointments ranging from hair stylists and manicurists to dental and fitness trainers, as well as bookings for lunch and dinners at top restaurants. Some names were underlined in red, and there were also notes about purchase dates and deliveries. Yet again he switched on his phone, filming as much of the contents as he could.

The diary's most recent pages were almost empty. Across each day, there was a note stating that Detmar was unavailable, along with contact numbers for him in France and Germany. There was also a sheet that appeared to be a list of large financial transactions and deposits in the Cayman Islands.

Jack put the diary back where he found it. He searched the other two drawers but found nothing of interest. Unable to open the locked filing cabinets, he decided to return to the gallery. As he turned towards the door, he noticed a faint scrape mark on the wooden floor next to the panelled wall. This immediately suggested that one of the panels was actually a door which dragged on the floor as it opened. After some exploration, he discovered a concealed lever on the wall. He pushed it and the hidden door clicked open.

As it closed behind him, his eyes adjusted to the darkness. He felt a thick carpet beneath his feet. Jack edged further into the room, arms outstretched for safety, and stopped when a small night light on the skirting board illuminated, obviously triggered by his movement. Its light revealed the room's contents. There was a carved single bed, with satin duvet covers and matching pillows, and two antique cabinets on either side. On the bed was a pinstriped navy suit, a crumpled shirt and suede shoes. He walked round the bed opened a wardrobe filled with high-end shirts, suits and shoes. Many items of clothing had Detmar's initials.

Beside the built-in wardrobe was another door, leading into a luxuriously appointed marble bathroom. He found a light switch as the night lights went out in the bedroom. Opening the cabinets, he found rows of vitamins alongside prescription drugs, sleeping tablets, Viagra and, in a small plastic bag with a silver spoon, a white powder he assumed to be cocaine. Hypodermic needles were still in their packages, and he thought one small dark brown glass jar could contain heroin. The second cabinet contained bottles of cologne and body creams, plus a silver-backed hairbrush and matching silver-edged comb.

Inspecting the hairbrush, he found a few long strands of hair caught between the bristles, also a number still attached to the comb. He took some sheets of toilet paper and folded some of the hairs inside, then put them in his pocket. Looking down at the wastebin, he saw that beneath crumpled tissues and used hypodermic needles was an empty leather case. Jack recognised it immediately and knew it had contained a G18 Glock 9 mm automatic. He straightened up fast as he heard Ester's voice, quickly turning off the light and stepping back into the dark bedroom area. He stood motionless against the wall so as not to activate the sensor lights and felt for the silver paper knife he'd taken from the desk.

Ester was shouting. 'You are insane! I don't know how the hell you got in here! I don't believe you! Get out or I will get the police to remove you.' Although Jack recognised Ester's voice, and he assumed the other person was Kurt, until he too started shouting.

'I want the money he promised me, or never mind you calling them, I will go to the fucking police myself. They've questioned me already, and I've kept my mouth shut, but they are now looking into the shipment at Southampton . . . you want to know what crazy is? I've got his bloody clothes. He slaughtered him like the mad dog he is and, yes, I never got rid of his clothes. So, if that bastard doesn't pay up tonight, I'll take them to the cops.'

Jack recognised the voice as O'Reilly's.

Ester sounded utterly confused. 'I don't know what you're talking about. I know nothing about any shipment at Southampton, and what clothes are you talking about? Who is dead?'

'Don't play the fucking innocent with me, you two-faced bitch. You're in it up to your fucking eyeballs. I go down, I'll make sure you go down with me.'

'I don't want any trouble, please let me talk to him for you. Detmar will pay you whatever he owes you. *Let go of me!*'

'He's fucking dead, you stupid bitch! He nailed him up!'

As Ester started screaming, Jack ran across to the hidden door, kicking it open to reveal Ester, curled up and terrified, with O'Reilly punching her. O'Reilly spun, leaving Ester and lunging at Jack. Jack parried a haymaker and went to stab him with the paper knife, but O'Reilly quickly headbutted him and the knife clattered to the floor as Jack fell to his knees then onto his back. O'Reilly made to kick him in the head, but Jack brought his foot up and kicked as hard he could between the legs. Screaming in agony, O'Reilly hunched over clutching his balls, but he still didn't crumple. Instead, O'Reilly ran out before Jack could stagger to his feet.

He had to hold onto the edge of the desk for a second to get his breath. Ester was hysterical. 'I don't know who that creature is . . . he somehow got into the second floor, threatening me and dragging me up here. He says Kurt owes him money . . .'

Jack was on his mobile, holding up his hand for her to stop talking. 'Just stay calm, go down and get your security guys lined up, but do it quietly, don't sound any alarms, say you want them on floor three and wait for instructions. And get as many of the guests out as you can.'

'I don't know what to say to them, what do I do?'

Jack gripped her by her elbow, shoving her towards the door. 'Get down there and do as I tell you. All the security guards to floor three. *Do it!*'

Jack's call was connected to the Fulham police station control room. 'This is an urgent call. I need to talk to DI Collingwood. I have information about the crucifixion case. *Yes*, you heard correctly. DI Collingwood. Transfer me to his mobile.'

DI Collingwood had just got home and was parking his car after another long, frustrating day. Recognising the station number, he answered immediately. 'DI Collingwood.'

'I don't have long, it's Jack Warr.'

Collingwood listened as Jack told him that he was about to make his career go up several notches. 'You need to get a team together, pronto.'

Collingwood perched on the hood of his car with his phone to his ear, hardly able to believe what he was hearing as Jack told him he had the identities of their victim and the perpetrator and if Collingwood moved fast, he could make an arrest. He gave him the address of the gallery and said that he would detain the suspect until backup arrived. He also instructed the now shaken Collingwood to get a search warrant for Norman O'Reilly's home where they would find their victim's clothes.

'Hang on, Jack, let me contact Morrison first as he's the SIO . . .'

'Fuck him. Just move as fast as you can. It won't be long before things kick off here.'

Collingwood leapt back into his car and was straight on the speaker phone as he reversed out of his drive, barking instructions to the Fulham station incident room as the adrenalin started surging through him. He slapped on the siren and tore his way through the Saturday night traffic.

CHAPTER 26

After making his phone call to Collingwood, Jack found Ester on the stairs crying. He pulled her to her feet. Time was against them and he needed her to listen. She still seemed badly shaken.

'He was saying I'm involved but I'm not, I'm not. I don't understand.'

Jack put his hands on her shoulders, making her listen to him. 'Don't play any more games with me. Your boss is dead. You need to salvage what you can from this, because you will need protection.'

'Why would I need protection? He's not dead. He's not.'

'Listen to me, Detmar's dead. Take that in, Ester, he's dead. Now go and do what I asked you because time is running out.'

'Stop shouting at me! I can't take any of this in.'

'You better had, because any minute now Kurt will be getting people into the floor three gallery, and Christ only knows his intentions. Do you know if any of the security team are armed?'

'I don't think so. I don't know.'

'Go now. Do what I told you. I will be right behind you.'

Ester took several deep breaths, wiped away her tears and then nodded, before heading down to the ground floor to speak to the security men.

Jack found the doorman and took him to one side, explaining that he was with the Met police, and that when a team of officers arrived he was to direct them to the third floor.

'Has some bugger stolen one of the artworks?' he asked.

'More serious than that, I'm afraid. Just keep the entrance clear.'

Returning to the reception, Jack passed a few of the guests on their way out, some loudly complaining about their evening having been curtailed. They were not impressed with having half-full champagne flutes taken from their hands and being ushered out without explanation. Jack headed up to the second floor to find Ester standing by the entrance.

'I've got the two security men from here up on the third floor, but there's a lot of guests and I can't talk to them all discreetly. What about sounding the fire alarm?'

They both stopped in their tracks as they heard the taped announcement. 'Ladies, Gentlemen, honoured guests, please make your way to the third-floor gallery as the exhibition is about to begin. Detmar's protégé and partner Kurt Neilson will present his groundbreaking works using oils, acrylic and collages that have never been displayed before this evening.'

'I don't believe this!' Ester barked, her face contorted with fury as her hands clenched into fists. 'Kurt is a pathetic amateur with no talent whatsoever, and his sexual obsession with Detmar is sickening, I can't believe that he would have the guts to harm him. *This is his only way of hurting him because Detmar has genuine talent for discovering great young artists, promoting and exhibiting their work . . .'*

Jack gripped her by her shoulders. 'We don't have time to list all Detmar's bloody virtues. If you can't control yourself, you'll create panic . . .'

She hunched up, bowing her head, her voice muffled as she pressed herself against him. 'I don't know what to do. Please help me.'

Jack took her face in his hands, his voice calm. 'There was a gun in the bedroom upstairs, Ester. Look at me, do you know if Kurt has taken it?'

'I don't know, I don't know. He was in there; he was in there earlier.'

Jack gestured to the young woman who had been passing out cloakroom tickets. She looked very confused at so many guests leaving. 'Take care of her, get her a brandy or something.' Before she could ask why, he barked, 'Just do it!'

Jack moved to the stairs, looking upwards to the remaining guests casually making their way to the third-floor gallery. He saw the glass-walled lift door opening and recognised the long blond braided hair, tonight worn with silk ribbons and a long backless dress, stepping into it. Jack darted forward to grab the door before it closed. Helga looked shocked for a moment before pressing her back against the glass wall as he jabbed at the button to stop the lift.

'You need to get out, and fast,' Jack told her. 'Detmar is dead, and any connection you have with him or this gallery will get you arrested and charged with forgery.'

Helga showed little reaction, so he moved closer to her. 'I know more about you now, Helga, and if you want to save Adam Border from being brought into this, don't lie to me anymore.'

'I don't believe you. Detmar owes me a lot of money.'

Jack pressed the button to open the gate, grabbed her by her shoulder and shoved her out; she even tried to hang onto his jacket before he gave another hard shove and she stumbled backwards as he pressed for the lift door to close. As the lift moved upwards, Helga was approached by one of the security guards encouraging her to leave. This time she didn't hesitate, hurrying out and hailing a passing taxi without even collecting her wrap from the cloakroom.

By the time Jack got out on the third floor, the double doors to the gallery were wide open and the guests were filing up the stairs. Two security guards were in position as Jack approached. He told them to stop anyone from going inside; there was a fire and they needed to leave the building. There were some very disgruntled and argumentative guests as Jack walked past them to go into the gallery and shut the double doors behind him. The platform was empty but at least twenty people were standing around the draped easels in some confusion. Then through a door at the back of the room, Kurt Neilson swept in, stepping onto the platform and opening his arms wide.

'Welcome. I am Kurt Neilson.' He squinted critically at the meagre crowd in front of him but continued regardless. 'You have been invited to see my first and only exhibition. I am very proud to show you the results of my creative endeavours, many works in oils and acrylic, as well as collages.' The crowd might have been sparse, but there was a palpable sense of anticipation in the room, the excitement of art collectors about to get in on the ground floor.

Kurt stepped down from the platform to remove the drape from his first painting. Everyone moved closer. It was a portrait of a woman; her hair had been styled with hundreds of tiny seashells, and in her arms was a small piglet, which she was suckling. He withdrew a drape from a second painting, and this one created more of a murmur. It was a mermaid, her webbed tail and fin covered in pieces of tin foil. Her blond hair was brilliant yellow seaweed, and out of her wide-lipped mouth emerged a fish with a phallic tail.

The astonished guests began whispering, even sniggering, as Jack eased his way around the room. He kept his eyes on Kurt, but he could see no obvious weapon. Jack noted that the two security men were now inside.

Kurt started laughing, then pivoted to the third canvas. Someone said loudly that they had seen enough and this made everyone laugh. Kurt stopped in his tracks, his face twisted with disbelief.

'You have not seen my best work. I was keeping it for the end. But I will quickly show you some of my most recent pieces first.' The third painting was of a red brick building with dolls' faces smeared with makeup at the windows. People began to walk out. Now Kurt was really becoming agitated, swirling around in his robe, his face glistening with sweat as he screamed,

'Wait! I have saved the best for last.' There was laughter around the room. 'You two-faced condescending . . . *Look!* This is my masterwork: my beloved mentor Detmar Steinburg, Ladies and Gentlemen.'

Kurt had to jump up to unhook the drape from the top of the six-foot canvas. As soon as it was revealed, the laughter instantly stopped, to be replaced with gasps of horror. The figure was crudely painted, his crossed ankles and outstretched hands nailed to the cross with silver bolts. Naked and with deep knife wounds gushing blood, the most appalling part was the head. The figure's long hair hung loosely to the shoulders but couldn't disguise the destroyed face, with blood spurting from empty eye sockets, the nose flattened to a pulp and the mouth a mass of broken teeth.

Jack gestured as unobtrusively as possible for the two security guards to move closer. They were now standing on either side of the painting, and Jack was easing into position behind it. After the initial shock, people began to find their voices and they were all angry. There were shouts of 'Rubbish!', 'Disgusting!' and 'Sickening!' Some of the guests were using their mobiles to take photographs, as others made for the doors to get away from the terrible sight as quickly as they could.

Jack saw Kurt reaching into one of the kaftan's deep pockets and shouted out for the security guards to grab him. But, in that instant, Jack knew Kurt would get to the gun first. As he hurled his body at Kurt, he could see the silver Glock pistol butt. Jack knocked him sideways as the two security guards grabbed an arm each. Kurt was kicking and writhing, but the three of them managed to hold him down while Jack wrenched the Glock from his hands and pushed it out of reach.

They flipped Kurt onto his front so that the security guards could cuff him, allowing Jack to retrieve the weapon and flick the safety catch on.

'Shoot me! Go on!' Kurt screamed, as Jack grabbed one of the cords that had been holding the painting's drapes to tie Kurt's feet.

Jack turned to the stunned guests. 'You all need to exit the gallery – *now*!' Only then did he hear the police sirens wailing, but it was still a few minutes before DI Collingwood and three uniformed officers burst into the room.

Collingwood had done his best in the time he had but had only brought six officers. Three were downstairs in the reception area as the guests were all pushing to leave. It was pandemonium, with screams and shouts from those who had witnessed the horrific unveiling. Eventually Collingwood gave instructions for everyone to remain in the main gallery until he had taken their statements.

Jack remained with the two security guards standing over the hysterical Kurt, his hands and feet now restrained, but still twisting his body back and forth like a captured animal, until Collingwood instructed his officers to take him into custody. They replaced the cord with leg straps before dragging Kurt to his feet, ready to bundle him into the waiting patrol car, while he continued swearing, spitting and trying to bite them. As they pulled a spit hood down over his face, Kurt turned his venom onto Jack, alternately snarling and sobbing while repeating over and over, 'Kill Me! Kill me!'

Jack remained with Collingwood as he explained in more detail what had happened, handing him the hairs from the brush and comb for DNA analysis to verify that their victim was Detmar Steinburg.

Even if the painting made it obvious that Kurt Neilson had committed the murder, everything would still have to be proven beyond doubt. Collingwood was finding it difficult to take in everything Jack was saying. He made copious notes, while constantly taking deep breaths and wiping sweat from his palms.

'You have to arrest O'Reilly and search his address asap.'

'I'm still waiting for the warrant.' Collingwood saw Jack roll his eyes in disbelief. 'It's a Saturday evening, Jack. Trying to find a bloody magistrate is murder.'

Jack nodded. 'When you do get it, you'll find even more evidence in O'Reilly's house. And he was here tonight demanding money.'

'O'Reilly was here?'

'Yes, I won't waste your time with all the details now. But I am pretty certain he's the one who cleaned up the framer's shop and is also involved in Detmar's other business . . . the illegal sale of forged paintings.'

Collingwood took another deep breath. This case was getting stranger by the minute. 'Listen Jack, I have to ask you this, because it seems like you're right at the heart of it—'

Jack interjected. 'I was suspicious after seeing you all at the ICU. Don't forget bloody Morrison has been questioning me about being caught on CCTV at the murder site! I wasn't going to do nothing. I just started to put a few things together, but you take the kudos. Say it was an anonymous tip-off, because I'm out of here.'

'Jack, wait, you can't just walk away.'

'Yes I can. There's a woman here, Ester. She was Steinburg's personal assistant for a long time. She should be taken in for questioning. For Christ's sake Collingwood, don't waste any more time. She's loyal, so right now she'll be clearing out anything incriminating. She cries easily, but she's a good liar so don't be fooled. Detmar Steinburg was a very rich man. There's a hidden room off the office. You'll find it.'

Collingwood watched Jack walk away, wondering whether he should have allowed him to do so. But he had so much to deal with already, he really had no choice. First off, he needed to find O'Reilly. He would use the 'anonymous tip' angle and made a note to talk to whoever had received the call at the station, hoping it would not be traceable back to him. Collingwood had not felt such an adrenalin buzz before in his entire career. Now that his team had secured the gallery and the surrounding scene and were starting to take statements, he decided to go up to the fourth floor and find Steinburg's assistant. One of his officers was coming down as he headed up the stairs.

'Anyone up here?'

'Yes, Sir, woman in the office. She refused to come out; I was just coming down to get a female officer.'

Collingwood continued up to the fourth floor, recalling what Jack said about a hidden room. He did a quick check of the bathroom, toilets and secretaries' office before entering into the main office.

'Ester?'

She was taken aback, staring at him, standing by the shredding machine. He moved quickly towards her. 'I'm Detective Inspector Collingwood. Stop what you're doing.' Ester hit the stop button. 'Are you Ester?'

'Yes. I'm Ester Langton.'

'I'll need a statement from you, and I'll also need your passport.'

'I'm afraid I don't have it here. Why do you want it? I'm not involved.'

'This is a murder investigation, Miss Langton, and as you were Mr Steinburg's personal assistant, you most certainly are involved.

I just need to find out how.' As Collingwood reached out to take the bag from her, she stepped back.

'These are personal items and if you want them, I will need to see a warrant.'

'Miss Langton, I can arrest you.'

'For?'

He was becoming impatient with her now and reached behind him to remove the handcuffs from his back pocket.

'Ester Langton, I'm arresting you on suspicion of art fraud and . . .'

She took him by surprise by darting past him. He didn't bother to chase after her, he simply got on his radio with instructions to detain the woman legging it from the fourth floor.

Collingwood checked through the shredded papers, which appeared to be letters and there was a further stack ready to be shredded. He left everything in place to be collected by uniformed officers.

By the time he reached the ground floor, Ester was handcuffed and being led out. Her hair had fallen loose from the coil at the nape of her neck and now hung limply to her shoulders. Her eye makeup had run, making dark black circles around her eyes, and even her lipstick was smudged. The usually immaculate, controlling woman running the most prestigious gallery alongside the handsome Detmar Steinburg was a mess.

* * *

Jack stood in the shadows, watching as Ester was led to a police car in handcuffs and smiling to himself. He would have liked to see her try and cry her way out of being arrested.

He suddenly felt drained and couldn't wait to get home. He reckoned the shit would hit the fan at Fulham police station tonight and he hoped Collingwood would hold firm and keep his name out of it. The one moment he would have liked to witness was DCI Morrison's reaction when told by Collingwood that not only had their victim been identified but the killer was in custody.

By the time Jack returned home, he had to sit in his parked car for half an hour to calm himself down. It was after eleven and the house was in darkness, so he quietly let himself in, closing the front door without making a sound. He didn't even turn the kitchen lights on but remained in darkness as he poured himself a brandy. He sat at the table going over the entire night, as if watching a film; from the moment he had arrived at the gallery, to when he had finally left. He sighed, closing his eyes, questioning if he had done the right thing by walking away. If his involvement got out now, he'd be in serious trouble. Once again, he wondered if Adam Border had drawn him in, like a moth to a flame, and he was about to get badly burnt.

CHAPTER 27

Ester Langton sobbed hysterically during most of her interview with Collingwood. She admitted that she had been shredding private correspondence when he found her, desperate to avoid any further scandal, but claimed to know nothing about Steinburg's death.

'He had no family. We had worked together for ten years . . . I was the person closest to him,' she said, visibly upset.

Collingwood hesitated before asking his next question, knowing the horrific state of Steinburg's injuries. 'Would you be willing to identify him?'

'Yes,' she said without hesitation, then added. 'I want to do it now.'

'Interview suspended,' Collingwood said, turning the recorder off.

'Kurt killed him, didn't he?' Ester said, tight-lipped.

'We have reason to believe so,' Collingwood admitted. 'But he hasn't been interviewed yet. Thank you for agreeing to make the identification. There are some things I need to do first. Please bear with me.'

Collingwood left the interview room and rang the mortuary at St Thomas's Hospital. The night staff were not very cooperative, but at his insistence, they agreed to move the body to their viewing area despite the lateness of the hour. Ester's lawyer followed them in her car and Collingwood sat beside Ester in the patrol car, explaining it was likely to be a very disturbing experience. He hoped Ester would be able to make the identification without having to see his ruined face.

Ester held her lawyer's hand as they arrived at the mortuary and remained silent as they signed the necessary paperwork before being allowed through to the viewing room. There was one mortuary attendant, a young man with round glasses, who took a long time to find the switch for the lights. The body was lying on a gurney entirely covered by a white linen sheet. They stood to one side as the attendant removed the covering from Detmar's head before Collingwood could stop him.

They had done their best to disguise the injuries. His eyelids were sewn closed, as was his mouth, so his smashed and broken teeth could not be seen. His broken, flattened nose had been filled with wadding, but nothing could disguise the bruising and disfigurement.

'Is this Detmar Steinburg?' Collingwood asked quietly.

Ester cocked her head from side to side, leaning forwards and showing no emotion, taking a long time staring from one side to the other of the dead man.

'Can I see his left hand?'

The cloth was lifted. This time the assistant was careful not to show the wound where the iron nail had impaled his wrist, and Ester, for the first time, showed a reaction.

'He wore a large gold signet ring on his little finger.'

'That was not with his body,' Collingwood confirmed before asking her again if it was Detmar Steinburg. Ester looked at the battered face again. Her 'yes' was hardly audible as she turned and hurried out with her lawyer.

Collingwood had to walk briskly after them to the car park and only just managed to thank Ester for her cooperation before they drove out. Although he had done a few identification viewings, he had never experienced one where there was such a lack of visible emotion.

* * *

Jack had stopped drinking, but remained sitting in the darkness replaying the moment Kurt had drawn the gun. He guessed that Kurt had not intended to shoot him or any of the guests, and the entire scenario he had set up, with the damning evidence of the crucifixion depicting his guilt, was to climax with him committing suicide. The more he thought about it, the more anxious he felt. He knew there were CCTV cameras both outside and inside the gallery, and when the footage was checked, he would be on it. He also recalled seeing some of the guests using their mobile phones to take pictures and videos. He got up and started pacing round the kitchen. He realised he'd been foolish to think Collingwood would be able to keep him out of it even if he wanted to. It was just a matter of time before Morrison learnt of Jack's presence at the gallery and he needed to get ready for the inevitable questioning.

But what halfway plausible story could he come up with?

* * *

At that moment Morrison was giving Collingwood a fierce grilling, demanding to know why he hadn't been informed of the situation at the gallery. Collingwood explained that he'd tried to locate his DCI, but the urgency of the situation left him with no choice but to take charge himself.

'You did all this on the basis of an anonymous tip-off?'

'I did, Sir. I've tried to trace the caller, but they used a burner phone. The Fulham control room forwarded the caller to me. I felt I had no option but to take it seriously and thank God I did. I could only drum up six uniform officers with it being Saturday night, and I really felt the need to get to the gallery asap, Sir.'

Morrison looked sceptical. 'So how did you get the connection to O'Reilly?'

'He was seen leaving the gallery, Sir. I sent a team to arrest him, but he was not at his residence and we've still not tracked him down. We have a warrant to search his flat.'

'That still doesn't answer my question. How do you know that O'Reilly is involved in the murder, or was this anonymous caller also a psychic? We've had him in our sights from day one, but he has an alibi we haven't been able to break.' He was about to continue when Collingwood's mobile rang. Morrison paused, grinding his teeth, forced to listen to the one-sided call.

Collingwood spoke briefly to the caller and congratulated them before ending the call. 'That was DC Harrow, he's at O'Reilly's flat. He wasn't there, but they found a carrier bag stuffed full of bloodstained clothing in a dog kennel. Ester Langton identified the body, Sir. I also have an all-ports alert out for O'Reilly, so hopefully, we'll nab him soon.'

Morrison knew he had to step up fast and take over. He was about to suggest their priority was to issue a press release Collingwood continued.

'Another thing, Sir. We may need to involve the fraud squad.'

'What are you bloody talking about now?'

'Well, it's on the cards that Detmar Steinburg was involved in the sale of fake paintings.'

Morrison cracked his knuckles then leaned forward so Collingwood was forced to back away. 'As from this moment, I am taking over, and it will be my decision to bring in the fraud squad if necessary. Right now, we have to clear up last night's debacle before it gets splattered over the front pages. I want the gallery's CCTV footage, and I will put out a press release when requesting anyone present who has information or mobile footage to contact us immediately.' He shook his head. 'The media are going to be on this like a pack of dogs. If we don't tie things up quickly, we're going to be bloody crucified.'

* * *

Jack was on the sofa, having drunk too much brandy the night before. He was still in his evening suit and had a terrible hangover. Maggie brought him a mug of coffee. She had her hair in rollers and was wearing her dressing gown. He struggled to sit up.

'So how did James Bond do last night?'

'He did good, Mags, but your tip-off was brilliant . . . if you hadn't brought it up . . . Christ I've got one hell of a headache, didn't want to wake you when I got back.'

'So, were you right?'

'Yeah, the victim was Detmar Steinburg and . . . I really need something for my headache.'

'Tell me all about it later. Come up to the bedroom and I'll get you some painkillers, because you need to get ready for church.'

'Church? What are you talking about?'

'We have to go to the morning service. It's to do with Charlie's christening.'

Jack was aghast. 'You mean we all have to go?' He carefully stood up and followed her up the stairs and into the bedroom.

She explained as they went. 'You and I, and Penny, Hannah and Charlie are all going. The vicar has agreed to meet us after the service so we can discuss the christening. I mean, he was very pleasant, but we are obviously not regular churchgoers, so we are going to have to put in a few appearances before the christening.'

Maggie went into the bathroom and came out with a glass of water and a packet of paracetamol. Jack was now sitting on the bed, his bow tie hanging loose and his shirt unbuttoned. He decided not to elaborate on what had taken place at the gallery. Instead, he watched Maggie looking through her wardrobe.

She turned to him with a straw hat perched on her head. 'What about a hat? I want to make a good impression.'

'That looks like you're going to the beach. Haven't you got anything a bit more churchy? He went into the bathroom to get more water. 'What do you think I should wear?'

'Not jeans or that old leather jacket,' Maggie said firmly. 'I'd suggest the tweed jacket, your grey trousers and a white shirt, but you will have to get a move on. We need to leave at ten forty-five.'

It was fortunate that she had walked out of the bedroom then, so didn't hear him throwing up in the sink.

Half an hour later he had managed to straighten himself out. He had taken some Andrews Liver Salts, another three paracetamols, showered, shaved and put on one of his best suits. Although his head was still throbbing, he no longer felt nauseous; in fact, seeing the whole family gathered in the hall, he almost started to feel good.

Maggie was looking as stunning as ever, Penny was in her favourite felt hat with a turned-up brim. Hannah was in a smart new coat and her best patent leather shoes. Even Charlie was looking spiffy dressed in a new padded coat with a hood. Jack insisted on taking a snap of them grouped in the hallway on his mobile. 'My family,' he said with pride before Maggie had to check that he hadn't cropped their heads off. Jack then stood by Maggie's side and they all bunched up for a selfie.

At the church, they waited in the vestry after the morning service. The vicar was young and fresh-faced with thinning blond hair. He took them into a private room to discuss possible dates and what would happen at the christening. Maggie was not keen to have a group christening with other families. She wanted Charlie's day to be very special, with just their chosen godparents present and a few family friends. Through it all, Charlie behaved like a little angel, quietly sleeping; Hannah was not quite so well behaved, however, and was asked to sit still and be quiet a few times when she said she wanted to hold Charlie. Jack whispered to her that they would all go to McDonalds' afterwards if she behaved, which did the trick.

Forty-five minutes later, as they sat munching their burgers and fries, Maggie proposed that since they would all be going to Church more often before the christening, they could make this a routine. Hannah clapped her hands. 'Mother of God, that would be so good!'

Maggie warned Jack not to laugh. 'You can say grace next time we come,' he said, managing to keep a straight face.

'Who's Grace?' Hannah asked. 'Does she live in the church with that vicar man?'

Charlie had been well behaved, sucking on a chip, but now he became very restless and started crying, so Jack scooped him up in his arms and they all got ready to leave. As Jack carried his son back to the car, it began to feel like the calm before the storm.

CHAPTER 28

Jack was in his office surfing the internet for news coverage of the gallery incident when Maggie started shouting for him to come downstairs.

'It's the news,' she declared. 'It just started a second ago.'

'Christ, I thought something was wrong.' He moved to her side in front of their latest purchase, a wall-mounted TV. On screen, a senior Scotland Yard officer was standing with DCI Mark Morrison at a press conference. Jack just caught the last few moments as they announced that they had identified the framer's shop victim as the art dealer Detmar Steinburg. A suspect had been charged and was due before the magistrates' court, where he would be remanded in custody pending trial. DCI Morrison then said that anyone who had been at Steinburg's Bond Street gallery the previous evening should contact Fulham police station if they had any mobile phone footage that might assist in their enquiry.

The programme then continued with news of further rail strikes before Maggie turned the sound down. 'You haven't told me what happened there last night. Who's their suspect?'

'He was Steinburg's partner, Kurt Neilson, a real nutcase who'd taken over the gallery for a private showing of his own paintings. I have to say, if you saw it, you'd understand why it had never been exhibited before. It was all truly awful. But the last one was really sick ... he'd painted his lover on the cross.'

'What?'

'You've never seen anything like it. It caused pandemonium, and things got worse when he pulled a gun. I think he was about to shoot himself rather than anyone else. Anyway, he was arrested and carted out.'

'That call I made to you . . . let me get it up on my laptop because it's freaky.'

He hesitated before following Maggie out. 'I told you last night about how important it was, Mags. You hit the nail on the head. I'm sure I don't need to see it.' But Maggie wasn't going to be deterred.

Maggie had left her laptop on Jack's desk. She sat in his chair as she brought up the articles on Joe Orton, his murder and the suicide of his partner Kenneth Halliwell. Jack leaned in as she scrolled through one article after another, and then, on the screen, they saw Halliwell's paintings.

'Ironic, isn't it? Because of the murder, Halliwell's paintings have finally become worth buying, not that I think they're very nice.' Maggie turned off her laptop. 'You know something, Jack. You didn't watch the whole of *The Third Man*; and I know you were too tired to listen the last time I explained it to you. But the film is basically about a friendship. One man tries to trace his friend in Vienna after the Second World War and discovers he's now a criminal, involved in the drug trade, so he hunts him down, finally cornering him in the sewers.'

'And?' Jack said, getting up from the desk.

'Well, I have a theory. Adam actually describes Detmar Steinburg, or whatever his name is, as being in a similar relationship to Joe Orton. He was his dealer, wasn't he?'

Jack nodded, frowning.

'Mags, where are you going with this?'

'Let me just think this through. I asked if you thought Adam could have been involved in Steinburg's murder. Only then you weren't sure he was even the victim.'

'That's why I went to the gallery. To find out if Steinburg was alive. To be honest, until I saw the body in the ICU, I wasn't sure whether Adam was the victim.'

Maggie swung round in Jack's swivel chair and reached out to take his hand. 'You know something, Jack. I think Adam was warning you not to trust him, and at the same time, I think he was tipping you off . . . no, that's not the right word . . . giving you some insight into his dealer because he was already planning to leave him.'

'You could be right.'

'I think he cares for you too, Jack, in whatever blunted emotional way he can.'

He took her by the hands and drew her up to stand, wrapping his arms around her. 'Maybe,' he said dubiously. 'And I didn't tell you about Helga.'

'She was at the gallery trying to collect money she was owed, a hundred thousand quid . . . in fact, I told her to get out before the police arrived. According to Ester, she was a valued client, making introductions to rich collectors. She was obviously working for Steinburg . . . he even rented the property in Haslemere for her. She lied, of course, denying ever knowing him and swore she did not know where Adam was. She said vanishing was what he always did.'

Maggie shook her head. 'I think the further away you are from this entire situation, the better. You mustn't get roped in any more than you already have been.'

'Yeah, I know.' Jack tapped her laptop. 'And thank you for this. It's incredible that a woman as intelligent as you can be bothered with an ignorant prat like me.'

'I am bothered because I love you. And yes, you may be ignorant, but you're good, kind . . . and sexy as hell in that James Bond get-up you had on last night. I couldn't wait for you to come home.'

'When I did you were fast asleep.'
'I'm wide awake now, Detective Warr.'

* * *

Collingwood and Morrison were searching Steinburg's luxurious penthouse apartment overlooking the river by Chelsea Bridge. Two forensic officers were also present, moving from one exquisitely furnished room to another. Collingwood stood in the centre of a huge drawing room, where large portraits dominated the walls, while Persian rugs were scattered over a polished, wide-planked mahogany floor. Dominating the room was a white marble-topped coffee table stacked with design and art books, with a Murano glass bowl filled with fruit in the centre.

'How the other half lives,' Collingwood muttered as he wandered around the room. Morrison picked at his nose, looking around in distaste. 'This apartment block is mostly occupied by Russians. There's an underground car park with more flash motors in there than you'd get at a motor show, and I bet these paintings are all worth millions.'

Morrison walked out into the corridor and stood by the entrance to the kitchen, which was yet another designer showcase with floor-to-ceiling glass-fronted cabinets and a chrome double-doored fridge alongside a marble-topped island with four high stools.

'It's so clean, it looks as if no one uses it,' Collingwood said, opening a cupboard to see stacked tins of caviar. But Morrison had already walked out.

They next toured the two bedrooms, and again, the decor was extraordinary, with the draped floor-to-ceiling velvet curtain matching the ornate bed canopy. More paintings were hanging on the walls, and when they opened the wardrobe doors, the array of garments was like a high-end gentlemen's outfitters. Opening the bedside drawers, they found an array of drugs and, to Morrison's obvious disgust, a variety of sex toys including enormous strap-on dildos.

They found more drugs in the white marble bathroom en suite. One cabinet was filled with hair treatments and shampoos. Morrison held up a hairpiece, grinning. 'This is called a spider, I think. Imagine all this money, and he's freaked out about going bald.'

Collingwood was too tired to laugh. He had only managed a couple of hours sleep at the station before starting again early that morning.

The forensic officers, wearing white protective suits, were working in Detmar Steinburg's office when Collingwood and Morrison joined them. Like the rest of the apartment, it was beautifully furnished with an antique desk and wall-to-wall cabinets. A large wall safe had been revealed behind a large oil painting. The officers had emptied the drawers of the desk, and numerous documents were already bagged and tagged, ready to be examined at the station.

'Can you open the safe?' Morrison asked.

'Still working on it,' one of the SOCOs told him.

Morrison followed Collingwood into the one room they had not yet looked through. This, they quickly ascertained, was Kurt Neilson's. Although it had been fashionably decorated, it was dominated by his hideous paintings and collages, along with an easel and boxes of paints and brushes. The fitted carpet was covered in paint stains, and numerous half-squeezed tubes of oil paint littered the floor.

Collingwood searched around the bed, wrinkling his nose in distaste at the smell of urine and the dark stains. Beside it was a leather overnight case. Collingwood gestured to Morrison as he lifted it onto the bed and got a wave of musky perfume as he opened it. He carefully removed two silk monogrammed cream shirts, underwear, socks, folded grey cashmere trousers and a white silk-lined jacket. In a small leather zipped case was cologne, shaving equipment, a brush and a comb.

'These have to be Steinburg's,' Collingwood said.

'Could be Kurt's ready-to-run case,' Morrison suggested.

'I doubt that, Sir. The shirts are monogrammed and too small for him. He's six feet four. Plus, they're too expensive for Kurt.'

Next, Collingwood unzipped the side panel and took out a passport in Detmar's name, plus Eurostar tickets for Paris, invitations to various formal events and a hotel booking at the Ritz, all dated days before the victim had been found.

'Ester Langton said she'd been trying to trace him for weeks, believing he was abroad. He never left London,' Collingwood said.

They were called back into the master bedroom as one of the techies had finally managed to open the safe. It was stuffed with cash: stacks of banknotes in various currencies, each secured with a banker's strip.

'How much do you reckon we're looking at?' Morrison asked.

'A few hundred thousand at least.' He sighed. 'I hope you're not going to ask me to count it. I need to go and get some sleep.'

Morrison patted him on the shoulder. 'That's what I was gonna say. You head off and I'll stay here until we get some more back-up.'

'Thank you, Sir.'

Collingwood knew he was too exhausted to drive. In the back of the squad car, he closed his eyes, but tired as he was, he doubted he would get much sleep. So far he'd kept his word to Jack Warr, but when Jack turned up on the CCTV footage from the gallery, Morrison would go mental. Jack had put him in a spot, and he had no idea how he was going to get out of it.

* * *

Jack and Maggie had just made some toasted sandwiches. They were both wearing dressing gowns after role-playing 'James Bond' in the bedroom. Maggie was still giggling at the memory of being called Miss Moneypenny in a terrible Scottish accent. Sex between them used to be hot, intense and full of passion, but as they got older it had become more relaxed. More loving. More fun.

Jack sipped his whisky, and Maggie hugged her mug of tea. She mentioned that she would need the car in the morning because she had an early start and wanted to take Hannah to school to give Penny a break.

Suddenly, Jack remembered that his burner phone was still in the car's glove compartment. He quickly got up. 'I'd better check if we need some petrol.' Before Maggie could point out he was still in his dressing gown, he had picked up the car keys and hurried out.

He missed Marius coming down with the tray from his TV dinner with Penny. 'I marked out the wall, Maggie, if you want to come and have a look. It'll mean we take out the dining room door, board it all up, and make the hall much bigger. We open an arch here in the kitchen. It's a supporting wall, so I'll need an RSJ, but it'll just be a couple of days, and we'll do it for mates' rates, of course.' Marius demonstrated where the arch would be, then they went out into the hall to look at the door to the dining room. 'It's easy to block it off. Brick up the hole, plaster over it. It'll really make the hallway bigger, and I could maybe put up a row of coat hooks.'

'I think it'll be perfect,' Maggie said. 'Which is good, because I've decided that when Charlie has his christening, instead of booking a restaurant, we can have a buffet here at the house. All I need to do is persuade Jack . . . you know what he's like.'

As Marius went to his van he saw Jack driving off down the road but thought nothing of it. A few minutes later, heading towards

Putney High Street, he was surprised to see saw Jack, in his dressing gown, leaning into a builder's skip. Marius thought of pulling over, but then decided against it as he guessed Jack might be embarrassed to be caught late-night tipping. He smiled, shaking his head. 'And him a cop'.

Jack smacked the burner phone hard against the side of the skip before it shattered. He then spread the pieces around the skip among broken window frames and general rubbish. Finally satisfied, he headed back home. He'd remembered to transfer all the photos and videos of the paintings in the back room at the gallery to his laptop, he'd just forgotten to get rid of the phone itself.

At the same time, three fire engines had finally got the fire at the Bond Street gallery under control. Ester Langton, wearing a hooded raincoat, stood on the opposite side of the road, watching a firefighter at the top of the turntable ladder pumping water through the smashed windows. The lower floors had mainly been untouched by the fire, while the two rooms on the top floor, where the fire had started, had been completely destroyed. But the water flooding down through the building was now destroying everything anyway.

Ester had remained calm, only becoming agitated when refused entry to the gallery. She closed her eyes, hoping she had already salvaged enough to finance her life without Detmar.

When Collingwood was woken at five in the morning by an irate Morrison, he immediately thought it was about Jack, but he quickly realised Morrison was ranting about a fire at the gallery.

'It's a fucking catastrophe. Get over there, Collingwood, and oversee the clean-up, check out the damage and get the CCTV footage. I'll meet you at the station.'

Morrison hung up before Collingwood could reply.

CHAPTER 29

Jack arrived at the station after a frustrating journey, as the tube had been delayed and the bus was not even running. The canteen was not that busy, so he grabbed a tray and was passing along the line when Laura walked in.

'Jack, can you grab me some brown toast? I'll get us coffee.'

He ordered two more rounds of brown toast before his order of scrambled eggs and bacon was served.

'Did you hear the news?' she asked excitedly as he sat down with the tray.

'It's been a busy weekend; we had to take the family to meet the vicar for Charlie's christening.'

'For goodness' sake, don't tell me you haven't seen it in this morning's papers.' Laura started spreading butter on her toast. 'DCI Morrison identified the victim, the one from Portobello Road that you were asking about; turns out he's a famous art dealer. And his boyfriend was arrested for the murder. It's all over the news this morning and Morrison was on TV yesterday speaking from Scotland Yard.'

'He must be creaming himself,' Jack smiled. 'That's a big arrest.'

'I know. And . . .' She rooted around in her bag. 'You'll probably get one as well.' Laura handed Jack a postcard. 'It's from Josh. He's retired to Florida.'

Jack looked at the postcard, turning it over to read Josh's message. This was the second thing in as many minutes Jack had to feign ignorance about.

'He deserves it. I owe him a lot.'

'So have you got a date for the christening?' she asked, munching her toast.

'A couple of months' time. Maybe there's a rehearsal too? We do one of those, don't we? I wasn't really listening. I guess you'll be at that. And we'll probably hire out a restaurant for a party afterwards. I think that's what Maggie has in mind.' Jack had eaten his large breakfast in the same time it had taken for Laura to eat her small one and he now had indigestion. He burped, apologised, then picked up his coffee. He really didn't want to talk about the Detmar Steinburg murder anymore.

'See you up there,' he said, moving off.

Laura picked up the bacon fat he had left and folded a slice of brown toast around it. She thought about Jack's interest in the man she now knew to be Detmar Steinburg. She knew something didn't quite add up, but then, hardly anything did if Jack Warr was involved.

In the incident room, Jack, along with several other officers, was soon dealing with social services and legal aid for two teenage boys they were holding, while knives found in their son's bedrooms were still being brought in by concerned parents. Each item had to be logged, dated and confiscated safely. Armani had been in DCI Clarke's office for forty minutes, and Jack assumed they were discussing the possible repercussions from the death of the teenage gang member who had been questioned and released.

Laura was assigned a burglary that had occurred at a local pub early on Sunday morning. Thieves had broken in and attempted to smash open the till but the pub had very good CCTV cameras and, as the pub closed at eleven, it was quite an easy process to forward the footage to the right point, as the alarm had been activated at 2.15 a.m.

It was late afternoon when Laura returned from the viewing room. By now, she had numerous photographs of the burglars which she was pinning up on the big noticeboard as Jack passed her desk on his way to the cells.

'Look at these, Jack. The two girls don't look over twelve or thirteen years old, and the boy can't be more than, what, fourteen?'

'I know who and where he is,' Jack said, pointing to the boy. Even with a black hoodie on, he recognised him as Jason Marks, aged 18. 'He was arrested for carrying a machete and is still down in the cells.'

'Bloody brilliant, thank you, does he have any previous?'

Jack smiled as he passed her the file. 'He's already lawyered up with the fragrant Sonia Billings. I'd get him brought up for more questioning.'

'Will do. You heard anything further about Morrison's arrest? Oh, I meant to tell you . . .' She leaned in close. 'After you left for the weekend, Cruella caught me in the loo, said she wanted a word. She almost pinned me up against the washbasin. Anyway, she said it was unethical for me to be at Fulham. I really saw red and told her it was none of her business, then she said she knew about my relationship with a married DCI.'

'What, Morrison?'

'Yeah. I was gobsmacked. Apparently, she found out before she dumped him. I'm regretting that quickie we had after the Italian. Never again, right? Always knew he was a shithead.' Laura took the file, giving Jack the thumbs-up. She went over to the probationary officer she had been working alongside, to get Jason Marks brought from the cells and into an interview room.

* * *

Fulham station was under siege from the press. Kurt Neilson had been charged with murder and taken to the magistrates' court.

After giving his name, age and address, he shouted that he was guilty and became hysterical, foaming at the mouth as he banged his handcuffed wrists against the dock until they were bleeding. He screamed out that he had crucified his lover, Detmar Steinburg, and babbled about needing to be punished. He was remanded in custody, but before he was taken to prison, a doctor was called to give him a sedative and check his injured wrists. The doctor recommended Kurt be kept under medical supervision in prison while awaiting trial as he was a suicide risk.

The press now had a name to go along with the image of Kurt being walked from the courthouse, hands cuffed, his head beneath a blanket. By the time Neilson arrived at the prison, they had tracked down his doctor via the prescriptions found in his bedroom. He told them Neilson suffered with severe anxiety and had been diagnosed as a paranoid schizophrenic with narcissistic traits for which he'd been on medication for several years. It was assumed he hadn't taken his meds for a while.

Neilson was taken to the prison's secure hospital facility, where he was put on 'suicide watch' in a single bare cell.

* * *

It was five o'clock and Jack was getting ready to head home as Laura returned from questioning Jason Marks, after arresting him on suspicion of the pub burglary. He had refused to name the two girls caught on CCTV, and his lawyer had asked for a break to discuss the situation with her client.

'It really pissed me off,' Laura said. 'I told her, you can clearly see it's him on CCTV smashing the fucking place up with a crowbar!'

Jack frowned, suddenly concerned by the ease with which he had identified Jason Marks from the pub's CCTV footage. He was certain that Fulham would contact him any day now and he still hadn't thought up a plausible reason for being at the gallery. He had a quick look around before Googling the latest news. The first article he saw had the headline: 'Murdered Art Dealer's Gallery Ablaze'.

'Bloody hell,' he muttered. Jack could hardly believe it! Not that the article was very informative, just that the fire had started on the top floor and the damage was extensive, with dozens of valuable paintings destroyed. He leaned back in his chair reading on. There was no mention of how the fire had started or even whether it was suspected arson.

* * *

The situation at Fulham after Neilson's uncontrollable behaviour at the magistrates' court had, as they had been warned, created a media frenzy. Reporters and photographers were outside the station, and anyone entering or leaving felt harassed.

Morrison's frustration gave his delivery a sarcastic edge as he confronted the team with details from the forensic lab.

'Surprise, surprise, DNA testing on the bloodstained clothing found in the dog kennel at Norman O'Reilly's address matches the blood sample taken from Detmar Steinburg's body. His clothes were in a plastic bag, with a newspaper dated the Friday, the day before he was discovered.' Morrison put his hands on his hips and glared at the twenty gathered officers. 'He's bloody asking to be nicked, so why the hell haven't you found him yet?' He shook his head in exasperation. 'Talk to the girlfriend again. See if you can shake his alibi.' He gestured to Collingwood, who had arrived late after visiting the gallery.

'I'm sorry, Sir, but even as an officer on the murder case, I wasn't allowed entry as the forensic officers were still examining the gutted top floor. I'd waited in order to acquire the CCTV footage but was told that Miss Langton was expected in around an hour and so I should return then.' He didn't mention that he had stopped off for breakfast first.

'Bollocks to that,' Morrison said. 'Right, you and me are going back there now. We've got search warrants for the whole building, plus the yard, and I'm not taking any bullshit about not being allowed in.'

As Morrison and Collingwood drove to the gallery, Morrison asked about Ester Langton.

'She's been very strange from the off, Sir. Like agreeing to go to the mortuary to identify him; strange lack of emotion.'

Morrison got out of the patrol car and stood on the pavement, looking up at the four-storey art gallery. The windows had been blown out on the top floor and the entire frontage had been drenched with the hoses, so where it wasn't blackened with smoke, the once pristine white stucco walls were grey and water stained. Morrison shook his head. 'Reckon it's gonna cost millions to clean this lot up.'

They entered through the double glass doors, to be greeted by a large sign stating the obvious: 'Closed until further notice'. A uniformed officer was sitting on one of the velvet-covered benches with a mug of tea. He quickly got to his feet, explaining that he had been there since nine and it had been freezing cold as the building now had no windows. He gestured to the mug of tea, saying that one of Miss Langton's security guards had made it for him. Morrison waved his hand dismissively.

'Where's Miss Langton now?'

'Fourth-floor office, Sir, or what's left of it.'

Morrison threw him a disparaging glance as he headed along the corridor, pausing at two large open doors to the reception gallery. He stood for a moment, looking into the room at the display of oil paintings along the walls. He then continued towards the staircase, pausing by the glass-walled lift, then headed up the stairs. Everywhere showed the damage from the water: sodden carpets and dripping walls.

On the second floor, Morrison walked into the gallery with Collingwood trailing in his wake. It was now devoid of any paintings, although the gilt-backed chairs were still lined up, some with sodden leaflets on them. There was a trestle table covered in a stained white cloth, half-empty crates of champagne and broken champagne flutes. He noticed a large reel of bubble wrap against a wall beside a thick roll of heavy-duty brown paper. The room itself looked comparatively undamaged, although the carpet on the stairs was waterlogged.

Collingwood had to hurry after Morrison who was quickly on the third floor, standing by the open door. 'So, this is where Neilson had his art show, third-floor gallery, right?' Morrison's question was rhetorical. 'Well, there's fuck all in here now, just a stack of easels and what looks like smashed frames.'

'I removed Neilson's paintings,' Collingwood told him. 'They're wrapped and ready to be taken away. And, of course, the main event painting is already at the station.'

Ester Langton was at the top of the next set of stairs, wearing a tight-fitting black cashmere dress and high-heeled black boots with plastic rain covers. Her black hair was drawn into an elaborate coil at the nape of her slender neck. She wore a string of pearls with matching pearl earrings, and her thick makeup disguised not only the bruise on her forehead but any sign of the trauma she had been through.

She stood patiently waiting as they squelched along the sodden carpet towards her. They could now see the extent of the damage:

some of the carpets had been rolled up, exposing the bare boards, and what remained of the burnt doors were stacked to one side. The whole area smelt of acrid smoke, with blackened walls, broken furniture and charred door frames.

'Be careful,' she warned. 'The floors are quite uneven. You can look into what was the office, and you'll see, the private bedroom is completely trashed.'

Morrison was not prepared to risk entering what was left of the office, although Collingwood edged towards what had been the staff storage area. It now had 'danger' tape where the door had been. The only area that had not been affected was the toilets, but the door was burnt and hanging loose.

Morrison had seen enough, unable to stop coughing as the acrid stench burnt his throat. They all went back down the stairs, into the room where the large paintings were still intact with little sign of damage from the fire.

Ester stood back to allow them to enter first. 'Please do sit down. Can I offer you refreshments?' She moved around a trestle table indicating a silver tray with a thermos of coffee and a jug of cream, a bowl of sugar cubes and a plate filled with pastries. There was a neat file of documents beside the tray. Collingwood stood to one side as Morrison drew up a velvet-covered hard-backed chair to sit down on. He noticed that although Ester looked perfectly turned out, as she gestured to the tray, her nails were chipped and broken.

'I have, as my lawyer instructed, compiled a list of all the guests,' Ester told them. 'We also had a young girl checking off their names as they arrived, so we know who turned up and who didn't. The invitations were printed before Detmar left for Europe; he was already planning the exhibition and was hoping to acquire new pieces to show. Kurt must have taken them and sent them out himself because I know Detmar would not have considered exhibiting his work. But as I said in my statement, Kurt had taken over the gallery whether I liked it or not.'

'Had he ever done that before?'

'No, he would not have dared. Our clients have been carefully selected over many years; discerning buyers and dealers and art critics. I noticed from the list of attendants that there was not the usual number of guests.'

Morrison reached out to take a pastry, and she passed him a small napkin. 'Miss Langton, I noticed you have a number of CCTV cameras. I will require the footage from Saturday night.'

She leaned forward, holding both hands out in a helpless gesture. 'I knew you would want them, and I can't tell you how horrified I was when I discovered they had all been muted, turned to the wall or damaged, and that the main electrical hub in the basement was smashed. Obviously, Kurt had done all this as he knew what was going to happen. I have called the company, and they are going to send an engineer to check if there is any salvageable footage. I understand its importance.'

Morrison nodded. 'It's vital. We haven't yet had the report from the forensic fire team. Do you have any indication of how the fire started?'

'Not really. I know the fire started on the top floor, possibly in the storage room. It could have been a stray cigarette I suppose. I don't know. There was such panic, and it was such a terrible night.'

Morrison nodded his understanding. 'I'm afraid I would like you to take me through the events of Saturday evening. I'm sorry to make you repeat everything.'

They both listened intently as Ester explained again how she was assaulted by the man she later identified as Norman O'Reilly; he had been demanding money and said he had kept hold of some bloodied clothing that he would hand to the police if Neilson didn't come good. She then explained how she was rescued from O'Reilly by one of the guests who had witnessed the assault. Collingwood strongly suspected this man was Jack.

'Tell me more about Kurt Neilson,' Morrison said.

'I can only tell you that he was in a long, often violent relationship with Detmar. I think I was told he had once been a boxer, but I never socialised with him. I disliked his hold over Detmar, who took him around the world and gave him whatever he wanted.'

'But he refused to exhibit his paintings?'

'Detective Morrison, if you saw them, you would understand why – they were pitiful. He had no talent whatsoever.'

'What about your relationship with Mr Steinburg?'

She sat upright in her chair. 'I was his secretary to begin with and then became his personal assistant. He was a wonderful man. I have been with him for ten years.'

'Did you ever have a sexual relationship with him?'

'I find that insulting. I was inordinately fond of him, but not in that way.'

Morrison nodded. 'Going back to Kurt Neilson. As you've told us, it sounds as if he was pampered by Mr Steinburg, with a luxurious lifestyle.'

She shook her head emphatically. 'I would say that was all about to fall apart because Detmar was quite a promiscuous man, and Kurt was a very jealous one. I have something that I think will be of interest to you, detectives.' She sifted through the neat stack of notes she had prepared for them and withdrew a single receipt. 'This is from a theatrical prop department, paid for by Kurt Neilson. It was used in an epic film about the Nativity and was delivered to one of the shops Detmar used.'

She held up the receipt between thumb and forefinger. It was for a giant wooden cross, to be delivered to the framer's where

O'Reilly worked. It had cost one thousand four hundred pounds, with an extra two hundred for the delivery, which included chains and hooks. As Morrison and Collingwood looked over the receipt, she filled a large manila envelope with all the papers.

'You have been very accommodating, Miss Langton, and I appreciate your assistance. I just have one more thing to ask. Would you help confirm something we are still looking into?'

She smiled and gave the same open-handed gesture. 'Of course.'

'We have found a considerable amount of cash in various currencies in Detmar's apartment.'

She shrugged. 'Detmar always liked to have money on hand, and I can obviously provide you with all his bank statements should that be legally requested. These would have been in my files, but of course due to fire . . .'

Morrison rubbed his hands together, crumpled the little napkin he had used into a ball and tossed it onto the desk. 'You see, all that cash makes me wonder if Mr Steinburg was engaged in another kind of business. Dealing in forgeries to be precise.'

She stood up quickly, her eyes blazing. 'How dare you even suggest that . . . let me tell you, if ever I discovered that we had acquired a fake artwork, I would not only report it to the authorities but ensure the artist was arrested. We employ renowned art experts to ensure the authenticity of every one of our paintings. Detmar does not ever . . .' She stopped, heaving for breath, having spoken about him as if he was still alive. As the tears came, she snatched a paper napkin from the table. 'I think you should leave. If you want any further information from me, I will insist my lawyer be present.'

Morrison stood, picking up the envelope. 'Thank you for your time, Miss Langton. We have a search warrant,' he added, holding it out to her, 'and I'd like to go down to the basement before we go.'

'As you wish,' she said curtly. 'I'll call one of the security guards to take you down there.' She led the way out into the reception area.

Ester gestured to a security guard carrying a ring of keys. 'This is Eric. He'll take you into the basement. If you'll excuse me, I have a great deal to sort out.' She turned and walked away.

Morrison reached out for the keys. 'I think we can handle it from here, thanks, Eric.' He noticed large sweat stains on the security guard's shirt. Morrison took the keys and the black rubber torch from Eric's belt. 'A couple of questions before we go,' Morrison said, pausing. 'I understand you were not on the third floor and didn't witness the incident.'

'That's right,' Eric nodded.

'Did you see anything unusual before that?'

'Yeah, this guy, one of the guests, he was shouting orders, taking control of things. Then he legged it when the police arrived.'

Morrison sucked his teeth. 'Interesting. That's all. Thanks.'

'No problem.' Eric gestured to a door. 'Basement's through there.'

The basement smelt strongly of damp. The ceiling light, once they found the switch, gave only a faint glimmer. Morrison clicked his fingers for the torch, and Collingwood handed it over. Slowly moving the beam around the vast space, they could see tangled cables leading to what was left of a box with rows of switches. The box had been smashed to pieces.

'That'll be the CCTV,' Morrison sighed. 'Kurt was certainly busy down here. Get one of our tech specialists down asap to see if they can retrieve anything.'

Frames of every shape and size were stacked along the walls, along with dozens of narrow wooden crates. Most were damaged. Morrison shone the torch around the walls and then the stone floor; it was evident that, at some point, something heavy had been pushed along it. There were distinct scrapes about six feet apart, leading to a double warehouse-style door which had an unlocked padlock hanging by a chain. He wrenched it open a few inches and peered out into the backyard.

Collingwood started looking through the bins. 'You won't find anything in there,' Morrison told him. 'Anything that was there will be gone by now. But that backyard could have been a way to get in if it was arson. With just two officers covering the place I'd put money on them not checking out the backyard.'

Back in the car, he asked Collingwood for his thoughts. 'I'm not sure, Sir. But I think you are right about whatever they had in that cellar being shipped out fast. I noticed Ester's hands were in a rough state, and the security guard was sweating like a pig.'

Morrison nodded. 'Yeah, she only really started to lose it when I mentioned the forgeries. I mean, we have fuck all on that, I was just trying it on, but it looks like we hit a nerve. I reckon our Mr Steinburg was definitely running some sort of scam; with all of his properties, skipping around the world buying and selling. I don't know and, to be honest, I can't at this stage bring myself to give a fuck. More important we got the receipt for the cross, indicating premeditation; that was a good result.'

Collingwood nodded. His mobile gave multiple pings as Morrison continued. 'And we need the fingerprint blokes down in that cellar to check the damaged CCTV unit. When you get back to the station, double-check if any dumpsters were hired either Sunday or today at the gallery. Something heavy-duty was parked in that backyard, must have shifted a lot of gear out of there.'

'Yes, Sir. I just got a text. They're bringing in Norman O'Reilly's girlfriend first thing in the morning. Maybe she'll give us something.'

Morrison nodded, then frowned as another loose end popped into his head. 'I'd like to know who that anonymous caller was that tipped you off about what was about to go down.'

'Yeah ... right,' Collingwood murmured his agreement. His anxiety levels were going up again. As well as the text about O'Reilly's girlfriend being brought in, he'd also been told that the station was receiving streams of mobile phone film footage from people present at the gallery. What were the chances at least one had caught Jack?

CHAPTER 30

Jack had stopped off for a quick pint in his local pub, and to read the *Evening Standard* for any update on the fire at the gallery. It didn't take long to discover there was no real news, and he tossed the paper into a bin as he started the fifteen-minute walk home. It was getting dark when he turned into his street and saw the car. About twenty yards ahead, a black Mercedes flashed its headlights. He paused, and the car flashed its lights again. He quickened his pace, coming abreast of the car. There was a driver wearing a chauffeur's hat looking straight ahead, and Jack was about to rap on the window when the rear passenger door opened, and the interior lights came on.

Helga was sitting on the far side of the back seat, swathed in some kind of white fur. She gestured for Jack to get into the car. When he hesitated, she leaned across. 'I do not have very much time.' He got in beside her and closed the door. The interior light went out, and Helga leaned forward to the driver. 'Do you mind leaving us for five minutes? I need a private conversation.' Her driver half turned towards her, clearly not liking the instruction, then got out and closed the door.

'What are you doing here?' Jack asked angrily.

'Don't get tetchy with me,' she said calmly. 'I spoke to a very nice lady this morning and she told me you were due back early this evening, so here I am. I have been waiting for quite some time.'

She rummaged briefly in her handbag. 'I also promise you that this time, I do have a plane to catch. I am on my way to Dubai. Here, this is my ticket,' she waved it in front of him.

'What do you want?'

'Two things, first to tell you some good news and the reason there was some urgency in being paid what was owed to me. Adam has found a young man, a scientist, who has discovered a way around the problem he was so concerned about. Do you remember we discussed that art experts have discovered radiocarbon as a method of dating paintings?'

Jack nodded, hating the fact he was sitting next to her right outside his family home.

'Well, there has been some satisfactory development, but it is very expensive and obviously illegal. Without having that as surety, the thought of taking two or more years before his work is completed was something he was concerned about.'

'Where is he?'

'He was in Arizona, I think he was perhaps in Berlin also, but I have no idea if Adam is still there or not.'

Jack reached out to open the door.

'Wait,' she said sharply. 'Please, I doubt if I will be returning to London for a long time, and I wanted to explain something about what I do. It has taken me years to build up my list of wealthy clients. They are billionaires that want a Renoir or whatever and can pay for it. I connect them with someone who can find what they want.'

'Is that what you have been doing for Detmar?'

'Yes, for many years, but recently he was becoming too greedy. You have to understand that Detmar had to spend a vast amount of money to show that he was wealthy and successful.' She gave a soft laugh. 'In reality he owned nothing. His properties were all short-term leases, and that included his galleries. It was all a house of cards.'

'So how do you make your money?'

'I get a cut of the sales, that is if my introductions pay dividends.'

'Even if you are selling fakes?'

'I am not selling any such thing. I am simply introducing people with great wealth to exclusive dealers. Whether or not they proceed to pass on a fake work of art has nothing to do with me.'

Jack shook his head, laughing, and again he went to open the door when she reached out and held his arm.

'I also want to thank you, Jack. I could have been involved in that horror on Saturday night. Ester made sure I was paid off and more this morning. But she cannot be trusted, and right now, with Detmar gone, she will be stealing anything she can lay her nasty hands on.'

'You mean what's left after the fire?'

Helga laughed again. 'Convenient, that it was only the top floor, no?'

He was unsure what to say to that. She reached into her bag again. 'I must go, and by the way, this is not my car or my chauffeur ... it's only a top-of-the-range Uber.' She took out a thick white envelope. 'This is for you. I doubt we will meet again, so this is me thanking you.' She signalled to the driver who opened the driver's door and got in. She turned away and Jack got out.

He stood on the pavement with the envelope in his hand as the car glided away. There was so much more he had wanted to ask – should have asked – but he hadn't wanted to spend any more time than he had to in her company, just yards from his front door. He opened the envelope. Inside were several bundles of crisp new fifty-pound notes tied with an elastic band. He quickly counted it. Twenty thousand pounds. He put the money back in the envelope and stuffed it into his jacket pocket. 'Fuckin' hell,' he muttered, quickly looking around, to make sure no one had seen.

As soon as Jack walked in, Maggie shouted for him to come into the dining room where Penny and Hannah were waiting, along with a smiling Marius.

'Now don't get angry,' Maggie began, 'but with you earning again and my wages, and we have a few quid left in the joint account, what do you think? Marius says he can break through this wall and . . .'

'Just wait a minute. It looks to me as if you've already decided. To my mind, we don't really need all this extra work done.'

'The reason is, Jack, I've decided to save money for the christening party. We'll have everyone here, which means we'll need a bigger space.'

Jack sighed, shaking his head. He turned to Marius. 'What'll it cost?'

Marius stroked his chin. 'I'd say for a cash deal, two and a half thousand, and that'll include the plastering and RSJ for the main wall.'

Jack felt the weight of the money in his jacket pocket. He was eager to get up to his office to stash the money somewhere safe. 'OK, I give in.'

Maggie clapped her hands and gave Marius a high-five.

Upstairs, Jack duct-taped the cash under the seats of a plastic toy cart that Hannah had grown out of and stuffed it in a corner. Only then did he start to relax. He physically jumped when Maggie came in carrying Charlie.

'Wait until you see how fast he can crawl now,' she said, putting him gently down. He quickly started beetling around the office on all fours.

Jack laughed. 'Very impressive.' He scooped Charlie into his arms before he could get stuck under the desk.

'By the way, did you take a call for me this morning?' Jack asked.

'At the house? I was at work.' She held her arms out. 'Let me take him and get him ready for bed.' She was almost out of the door when she turned. 'I know it will really look terrific, Jack, and thank you for agreeing. Oh, did you have a good day at work?'

'Not so bad . . . I'm on a late tomorrow, so I won't be back until after nine.'

'Put it on the diary board. I'm on the early shift. Oh, I saw it was on the six o'clock news about the fire at the gallery.'

'Yeah, there was something in the *Standard*,' he said as she went downstairs. He took a couple of deep breaths before following her down to the kitchen. Penny was feeding Hannah at the table as he went over to check this latest family schedule.

'Did you take a call for me this morning, Mum?'

'No, dear, I went to do a grocery shop after taking Hannah to school, I think Gladys may have as there was a message, but it just said someone had called for you. I told her to always put down the name of the caller but to be honest, I don't think she really understands very well, and her writing is shocking.'

'I am doing joined writing,' Hannah said.

Penny nodded and smiled at her. 'She is doing very well at this new school – oh, and there's a parents' meeting next week. I've put it on the board, so you and Maggie can hopefully both go.'

'I am going to do ballet, and I have to wear a tutu and ballet shoes and a pink stretchy thing,' Hannah said.

'Oh yes, I need to ask Maggie about that,' Penny said. 'There's a shop in the West End that sells ballet shoes and leotards. It's a bit expensive, but we don't want her to be the odd one out. It's also after school – the ballet teacher is a professional. From the stage. It's ten pounds a lesson.'

'Fine, whatever she needs,' Jack said.

'Well, I thought it was a tad expensive, but if you agree, I'll tell Maggie and organise it with her class teacher.'

Jack shrugged, looking at the markings on the wall indicating where the hole would be knocked through into the dining room. He could not imagine what it was going to be like. All he could think of was that cash strapped under the cart in his office. 'Thank you, Helga,' he murmured under his breath.

* * *

Early the following morning, Collingwood and Morrison were waiting for O'Reilly's girlfriend to be brought in. Collingwood was scanning one of the morning papers, and it gave him an uneasy feeling.

'You know, Guv, the description of the painting is out there now, even though there are no photos, thank God, but with all the mobile footage, I'm sure it's only a matter of time.'

Morrison shrugged. 'Listen, we were told not to broadcast any fucking details about the crucifixion, and we've done our damnedest . . . are they worried there's going to be a fucking copycat murder or something?'

'I guess it's because the details are so horrific.'

'Yeah, like Jack the Ripper, ripping out his victim's insides. They never disclosed half of what he'd done at the time. Anyway, it'll all come out at the trial.'

'Maybe not. If Neilson pleads guilty, there won't be a jury trial, so . . .'

'Listen, pal, word is he's got a shit-hot legal team lined up, and they'll want to get as much expensive court time as possible. Anyway, forget about the painting – right now, we look like fucking idiots for letting O'Reilly slip through our fingers.'

Collingwood looked at a text on his mobile. 'She's here, Sir.'

'Right, let's get to it,' Morrison said.

Collingwood looked uneasy. 'Before we do, Sir, I just thought I'd mention to you that she is physically challenged.'

'What the fuck do you mean by that?'

'Well, Sir, she's very small. It could be dwarfism, I'm not sure.'

Morrison got the insinuation. 'Right, you think I'm going to make a joke about her being a small-arse.'

'No, I—' Before Collingwood could finish, there was a tap on the door. He went to open it and stood back as a uniformed officer ushered in Rhonda Curtis, who was three and a half feet tall and very pretty, with thick blond wavy hair. She had large blue eyes with false eyelashes and her bright pink lipstick set off her flawless skin.

'Thank you so much for coming to the station,' Morrison said. Collingwood brought a chair for her to sit across from Morrison, but that only made her the same height as when standing, with her head only just appearing over the desk.

'Have you got a cushion?' she asked, in a low, throaty voice that belied her childlike appearance. Collingwood silently cursed himself for not having thought of it. He hurried out and quickly reappeared with one.

'Thank you,' she said, smiling sweetly as she sat down.

'I'm Detective Chief Inspector Mark Morrison. Again, thank you for coming in.'

'I didn't have much option when they came to my flat. Very nice officers though. Now I need to get something sorted. I watch a lot of real-life crime shows, and I know they always refuse to say anything unless they get legal representation.'

'Miss Curtis, at present this is an informal interview. You can leave any time you want and speak with a solicitor at any time...'

'So, I'm not under arrest?'

'At present no, but if we discover you have lied to us you may well be arrested.'

She pursed her lips, opening her handbag to take out a tissue. 'Is he going to witness everything?' She pointed at Collingwood.

'Yes, Miss Curtis, Detective Inspector Collingwood will remain in the room. Now, you have stated that Norman O'Reilly was with you in Southampton on two specific nights and that he remained with you throughout Friday 14th and Saturday 15th of March. We are now aware that Mr O'Reilly is prone to violence ... perhaps you were coerced into making this statement, fearing physical repercussions if you did not?'

'Oh, I was coerced all right. He threatened to beat me up and he terrified me, but I was stupid, you know, getting myself into that situation. I'd only met him a few weeks ago. I work in the market on Saturdays, and he was always very friendly We struck up a friendship.'

'So, you'd only known Mr O'Reilly for a short time.'

'I just said so. We had a couple of dates, which I never told Dad about 'cause he definitely wouldn't have approved. Then, on Thursday, he came into the cafe and said he was going to do some business in Southampton at the weekend and stay in a nice hotel, and did I want to come. I had to tell my friend in the market I'd not be working, but it was my weekend off from the cafe anyway, so I thought why not.'

'Tell me about the Friday when you travelled to Southampton.' Morrison tried hard not to let his impatience show.

'He was late picking me up and left me standing around until just before lunchtime. He had a white rental van and was very het up because he had to make this delivery at the docks; some crates he had in the back of the van, and he was worried he was gonna miss the pick-up. We got there, and it wasn't a posh hotel or anything, just a cheap B&B. We'd only just arrived when he got a call on his mobile. He said he had to deliver the crates and for me to order in a takeaway.'

'So, he left you at the hotel. What time did he return?'

'Well, I was dead angry because he never got back until about midnight. I'd had the takeaway and I was going to go home, but he bought a bottle of gin. He calmed me down and said he was sorry, but he had to do a big job which was going to make him a lot of money.'

'So, you were with Mr O'Reilly for that Friday night or what was left of it, and throughout Saturday.'

'Yes, we eventually went back to London late Saturday, after he'd unloaded the crates. He made me promise to say about him being with me all weekend and that I would get five hundred quid.'

'When you left, was it in the white van again?'

'Yes, and when I went to put my case in the back, I had the door open and he snatched it from me. The van didn't have the crates in no more, but it smelt of bleach, and there was something in a plastic bag.'

'Can you describe it?'

'No, not really. It was about this big.' She indicated with her hands. 'There's something else. When he got back to the B&B, he smelt of bleach, and he had to take a shower and change his clothes.'

'Did you get paid the five hundred?'

'Well, not straightaway. It was a few days later, and there was this murder in Portobello Road and everyone was talking about it. That's when he came into the cafe and said if anyone asked me about the weekend, I had to promise that I was with him, and I would get another two hundred. He threatened that if I didn't, I'd be very sorry, you know, like you said, coercion. If my dad found out, all hell would break loose.'

'Did you ever meet Kurt Neilson?'

'No, I never met anyone when I was with Norman. I never went into that shop either, full of old junk.'

'Have you any idea where he might be?'

'Now?'

'Yes, Miss Curtis, we are trying to track him down.'

'I don't know, like I said; I'm ashamed to admit I didn't know him that well. He was lousy in bed, too, so I was never going to have another date with him.'

'Have you seen him recently?'

'Why would I? There were police all around his shop, and I was told something terrible had happened in there. I think he's got a brother in Cork, and the bloke who rented the white van was a friend. He said he got a cheap rate.'

'Can you recall anything about the van that would help us trace it?'

'Not really. It was a white rental van with an address and contact numbers on the side, but I can't remember what they were. He said he used them a lot for driving these crates to Southampton.'

Morrison stood up as Collingwood went to help Miss Curtis down from her chair, although he wasn't sure how. He offered her his hand, which she took, allowing her to slide gently to the floor with a giggle. He walked her to the door and then accompanied her out into the corridor, closing the door after them.

Morrison got onto the team to trace the rental van, then flipped open Rhonda Curtis's file. 'She might look like a little girl, but bloody hell . . .' he muttered, noting that she was thirty-five years old and had a previous conviction for sex work.

As Collingwood was heading back to Morrison's office, Ralph Jordan came running down the stairs from the office being used to check the CCTV and mobile footage. He seemed very agitated.

'Mike, you'd better come up and have a look at what we've got. I don't know what the hell to do about it.'

Collingwood was about to follow him, when Morrison appeared and said they'd had a hit with the van. 'It's registered to a company in White City run by a Frank Jones. A patrol car's waiting for you. I'll organise a forensic team to be on standby.'

* * *

The van rental company was located in a run-down yard with a cheap corrugated lean-to. The yard was attached to residential property and used the front room as their office. Collingwood's patrol car drove in through the old wooden double gates to see two young kids using a hose-pipe to wash down one of three vans. Collingwood stepped out, a uniformed officer alongside him. The third officer started looking closely at the vans.

'Frank Jones, need a word,' Collingwood said to one of the boys. The boy turned with the hose full on and nearly soaked him.

'He was taking his kid to school, but he might be back in the office.' He jerked a thumb.

Collingwood, accompanied by the officer, were walking towards the indicated door when there was a shout from the yard behind them.

The officer was struggling to hold onto a screaming Norman O'Reilly. The two boys were not giving any assistance but staring wide-eyed as Collingwood and the other officer piled in to drag O'Reilly face down and put the handcuffs on him. By the time they had dragged him onto his feet and got him into the patrol car, Frank Jones, driving an old jeep, drove into the yard.

Collingwood sent the patrol car with Norman O'Reilly back to the station and led a worried-looking Jones into his office.

'I had no idea he was hiding in one of my vans. I just got the boys to start hosing them down this morning.'

Collingwood called for backup, and when they arrived, they found a sleeping bag and food cartons left in the back of the van Norman had just been dragged from, along with some clothes and a mobile phone. A further search revealed his passport and tickets for the ferry over to Ireland. Jones identified the van O'Reilly had used on the trip to Southampton, which still had a strong smell of bleach. Collingwood called for a flatbed truck to take it to the forensic lab to be examined.

By the time Collingwood returned to the station, he had a statement from Frank Jones and the dates and times he had rented one or other of his vans to O'Reilly over the last two years. He claimed that he only ever did business with O'Reilly himself, and it was always a cash deal, never having met anyone from the framer's shop.

CHAPTER 31

In the incident room, Jack was working through another set of statements, court dates and magistrates' schedules, trying hard to stay awake. Laura on the other hand couldn't sit still, she was so frustrated with the Jason Marks case.

'That slippery lawyer of his is going to spring him, even though he was caught on camera red-handed. He's got previous, I just know it.'

'Why don't you just let it go,' Jack said.

Laura showed no sign she'd heard him. 'I'm going to have one more search. I'd really like to get one over that bloody woman.'

Laura went off to the records department as Jack continued working at his desk. He would have to have a meeting with DCI Clarke to talk about the overload of cases instigated by Armani's gang strategy.

Laura logged into the main records computer and immediately noticed that Jack Warr had also been down there recently, as everyone using the computer had to log the date and time of access. Curious to know what he had been checking out, she brought up the old case that both of them had worked on. It had been a major double operation with the drug squad and Ridley, investigating the murder of an elderly woman. She was fast forwarding through details about the lengthy search for a suspect, Adam Border, the victim's son. About to close the file, she stopped, as photographs of Border from childhood to his teenage years came up on the screen. She sat back, frowning, moving the curser back and forth until she enlarged one profile, the teenager wearing a baseball cap. Laura suddenly remembered having déjà vu at Fulham station as she looked at the photograph of a man wanted for questioning in connection with the murder at the framer's shop. It was Adam Border.

At the same time, O'Reilly was being brought up from the cells and taken into an interview room. Morrison was waiting for him. After Collingwood had gone through the usual preliminaries, Morrison told O'Reilly he was under arrest on suspicion of aiding and abetting Kurt Neilson in the murder of Detmar Steinburg, perverting the course of justice and assaulting Ester Langton on the night of the art show in the Steinburg gallery.

'Right, Norman, let's start from what happened on the night of the 14th. You have previously claimed that you were in Southampton all afternoon and evening, but we now know that was a lie. So tell us exactly what occurred that evening.'

'Right, I had only just arrived. As far as I was concerned, I'd missed the pick-up for the crates. Then I got a call, saying it was urgent I return to London.'

'Who was the caller?'

'It was Kurt Neilson, and he was blazing angry because I had locked the door into the main sales room of the shop. I'd left the back door open to the yard because a market stall-holder used to leave her trestle table in the shop for her to set up on the Saturday.'

Morrison tapped the table with a pencil. 'But you knew you were not returning that Saturday.'

'That's right, but I forgot, and to be honest, I was nervous because I was worried about not making it to Southampton in time for the collection. I had already had a run-in with Kurt on Friday morning. He had this cross delivered, enormous bloody thing, and it was taking up a lot of space in the shop. I had asked when it was being moved out. I never knew, you see, when I'd get a delivery of frames, they could come without any warning, and that's another reason I left the yard gates open because they sometimes delivered them at night.'

'Get back to the Friday, Mr O'Reilly.'

'Right, well, he's screaming at me that I was going to be out of a job because he'd left some important invitations in the shop when he'd been there earlier, and I was even more stressed because I'd forgotten I'd picked them up and put them into my big shoulder bag.'

'Friday, Mr O'Reilly. I'm getting impatient.'

'I drove straight there. I needed this job – it was good money, and I made good time; the doors to the yard were open, and I drove in. I had the keys to the front of the shop – it's a heavy-duty lock because that's where the good frames and paintings are kept.'

'Which entrance are you talking about? The main door of the shop or the internal one?'

'Both have strong locks and there's a bolt on the main front door. Portobello Road can be a dodgy place, thieves'll break in if you're not careful. The back's all storage, so leaving that open is less of a big deal really. You can't get into the main part of the shop through the yard, you need to go through an inside, locked door.'

'So, you were there to open the internal door, right?'

'Yes, exactly. But Kurt had smashed in the door from the yard, so I got out of the van and walked in. He must have used a jemmy or something. Anyway, he was in there, and he looked madder than ever. I was shaking when I searched in my bag for the keys because no lights were on, and I said I'd got the invitations and . . .' He paused.

'Go on.' Morrison leaned forwards over the table.

'He said he needed me to do something for him. He said he had some cash, but there would be a lot more. He said he would pay fifty thousand quid if I agreed to help him. I mean, that is a lot of money. I asked how I could trust him for that amount of money, and then he switched the light on.'

If O'Reilly was acting, Morrison thought he was doing it very well as his whole body was shaking. He tried to catch his breath, opening and shutting his mouth like a fish. Morrison glanced at Collingwood as they waited.

'The floor was covered in blood, pools of it. I mean, it was everywhere, and that's when I saw his suit was splattered with it. He said if I cleared the place up, he'd pay me the fifty grand. There had been some sexual thing that had got out of hand . . .'

'Did you see the victim?'

'No, well, not exactly. There was a rolled-up carpet in a corner. It could have been in there.'

'So, what happened next?'

'I had some containers of bleach, and I got a mop and buckets and started cleaning whatever I could and then used a hose pipe that was attached to a tap in the yard. I was out in the yard brushing the water down the drain, then, when I went back in, the carpet had been moved into the main shop because he'd opened the door. I was still spraying more bleach everywhere and using the mop to wipe down the walls. It took about two hours before he was satisfied, and then he said that I'd done a good job but there was one more thing I had to do.'

O'Reilly was sweating, constantly wiping his face with the back of his hands. Morrison passed him a bottle of water. He drank a few gulps before putting the bottle down.

'I had to get rid of the carpet, and he handed me this carrier bag full of stuff, he said not to chuck it all in the same place but to spread it around. I heaved the carpet into a dumpster in White City as I was heading back to Southampton. I was driving around looking for somewhere else and was at Shepherds Bush . . . there were a lot of waste bins, so I reckoned it would be as good as anywhere. I parked up and opened the back of the van. The bag was full of bloodstained clothes, and that's when I had second thoughts. I reckoned I should keep them as evidence if Kurt didn't pay up, so I would have a bargaining chip.'

Morrison nodded, picked up his pen and tapped the desk again. 'So where did you get the money to pay Miss Curtis? Five hundred pounds, right?'

'Oh, right, yes, he gave me that before I left.'

'So, what else was in the carrier bag? Did you look through it?'

'No, I did not. I was still scared shitless, excuse me, but I wanted to get back to Southampton.'

'No credit cards, driving licence, no kind of identification?'

'That's right, and I gave Miss Curtis the money I'd promised her later in the week after I'd hidden the bag in the dog kennel out in my backyard because by now, I knew I was going to be in big trouble about what had gone down in the shop. You know, Kurt had always been helpful, and we got on because, in the old days, I'd done a bit of boxing, not in his league, he was a middleweight and could have been a champion, used to be known as The Panther, the way he moved like a dancer. But on his first big amateur fight before turning pro he got, not a really hard punch, but more of a winger to his jaw and he was out like a light. They found out he'd got a glass chin, so that was the end of his fight career. With his looks, I think he did some modelling, but I also knew not to question him on all the money he flashed around, 'cause he could turn on you and get very nasty.' He paused as if thinking something over. 'I suppose that was what happened to the bloke in the carpet.'

* * *

Laura had been waiting for Jack in the incident room for half an hour, but he was still in DCI Clarke's office. Why had Jack been looking at that case file? Had he also recognised Adam Border? She recalled how the case had finally been closed, when Ridley had discovered vital CCTV footage from Ireland. She couldn't remember Jack's part in it, but she was certain Adam Border remained on the wanted lists.

Jack eventually exited DCI Clarke's office, but before Laura could talk to him, DI Armani appeared and instructed Laura and Jack to attend a possible murder enquiry. They were assigned different cars, frustrating her even more.

* * *

Collingwood was eager to find out how much O'Reilly knew about the gallery's connection to art fraud. Once Morrison had finished with his questions, Collingwood asked O'Reilly about the deliveries he had made recently. He put the CCTV photo of the man with the baseball cap on the desk in front of him. O'Reilly started to look nervous.

'I never made any personal deliveries to anyone. The crates were delivered to me with instructions about shipping them on.' He paused, then leaned forwards pointing at the photo. 'Him, that bloke, he was a regular, but I had a delivery to him, it was a huge painting with a gold frame.'

'You claimed not to know him,' Collingwood said.

'I don't. He came in and collected what was delivered to the shop for him and left. That was the only time I had to take a frame to him.'

'Do you know his address?'

'Yeah, I do, not the exact one, it was an old comprehensive school near Westbourne Grove. I unloaded it, but I wasn't gonna help carry it in there for him, 'cause it weighed a ton and I've got lower back problems.'

Morrison nodded to Collingwood to organise someone to go and check out the school. He was not that interested, wanting to move the interview on to the night at the gallery. O'Reilly soon admitted he'd been there.

'I'd run out of money. I didn't even know there was an exhibition going on, I just wanted to ask Kurt for the money he promised. I was trying to get Ester Langton to talk to Kurt when some bloke attacked me. He looked a bit familiar but I don't know who he was. When the police arrived, I legged it. I couldn't think where else to go so I went and hid at the Rent-a-Van company. Frank Jones didn't know nothing about it.

Collingwood came back in with a photograph of the now demolished school on his mobile. He held it out to O'Reilly. 'Yeah, it looks like the place I delivered the painting to, but it hadn't been demolished then.'

'So, you say this man, the one in the baseball cap, was at the school. Was he waiting for the delivery?' Collingwood asked.

'Yeah, didn't tip me when I got it out either.'

'But you don't know his name?'

'No, like I keep sayin', he was just a regular customer.'

Morrison had had enough of this line of questioning. 'How well did you know Detmar Steinburg?'

'Listen, I never met him, and I never had any dealings with him. I knew he owned galleries and was as rich as Croesus and that Kurt was his boyfriend. I knew they were perverts, you know, they liked young boys, but I just kept my nose out of their business. Like I said, I got paid well.'

Collingwood sat back, folding his arms. 'If I was to suggest to you that your shop was dealing in fake paintings and shipping them out to Europe and the States for considerable sums of money, and that you had to have been fully aware of this illegal transaction for some time, what would you say?'

O'Reilly shook his head several times. 'Listen to me, if I'd known there was another fucking business going on right under my fucking nose and making other people a lot of cash, I'd have been pissed off. I don't know anything about any fake paintings, I was just a gofer, a small-time fuckwit that got caught up in that bastard's sick murder.'

Collingwood noticed O'Reilly looking furtively down at his feet. He got up and went round the table. 'Stand up,' he told him. O'Reilly was wearing a pair of expensive-looking designer suede shoes.

'They were the only things my size,' he said plaintively.

O'Reilly was standing in the dead man's shoes.

* * *

Morrison was tired out and wanted to get something to eat, so he went to the canteen. Collingwood took the opportunity to head up to the office used for viewing CCTV and mobile footage. Two officers, including Ralph, were still working as Collingwood walked in.

'We've checked O'Reilly's mobile phone record and verified that he did receive a call from a mobile phone belonging to Kurt Neilson at one forty-five on Friday the 14th . . .'

Collingwood nodded. 'Good work. If you guys need a break, take one now. I'll stay here with Ralph.'

He didn't have to ask twice; everyone was tired from being glued to the monitors all morning. They hurried out as Collingwood took over one of their chairs. Ralph waited until the door closed behind them and then leaned in close.

'About bloody time. I've been fending off queries all fucking day.'

'Yeah, well, we had Norman O'Reilly in. So what's getting your knickers in such a twist?'

'It's no joke, Mike... this is all footage recorded on people's phones at the gallery.' Ralph plugged the hard drive into a desktop computer. Collingwood leaned back in his chair as one of the screens on a bank of six lit up, with the date and time stamp. After a few moments, Collingwood sat up, his back rigid as he watched footage of Jack Warr moving down the staircase at the gallery, exiting the glass lift, moving up the staircase and trying to herd people to move downstairs.

'Shit,' he said softly.

'You've not seen the best yet... this is from the gallery on floor three, and we've got four other sections from different people.'

The footage showed Kurt Neilson pulling the cover off one of his paintings, then the footage cut to Jack Warr tackling him to the ground as a gun spun away across the floor.

Collingwood sat back, feeling sick to his stomach. 'OK, leave it with me until I've had time to talk to Morrison. Don't mention it to anyone else.'

'It's dynamite, isn't it? I mean, what the hell was he doing there dressed up in his monkey suit? But I have to say he was bloody controlling the mayhem.'

'You do nothing until I tell you,' Collingwood snapped, eager now to get out and warn Jack what was coming. He pushed his chair back as Ralph turned to him.

'You know we got a rollicking about letting him into the ICU unit. I held my hand up about that. But after seeing this footage, I'm having second thoughts about it being a coincidence. He could be involved, Mike. I mean, Detmar Steinburg was bloody crucified...'

Collingwood slammed the door shut behind him, not wanting to listen to any more. But he had a stomach-churning feeling that Ralph was right.

CHAPTER 32

Collingwood had been trying to reach Jack all day. He called him at home and spoke to Penny, who told him he'd be at the station. At the station he was told Jack was unavailable. And the mobile number he had for Jack was dead. So far, Jack had been lucky. The officers working on the phone camera footage had tried to get Morrison's attention all morning and when he finally agreed to accompany them to the viewing room, he was called to a meeting with Detective Superintendent Broadbent. But Collingwood knew it couldn't last.

Unaware of all this, Jack, along with Laura, was taking a statement from a frail elderly woman who had called 999 to say she had murdered her husband. He had been found in his wing-back chair with a plastic bag tied around his head, his feet resting on the chair's footrest. She explained that they could not afford to send her terminally ill husband to Switzerland for the end-of-life programme, so when he had begged her to help him die, she had decided to do it herself. She said he was in terrible pain and had been for the past ten years. She said all this through quiet sobs as she sat on a sofa crying in the little drawing room, surrounded by officers. A doctor had already been called, and a care worker was also on the way.

Jack told them all to leave the crime scene, then crouched down in front of her, talking to her in a soothing voice, gently explaining that she would have to be taken to the station to be interviewed.

What a Jekyll and Hyde character you are, Jack Warr, Laura thought.

Eventually Jack and Laura left it to the uniforms and returned to the station. This time they were in the same squad car. Jack seemed tired, resting his head against the window and closing his eyes.

'I was down in the records department earlier,' Laura said. 'You know, still trying to find out about that little thug I've had in for the burglary. Are you listening?'

Jack grunted. 'Did you find anything?'

'I did, actually. But not what I was looking for. I noticed that you logged in a few days ago.' Jack turned to look at her, but she wouldn't meet his eye. She continued, still not looking at him. 'I don't know if you remember, I told you when I was at Fulham, in their incident room, I saw your photograph pinned up, alongside another man wanted for questioning.'

'Yes, I remember.' He still kept looking at her.

'I said I had a sort of déjà vu.'

'What are you trying to tell me Laura?'

'You accessed that file, the big drug bust when you and I spent months trying to trace the prime suspect.'

'Yeah, we did.'

'It was Adam Border, Jack. I recognised him from an old photo in the file. Ridley kept him on the wanted list. I think he still is.' Jack turned away and stared out of the window. 'You know it was him. I just don't understand why you never said. I mean, why?'

'He has nothing to do with the murder, they've got the killer, just forget it,' Jack said.

'Do you know what can happen to you if this gets out?' Laura persisted. 'Not only is he still wanted, but you could be charged with withholding evidence.'

'So what do you intend to do about it?' Jack asked her.

'You could lose your entire career if it got out Jack, I mean why have you lied?'

'Mind your own fuckin' business, Laura!' Jack said in a low voice. 'Just forget about it.'

She had never seen that quiet, icy anger before; his dark eyes frightened her. Could this really be the same man who had just treated the old lady with such gentleness? They passed the rest of the journey in silence.

* * *

The press coverage was creating a lot of anxiety among the top brass, and Morrison was still in a tense meeting with Broadbent and a high-ranking commander from Scotland Yard. The press seemed to have a lot of details about the guests at the gallery. Was there a leak at Fulham station? Or was Ester Langton the source? They debated whether to bring her in again.

Morrison explained that they had extensive footage from mobile phones sent to the station, which would hopefully make up for the fact that the CCTV cameras at the gallery had been destroyed. He explained that he had not yet had time to view them as he had been focusing on interviewing Norman O'Reilly, who was now in custody.

'That's all potentially positive,' Broadbent concluded. 'The important thing is that we appear to be making progress. We just need to make sure we control what details about the murder are released. We have to hope some of that mobile phone footage doesn't get into the press.'

After another half an hour, they had managed to draft a statement.

'Now's as good a time as any,' said Broadbent, 'with all the cameras outside the station. It's four o'clock now, so it'll make the six o'clock news. I'll read out the statement, and you, DCI Morrison, can take any questions.'

Morrison went to the washroom to splash his face with cold water, comb his hair and try to straighten out his crumpled suit. 'This is the bit I bloody hate,' he muttered to himself.

* * *

Jack and Laura had not spoken since they had returned to the station and written up their reports on the death of the old lady's husband. The body had been taken to the mortuary and the old lady, after being interviewed, was released into a care facility while the Crown Prosecution Service determined what charges, if any, she would have to face. By the time she had been taken from the flat, she seemed to no longer comprehend her situation, asking anxiously who would take care of her cat. The care worker, who had been responsible for the couple's welfare for the last two years, gently reminded her it had died years ago.

Jack was putting on his jacket. 'Well, that was a wretched day. I've had enough. I'm off home.' She stared at him. All the years they had worked together, and it had begun to dawn on her that she didn't really know him at all. 'See you tomorrow.'

'Yeah, bye Jack,' she said.

* * *

Morrison had started to sweat profusely as he sat watching the mobile footage. He turned to Collingwood in a fury.

'Why didn't you show me this earlier? This is fucking making me have heart palpitations. Warr's on a fucking shedload of recordings and I've just been out there on the bloody news. I should have had this hours ago.'

'I did try, Sir, but you were unavailable all afternoon, and I was unsure exactly what to do with this new evidence or what connection he has with the case. I mean, we have Kurt Neilson admitting his guilt, and we have confirmation from Norman O'Reilly that he was cleaning up blood in the shop with the bloke in the carpet.'

Morrison swivelled round in the chair to face him. 'Am I hearing you right? Don't you recall I interviewed Jack Warr about his presence at the ICU? He bullshitted his way out of that, and now we have him at the fucking gallery on the night Neilson was arrested! What the fuck do you think he was doing there, directing traffic?'

'I don't know, Sir.'

Morrison cocked his head to one side. 'Wait a minute . . . unless he was behind that anonymous phone call that got you running like a dog out of the traps to the gallery. Just think about it . . . if Kurt Neilson offered fifty grand to Norman O'Reilly, how much do you think he offered Jack Warr? I want him arrested and I want it done tonight, and I want him brought here in cuffs and chucked into a cell for withholding evidence.'

'But—' Collingwood started to protest.

'No fucking "buts",' Morrison cut him off. 'I'm telling you, the two-faced bastard will go down for this.'

CHAPTER 33

Seventy-year-old Henry Montgomery, art critic and collector, was being interviewed on the Channel Five news, and the story he had to tell was a sensational one. In a quietly authoritative tone, he described being behind a group of other guests when Neilson began showing his artworks. He then described the unveiling of the final painting, the crowd's shocked reaction and the moment Neilson pulled out a gun, before a young man literally hurled himself through the air to disarm him.

'Whoever that young man was, he was a hero. God knows how many lives he saved with his act of bravery.' That last quote soon went viral, but it was the mobile footage that went with it that really caused a sensation, clearly showing the ghastly painting and then, like a scene from an action movie, Jack recklessly throwing himself at the deranged artist.

When Jack arrived home, he had no idea that speculation about the gallery hero's identity was now spreading like wildfire on the internet. Maggie was not due home until seven, and Penny had collected Hannah at three with Charlie. Jack assumed they were up in the nursery, so made himself a coffee and was about to go and check on them when he heard a commotion upstairs. Penny rushed out of the nursery shouting for Hannah. Seeing Jack, she stopped in her tracks.

'Oh, Jack! You're on TV! I want Hannah to see you. Go in, hurry up!'

'What on earth are you . . . ?' Jack was about to follow her when his mobile rang and, at the same time, the doorbell went. He took his phone out of his pocket and he went back down the stairs to open the front door. Collingwood and a uniformed officer were on his doorstep and a patrol car with its blue light flashing was in the driveway.

'Sorry about this, Jack . . . I've been instructed to bring you to the station.'

'Am I under arrest? What the hell is going on?'

Collingwood stepped forward, motioning the officer to wait. 'Morrison is after you like a mad bull,' he said in a low voice. 'Mobile footage from the gallery has gone viral, and you're in loads of it. The media is going mental.' He leaned closer. 'Morrison will ask you if it was you who gave me the tip-off, but I've said nothing.'

The blue light on the patrol car had now drawn Penny to the stairs, and seeing Jack with Collingwood, she began to run down.

'What's happened? Is it Maggie?'

Jack turned to her with a calming gesture. 'It's nothing, Mum, I have to go into the station, something's come up. Tell Maggie I'll call her.'

Hannah came running down the stairs calling out 'Daddy! Daddy!' and hurled herself into his arms. 'I saw you on TV!'

'Daddy has to leave, you be a good girl and go with Nana.' Penny had to pull Hannah free from him, and held onto her as Jack grabbed his jacket from the hall stand and walked out with Collingwood.

Once they were in the car, Jack tuned to Collingwood. 'I've been caught up with a case all afternoon, what the hell is going on?'

Collingwood leaned back, closing his eyes. 'You haven't seen any TV news or the papers?'

'For Christ's sake, I've been at work all day . . . what's so urgent that you have to come to my home and take me out in front of my daughter?'

Collingwood kept his voice low. 'There's footage of you tackling Kurt Neilson to the floor all over the media. Everybody wants to know who the big hero is. You better get your story straight, Jack, or withholding information is going to be the least you get done for.'

* * *

At the station, the DS was hardly able to contain his fury. 'This bloody Montgomery interview has made our press release look like nonsense.' He jabbed his finger at Morrison. 'Are you telling me that this bloody "hero" was questioned by you previously and you had no knowledge of his presence at the gallery? And yet here he is, manhandling your killer and risking his own life, and you now tell me he's a Met police officer? And if that wasn't bad enough, Channel Five is showing the crucifixion painting which I categorically said must not be made public. I tell you right now, Scotland Yard is being humiliated.'

Morrison turned as there was a knock on the door and Ralph was standing in the doorway. 'Sir, Collingwood is bringing him in now. Just checking where you want him.'

'In the cells until I'm ready to interview him.'

The superintendent frowned. 'Is that strictly necessary? There may be an innocent explanation, so couldn't he be interviewed in your office initially?'

Morrison stood his ground. 'He needs to be interviewed under caution and on video. By withholding vital evidence, he's obstructed my investigation and perverted the course of justice. As to my previous interview with him, I had DI Armani from Warr's station confirming the reason he was in the ICU was not connected to the murder and, at that time, we still hadn't identified the victim as Detmar Steinburg.'

As the officer who had unwittingly encouraged Jack to join the team in the ICU sector, Ralph was eager to leave. 'Anything else,

Sir?' he said, backing out of the room. Morrison turned to dismiss him when Ralph remembered that he had received a message earlier in the afternoon.

'You had an officer checking out dumpsters that could have been used recently at the gallery. We have information that a company was hired twice this last week and . . .'

Morrison held up his hand dismissively. 'Thank you, I will deal with that later.'

'Hang on a minute, what's this about dumpsters?' the superintendent asked.

Ralph looked nervously towards Morrison, who was stacking files on his desk, pointedly ignoring the question. 'I'm not certain, Sir,' Ralph said. 'It appears some items may have been taken from the gallery, Sir.' He paused for a moment before sliding out and closing the door.

'Dear God, did you not have officers remain at the gallery?' the DS asked incredulously.

'Yes, I did, Sir,' Morrison said. 'And I did a thorough search with two officers, but due to the fire damage on the fourth floor we could only estimate which items had been removed, especially since we didn't have an inventory of the contents. We've also been hampered by Steinburg's legal team. We asked them to produce the deceased's will and details of the gallery's transactions, but they have so far not complied. And a lot of documents were destroyed in the fire, which doesn't help.'

'Then get a bloody warrant as soon as possible. I would also bring in Miss Langton. She could be holding documents back to line her own pockets.'

'I think she has been very cooperative,' Morrison said, trying to defend his handling of the investigation. 'She made the formal identification of Mr Steinburg.'

Their meeting was interrupted as Collingwood knocked and entered. 'DS Jack Warr is now in custody, Sir. As instructed, I've put him in the cells.'

'Did he kick up about it?' Morrison asked.

'No, Sir. He's confused but very calm, not argumentative in any way. He has not asked for a lawyer but would like to make a phone call.'

'Fine. He can make a call. I'll need some time to get ready, thank you.'

'Sir.' Collingwood closed the door behind him, then stood for a minute in the corridor. He could hear the DS loudly tearing a strip off Morrison, accusing him of mishandling the entire case.

'Now we've a detective sergeant being hailed as a hero who you didn't even know was there . . .' The irate superintendent clenched his fists. 'You didn't manage to identify the killer before he tried to shoot Christ knows how many people at the gallery, and you wouldn't have made an arrest if it wasn't for this DS Warr. Tread carefully, DCI Morrison. I am watching every fucking move you make from now on.'

Collingwood only made it a little further down the corridor before the superintendent slammed out of Morrison's office. He walked past, fuming with hands still clenched as he headed towards the incident room. Collingwood took the opportunity to make his way down to the cells. Sliding back the viewer, he saw Jack was sitting on the bunk bed. He stood up quickly, moving to the door.

'Morrison has been given a right dressing down and is now very jumpy. He's letting you make a phone call. I don't know if I'm going to be in the interview, but if the super decides he wants to be there he's maybe on your side. OK?'

Jack nodded. 'Is it just about withholding evidence?'

'So far, I think that's all he's going for, so he'll probably go back over the interview you had at your station.'

'Has he got any connection between me and Norman O'Reilly?'

'No, O'Reilly just said he cleaned the murder site for fifty grand, never got paid and he kept the victim's clothes as leverage.' Collingwood turned as the custody officer appeared.

'I'm to take him to make his phone call.'

'Right, I was just letting him know DCI Morrison will be interviewing him.' Collingwood left the cells, feeling less tense after overhearing the rollicking Morrison had taken. He knew it would be down to Jack to get himself off the hook, but he was now confident Jack would not implicate him.

* * *

Penny told Maggie what had happened as soon as she arrived home, and Maggie had been anxiously waiting for Jack to call ever since. It didn't help that Hannah kept on telling her excitedly that Daddy had been on TV.

Penny had recorded all the news programmes she could find, using her newly acquired technical abilities Marius had taught her.

'Good heaven, how many have you taped?' Maggie asked.

'As many as I could find, I've watched some on catch-up, and I've got recordings set for the late-night news programmes as well.'

'You are brilliant, thank you. Would you mind if I watched them by myself?'

'No, dear. I'll go and read to Hannah. She's so excited now that her father's famous.' She shook her head, knowing it was not good news at all.

Maggie had just sat down when Penny returned with a large glass of wine, quickly leaving again without a word and closing the door behind her.

CHAPTER 34

Maggie perched anxiously on the edge of the chair, watching all the footage, even pausing to go back and repeat some sequences, especially the interviews which had references to the mysterious man who had taken charge.

First there was the doorman. He had been shaken by the arrival of the police but had been warned by a young man to expect them and told to assist in ushering as many guests as possible from the premises.

Next came a young student who had been hired as a waitress. She recalled being told to lead guests out from the main reception area by one of the security guards and another man who she thought was working there. She said she became frightened when some guests left without claiming their coat tickets.

Maggie could not believe how many times Jack was visible, either shepherding guests down the staircase or standing at the top of another staircase shouting for people to get back. He seemed to be on virtually all the videos taken on mobile phones.

The most striking thing was that despite all the chaos, he always looked calm and in control, quietly assuring and encouraging the panicked guests. Together with the fact that they kept referring to him as 'the hero', it made her want to break down in tears. It shocked her that when he arrived home, he had not even mentioned the trauma he had been through, and it made her wretchedly sad and then angry. It reminded her of the feelings he had concealed during the period of his near breakdown.

Sometimes, it felt that she really didn't know him, how much he held in, how much he kept hidden from her and she felt not just hurt, but frightened. Their jokes about James Bond suddenly didn't seem funny anymore.

Maggie heard the landline ringing and ran down to the kitchen to pick it up.

'Mags, it's me.'

'Jack, are you all right?'

'Not too bad. They're holding me here at Fulham, and I wanted to tell you that I might not get home tonight, so don't worry.'

'Don't worry? Jack, I am worried sick. I've been watching all the footage . . .'

'Listen, I can't talk long, but I want you to check the pocket of my dinner jacket. There should be something in the side pocket. Don't say anything about it, not now . . . just keep it safe. It might be very important.'

'Jack, is this something to do with—'

He interrupted her before she could say Adam Border, his voice firm, almost angry. 'Don't say any names now, Mags. I know who you're referring to. Just wait until I call again, and in the meantime do the one thing for me.'

'Of course, but please don't protect him. This is serious, isn't it?'

'Just know I love you, and I'll be home soon.' He ended the call.

Maggie stood holding the phone in her hand for a moment, before slowly replacing it. She wanted to scream or shout or do *something* because she felt so useless. She went into the bedroom, opened the wardrobe, took out his dinner jacket, felt in one pocket after another, and finally found, stuffed into the inside pocket, the folded gold-embossed invitation. She took it into his office and was about to put it in one of the drawers, when she hesitated and decided to find a better hiding place.

A corner of the office, much to Jack's annoyance, had a stack of old toys and other items they intended on taking to the dump, unless she could sell them on eBay. Maggie picked up a broken plastic duck with a small trolley attached, which only had two wheels. The duck's plastic head had a hole in it, so she rolled the invitation up and stuck it down inside. She placed the duck among other broken toys then went back to the desk to shut the drawer. One of Jack's large brown envelopes, which he used to stash notes and memos to himself, was open. She eased it out of the drawer, tipping out everything onto the desk. Stapled together were several articles cut out of magazines like *Tatler*, *Vogue* and *Elle*, all featuring Detmar Steinburg at glamorous society events. There was also a Post-it note in Jack's handwriting with the words 'dealer' and 'forgeries' on it.

Penny peeped into the room and Maggie physically jumped. 'There's more news on – was that a call from Jack?'

'Yes, he's being held at Fulham police station. He said he won't be home tonight but will call again when he can.'

'You mean he's been arrested?'

'Just being questioned, Penny, nothing to worry about. Jack's not worried.'

'Should I call Marius and ask him to come over?'

'No, you carry on watching the TV.'

'They never said his name on all the news and interviews.'

'Please, Penny, just record anything else you see.'

'Yes, dear.' Penny left. As Maggie looked through the clippings, she heard her mobile. For a moment, she couldn't remember where she had left it. She was about to go and search for it, but the next moment the landline on Jack's desk rang. She snatched it up, hoping it would be Jack. It was Laura.

'Maggie? I just tried you on your mobile. I'm really getting worried because of all the news. I've tried to find out what's going on, and all I've found out is that Jack has been taken to Fulham station.'

'That's all I know too, Laura. He rang and said he was being held there probably overnight . . . can you find out what it's about?'

'It obviously has to do with what happened at the gallery. I couldn't believe Jack was there. You know he was previously questioned here at our station about getting access to the ICU where they were holding the victim? They accused him then of withholding evidence, but it was dismissed, so I reckon it must be connected. Listen, Maggie, maybe check out anything Jack might have been investigating on the QT. You know what he's like when he gets something that needles him. You need to understand, Maggie, this is really very serious, you have to get rid of anything incriminating, right now. Especially any reference to Adam Border, all right?'

'OK,' Maggie said. 'Thank you. And please call again if you find out anything else.' She put the phone down, then ran down into the hall and grabbed her coat, car keys and handbag.

Maggie drove to the nearest tube station and got out by the row of public telephones, which were all the new models requiring a credit card. She returned to the car and drove around the local areas until she found one that would take coins. She took out her purse and selected some coins, her hand shaking because she wasn't sure if she was doing the right thing or not. She had to use directory enquiries to get the numbers, writing them down on the back of her hand with a biro. She then placed the first call to the *Daily Mail* asking to be put through to the crime desk. Maggie made three further calls, always keeping the conversation brief.

'I recognised the man being called "the hero". He's Detective Sergeant Jack Warr of the Metropolitan Police.'

She did not give her name, hanging up each time as they asked for more details. Returning home, she went to Jack's office and searched the desk drawers for any more notes relating to Detmar Steinburg, then stuffed everything into a bin bag. Then she went down to the kitchen and opened the drawer in the big old dresser she used for all the family paperwork like mortgage documents, school reports and various receipts. She gathered them all up and returned to his office, stuffing them in the envelope Jack had used for his research into Steinburg and putting it into a drawer.

Trying to think of a good place to hide the bin bag, Maggie sat with it on her knee. She heard Penny's footsteps from the floor above and knew she should go and sit with her for a bit, even watch the late-night news. She put the bin bag on the floor and went into the corridor as Penny was coming down with Charlie's plastic waste bucket full of soiled nappies ready to be transferred to eco-friendly plastic bags that would go into the large collection bin provided by the council.

'Everything all right, Penny?'

'Yes, dear, Charlie was a bit ratty with his teething, so I've been sitting with him. I didn't want him to wake Hannah.'

'Let me take that out for you . . . we have a spare, don't we?'

'Yes, we've got two; one I've never used.'

Maggie took the plastic bucket from her and said she would bring her a hot chocolate. If Charlie was sleeping, they could watch TV together.

'I'd like that, dear. I've been worried sick.'

Maggie watched her return to the nursery and then went to her bedroom. She picked up the black bin bag and went down to the kitchen. She put most of the poo-filled nappies into the eco bags, tying them tightly. Then she went outside to the bins and put them in. Next, she pushed the black bin liner down into the bucket, placing two stinking nappies on top. With the secure plastic lid back on, she took it back upstairs and put it into the bathroom under the washbasin. Finally, she opened Jack's laptop and started trying out different passwords.

* * *

Jack had been held in the cell for three hours and had only just been brought a tray of sandwiches and coffee. He knew exactly how long anyone could be kept in custody without charge, but it was hard to remain patient. If they were going to accuse him of withholding evidence again, he suspected Morrison was carefully reviewing the notes of his previous interview. Admittedly, the fact that he had been left in the cell for so long had allowed him to think through how he was going to defend himself, but he was now beginning to lose his temper.

But it would be a while longer before he was interviewed. Morrison was now under renewed pressure after an anonymous caller identified the gallery 'hero' as Detective Sergeant Jack Warr. This revelation reached Morrison just as he was about to bring Jack up from the cells. The press was keen to find out if Detective Warr was an undercover officer working at the gallery or if his presence was just a coincidence. Morrison was under pressure to give them an answer and his now irate superintendent was not happy.

Broadbent walked straight into Morrison's office without knocking and kicked the door closed behind him. 'You have ten minutes to explain this latest development. DS Warr has now been named the hero at the art gallery, and you have him under arrest. How do you think that makes us look?'

Morrison struggled to find an answer. At that moment there was a tap on the door and Collingwood opened it. Morrison gestured for him to come in.

Broadbent continued. 'Let me get this straight – you're suggesting that Jack Warr knew who your victim was before you'd managed to identify him, and he was at the gallery because he also knew who had killed him?'

Morrison nodded. 'Exactly. He was withholding vital evidence.'

'For what reason?'

'Neilson promised to pay Norman O'Reilly fifty thousand to clean up the murder site. Maybe Warr was in on the action somehow too.'

Broadbent pursed his lips. 'I can't see how that makes any sense, given Warr's subsequent actions, but I'll admit he seems to have been one step ahead of you in terms of the investigation.'

'Shall I get him brought up from the cells, Sir?'

Broadbent thought for moment. 'We must tread carefully and make sure we have solid evidence before accusing a senior officer.'

'Yes, I think I have—' Morrison began.

Broadbent cut him off. 'It's all just circumstantial! He's a fucking hero right now, and now his identity is public, we cannot afford put a foot wrong. He's had a distinguished career to date . . . only last year, he solved a major serial murder case.'

Collingwood was waiting nervously for Morrison to bring up the anonymous phone call. He was about to interject when Broadbent ordered Morrison to get a search warrant for Jack Warr's home. 'And take a look at his desk here too.'

'Excuse me, Sir, but it's already after ten, and I know DS Warr has a new baby, and his wife is a doctor,' Collingwood said.

Broadbent gave a dismissive glare. 'No, we don't interview him until you've completed the search . . . if not tonight, then first thing in the morning. Scotland Yard has a team working with Steinburg's lawyers and accountants. They have agreed to produce all the relevant documents, including his will. Maybe that will tell us more about what the hell's been going on.'

* * *

Jack became even angrier when another hour passed and he was still not told what was happening. Collingwood had twice tried to get past the custody officer in the corridor to the cells, but it was getting dangerous to be seen talking to him – and then he was called away to try and get the search warrant signed by the on-call magistrate. It was eleven thirty, and Broadbent decided the search would go ahead at six o'clock the following morning.

Morrison was aware Jack had now been held in custody for six hours without charge, and another night would make it over sixteen hours. 'That's of no concern. We can get an extension from sixteen hours to twenty-four if we need to. That should give us plenty of time to get the evidence we need.'

Jack sat on the cot bed, trying to figure out their intentions. He lay back, closed his eyes, and began thinking through what Morrison had discovered. He knew he had got away by the skin of his teeth when they had tried to nail him for withholding evidence after his visit to the ICU. But he had to at least consider the possibility that Collingwood had grassed him up about the anonymous phone call. For the first time, he asked himself why he had kept his suspicions – and, ultimately, critical evidence – to himself. He had to face the truth. Maggie had been right: it was because he had been protecting Adam Border, instead of protecting his career and his family.

CHAPTER 35

Kurt Neilson had been under constant surveillance since being placed on suicide watch. Despite taking his medication, strict precautions were still in place. His requests for a visit from his mother were denied, and he was only allowed to speak with his lawyer via telephone in a protected booth, closely monitored by officers and medical staff. He barely spoke at first but soon became animated as, unprompted, he started describing his elaborate plans to murder his lover.

Although she had not visited Neilson in prison, Ester Langton had organised his legal team, who had initially reported that they were confident Neilson could claim diminished responsibility at trial, arguing that he had been mentally unbalanced at the time of the murder. The only problem with this strategy was Neilson's insistence on his guilt and tendency to describe the more horrific details of the murder with evident relish.

* * *

The following morning at six o'clock, Morrison, Collingwood, and two officers rang the doorbell and banged loudly on Jack's front door. Penny, wearing her dressing gown, opened the door looking terrified. They showed her the search warrant, but she seemed confused and distressed as they prepared to search the property. Tearfully, Penny went up to the bedroom and told Maggie that there were officers downstairs and that they had a warrant to search the house.

'Go and get Hannah dressed and Charlie ready for his feed. I'll get the pram out for you to walk them to school,' Maggie told her.

'But it's only six o'clock!' Penny wailed.

'Yes, I know, but after you've got their breakfast, you need to go . . . go to the play area in the park. I don't want Hannah upset or frightened. Go and tell them they can do whatever they need to and that I'm taking a shower.'

Penny did what she was told, hurrying to the nursery when she saw the officers entering the kitchen. By now, Hannah was shouting, and Charlie was screaming.

Wearing a dressing gown and with her wet hair wrapped in a towel, Maggie headed down the stairs. Collingwood stood at the bottom, looking apologetic.

'Does your husband have a home office?' he asked. Pulling her dressing gown even tighter around her, Maggie pointed to the office.

Maggie opened the hall closet and pulled out Charlie's pram, tucking the pillowed lining and blanket in ready for him to be put inside. She then went into the kitchen, where they were searching through the drawers and even the cutlery box. Morrison introduced himself, looking ill at ease.

'Will my mother-in-law be allowed to make the children breakfast? She always walks them to school. I'm shocked you're doing this to be frank. Has something happened to Jack? I thought he was helping you with your enquiries.'

'He's at the station and I'm sure he'll call you soon to explain in more detail,' Morrison said, eager to get away from her. She followed him up the stairs as Collingwood entered Jack's office.

'Are you allowed to do this? Jack's a police officer and that is his private home office.'

Morrison ignored her. But Collingwood showed her a copy of their search warrant. 'We're allowed to search the entire house,' he told her, without being able to meet her eye. He turned away and started with the drawers of Jack's desk.

Penny had been allowed to make breakfast, then she put Charlie into his pram and left the house with Hannah. As the search continued, Maggie dressed then brewed some coffee in the kitchen. She rang the hospital and told them she wouldn't be in that morning due to a family matter but hoped to be in later that afternoon.

Heading up the stairs, she could see Jack's office door was partly open. Morrison and Collingwood were searching his desk, all the drawers open. Morrison turned to her. 'Does Jack have a laptop?'

She hesitated. 'He used to have one; it may be at the station.' She continued on to her bedroom, and Collingwood followed her sheepishly. As he walked in, she turned, holding the plastic nappy container.

'I was just taking this out to the bins.' Maggie went closer, then opened the lid of the container. 'If you want to search it, go ahead.' He shifted his weight as she withdrew the lid and held it out. He peered inside, trying not to gag, then shook his head. Looking over to the bed, he saw Maggie's laptop.

'I can't allow you to take that. It is my personal laptop containing information from some of my patients. It does not belong to Jack, and I am sure your search warrant only allows you to remove my husband's belongings.'

'I'm sorry, but we need to take it, and the computer from his office.'

Maggie sighed heavily, heading to the door as Collingwood began to search through Jack's clothes in the wardrobe, checking pockets and taking out the evening suit jacket. She walked out, and passing the office door, she saw Morrison sifting through the stack of documents she had left in the drawer. He didn't even turn to look at her as she carried the plastic container down to the kitchen.

They had left most of the drawers and the cupboards open, stacked the clean tea-towels and left them on the floor. She placed the bin by the big ceramic flowerpots, astonished that they even appeared to have dug around in them, leaving soil all over the floor.

The two officers who had searched the top-floor nursery, Penny's room, and the bathrooms, were now in the loft. Maggie found a brush and began clearing the soil, leaving the back door open.

Collingwood returned to Jack's office, holding Maggie's laptop.

Morrison nodded. 'Don't forget to get the password, so we don't waste any more time.'

'Yes, Sir. You found anything?'

'He's mortgaged up to the hilt with fuck all in his bank accounts. She's earning good money, but as soon as it comes in it looks like it goes straight out. Right, let's get this lot back to the station.' The evidence boxes containing all the items they had removed were being carried down the stairs.

'I'm sorry Doctor Warr, but we need to take this into the station as it could also have been used by your husband.'

She threw up her hands and strode past him. 'The house is a mess. You could at least clean up before you go.' Maggie remained in the bedroom until she heard the front door slam and the patrol cars moving off. She went into Jack's office, where papers were strewn over the desk and floor. It looked as if they had kicked over the toys she had intended to get rid of. The little duck was on its side, and among other overturned items was the old plastic cart. Suddenly she felt the tears welling up and was about to burst into sobs when she heard Penny shouting. She hurried to the window. Penny was outside on the path with Charlie in his pram, furiously telling two journalists they were on private property and to get out or she would call the police.

When Maggie got downstairs, Penny was inside, slamming the front door shut behind her. She was fuming. 'One was hiding in the bushes! If they're still there, I'll go upstairs and throw a bucket of water over them. One had a camera, trying to take our photographs.'

Maggie told her to take Charlie upstairs and not to bother throwing water over anybody as she folded the pram. Next, she checked the nappy bin and removed the bin liner before taking the bucket to the bins.

A short while later, Penny came down. Charlie had been fed and was much calmer, so she carried him to his swing seat and hooked his safety harness around him. Charlie was instantly a happy little soul bouncing up and down.

Maggie walked in, and Penny immediately saw that she'd been crying. She held out her arms. 'Come here, love, give me a hug . . . you look as if you need one.'

Maggie sat on Penny's knee, wrapping her arms around her and resting her face on her neck as she cried. Penny gently rocked her just as she did her granddaughter, telling her softly that everything was going to be all right.

'Jack's been in trouble before, but he always comes out on top. He'll be home soon, and everything will be sorted out. You just have to calm yourself and be here for him when he needs you.'

Maggie sniffed. 'I don't know what I'd do without you, Mum.' Maggie had never referred to Penny as 'Mum' before, and it made Penny cry. Then the pair of them started to laugh. It was a childlike moment between the two women before Penny cupped Maggie's face in her hands.

'We're here for him. I know this is serious, but we never show that we are scared for our boy.'

* * *

Jack had finally been allowed to take a shower. He was still in the clothes he had been wearing when they brought him in, but he felt a little better. He was returned to his cell and this time, a young, uniformed officer was assigned to take him back. When Jack asked how long it was going to be before someone told him what was going on, he got an embarrassed shrug.

'Morrison's back from the search, so . . .'

'Search? Are you telling me they've been searching my home?'

'All I know is there's a lot of people up in the incident room, some of them from Scotland Yard.'

* * *

Morrison stood up behind his desk as Broadbent came in with a thick file, followed by Collingwood carrying another file.

'So, what did you find at his house?' Broadbent demanded. 'Anything connecting him to Detmar Steinburg?'

Morrison looked uncomfortable. 'We removed his computer and a laptop from the address, both of which are being examined by the digital technology blokes.'

'That's it? A laptop . . . and is it Jack Warr's?'

'It's his wife's.'

'She gave you permission to take it?'

'Warr could also be using it. Plus, his home PC had data on it that he must have illegally downloaded from the HOLMES major incident database.'

'Show me a fucking officer who hasn't done that, so they can complete their work at home,' snapped Broadbent. He sat down in front of Morrison.

'We have some new information, first up the contents of Steinburg's will. His main beneficiary is Ester Langton: she gains all his personal property, including his art collection. However, there is a proviso attached: Miss Langton will only receive the bequests if she takes care of Kurt Neilson financially and pays all his medical bills.'

Broadbent shook his head and gave a grunt of a laugh. 'Given his mental health issues, that might put quite a dent in her finances. And she definitely won't be inheriting any cash from Steinburg. In fact, all she may be inheriting is crippling debt. It looks like his whole global business empire was a house of cards. He didn't own any of the galleries or the penthouse – they were all on short-term leases and he died owing a staggering amount of money. I'll be handing all the documents over to the fraud squad, let them sort it all out.' He closed the file in front of him. 'So, tell me, what else did the search of Jack Warr's home turn up, apart from his wife's laptop? Uncovered any connection to Steinburg?'

Morrison was sweating again. 'I'm afraid not – not so far, anyway – but the search history on his wife's laptop is interesting. Lots of articles about art fraud and books about it ordered from Amazon.

Broadbent was studying his nails. 'That's it?'

'To date, yes it is, but we are still working on it.'

'OK, might as well interview him now. But I'd say so far you have fuck all on him. I hope you're going to prove me wrong.'

It was decided they would interview Jack in the largest interview room. The meeting would be recorded, and as he had not requested a lawyer, Broadbent and Collingwood would also be present. Accompanied by a young, uniformed officer, Collingwood headed down to the cells. He stood to one side as the cell was unlocked and waited as Jack casually walked out. As all three reached the stairs, Collingwood told the officer in front to go up ahead of them, giving Jack and Collingwood a few seconds alone.

'We found nothing, Jack. And you're in the clear on the anonymous call.'

In the interview room, Morrison was seated next to Broadbent, and Collingwood was left to stand behind them. The table was stacked with files.

'Right,' Morrison began, looking at Jack seated opposite him. 'You've been arrested for obstructing a police investigation by withholding vital evidence pertaining to the arrest of Kurt Neilson and the murder of Detmar Steinburg.' Jack sat back in the chair, his hands resting on his knees, appearing relaxed. Morrison coughed then continued. 'Firstly, can you explain how you financed two large extension projects in your house?'

'What? How do you know about that?'

'We had a search warrant, and we were at your property this morning.'

'A search warrant? What the hell is going on? You've been holding me here since yesterday afternoon. Why did you need a fucking search warrant? What could I possibly have that you hoped to find at my family home?'

'I'm asking you again, Jack. How did you pay for the building work at your property?'

Jack banged the desk with the flat of his hand. 'I had paternity leave; my mother's partner is a retired builder and we did the work between us. My wife will be able to provide you with the breakdown of costs as she handled the finances.'

Broadbent tapped the table for Morrison to change the subject.

'All right,' Morrison said, clearly annoyed. 'How can you explain your presence at Steinburg's gallery on the night of Kurt Neilson's arrest?'

'Jesus Christ! Is this what it's all about? I had an invitation.'

'Explain how you acquired this invitation. We have a list of all the guests, and your name wasn't on it.'

'Well, on a Friday morning, a few weeks before the exhibition, I was at the framer's shop in Portobello Road. I asked the man in the shop the price of a small gilt frame, and he told me it was ten pounds. I offered him five. He got irate and snatched the frame out of my hands, then told me to get out. I was standing by a cabinet and noticed there was a stack of invitations. Honestly, at the time, I didn't know what they were, but I was so angry at the way he had spoken to me that I took an invite without thinking.'

'Did you notice anything unusual inside the shop at this time?'

'Yes, I did. There was an enormous cross that took up a huge amount of room. In fact, I recall making a joke about whether or not it had been bought from *Jesus Christ Superstar*.'

'So, now you had this invitation for the show at Steinburg's gallery, what did you do with it?'

'Well, it was a coincidence because my wife and I had recently become very interested in art. It's become a bit of a hobby we share outside our work. Around this time, I think there was also a lot of coverage about a painting being valued at sixty or more million, and we started to get interested in how paintings are valued and then the whole business of art fraud.'

'Detective Warr, you recall our previous interview regarding your presence at the ICU where Detmar Steinburg was being treated?'

'Of course. At that time, Detective Morrison, you had not identified him. You made an accusation that I was somehow attempting to gain information about him when I was there on another case at the request of DI Armani. My presence there was totally and utterly coincidental. I made no effort to see the victim but was encouraged by two of your officers to join them for a cup of coffee. I don't know why you don't accept my explanation. Have you got some personal grievance against me?'

'I'm investigating a brutal murder,' Morrison snapped. 'And you still have a lot of explaining to do. Do you expect us to believe that your presence at the Steinburg gallery was another coincidence, because you just happened to pick up an invitation?' Morrison said, trying to control his temper.

'Yes, it was. Whether or not you believe me is up to you.'

Broadbent tapped the table with his pen. 'Did the name Detmar Steinburg mean anything to you?'

'No, I had no idea who he was. Though I must admit I was hoping I might meet him, after we did a bit of research and found out he was a famous collector and dealer.' Jack leaned back, chuckling. 'I nearly got stopped at the door, even though I was all togged up, but there was quite a crowd, and I managed to slip through.'

Broadbent leaned forward, tapping the table again with his pen. 'You may be amused, Jack, but believe me, I am not. Finding yourself in close proximity to the victim and then to the killer smacks of more than mere coincidence.'

'But along with DCI Morrison, when I was in the ICU, I didn't know the victim *was* Detmar Steinburg. Likewise when I picked up the invitation. I had no idea there was a connection.'

Broadbent leaned back, looking annoyed and frustrated. Morrison took over. 'OK, tell us what occurred at the gallery while you were innocently looking at the paintings?'

Jack thought for a moment. 'I went into the first gallery and then moved up to the second floor. There was another display, but the exhibition of new work was taking place on the third floor, and there was a chain and padlock on the doors. This time, I didn't walk down the stairs but used the lift. I intended to go back down to the ground floor, but by mistake I pressed the button to go up.' He glanced from Broadbent to Morrison. Both were stony-faced. 'So, I was now on the fourth floor. I heard someone screaming, then

I saw a woman, I now know her name is Ester . . . something, she was being assaulted by this man, he was punching her and shouting. I ran into the office. He had hit her in the face and she was bleeding. He then turned and tried to punch me. I recognised him as the man from the framer's shop. He was frothing at the mouth with rage, shouting that he was owed money. I punched him hard, and he ran down the stairs. I helped Ester into the bathroom and cleaned her up with some paper towels. She was very shaken, and I think I told her she should call the police.'

'Did you see her make the call?'

'No. She went back into her office.'

Broadbent was checking through Norman O'Reilly's statement. It tallied with what Jack had just described. 'When did you meet Kurt Neilson?'

'I wouldn't describe it as meeting him. I left the bathroom after looking after Ester . . . ah, I think her surname is Langton. I was going to use the lift to go down as I heard a loudspeaker announcement encouraging the guests to go to the third floor as the exhibition was about to open. I had no idea it was Kurt Neilson, but when I came out of the bathroom, I saw a big man wearing this long robe. He was screeching at Ester, something about it being his exhibition, and then he ran to the stairs and she came out in a terrible state. She asked me to get the security guards, said he was crazy and she was afraid of what he was going to do. She didn't need to tell me twice. He seemed completely crazed. She went down in the lift to the first floor.'

'Did she call the police then?'

'She must have, because they arrived not long after, and by that time I had the guards with me in gallery three. We'd tried to stop people coming up. It was already obvious Neilson was out of control.'

Morrison began to lay out the photographs taken from the mobile phone video footage.

Jack leaned forward, looking from one to the other, then picking one up and staring at it, said, 'My God, that is me. I'd manoeuvred to stand behind him, and the two guards were on either side of me, and then when he unveiled this huge canvas, all hell broke loose. I saw his right hand go into the pocket of his robe, and he took out a Glock pistol. I was convinced he was going to either fire into the crowd or shoot himself and . . .' Jack turned the photograph around, showing himself flying through the air towards Kurt Neilson. 'I'd like to know how long you have had this evidence . . . you brought me in and left me for how many hours in a cell when you had all this?' Jack started to stand.

'Sit down!' Morrison barked.

'When did you identify your victim as Detmar Steinburg?' Jack asked him.

'I'm asking the questions!' Morrison snapped.

'That night? You had me arrested and for what? Not staying at the scene? I want a damned good explanation for what you have subjected me to, not to mention my family.'

Morrison looked to Broadbent, who was tapping the last page in his file.

'Why did you leave the gallery?'

'As far as I can recall,' Jack said slowly, 'I believe DI Collingwood and a team of officers were at the gallery. He had the place surrounded and, after the experience of dealing with that crazed man, I just wanted to get out of there and be with my family'.

Morrison asked the next question staring hard at Jack, as if daring him to lie. 'Did you make the anonymous call to Fulham police station control room that night, Detective Warr?'

'No, I did not. Now I think it's about time I called a lawyer as I have been subjected to what I would describe as harassment from a senior officer who clearly bears some personal grudge against me.' Jack wondered for a beat if he had overstepped the mark. His biggest fear was that they had found the stash of money hidden in the child's toy, but as it had not been mentioned, he assumed it was still safely hidden.

Broadbent stood up. 'I would ask you to be patient, DS Warr, while I re-assess the whole situation.' He turned to Collingwood, who had been standing behind them. 'Is there anything you would like to add?'

'I would just like to say, on DS Warr's behalf, although at the time I was unaware of not only who he was or that he was in fact a police officer, his calmness and courage in a chaotic and potentially highly dangerous situation were admirable. By the time we put the cuffs on Neilson, the situation was well in hand.'

Broadbent nodded as if satisfied, then suddenly said, 'But surely you must have recognised him because you had met him before in the ICU viewing room?'

Collingwood hesitated, licking his lips nervously, and for a moment Jack thought he was going to fold. 'The thing is ... as I said earlier, it was a chaotic scene, a lot of panicked people milling about, and he was dressed in an evening suit, so I just assumed he was one of the guests. I simply didn't make the connection at the time with the officer I'd met in the ICU.'

Jack held his breath, but Broadbent seemed satisfied with Collingwood's answer, even though Morrison was shaking his head in disbelief.

Broadbent stood. 'Right. Better organise a patrol car to take DS Warr home.'

Collingwood held the door open and followed Jack out. As the door closed behind them, Broadbent turned to Morrison. 'I don't believe in coincidences any more than you do. But I'm afraid we just don't have any hard evidence that Warr did anything wrong.

And I don't want him suing the department for harassment. The plain fact is that without his intervention at the gallery, there could have been numerous casualties. He risked his life and then just wanted to return home to his wife and children.'

'I still don't trust him,' Morrison said plaintively.

Broadbent opened the door, saying quietly, 'Neither do I. He's a clever bugger ... and now he's a hero. But even clever buggers make mistakes. Just be patient.'

CHAPTER 36

It was three thirty and Jack was heading for the station's main reception with a spring in his step, but Collingwood put a hand on his arm. 'Better to use the back entrance and leave through the station yard, Jack. The press are out front in force. No doubt they want to get a few quotes from the hero of the hour.'

'Bloody hell,' Jack said.

'Somehow they got wind of your name and rank and since then they've been laying siege to the place.'

Jack patted Collingwood's arm. 'I've got a lot to thank you for, Mike.' He shook his head. 'I can't believe Morrison searched my house.'

'I'd say it's your wife you need to thank, Jack – big time. Come on, I've got a car waiting.' As the patrol car swept out, Jack looked back and saw the scrum of reporters and photographers milling around outside. But his relief at having dodged them was short-lived. As the patrol car parked up outside his house, a journalist popped up, seemingly out of nowhere, with a photographer close behind.

'Detective Jack Warr, I'm from the *Daily Mail*, and I have a few questions . . .' Jack resisted the temptation to push the photographer out of his way. Instead, he kept his head down and sidestepped him as he hurried to the front door. He fumbled to get his keys out as the photographer started snapping away, finally managing to open the door and slam it shut behind him. He stood in the hall for a few moments, taking deep breaths.

'Maggie?' he called out, walking into the kitchen. It was a mess. All the drawers had been emptied and the contents left scattered on the floor, along with grocery lists and takeaway leaflets. The sink was full of dirty pans and crockery, and there was a pile of dirty washing beside the washing machine.

Jack hurried up the stairs. 'Maggie! Mum!' Their bed had been left unmade, and going into the nursery, he found a pile of Charlie's dirty clothes beside his cot, while his changing table was littered with empty bottles of milk and dirty food bowls. He could feel his heart pounding as he went into Hannah's bedroom and saw the same disarray. Even Penny's room looked as if it had been ransacked, with an unmade bed, drawers open and clothes strewn across the bed as if she'd left in a hurry. The whole house was like the *Marie Celeste*.

Going back down to the kitchen, he called the hospital, pacing anxiously while he was put on hold. 'I've just come out of surgery. I've only got a minute,' she said curtly.

'I'm home, Maggie, everything's fine . . .'

'We have a lot to sort out, Jack,' she said, as if she hadn't heard him. 'I'll be home around seven. Penny's taken Hannah to a dance class, and Charlie's with a baby minder at the school. Marius is with them. I have to go . . . we'll talk later.'

Jack stood holding the receiver. Never in the entire time he had been with Maggie had he heard that cold, dismissive tone in her voice. He stood there, unsure how to deal with it, before replacing the receiver and running up the stairs to his office. He was expecting the worst, but he was still shocked by the state of it. It looked as if the contents of all his drawers and what had been on his desk had been tipped onto the floor, along with the phone, but what made him really furious was the way the old children's toys had clearly been kicked around. He picked up one of Hannah's old broken dolls, now with its arms ripped off, and flushed with anger.

He took a moment to calm himself, then got down on all fours and searched through the debris for the plastic cart. He turned it over and sighed with relief when he saw the duct tape was still in place. Getting to his feet, he took another deep breath and returned to the kitchen.

After making himself a cup of tea, he went back upstairs and took a shower, washed his hair, shaved and put on a clean T-shirt and jeans. It was now after six, and he was expecting Penny and the children to be home before Maggie. Suddenly he heard Hannah singing at the top of her voice. He hurried down the stairs; Hannah was twirling round and round, wearing a pink leotard, white tights and ballet shoes, while Penny was taking Charlie out of his pram. When she saw him, she ran into his arms with an excited yelp.

'I've been at ballet class, Daddy!'

Penny gave Jack a disapproving look. 'She wouldn't get changed,' she said.

'You were on TV... I saw you on TV!' Hannah shrieked.

'I was going to order a takeaway,' Jack said, giving Hannah a hug.

'We've already eaten, and this little boy needs changing so I'll take him straight upstairs,' Penny said coldly.

'Mum, everything's all right. I'm home, and it's over.'

'You've got a lot of explaining to do... we've had a terrible time here,' Penny said, shaking her head.

'I can make some hot chocolate for everyone,' Jack suggested.

'We had some at McDonald's. Mustn't have too much sugar when they have to go to bed.'

It was obvious Penny wasn't going to talk to him, so he went up to his office to see what Maggie had done with all his research on Detmar Steinburg. He heard the front door closing and ran downstairs. Maggie was taking off her coat in the hall. Ignoring him, she went straight into the kitchen, putting a pizza box down on the table.

'Mags . . .' He went to embrace her, but she pushed him away.

'Go up and ask Penny to show you all the TV footage and newspaper articles, then come down and we'll have pizza.' Jack did as he was told.

Fifteen minutes later, he came back down to find Maggie had opened a bottle of wine. 'OK, I've seen enough,' he said.

'Sit down,' Maggie told him. 'I'll put the pizza in the oven, and you can pour me a glass of wine.' Jack poured two glasses of wine. Maggie took two warmed plates out of the oven and searched a drawer for the pizza cutter.

'So, what did they arrest you for?'

'Obstructing an investigation and withholding evidence.'

'Those are criminal offences, right?'

Jack shrugged. 'Sure, but that prick DCI Morrison already tried and failed to pin them on me. I don't know why, but he's got it in for me.'

'So, it was not until the footage from the gallery was released that they suspected you of withholding evidence for the second time.'

'Yeah, someone at the gallery was bound to have got me on their mobile.'

'So, after you had done your hero bit, you just walked out?'

Jack shrugged and took a sip of wine. 'Yeah, by then Mike Collingwood was in control of the situation. I just wanted to get home.'

'So it was very fortunate he was there in good time,' Maggie said.

'Well, it was kind of down to me. I told him to get as many officers as possible to the gallery asap because I knew something was going down.'

'You contacted him?'

'I made an anonymous call to the station and got through to Mike. I didn't want that shit Morrison getting the kudos.'

Maggie took out the pizza and cut it into slices.

'This looks great,' Jack said, rubbing his hands. 'All I've had is a few biscuits in the last twenty-four hours.'

'At what point did you know, as you put it, something was going down?'

Jack took a bite of pizza and chewed for a moment before he answered. 'I thought I was right about the victim being Detmar Steinburg, but without your brainwave about that guy Joe Orton, I'd never have pieced the whole thing together. As soon as I saw Kurt running around like a nutcase, I knew he'd done it.'

Jack finished his first slice; Maggie just nibbled on one of hers and then sipped her wine. 'So, you suspected that Morrison's unidentified victim was Detmar Steinburg, and you went to the gallery to prove you were right.'

'Yes.'

'You had no other reason than that?'

Jack put down his second slice of pizza. 'Where are you going with this?'

'You know exactly where I'm going.'

'No, I don't.'

'Yes, you do.'

'OK, Mrs Detective, tell me. You think I had some ulterior motive?'

'I know you did. And you were prepared to risk your career and your family for it.'

Jack tensed. 'What the hell are you talking about?'

'Adam Border. I think you withheld evidence until you could find out, one: if the victim was Adam Border, and two: if he wasn't, had he committed the murder.'

Jack was speechless. Suddenly he felt like he was back in the interview room, only this time he was being grilled by his wife. Maggie got up and picked up a suitcase on the floor by the door. She carried it over and banged it down onto the table. Opening it, she took out Jack's laptop.

'I managed to get this out of the house, right under their noses. I put it in Charlie's pram beneath the covers. Penny took him and Hannah out of the house because they were scared out of their minds with the police banging around and tipping things out of drawers.'

Next, Maggie took out of the black bin liner, tipping the contents onto the table. 'All your notes and press cuttings about Detmar Steinburg.' Jack looked on in shocked silence. Maggie picked up her wine glass and took a long gulp. 'I cleared out your desk drawers and put all this into a nappy bin, leaving two of Charlie's dirty ones on top. Then I called the papers and told them you were the unnamed man at the gallery.'

'Did you give your name?'

'*No!* Of course not. Then I retrieved the invitation from your evening suit jacket pocket and hid it, like you asked me.'

'Did they find it?'

'I stuffed it in the plastic wheelie duck . . . it's still there.' Jack was about to speak when she snapped. 'I haven't finished. I removed all my receipts, mortgage documents and bank statements from the kitchen drawers and put them in your office. When they searched in there, they removed the lot.'

Maggie grabbed everything from the table to shove back into the case, then slammed it shut and carried it back to the doorway.

'If I hadn't managed to hide everything, especially your laptop, they could have found a lot of incriminating evidence, probably enough to charge you. They took my laptop, in case you'd used it, but I doubt there was anything incriminating. I am taking legal advice as it is predominantly used for my work, so it is an invasion of medical records privacy.'

'I don't know what to say. I might not be here now without what you did.'

'You need to think about everything, Jack. I refuse to have you jeopardise my life, my career, our family and your own career. Sleep in the loft tonight because no matter how much I love you and want to protect you, I can never go through this again.'

She walked out, leaving him sitting at the table with the rest of the now cold pizza.

CHAPTER 37

Jack lay on the small single bed they'd bought from Portobello market feeling utterly wretched. He went over the entire discussion he'd had with Maggie. He'd always known she was far more intelligent than he was, and tonight, she had once again given proof of her many talents. Her quick thinking and determination to protect him made him feel like weeping. He immediately considered giving in his notice and leaving the Met, but then what other options would he have?

He was trying to avoid facing the truth of her accusation. He had risked so much, and it wasn't the first time. He closed his eyes, hoping to sleep, but his brain kept spinning, trying to figure out his next move. He knew if he went back to the station, the boredom would only get worse and he'd never get the respect he felt he deserved. Reflecting on his emotional breakdown and how Maggie had protected him, he said to himself, 'I have to make some changes in my life.'

One thing was for sure, he didn't want to change his family. Maggie and the children were the best part of his life. Losing them would destroy him and he'd only have himself to blame. He began to go over everything that had happened over the last few weeks, eventually falling into a deep sleep as exhaustion overtook him.

Maggie had an early start at the hospital. Penny was preparing for the walk to school with the children when she saw Maggie was getting ready to leave. 'Is everything all right, dear?' she asked tentatively.

'No, Mum, it isn't, but I don't want to talk about it now.'

Penny quickly changed the subject. 'Marius was asking about knocking down the walls.'

'Fine, let him come in and smash them down. It might wake the hero.'

'Oh, I wanted to tell you that his computer, his mobile phone and your laptop were delivered late last night. They're in Jack's office. It was so late I didn't want to disturb you,' Penny said.

Maggie shrugged, collecting her medical bag and briefcase before walking out of the kitchen, fighting back the tears. Penny sighed deeply, then got on with getting Hannah ready and Charlie settled in his pram.

Jack heard the movements downstairs and waited for Penny and the kids to leave the house. He had a shower and put on his best suit. In his office, he found the invitation hidden inside the plastic duck. He charged his mobile and then made a to-do list before making some calls. He got through to DCI Clarke, briefly explained that he wanted a transfer, and ended the call before Clarke could ask any questions. He then called DCI Broadbent at Scotland Yard.

'Good morning, Sir. I wanted to let you know that although my mobile phone and laptop have been returned, along with my wife's laptop, she is taking legal advice for misappropriating her confidential medical reports.'

Broadbent was taken aback by Jack's aggressive tone. 'I do hope we can avoid getting into any kind of legal situation, DS Warr.'

Jack continued. 'As you know, the press is still very eager to interview me. I have declined to speak with them up to this point, but before I make a final decision, I would like to know the Yard's intentions regarding my presence at the art gallery.'

'I believe it is under discussion this morning.'

'That's good. I hope it will be satisfactory. I really don't want to broadcast the fact that I was in a cell for over sixteen hours and subsequently released with no charges.'

'As I said, we are discussing the entire situation at eleven o'clock this morning.' Broadbent was trying his best to sound reassuring.

'Good. I have also resigned this morning and would like to suggest an alternative position. Perhaps this would be a good time to discuss—'

'I'm sorry, are you saying you have resigned?'

'As a homicide detective, not from the police service. I was hoping there might be another more suitable position within the Met.'

Broadbent was struggling to assimilate everything Jack was saying. All he could do was to try and pacify him. 'I believe DCI Morrison will not be present at the meeting this morning.'

'He shouldn't be. He's an incompetent officer with a personal grudge against me. If you examine my records and the many murder cases I have headed up, you'll realise it was a deplorable act to accuse me of misconduct. His outrageous treatment of me as a highly respected officer should be part of your discussion this morning. And perhaps his extra-marital affairs should also be mentioned while you're at it. My home was invaded and you found no incriminating evidence against me. To be treated like a common criminal, arrested and put in a cell for what have been described as heroic actions is beyond belief. And let's not forget that my actions led to the arrest of a very dangerous killer.'

'Thank you for calling, Jack, I will endeavour to convey what you've said to the commissioner this morning.'

'Thank you, Sir, but I would appreciate it if I could be present.'

'I doubt that will be possible . . .'

'I'll be at Scotland Yard this morning for you to update me,' Jack said, ending the call before Broadbent could argue further.

Jack pushed back his chair and stood up. He was beginning to feel better about things. For the first time in his career, he had spoken up for himself, and it felt good. He hoped he could keep it up in front of the commissioner and the rest of the brass later. In the kitchen he saw that Penny had left the ironing board up beside a basket of laundry. He took the rolled-up invitation out of his pocket and switched on the iron. He waited only until the iron was warm enough, then ironed out the creases and slipped it back into his pocket.

* * *

After checking Morrison's office, Collingwood tracked him down to the canteen. He was sitting at a corner table, his unfinished breakfast pushed to one side.

'Morning, Sir, do you want the good news or the bad news?'

Morrison's red-rimmed eyes glared at him. 'Don't try and be funny with me.'

'Sorry, Sir, but I've just had the fire department's forensic results from the gallery.'

'Christ, was it fucking arson?'

'They don't think so. No accelerants were discovered.'

Morrison nodded. 'That's one less problem then.'

'Seems so, Sir.' Collingwood handed Morrison the file and went to the counter to get some breakfast.

* * *

Jack got an Uber and grabbed breakfast at a coffee bar near Scotland Yard. It was only 9.45 a.m. so he took his time finishing his macchiato and bagel before taking the short walk to the Yard.

Approaching the main desk, he showed his ID and explained that he was scheduled to meet with Detective Superintendent Broadbent and the commissioner. The young female uniformed officer checked the scheduled meetings on her computer. As Jack had hoped, he was now slated to attend.

'You're a bit late, I'm afraid,' she said, frowning. 'They've been in the main boardroom since nine.' She gave him a lanyard and instructed him to go to the third-floor reception desk. Jack went through security, which included a thorough check of his briefcase, and took the lift. On the third floor he walked past the reception desk and straight to the double doors of the boardroom. He took a deep breath, then opened the doors and strode in.

Seated at one end of the oval-shaped table were Broadbent, the uniformed commander and the commissioner. They turned in surprise as Jack closed the door behind him and approached the table. Judging by the array of coffee mugs and empty plates, it was obvious to him that they had been closeted together for some time.

Broadbent stood up. 'I was not expecting you until later this morning, Detective Warr.'

'I wanted to be here as soon as possible after our conversation.'

Broadbent turned to introduce the two senior officers, who gave cold, hard stares but said nothing as Jack drew out a chair at the other end of the table.

The commissioner nodded for Broadbent to remain seated. He had a large file open in front of him. He laid his right hand on top of the thick stack of documents. 'We have been looking at your career, which I find very impressive. You have proven yourself to be a skilled investigator with a strong understanding of forensic science and an excellent team spirit. The recent situation has been a shocking and damaging development for the Met's policing. I have thoroughly reviewed the facts of the case and your subsequent wrongful arrest. I want to express my sincere regret for the distress it has caused you and your family. I have also taken into account your involvement in the arrest of Kurt Neilson and your determination to protect the many innocent lives that were at risk.'

Jack leaned back in his chair. The three men exchanged glances as if they had already discussed exactly what the commissioner would say. When he got no response from Jack, he coughed and after a pause, continued.

'Detective Warr, we have prepared a statement for the press that we want you to review. We need to put a lid on all the speculation instigated by your disappearing act, for want of a better description.'

Broadbent was handed a typed single page with a Scotland Yard logo. He walked down the table to pass it to Jack and then returned to his seat.

Jack leaned on his elbows as he read over the statement. It was bullshit, explaining that to avoid identifying a senior undercover detective, they had withheld his identity for his safety. Jack finished reading and slid the page back down the table.

The commissioner then looked at Broadbent before he coughed. 'Regarding your future within the Met, you informed DCI Broadbent in a call early this morning that you had every intention of resigning; understandable, as you were still under pressure from the media and had no wish to return to your present station.'

Jack nodded, keeping his thoughts to himself, while frequent glances were exchanged between the three senior officers. He could feel the tension in the room.

The commissioner continued. 'We have thoroughly evaluated your actions and concluded that although you took some risks, they were justified by the outcome. After careful consideration, we have decided on the best course of action. Although it hasn't been officially announced, we will soon be forming an elite team of highly experienced officers on a new homicide squad. This squad will focus solely on handling category A murder cases and will operate directly from Scotland Yard.'

He waited for Jack's response and not getting one, continued. 'We think it will be a very beneficial career move for you to be allocated a position on this squad. We all agree that you would be a valued addition, and so we are offering you this opportunity.'

Jack leaned back in his chair and gave them a polite nod. 'I'd like to thank you for offering me this opportunity, but I'm afraid I cannot accept. I have thought a great deal about my future. Right now, at my last station, they are processing a manslaughter charge for an elderly widow whose pain-wracked husband begged her to take his life. I have found the emotional impact of dealing with these types of cases very disturbing, especially after the horrors of the Rodney Middleton case. That investigation, and the subsequent trial, took a heavy toll on me and my family, and so regretfully I am turning down the opportunity of working with a squad that only deals with murder investigations.'

The tension went up a notch as they looked at each other. Broadbent pushed his chair back before speaking. 'In that case, Detective Warr, are you intent on resigning?'

'Not at all, Sir. I hope to be able to work in an area I've become very interested in. When I was arrested, I made it clear that my reason for being present at Detmar Steinburg's gallery was my interest in art. More specifically, the business of art fraud.'

The commissioner held up his pen. 'I'm sorry, what has this got to do with wanting a transfer?'

'Just as you are organising an elite murder squad, I want to head up an elite fraud squad specialising in uncovering fake artworks.'

Broadbent blinked rapidly and turned to the commissioner, who seemed equally taken aback. 'As I'm sure you're aware, Detective

Warr, we already have a squad that deals with all types of fraud, and I believe this includes the sale of forged paintings.'

'Not to the degree I want to focus on it, Sir. Right now, Sotheby's employ, on a permanent basis, an art specialist who uses scientific methods to determine whether they are selling legitimate masterpieces or fakes. The market is huge and getting bigger. We need to keep pace with it.'

Jack was asked to leave the boardroom for fifteen minutes so that they could discuss his request. He correctly guessed that they would be reluctant, believing that the current fraud squad was up to the task. But they would also prefer to keep Jack in-house where they could keep an eye on him. And Jack's new team could always be disbanded if it proved to be a waste of time.

* * *

Two hours later, Jack left Scotland Yard with a spring in his step. He flagged down a taxi to take him to Bond Street. The gallery was covered in scaffolding, with a notice saying it was closed for refurbishment. Looking up at the empty, fire-blackened windows, he realised how fierce the fire must have been. Peering through the entrance, he noticed a light on in the reception area. After pressing several different buttons, the door finally buzzed open and he stepped inside.

The gallery looked nothing like it had when Jack had first blagged his way in among the throng of well-heeled art lovers. The walls had been stripped bare, the carpets removed and the huge chandelier was missing. And at first, he didn't recognise Ester when she walked out of the first gallery wearing fawn trousers and high-heeled boots with a matching draped cashmere sweater. It was not just the different clothes, she had also cut her hair short and was wearing very little makeup.

'I saw you getting out of the taxi,' she said. 'I am waiting for the new leaseholder's assessor to check the building, which, as you see, is now back to the way it was before we made it into an art gallery. They are very unpleasant. And it is frankly going to bankrupt me to get the fourth floor rebuilt. At least the paintings lost in the fire were covered by the insurance.'

She cocked her head to one side as if expecting him to leave; when he didn't, she went over to a small table and opened a file. A briefcase was propped beside the table. He slowly walked towards her, and she pursed her lips.

'What do you want?'

'To talk. Is there anywhere else we can go, or is this all that's left?' He gestured to the table, and she shrugged.

'As I said, I am waiting for the assessor.'

'It won't take long. We can talk here,' Jack said.

She sighed, sitting down on the only chair behind the table while he perched on the edge.

'I know who you are, Detective. You've had quite a lot of press recently. If this is an official police visit, I refuse to have any further conversation with you without my lawyer present.'

'I wouldn't call it official,' Jack said. 'It's more like move three places and pick up a get-out-of-jail-free card.'

She tightened her smile. 'I've never played Monopoly. So why don't you just tell me what you want from me.'

'How is Kurt Neilson?'

'Mad.'

She laughed softly. 'You know the value of his sick paintings have gone through the roof. Eventually, as Detmar's main beneficiary, I will get them, with a proviso that I take care of the madman until his death.'

'So you are a very wealthy woman.'

She laughed again, shaking her head. 'Not really, maybe just a little more financially secure. I am still waiting for the money taken from his penthouse to be handed over to me.'

Jack smiled. He noticed that she had perfect, very white teeth. She looked prettier than when he had last seen her. 'Your new haircut suits you,' Jack said with a smile, trying to put her at her ease.

'Thank you.' She smiled. 'With Detmar gone, I no longer need to look like the dominatrix. He was very particular about how I dressed. He said his clients liked the steely, sophisticated approach.' Reaching down, she opened the briefcase and took out a silver vape. She breathed in and exhaled, releasing a fine white trail.

'I'll get to the reason I am here, Ester. And don't even think about lying because I know very well that Detmar's real source of income was dealing in forgeries.'

'That is ridiculous,' she said, shaking her head. 'Detmar was an astute collector. He bought well and sold even better. His knowledge of art was—'

'Don't bullshit me,' Jack interrupted. 'I don't have the time and neither do you. You need to listen to me carefully, Ester. I know you were involved in every aspect of his illegal business. But I'm here to offer you a deal.'

She sucked hard on her vape but didn't protest. He leaned closer. 'The deal will be that you agree to work with me and pass on your knowledge, because I'm certain you intend to carry on Detmar's business when the publicity around his murder has died down'.

'You are wrong. I was never involved . . . I was just instructed to organise the shipping.'

'Stop it, don't lie to me because I have enough evidence already to have you arrested. It's not an empty threat, Ester . . . it's a reality.'

She blew out another puff of the vape. 'Aren't you overplaying the hard man act a little? I think you should just fuck off.'

Jack swiped her briefcase off the table and put his own down. He clicked it open and took out his laptop, while she pressed back in her chair. Jack turned the laptop around so she could see the images on the screen – photos of all the information detailed on the walls: sales, shipments, names, along with the crates with their delivery labels, in particular the open crate clearly showing a section of the oil painting he had seen previously at Adam Border's studio, *Lady with a Fan*. It amused him to watch her face, her tight lips, her eyes glued to the images on the screen. He switched it off.

'Seen enough, Ester? If you agree to my proposition, it will also give you some leverage over me. Do you understand?'

'I am trying.'

'You tell me everything about how Detmar ran his business, including his artists and contacts in Europe and the USA. Just one of the paintings I've filmed gets sold, any one you claim was destroyed in the fire, and I will release this footage, unless you agree. And I want a percentage of every sale. Do you understand now?'

She nodded, taking another heavy pull on her vape.

'I also want you to contact Helga Meirling and schedule a meeting with her as soon as possible.'

'That will be difficult. She is abroad. I don't know where. And you should know she is a very astute businesswoman. She has immensely rich friends, who are very careful about protecting her, just as you should be very careful about threatening me.'

'All right, let me tell you how well I know Adam Border.' Jack saw the glimmer in her eyes as he said Adam's name.

'I don't know any Adam Border,' she said. He reached over and took hold of her chin.

'Don't lie, Ester. I know about Adam and Helga, so just do as I ask, or be prepared to take the consequences . . .' He released his hold on her chin and clicked his fingers.

'I don't know where Adam is,' she said finally. 'He's as dangerous and as untrustworthy as she is.'

It took Jack another half an hour to explain everything he wanted her to do, starting with how they would arrange their meetings. 'I will always contact you, not the other way round,' he said.

She nodded.

'Do you trust me, Ester?'

She laughed softly. 'Do I have an option?'

'Not really.'

'You have a lot to learn.'

'That's why I need you, Ester.' He stood up, putting his laptop back in his briefcase. She walked around the table to show him out, and he was surprised when she hooked her arm through his.

'Shall I tell you something funny? After it happened, I had to move everything from the fourth floor, moving the paintings down in the lift, getting them all out and hidden before the sales could go through. Then I had to clear the rest of the basement; the crates of unsold paintings had to be moved. I organised skips to be loaded with all the wooden crates and taken to the main tip. Eric, one of the old security guards, a good man, stayed close to see them destroyed. You know they separate all the wood items to be pulverised by this big heavy machine that smashes them to bits, and he watched as one after the other was crushed.'

She withdrew her arm and laughed. 'He said he became concerned as one of the crates opened and he saw part of an oil painting. The guy on the machine stopped, looked down, then said it wasn't anything worth saving, just a gloomy picture of an old man in a broken frame. That was a Rembrandt self-portrait; Adam painted several of them, as did Rembrandt.'

Before Jack could react, two men arrived at the glass reception doors. Both were smartly suited and carrying briefcases, one bald with glasses, the other gaunt and older.

Ester gave Jack a brilliant smile, thanking him loudly for his estimate, before standing back to welcome the two men inside. 'Good afternoon, gentlemen,' she said, closing the door behind them.

CHAPTER 38

Jack hailed a taxi to take him home. He stopped at the local supermarket and brought a bottle of champagne, then stopped the driver again as they passed a flower stall on Fulham Road; he told the stall-holder he wanted a bucket-full. Arriving home with his arms full of roses and lilies, he didn't need his keys as the front door was wide open. Outside was a skip full of debris. Inside, the hall now had a very large hole in the wall, while protective sheets had been laid along the carpet leading to the kitchen where there was another big hole. Marius was sweeping brick dust into the garden via the open doors.

'Where is everyone?' Jack asked, taking the flowers to the sink.

'Your mum has got a picnic going up in the nursery. I'm finishing up for the day. I'll be back first thing tomorrow to start plastering. The RSJ was a right bugger to fit, but we did it, and I'll be getting a carpenter in to make a nice archway. I'm using the dining room door to make two safety gates for Charlie.'

'All looking good to me,' Jack said, already covered in white brick dust.

Marius slipped him a dusty scrap of paper with the estimate, then tapped his nose and winked that it was just between them, cash for himself and his lads. By the time Marius had cleaned up as much as he could and left in his van, Jack had found various vases and jugs to carry the flowers to the bedroom. He joined Penny and the children in the nursery, watched some TV with them, and had a banana sandwich before returning to the kitchen. Fetching the bottle of champagne from the fridge, he took two glasses from the cabinet and went up to the bedroom.

It was after seven when Maggie arrived home. She went straight to the kitchen and stood looking at the massive hole in the wall for a few moments before going up to the nursery. Penny was reading to Hannah, while Charlie crawled around on the floor.

'Have you heard anything from Jack?' she asked.

'He was with us earlier,' Penny said. 'We had tea up here because of all the dust. Will you order something for your dinner?'

'Yes. I think Marius is doing a good job, by the way.'

'He and his lads have worked their socks off, but it was a real bugger getting that RSJ into place.'

Maggie nodded. 'I think I'll take a shower, then say goodnight to Hannah and Charlie.'

Maggie was stunned when she walked into the bedroom to see flowers wherever she looked. She was even more stunned when Jack, in his dressing gown, held up the bottle of champagne, grinning like a Cheshire cat. She sighed, kicking off her shoes.

'This had better be good, Jack. It smells like a florist's shop in here.'

'I'll open this after I tell you about my day at Scotland Yard.'

She unbuttoned her blouse, refusing to play along, as he put the unopened bottle on the bedside table. He sat on the bed, watching her undress, and told her about the offer of a role in an elite new murder squad, dealing only with first-degree murder cases.

'I respectfully turned them down.'

'What? Did you hand in your resignation? Is that what this is all about?'

'No. Let me finish. Damn, seeing you getting naked makes it difficult to concentrate.'

'Oh, for God's sake, you are beginning to piss me off.' She went into the bathroom and he followed, watching her cleaning her makeup off and then washing her face. He leaned against the open door as she cleaned her teeth.

'I asked to be given a team of officers to set up a new division in the fraud squad concentrating on art fraud. After a lot of huffing and puffing, they agreed to it. I'll be working out of an office in Scotland Yard. It'll take a few weeks to set up, with all the specialist equipment, but I'll have three fraud officers already working there as my team.'

Maggie spat out the toothpaste and rinsed her mouth. 'Is this for real, Jack? Or is it fantasy? Because to me, it doesn't make any sense.'

She walked past him and took off her bra and pants to put on her nightdress. He was disappointed by her reaction. She didn't seem to understand how serious he was. He switched off the bathroom light, following her into the bedroom.

'What doesn't make any sense to you, Maggie?'

'Moving into a completely different area of the Met after your past record tracking down killers and bringing them to justice.'

'I thought you would approve,' he said quietly.

They were silent for a while. Then she watched him pick up the bottle of champagne. 'Don't open that now, Jack.'

'You might not want to celebrate, but I do. My dad, Charlie, encouraged me to join the local force when I was eighteen. I'd never even thought of it. I just went ahead to make him proud of me. When we met and you had the offer of the position here in London, I just followed and got transferred to the Met. I never had any ambition, and truthfully, if it hadn't been for my old boss, I would more than likely have quit, but Ridley became a sort of substitute for my dad, with me wanting to make him proud, and so I carried on and on and on, bored out of my skull most of the time, having to deal with the incident room arseholes. The further I moved up, taking on one murder investigation after another, the more I felt trapped, as if I was hiding who I really was.'

Maggie watched him in the mirror. Speaking quietly, his usual boyish expression was gone. His dark eyes now appeared hooded, and there were shadows under his chiselled cheekbones. She felt her heartbeat quicken, afraid of what he was going to say next or how to comfort him.

'The first time I felt it was when I had to knock on the parents' door to tell them their sixteen-year-old daughter had been murdered. Asking them to sit down before telling them why I was there. Then the anguish in their eyes, and having to be with them when they identified her, her face made up to hide the lacerations. I have had to deal with that torment repeatedly. Then the obsession with tracking down the killers, hoping to bring some justice but knowing there isn't any. I cannot go back to all that because I can't deal with it anymore.'

Maggie wanted to reach out to him, but the fact that he had hidden so much from her was painful to accept.

He was staring at the floor, then he looked up and smiled. 'You know you're always asking me about Adam Border. Why I protect him. I'll tell you why. Being with him for even a short while gave me a strange sense of hope. He taught me, without even knowing that I was depressed, that there was another option. I want, like him, to do something I'm passionate about.' He smiled. 'And then I want to prove I can outwit him.'

Maggie got up and wrapped her arms around him. Some of it still didn't make sense to her, but she didn't care. They opened the bottle of champagne, and she held up her glass before he could say anything else.

'To you, Jack, and to your new position, because all I want is for you to—' Maggie never finished, as there was a loud boom and sound of falling debris from right beneath their bedroom, making it feel for one terrifying moment as if the floor was about to fall in underneath them. They ran into the corridor shouting for Penny, and heard Hannah screaming as Penny came down holding the baby. As they reached the ground floor, loose bricks littered the floor by the stairs and inside the kitchen the hole was now massive. One end of the RSJ had broken loose and fallen with a mound of bricks.

Penny looked fearfully at them both as if it was somehow her fault. They were gaping in shock with brick dust in their hair, when Hannah picked up a brick and said, 'Nana said it was a bugger to put up.'

Jack and Maggie glanced at each other and started laughing.

* * *

Work resumed the following morning, and Marius and his team, assisted by Jack, managed to manoeuvre the massive RSJ back into position. Marius couldn't apologise enough.

While Jack was brewing coffee, he got a call from Laura, upset at the news he would not be returning to the station.

'What are you going to do?'

'I can't give you any details yet, Laura. But it's a positive move. Very liberating.'

'Mysterious as ever, eh Jack?' she laughed. 'But positive and liberating sounds good.'

'Gotta go, that's the doorbell,' Jack said. 'Look out for your christening invitation.' He opened the front door and the postman handed him a small parcel. It was a square box, around six by ten inches, wrapped in brown paper secured with packing tape. The postmark was blurred so Jack couldn't tell where it had come from and the address was printed in thick black felt-tip. Jack took it up to his office, then went to give Maggie her coffee. She was in the shower so he left the mug at her bedside and returned to the office.

Opening a drawer, he took a pair of scissors and cut through the tape. The box itself was slightly battered, as if it had been used before. He carefully eased off the lid. Inside, something oval-shaped was covered in bubble wrap. He cut through the plastic and then eased out a dark red leather photograph case that opened like a small book. Horatio Nelson was written in elegant gold lettering on one side. There was also a tiny, folded slip of yellowing parchment. On the facing side was an exquisite drawing of Nelson, not in uniform but in a high-necked shirt with his hair tied back. Jack carefully unfolded the note. The writing was very faded, but he could make out the date, 1799, and the name Emma Hamilton. Jack took a deep breath. The portrait had belonged to Lady Hamilton. He searched through the wrappings, then the worn cardboard box for any message. There was something written in ink at the bottom of the box: *First, gain the victory and then make the best of it you can.*

Jack tried to recall if he had ever mentioned to Adam his choice of name for his son. The gift he assumed would be of great value. He studied the leather case and the perfect drawing, certain it had to be the original. Spreading out the brown wrapping paper he had removed, he tried again to see where it had been sent from, and although it was very smudged, he thought it might be Berlin.

Next, he Googled the quote, which of course was from Nelson himself. Repeating the words, he concluded that Adam was warning him. He did feel as if he had won a victory. But he knew the fight was not over. He also knew with certainty for the first time that Adam Border was not his friend but his adversary.

The darkness that had clung to him was gone; it was a new beginning and the contest between them had already commenced. Now they would see which of them would win.

ACKNOWLEDGEMENTS

I would like to thank Nigel Stoneman and Tory Macdonald, the team I work with at La Plante Global.

The forensic scientists and members of the Met Police who help with my research. I could not write without their valuable input.

Cass Sutherland for his valuable advice on police procedures and forensics.

The entire team at my publisher, Bonnier Books UK, who work together to have my books edited, marketed, publicised and sold.

A special thank you to Ben Willis and Bill Massey for their great editorial advice and guidance.

Allen and Unwin in Australia and Jonathan Ball in South Africa, thank you for doing such fantastic work.

All the reviewers, journalists, bloggers and broadcasters who interview me, write reviews and promote my books. Thank you for your time and work.

My readers, without you I would not be able to do a job I love, sincerest thanks.

ENTER THE WORLD OF Lynda La Plante

ALL THE LATEST NEWS FROM THE QUEEN OF CRIME DRAMA

DISCOVER THE THRILLING TRUE STORIES BEHIND THE BOOKS

ENJOY EXCLUSIVE CONTENT AND OPPORTUNITIES

JOIN THE READERS' CLUB TODAY AT
WWW.LYNDALAPLANTE.COM

Dear Reader,

Thank you very much for picking up *Crucified*, the fifth book in the DC Jack Warr series. I hope you enjoyed reading the book as much as I enjoyed writing it.

In *Crucified*, Jack not only has to hunt a killer who's terrorising the fascinating world of art, he must also contend with the nightmares that have plagued him since putting away serial killer, Rodney Middleton. It is always such a joy to write about Jack – a brilliant detective with a burning desire to bring justice no matter the cost, who often blurs the lines of the law. But in *Crucified*, Jack has reached breaking point – even more so than at any other point in the series. My aim with the story is to keep you guessing at every stage – I hope you enjoy the twists and turns!

If you enjoyed *Crucified*, then please do keep an eye out for news about the next book in the series. If you want to catch up on Jack Warr's story so far, the first four books in the series, *Buried, Judas Horse, Vanished* and *Pure Evil* are available now. And if you would like to delve into the Tennison series, all ten novels – *Tennison, Hidden Killers, Good Friday, Murder Mile, The Dirty Dozen, Blunt Force, Unholy Murder, Dark Rooms, Taste of Blood* and *Whole Life Sentence* – are available to buy in paperback, ebook and audio. I've been so pleased by the response I've had from the many readers who have been curious about the beginnings of Jane's police career. It's been great fun for me to explore how she became the woman we know in middle and later life from the Prime Suspect series. It's been a pleasure to revisit the Trial and Retribution series after its television success and I am thrilled to return to it in print – the first two books in the series are available to buy now.

To discover more about my life and career, please do pick up a copy of my brand-new memoir, *Getting Away With Murder*. It was such fun to write, and I'd love to hear what you think.

If you would like more information on what I'm working on, about the Jane Tennison thriller series or the new series featuring Jack Warr, you can visit www.bit.ly/LyndaLaPlanteClub where you can join my Readers' Club. It only takes a few moments to sign up, there are no catches or costs, and new members will automatically receive an exclusive message from me. Bonnier Books UK will keep your data private and confidential, and it will never be passed on to a third party. We won't spam you with loads of emails, just get in touch now and again with news about my books, and you can unsubscribe any time you want.

Finally, if you would like to get involved in a wider conversation about my books, please do review *Crucified* on Amazon.co.uk, Waterstones.com or on Goodreads, on any other e-store, on your own blog and social media accounts, or talk about it with friends, family or reader groups! Sharing your thoughts helps other readers, and I always enjoy hearing about what people experience from my writing.

With many thanks again for reading *Crucified*, and I hope you'll return for the next in the series.

With my very best wishes,
Lynda

INTRODUCING
JACK WARR

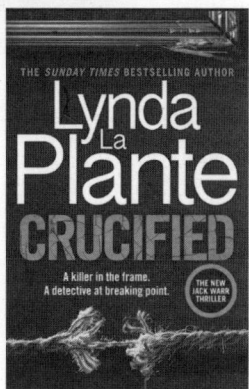

The gripping and twisty series
from the *Sunday Times* bestselling author
Lynda La Plante

BEFORE PRIME SUSPECT THERE WAS

TENNISON

DIVE INTO THE ICONIC *SUNDAY TIMES* BESTSELLING SERIES.

Now brought to a close with the final epic instalment...

WHOLE LIFE SENTENCE

THE
INSPIRATION
FOR THE MAJOR MOTION PICTURE
SOON TO BE A MAJOR FEATURE FILM
Lynda La Plante
WIDOWS
Facing life alone, they turned to crime together
FROM THE BESTSELLING AUTHOR OF WIDOWS
Lynda La Plante
WIDOWS' REVENGE
The brutal payback begins
OUT NOW

THE NEW PODCAST THAT PUTS YOU AT THE SCENE OF THE CRIME

LISTENING TO THE DEAD — The secret world of forensics

With Lynda La Plante and CSI Cass Sutherland

AVAILABLE NOW